GOING SOUTH

GOING SOUTH

By
MacArthur Johnson

"GOING SOUTH"

A term used by organizations to refer to individuals who are no longer abiding by or carrying out the policies and directives of the organization and are, therefore, out of control.

Synonym: Going Rogue

Published by Mammoth Star Publishing

Aspects of Writing, Inc.

Las Vegas, Nevada

ISBN 978-1-886726-22-2
PRINTED IN THE UNITED STATES OF AMERICA

DEDICATION

This book is dedicated to my mother, Jeanne M. Johnson, and to my wife, Ann. Both lived through the creation process but sadly did not see the efforts in print. Upon reading the initial rough draft, my mother was convinced the story was autobiographical. Nothing I could say would dissuade her of that impression. Ann survived through countless nights alone in the television room while I pounded on the computer keyboard and later helped with the first edit.

ACKNOWLEDGMENTS

For an effort that was Herculean to say the least, warm and enduring thanks go to my beautiful wife, Carol, for all her efforts, including reading, providing an initial edit of the novel, for her wonderful creative work on the cover design and creation, and generally for the patience she has shown and the encouragement she has given during these final days.

Thanks is given to my friends Cheryl Kaylor, Gail Baker, and my daughter Pam Schultz for their initial reading of the novel as well as the advices they gave as edit and plot consultants.

An immense amount of credit for the novel must go to my publisher, Mary Walker Owens, who not only stuck with me during the final edit, which she supplied, but also gave me encouragement concerning the value of the novel as a work of art. This novel could not have come to fruition without the sustaining efforts of Mary. Her knowledge and expertise was much appreciated and for which I will be eternally grateful.

PROLOGUE

The Nevada air was its usual hot and dry. There hadn't been rain in excess of 150 days. This was approaching a record for the area defined as Clark County, Nevada. My second-class hotel room, three long blocks from the famed Las Vegas Strip, was air-conditioned, or at least that's what the sign on the registration desk said. What air-conditioning there was worked noisily, and only periodically, with absolutely no logic as to when it would work and when it would not. I was sitting in a rumpled suit, damp from perspiration, eating Ritz crackers and waiting for my cell phone to ring. Strapped to my side, just inside my jacket, was a S&W nine mm. It was most uncomfortable, cutting into my side, as a result of the ill-fitting chair.

What choices in life had I made getting me to this place - at this time? What had occurred causing me to be here, in a second rate hotel registered under an alias with forged credentials. Eric Butler was the name I was using - a name I had become more accustomed to than my given name. I was not a fugitive, nor was I running from family problems or self- imposed addictions. I had in the vicinity of fifty thousand dollars, all cash, stored in various locations on my person and in my personal effects.

Only three blocks away was the Strip, where climate-controlled hotel rooms could be had for the price of a well-placed bet; where food to satisfy even the most discriminating palate was available for the asking; where the atmosphere – well, there were few, if any, places in the world that could compare. Why was I here?

By the way, my given name is William Jennings. As you can guess most people called me Bill. My early life was storybook in nature. I grew up in the middle of a large national forest, with a backyard easily constituting three million acres of virgin timber. I had all the amenities one would expect from being raised in a place and at a time when the development of the resort country in the Rocky Mountains was just beginning. I competed in sports in high school and college levels and was mildly successful in the amateur ranks. I graduated from college with good enough grades to get into law school, which I finished close to the top of my class. I practiced law for a short period of time with one of the major law firms located in Denver, Colorado, a city approximately one hundred miles from where I was raised.

Very early in my professional career, I became bored with the day-to-day drudgery thrust on an associate lawyer. It may have been the boredom that sparked the interest I experienced when I received a notice stating the Central Intelligence Agency was going to interview interested applicants at my alma mater. I signed up, not sure whether I was serious or was doing this as a lark. In any event, I soon found myself in the presence of three Central Intelligence Agency recruiters. *Interview* was what it was deemed on the invitation and in the notice. *Interrogation* would have been a more accurate description of the process. Questions were asked that would have been grossly inappropriate in any traditional setting, bordering on the illegal. I got up to leave several times, incensed at the level of knowledge the Agency already possessed concerning my past, including details of my family life. I can't tell you why I stayed. There was something, possibly the unstated promise of intrigue, which piqued my interest.

Following my experience with the agency, I returned to an associate's mundane life of practicing law, striving to adjust to the life of a city lawyer, a task that was becoming more and more burdensome. I had immediately dismissed the agency *interview* and three or four weeks later was attending a firm meeting where new business was discussed and associate responsibility was assigned. One case was introduced and identified as a case requiring three or four years to resolve. Massive amounts of research would be critical, all associates assigned to this project would be unavailable for other projects in the foreseeable future. I prayed I would not be chosen. The last thing I wanted was an assignment tying me to the library fifty to seventy hours a week - indefinitely!

As luck would have it, the managing partner chose me and two mousy individuals to assist in the case preparation. The mice were ecstatic. I was devastated - able to mask my feelings just long enough to get out of the meeting. I found myself making calls to other potential employers. I spoke with friends and relatives about my disappointment. I knew I had to get out of the firm - most probably out of the practice of law. A week passed. I was beginning to feel trapped.

I arrived home from the office, one Saturday, late as usual. Stopping at my mailbox, I realized I hadn't picked up my mail all week. The box was overflowing with several bills and accumulated junk mail. Struggling with my briefcase and the volume of mail, I finally reached my apartment, got the door open, and deposited my entire load on the kitchen table. An envelope from the Central Intelligence Agency briefly caught my attention. I got a beer from the small refrigerator in my apartment and first began opening the bills and credit card statements. It was my habit to pay immediately, upon receipt, so I spent the next twenty minutes writing checks, completing envelopes with my name, address, including those ungodly long account numbers all the companies want included on the check. I finally opened the Central Intelligence Agency envelope. I remember thinking the agency was simply writing to thank me for attending the interview, a *"thank you but no thank you letter."* I was amazed! The opening paragraph was the preface to an offer of employment.

Now I was interested! The Agency recruitment policy required prospects to attend an extended paid pre-employment briefing and pass a physical examination. It was clear they wouldn't allow applicants to maintain employment commitments during this time. The letter stated the commitment to pay new recruits was for six months, and I would be on the payroll ten days from acceptance The time remaining for acceptance, or rejection, of the offer was only three days. My response had to be in their hands within that time period which seemed exceedingly short. Now my head was spinning! For the first time in many months, I had the feeling life was going to get better. The letter indicated acceptance of the offer was to be made by e-mail. Travel documents would arrive within five days of acceptance. The decision to accept the offered employment was a foregone conclusion. My acceptance e-mail was dispatched immediately. I don't remember much of the remaining weekend.

On Monday I submitted my resignation to the firm. A condition of the Agency employment offer was my employer could not be told where, or for whom, I was going to work. I was only to tell them the position did not conflict with and would not compromise the firm or any firm business. My supervising attorney was not happy. He was sure a competing firm had *lured* me away. The end result was he immediately terminated my associate position. I was escorted out the door by the firm's security guard, burdened only by the few personal affects I had in my office. This experience turned out to be my first attempt at cloaking the real facts while, at the same time, giving enough plausible information to satisfy the inquirer. I wasn't as skilled in deception as I would later become.

Thus began the life which led me to this hotel room, at this time, and in this place.

PART ONE
THE ASSIGNMENT

CHAPTER ONE

The left breast pocket of my coat began to vibrate. It had to be the call I was waiting for. Only two others had the cell number. I punched the receive button. "Yes?" A refined male voice responded, simply stating Mr. Barajas was ready to meet me. I was to be at the fence in front of the Mirage Resort, by the volcano, in twenty minutes.

Jose Salvador Barajas was born in the Pyrenees Mountains. I knew every detail about Barajas that could be gleaned from the records of the Central Intelligence Agency and much which could not. Both history and his mother were unsure in which country he was born. The small town of his birth was in an area where borders change frequently. Mr. Barajas always insisted he was Spanish. That was consistent with his passport and his family names, one of which was the surname of his maternal grandfather and the other the sir name of his paternal grandfather. I had all of this information because it was my job. Barajas had been my project for the past three years. I knew him as well as I knew my own father. Yet, I had never met him face to face.

With just a little luck, and with the unknowing help of Barajas, I intended to bring down one of the most profitable of the underworld crime syndicates. It's hard to reconcile, under twenty-first century morays and standards, how such a large business could exist where the sole product is human misery. Drugs and the products of white slavery were what the syndicate marketed and it did it very well.

I was not operating within guidelines. In fact, I was probably committing a felony by conducting, even this small part of my operation, inside the borders of the United States - a risk I was willing to take. It was the only way I could wrangle my way into the complete confidence of Barajas. The arrangement for this meet had been made in Bogotá, Colombia two days ago. The choice to meet in Las Vegas was brilliant. If I were a CIA agent, I would have no jurisdiction within the borders of the U.S. To insist on meeting me here in the U.S., ironically, was his safety net.

As far as Barajas knew, I was the front man for a syndicate marketing enormous quantities of drugs in Europe and the Middle East. I was looking to establish a replacement supplier and to expand my lines of endeavor. We had dealt indirectly with each other on several occasions, but he had never allowed us to meet. I knew he was involved because the quantities were too great to be supplied by anyone else. Barajas never completed the transactions but was always aware I had the ability to pay for the large quantities he had been asked to supply. In less than twenty minutes Jose Salvador Barajas was going to be offered a schematic for the marketing of commodities he represented which would turn the drug and, if he chose - the flesh trade upside down. What he would not know was, it was going to be run by the CIA.

For three years I had portrayed a syndicate which operated in a part of the world that did not compete with his efforts and was as large, if not larger than his organization. Barajas believed, at least I hoped he believed, the purpose of our meeting was to arrange an enormous buy of processed cocaine to be delivered to a designated port in the Middle East. The small port was in a war torn area on the northern coast of Africa. The country had been so decimated, and the population so economically destroyed, that a moderate amount of money could buy any level of security necessary to assure success. As the result of our prior dealings, I hoped Barajas believed money was not a problem. What I intended to do was to propose a joint venture so large and all-encompassing, that in the future, all other syndicates would have to deal with us to get product. I would propose that we become the only illicit drug pipeline in the world, thereby controlling most of the drugs destined for the penthouses, streets, and gutters of the world.

In an effort to gain the confidence of Barajas, I knew I would have to make the buy. It was expected, and I was prepared to complete the arrangements. On my call and with the passing of some code words, the amount of money necessary to complete the deal would be transferred to an account of my choosing, including if necessary, Barajas's offshore bank accounts. I knew the location of many of these accounts because of our previous dealings. Arrangements had been made to have friendly bankers on the receiving end of my calls. The plan was that no real money would be transferred but the credits would appear. If circumstances dictated the friendly bankers could not be used, real money could be transferred to any account I designated. I never knew how this arrangement was accomplished, but then I never asked. In the business I was in, there were a lot of questions one never asked.

I figured I could get to the designated spot in eight or nine minutes. It was time to leave. I knew I could not risk being late, but being too early would also raise questions. I strolled toward the Strip - the famous Las Vegas Strip. I was on time by my calculations. I was nervous. Three long years of deep undercover work were at stake, not to mention my life. I knew they would have checked and rechecked my cover prior to this meet. If anything showed up, I was in deep trouble. I was in my own country and couldn't ask for help if things went wrong.

As I reached the fence, the volcano was just completing an eruption and the crowd was beginning to disperse. I leaned against one of the posts supporting the fence and lit a cigarette. I really didn't like to smoke, but over the years I'd found that lighting a cigarette gave me time to consider my options and not be too obvious. In my game, that can be lifesaving.

"Senor!" the voice was behind me and to my left. I turned to find a distinguished man in his early sixties.

"Yes," I said. "Can I help you?"

"You can, if you have some familiarity with the North African coast," he said. I somehow knew I was talking directly with Barajas.
He was wearing a light brown silk suit that would have made him stand out in any city in the world, but not in Las Vegas. Here he was just another high roller, looking for the adrenaline rush that can only be associated with high stakes gambling.

"I have some," I replied. "It's my understanding the ravages of war have created many opportunities in that part of the world."

"An unfortunate fact, but one which the astute business man must recognize," he replied.

I knew that it was time to move on with the apparent business. "I have a business in the area, but am in need of a partner to insure the raw materials I need are available."

Barajas looked at me with a gaze which made me feel extremely uncomfortable. The refined older gentleman seemed to have disappeared and in his place was a man with the eyes of a hawk - eyes silently promising me that lethal talons were instantly available.

"Are you telling me this, because you feel I may be of assistance in supplying your need?" he asked.

I knew at this point that I was either being tested or played with. I hoped it was a test, because if it was a game, I was dead. I felt I must get by the small talk quickly.

"Yes, but let's not play games. If you are interested, let's meet where we can do business. If not, I will seek another partner, and you can get back to the baccarat table."

My heart was in my mouth. Three years' work was in the balance. Barajas looked at me for a long time and then nodded to a man I hadn't noticed. He was located across the simulated volcanic lake and behind a small fenced-off area. This is it, I thought. I'm targeted. However, he continued with the same matter of fact approach exhibited from the beginning. "Serge will give you a key which will get you to my suite. Be there in four hours. By the way, a room has been arranged for you in my hotel. See Jeb, the bellman.

He will show you to your new accommodations. I don't do business with men staying in second rate hotels." He turned and left.

It occurred to me, as he walked away, that I didn't know which hotel. I looked over and the man Barajas had nodded to was in route, making every attempt to appear to be a star-gazed tourist. It took him easily four or five minutes to cover approximately a hundred yards. Upon reaching me, he passed me a key - actually a key card, and a note. He immediately proceeded south on the sidewalk. As I was placing the key card and the note in my suit coat pocket, I worked my way across the street and into Harrah's Casino.

To discover if I was being tailed, I took a seat at a twenty-one table and played about a dozen hands. In another circumstance I would have been thrilled, as I more than doubled my buy-in My attention was not on the game, however, but on the people around me. Was anyone paying an inordinate amount of attention to me? One man who had come to the table after I sat down was watching me. I concluded he was interested in how I was playing, nothing else. The dealer had called him Bill. He was probably just a regular guest. I asked the dealer where the closest men's room was located. He indicated it was up the escalator, just down the row of tables from me. I knew from previous trips to Vegas where the restrooms were, but I wanted Bill to know where I was going. If he followed me, I would know I was being monitored. If not, well at least the probability was he was not one of Barajas's men. Leaving my chips on the table, I started toward the escalator, then got on the escalator and glanced back. Bill was still at the table, now engaged in conversation with another customer.

I proceeded to the men's room. In the men's room I found myself in the company of a man in his early thirties with his small son. The boy was having trouble getting his pants zipped and his father was helping him. They completed the zipping and left. Now I was alone. I chose the first stall and entered, dropped my pants and sat down. If anyone entered the men's room I wanted to appear to be there for the appropriate reason.

I reached into my suit coat pocket and retrieved the note and card key. The key was to an elevator accessing an exclusive suite at Caesar's Palace. The note contained two short sentences,

"I'm in Suite C on the twenty-second floor.

Leave the 9mm in your room."

CHAPTER TWO

I had about three and a half hours left until the meeting. I needed to get my thoughts together and make the move to Caesar's Palace. I went back to the casino and sat down in front of my chips. "They don't seem to have grown any while I was gone," I said in an effort to appear to have the appropriate vacation spirit. The table laughed. I noticed Bill had left. I played three more hands and lost all of them. "Well, the luck has run out here. Time to move to greener pastures."

There wasn't a line at the cashiers' cage, so within five minutes I was on the street heading for my "second-rate" hotel room. For the second time in less than thirty-six hours, I had to marvel at the methods of Barajas. If he was being watched, a meeting with someone from a seedy hotel several blocks from Caesar's could be noticeable. A meet in which the participants were all guests of the same hotel might not be so evident. He'd also have better control of me. That was the real reason.

The walk back to my hotel was uneventful. I couldn't spot a tail, but instincts told me one was there. I arrived, letting myself into my room. As expected, the room was a mess. Someone had gone through my luggage. When I left the room, I had taken fifteen thousand dollars with me. I had left thirty-five thousand carefully secreted within various locations in my clothing and luggage. On the dresser, now, was a neatly stacked pile of three hundred and fifty hundred dollar bills. It was obvious who was responsible. What better calling card could Barajas have left! He had just made it clear that he was not to be taken lightly. The search was not for money, but for information, and he wanted me to know he had ordered it done. In the closet were three new pieces of luggage to replace the ones they had cut up.

The fact I was still alive was the best evidence that they had found nothing. If they wanted to get rid of me, they would do it in my backyard, not theirs. I gathered my clothes and_repacked, using my new luggage, and prepared to leave the hotel for my improved digs. At least I would arrive at Caesars in style. There was still something that bothered me and I couldn't put my finger on it. Was it something they said? A mannerism? What was it? I learned years ago these feelings were not to be ignored. They could save my life one day. I sat on the bed and nibbled on the last Ritz cracker left on the table.

Then it occurred to me. It was the note. They might expect that I would pack a piece, but how did they know the caliber? I ransacked my mind to recall the last time I had taken it out. It was here in this room, before the meet. It had become uncomfortable, so I adjusted it - and in doing so, took the piece out of its holster. They must have visual surveillance of this room. It wouldn't be hard to buy the management of this place. A bottle of cheap scotch would do the trick, but how did they know I was going to stay here. Not even I knew, until reaching Las Vegas. Then it occurred to me that the airport taxi cab driver had taken me out of turn. It seemed strange, at the time, but I chalked it up to cabbie competition and dismissed it. That had to be the answer.

I considered my circumstance while I lit up a cigarette and smoked it. The surveillance must be on going as I sat there. I must not allow Barajas to believe I was unaware of this. I must locate and destroy the camera - to do otherwise would show a lack of vigilance. A certain amount of twisted professionalism is required in my line of work. Thinking back on the adjustments I made to the piece, and the locations that would allow the surveillance necessary to determine the caliber, left only three possible locations: the fixture above the bed, the mirror above the dresser, and the window frame beside the chair I was sitting in. Then it hit me. They didn't have to place the camera themselves. This sleaze bag hotel management had done it for them long before I rented the room in an effort to satisfy some pervert's sick, prurient need. I jumped on the bed, pulled down the fixture, and bingo - an extra set of wires leading to an aging surveillance camera! I twisted the brittle wires until they broke, gathered my luggage, and left the room - and the hotel.

Reaching the sidewalk, I looked for a cab. Three blocks was not far, but with three pieces of luggage, it was out of the question. Up the street was a dark blue sedan, facing the same direction I was going. It had those dark tinted windows, so common in the desert - and illegal most other places. The light was just right to catch the passenger's profile. It was Serge again. So, why use a cab? If they wanted to watch me, they could do so. I walked to the sedan and rapped on the window. Serge rolled it down.

"Release the trunk," I said. "Rather than tail me to Caesars, you might as well take me."

Serge was dumbfounded. "Is this okay with Mr. Barajas?" he blurted.

"Shut your mouth and open the trunk. I'll take care of Barajas," I sneered. The driver reached for the trunk release. It clicked and the counter balance swung the trunk lid open.

I've seen surveillance equipment before, but never anything like what was in the trunk. Wherever the listening post was, this equipment could have transmitted a conversation through a two-foot concrete wall. There wasn't room for an overnight kit, let alone three full sized pieces of luggage.

I slammed the trunk and threw my bags in the back seat. "Hope that broke some eardrums!" I said, feigning anger. I opened the front passenger door, "Get out!"

Serge got out immediately.

I got in. The driver was pale. "Now get me to the hotel and when you get there find Jeb and get these bags to my room. I'll be in the first lounge I can find."

The driver looked confused. "What about Serge?"

"Does he know the way to the hotel?" I asked.

"Yes" "Then we can assume he will eventually get there. Now get this car moving!"

The driver responded, leaving Serge on the sidewalk, holding a bottle of commercial water and looking astonished.

The driver delivered me to the front door of Caesars Palace. I got out and went directly into the hotel, spotting a lounge across the foyer. The driver, whatever his name was, could easily find me there. I needed a drink. I needed to have some time to think. I looked at my watch. Two and a half hours.

The driver appeared at the entrance of the lounge. He was searching for me. I could make it easy for him, but, what the hell, he was supposed to be watching me! I did nothing and he finally saw me. He came directly to the table. I had obviously destroyed any feeling he may have had regarding the covert nature of his assignment.

"Jeb gave me the key to your room and took your luggage."

"Thanks, you can go now." He left the lounge only to meet Serge at the entrance. I couldn't hear what was being said, but I could tell Serge was not a happy camper. The driver was getting the brunt of it all.

I finished my drink. It was time to go to the room. I located the bank of elevators serving my floor, among several others, and found my room with little trouble. The room was small, a room designed for tourists. This was not going to work. I needed to be as equal to Barajas as I could appear. His obvious intent was to make it clear that he intended to be the boss. I picked up the phone and dialed the front desk.

"Caesars, front desk" an appealing female voice said. "What can I do for you, Mr. Butler?"

"This room is not adequate. Please move me to a suite."

"One moment please." At least a minute passed.

"Mr. Butler, I'm sorry for the wait, but it appears that your room is being paid for by Mr. Barajas, and there's not authorization for an upgrade. Would you like me to contact him for authorization? "
"No, and I don't want him to pay for my room or the suite. Just move me at once. I'll be down later to complete the financial arrangements."
"Your request is outside my authority, Mr. Butler. I'll get my supervisor."
After several seconds an officious sounding male came on the line. "What can I do for you, Mr. Butler?"
"I want to move to a suite, and I want to do it now. Is that a problem?"
"Well, yes - and no, Mr. Butler. We have a suite available and that's the good news, but because we don't have any registration materials completed, I'm afraid you'll have to come to the registration area to make the arrangements."
As usual, Las Vegas was run by money.
"Maybe this will help. My Gold American Express number is 97259 0942 987. That should satisfy any immediate need for arrangements. I'm also having two hundred-fifty thousand dollars wired to my account today. The deposit should relieve your concern for security on the account."
"That will be more than adequate, Mr. Butler. A bellman will be up shortly to move your luggage."
"I thought that would solve the problem. Just make sure the bellman, Jeb, is the one you send." Jeb was one sure way Barajas would get the message not to treat me lightly.
Now, I must arrange for the quarter million transfer. I needed a clean line and the only one available was my cell phone. Barajas had the number, but the cell phone had been set up to make it virtually impossible to trace or eavesdrop on the line.
Recalling the surveillance equipment, I realized I had to get to another location in order to make the call. I left the room and went to the casino area. I picked the noisiest crowd I could and dialed the number. It answered with the electronic security whine and I entered my security code.
"Yes," a familiar voice said. It was Howard Baker. I had known him for years. Howard had been in the field before me and had gotten badly cut up during an endeavor gone bad. His injuries had left him in administration, and he was now my assigned handler.
"I need two hundred fifty thousand wired to my account at Caesar's Palace in Las Vegas immediately. I know I'm not supposed to be in the country, but it couldn't be avoided. Hopefully, that's not a problem?"
"Country could be a problem down the road, but with your clearance, the money is not. Consider it done."
It was now time to act the role I could play so well. I took ten one hundred-dollar bills from my pocket and spread them at a five-dollar

blackjack table. There isn't a better way to get recognition than to play significantly above other players at the table. It worked - as I knew it would! Within a matter of a few minutes, a pit boss approached the table. "Caesars welcomes you, Sir. Do you have a players card with us?" Pit bosses were getting more and more attractive over the years and this one was no exception. She was a knockout.

"No, but I'm sure that you can remedy that."

"I can - if you will just give me your name and if you're staying here, I won't need anything further."

"Eric Butler, and, yes, I am staying here."

CHAPTER THREE

Bogotá, Colombia had been unseasonably hot and humid. Maybe it was *El Nino* but, in any event, it contributed to the circumstances making Sadie Anderson feel most uncomfortable. Sadie had been in the same hotel for more than a week. While the hotel was nice enough and well enough appointed, her training dictated she not stay at any location longer than absolutely necessary. She was waiting for word from Eric. Waiting for a signal the meet had gone well. Only then, would she make arrangements to join him. Until word was received, she had to sit and wait. Sadie was not a person who sat and waited with ease and comfort.

Sadie Anderson was raised in a Midwestern state by parents involved in law enforcement. Because of the times, and probably the place, justice according to Sadie's parents, often was simply pragmatic, sometimes at the expense of any concept of civil rights. Sadie hated the *justice above freedom* attitude she experienced while growing up, especially during her rebellious high school years. However, despite her adolescent principles, she later discovered a certain expediency was appropriate in covert operations. Sadie, while deeply involved and committed, also hated the term *black opps* and at every opportunity resisted the label.

After college Sadie joined the Central Intelligence Agency, based upon her extremely successful college career in accounting combined with a curriculum of courses in international business. Sadie joined, expecting the job would primarily consist of tracing and auditing foreign bank accounts and other accounting functions related to the apprehension of international criminals. She joined the agency, hoping there would be a moderate amount of foreign travel and, for several years, her hopes were fulfilled. She found the accounting very mundane, but, the travel was invigorating. One of the features exciting her was the need to utilize an alias when she traveled. Often, only the home office had the information as to her real identify. She attributed this clandestine circumstance the CIA's attempt to live up to its reputation and, at least in her case, little more. Little did she know that her accounting background and her knowledge of international institutions would become invaluable later in her career - a career destined to become infinitely more active.

For the last eighteen months Sadie had fulfilled the role of Eric's live-in girlfriend and as such, was his only safe contact with the home office. Eric may have been, and probably was, under constant surveillance. Posing as his girlfriend, she could occasionally arrange the freedom he needed to safely contact their handler. Like Eric, Sadie had a cell phone as safe to use as technology would allow. Like Eric, it was the only connection to a world she had left over a year ago - a connection that brought her back into a world which had some semblance of normalcy and sanity.

Living arrangements for the operatives were very strained at first. After all, a nice girl from the Midwest couldn't just prostitute herself for her job on a moment's notice. She felt an immediate attraction to Eric she could not deny. She realized, in a way only a woman can understand, Eric was not comfortable either, but he was also attracted to her. Company policy was very clear, forbidding internal fraternization. Policy aside, everybody knew - in the field, in deep cover, it was difficult, if not virtually impossible for relationships not to develop. Sadie wasn't sure when the relationship was acknowledged by both her and Eric, but it happened. Now the live-in arrangements were old hat, and for the most part, very comfortable. She was living, and enjoying, the role designed for her. The Company, as it did so often in other matters, just ignored reality

The cell phone rang. Sadie jumped with anticipation. "Yes."

"Howard here. I heard from Eric. He's in Las Vegas, and as far as I can tell from the size of the deposit he requested, everything is going well. The next contact will probably be with you and probably over land lines, so stay in character and contact me when you can."

The phone went dead. Howard always did lack social graces – and he knew the last directive was unnecessary. Following his injuries, and his resulting administrative assignment, Howard had become a real worrier where field agents were concerned – a sort of "Company Mother." Sadie was a professional and would never drop the facade necessary to the success of an assignment

"Thank you for holding the shoes, but I don't think I want them at this time. You keep the deposit for your trouble." Sadie hung up satisfied she had kept in character. Any listening post would not be suspicious.

A guarded feeling of relief came over Sadie as a result of the call. At least Eric was still operating and healthy. But then, she already knew that to be the case. If things had gone badly, she would have been eliminated immediately. That was what made her feel at least a little uneasy. She was a sitting duck, and could do nothing about it, at least not yet. She went to the window and looked at the street fronting the hotel. As expected, about one block away, was a stripped down old Ford. Inside were, what appeared to be, two men. They had been there for the last twelve to fourteen hours.

Sadie knew they would be there until this matter was concluded, one way or another.

Sadie was also aware of a man and woman stationed in the lobby. The apparent couple was so untrained; it was easy to recognize their intent.

She also had good reason to believe the bartender was being paid to report her movements. All avenues of escape appeared blocked.

CHAPTER FOUR

I've lost four hands in a row. I usually leave a table at this point," I said to the dealer, "but then I might win the next three hands."

"You might, but I've been hot all afternoon."

"Let's test a theory. I believe the probability of losing seven straight hands is really long. I will bet three hundred-dollars a hand. If I win two of the next three hands, you get a hundred dollar tip, and I walk away having cut my losses. If I don't win at least two, you don't get the tip and I walk away - an even bigger loser."

The dealer smiled, and the attentive pit boss seemed amused. I won the next three hands, tipped the dealer as advertised, and walked away having cut my losses. My high roller image was now solid and would be conveyed to all the other pits *via* the house computer.

"*Bill*," someone shouted across several gaming tables. I proceeded on, as though I had not heard the summons. Was one of my worst fears coming true? Was a person from my past going to blow my cover and the meeting? Before I could reach the main isle someone grabbed my shoulder. I spun around coming face to face with one of the associates I worked with at the law firm years ago. His name was Jerry Newberry.

"Bill, I thought it was you! Remember me - Jerry Newberry?"

"Yes, I remember you. It's been years, how've you been?"

"Just fine -made partner last year. Man - it's good to see you! You know after you quit you just dropped from sight. Nobody heard from you."

"Well, I meant to stay in touch, but got real busy fast and somehow didn't." I lied.

"How long you going to be in town?" he asked.

"Not more than a couple of days. Here on business." I could see where this was going - I needed to find a way out. "In fact, I'm late for a meeting now. It's good to see you again, Jerry, but I must move along. I'm sure you understand."

"You bet, but you can't get rid of me that quickly. How about meeting later, or maybe tomorrow? How about dinner tomorrow night?"

I realized I wasn't going to shake him easily, so I agreed to dinner the next night and promised I would contact him early, the following morning, to finalize the arrangements. Finally satisfied, he returned to the gaming area and I was free to continue to my room.

Thirty minutes. Just long enough to get to my room, shower, change clothes and collect my thoughts for the meet of my life, at least my life up until this time. I found the tower where the new room was located. The bank of elevators was busy. One was just leaving, two were arriving. My training surfaced, even when it didn't matter. I virtually jammed myself into the elevator that was leaving. For whatever it was worth, if I was being tailed, I had just lost the escort.

Reaching my room I found the standard suite arrangement; a large sitting room, a very luxurious bedroom and a large sunken bathtub for two or more. My luggage had been delivered. My suits and shirts already hung in the closet, a service not advanced to all guests. In my case, directed by a guest with much more clout than I possessed. I quickly showered, and dressed in the appropriate casual clothes. I strapped my 9mm S&W to its usual location, just under the left armpit, and slightly to the back. I wasn't sure how the scenario would play out, but Barajas, was not going establish himself as my superior, more importantly, I was not his lackey. If I was going to do business with him, it had to be after I gained his respect, and more importantly, after he realized he did not pull my strings

I glanced at my watch. I had eight minutes before I wanted to arrive at his suite. Timeliness was not a factor I could play with. In this business, punctuality was certainly a major factor determining longevity. Leaving my room, I entered an elevator, inserted the floor key I had been given, and pushed the button labeled twenty-two; one floor up. The door opened to an ornate lobby, serving only four suites. The appointments were lavish. Barajas occupied suite C, and as I approached, double doors swung open. Waiting for me inside were two of Barajas's personal soldiers. Behind them I could see the lackey driver, whom had so graciously provided my transportation to Caesar's earlier. Both of the soldiers stepped forward.

"Welcome, Mr. Butler. Mr. Barajas is waiting to see you. There are just a few formalities before entering," the larger one said. The smaller of the two began to step forward.

"Stop right there!" It was time for me to establish myself. "If you intend to frisk me to see if I'm carrying, forget it. One more step will be your last. Your boss has done enough research on me, and I'm sure he passed it on to you, to know that I can carry out this threat. For your information, however, I am carrying." I opened my jacket and showed the nine mm.

"If Barajas has a problem with this, he's not the man I want to do business with. No one instructs me when and where not to carry - including Barajas!." The soldiers froze, mostly out of surprise I'm sure. "Go tell your Boss my conditions. I'll wait here for three minutes. Be assured, if I leave I

won't be back, and if either of you follow me, you won't be back either."
The soldiers turned toward the suite.

"It won't be necessary for you to wait, Mr. Butler, your terms are more
than fair, in fact expected."

It was Barajas -- the meet was about to begin.

I entered Barajas's suite. The soldiers, including the lackey driver,
seemed to melt into nothing. All of a sudden it was just Barajas and myself.
The suite – well, it was spectacular! The reception room was a hall, easily
ten feet wide and sixteen to eighteen feet long. It was appointed with
straight back upholstered chairs, love seats along its perimeter interspersed
with antique tables accented with crystal lamps and silver ashtrays. Persian
tapestries were on the walls. The ceiling was abnormally high and was
adorned with a crystal chandelier surmounting the artistry of the lamps, The
room at the end of the hallway was half the size of a basketball court, with at
least three distinct conversational areas. At least three or four more areas
could easily become further centers of social activity, without affecting any
other area. In the approximate center of the room was a big flat screen
television - or should I say: *three* big flat screen televisions. The central unit
was a massive triangle with a television screen on each face; each television
was easily sixty inches. Couches, recliners, more love seats, and overstuffed
chairs were all nearby – along with appropriate tables and exquisite lamps.
Each of the television sets seemed to constitute its own, loosely arranged,
mini-theater.

At the far end was a wet bar stocked with, what appeared to be, every
conceivable brand of liquor. To the left of the bar was a slightly less
ostentatious hallway, which I assumed led to the bedrooms. Behind me, and
just to the right of the entry hall, was a closed doorway. I assume that's
where the soldiers disappeared.

I must have seemed preoccupied with the television complex.

"You probably have the same questions I had when I first saw the
televisions." Barajas said. "How could you hear one if they all were on
different channels? The hotel has solved that problem. All of the televisions
operate from one remote--- their programming is identical at all times."

"That's unique." I commented "Probably has something to do with the
obsession we Americans have with sporting events."

He nodded.

"Enough small talk. I'm not here to discuss the American television
culture," I said, attempting to move the conversation forward. "I'm here to
discuss the structure of a potential business arrangement which will benefit
both of our organizations."

Barajas indicated to the bar area. "Before we get started, let's fix ourselves a drink and get comfortable,"

"I don't ever drink and discuss business," I said, "but I will take a tonic and lime. Barajas poured my tonic, squeezed a prepared lime section, and fixed himself a moderate scotch. I took the liberty of finding an overstuffed leather chair, just off the bar, and directly across an ornate coffee table from its overstuffed mate. He joined me. "Okay, Mr. Butler, where do we go from here? It's your meeting."

Three years of preparation and deception were at stake. The beginnings of success or failure were to be determined in the next few minutes -- or hours.

"To effectively expand our mutual interests globally, it's become exceedingly clear, that our two organizations desperately need one another. You and your people have supply far exceeding your ability to market product. This phenomenon will eventually result in one of two unfavorable conditions in your market place. The first is: you will drop your price, becoming more aggressive in your sales efforts. Profits will drop and the exposure to enforcement organizations will increase, with large risk to you personally, not to mention your captains. The second condition is: you will remain static and risk losing the supply advantage you currently enjoy to a more aggressive organization."

"Would that 'more aggressive' organization be you and your people?" he asked. "Because if that's the thread supporting this proposal, I will consider what you just said a threat *or* an attempt to extort, and this meeting is over!"

"If I were intending to extort, I would not be here in person. There are better and certainly safer ways to deliver that message. I am attempting to accurately state the current circumstance. If candor offends you, it is I who will leave now. Or if you want to hear the balance of the proposal, I will proceed, *but only* if you will allow me to finish *before* you make further comments."

The room was silent for what seemed an eternity. His eyes never left mine. I realized, from the cold blue Spanish stare, he was not accustomed to being spoken to so directly. Decisions were being made not necessarily concerning the offer I was about to make.

"Proceed, Mr. Butler"

"My organization doesn't have a source of supply capable of supporting all of the markets we have opened. We originally intended to arrange for supply, much as a middleman would, in the traditional retail situation. We find this arrangement unreliable, given the commitments we must make to secure the market. We are able, without going into detail, to market to the entire world, but we must have the committed supply. The only way this can occur is to acquire a partner whose financial interest is tied to the success of our marketing abilities. Conversely, our financial interest would be tied to the successful supply stream for the markets. Your weakness is our strength and vice-versa. The resulting cartel-partnership will have no weaknesses. The details of the organization will have to be worked out, but that's not a function of this meet. I only wish to secure your interest or your lack of interest, to determine if it's advantageous to go forward."

Barajas was about to speak when he was interrupted by a commotion in the entry hall. The man who had driven me to the hotel appeared. He was flushed, and his clothes were in disarray. Barajas turned to face the soldier. "Did you locate Serge?" he said.

The driver-soldier nodded.

"Well, bring him in here!" At that point other men entered, none of whom I had seen before. They were virtually dragging Serge, who was protesting,

"It's all a lie," he sobbed, fear evident on his face.

Barajas looked at Serge, "How long have you been in my employ? Two - maybe three years?"

Serge nodded breathlessly. "And how many times have I told you not to promise your girlfriends a supply of product? *At least* two times --- would you agree?"

"Yes, Mr. Barajas," Serge replied. "I swear to you, I haven't broken my solemn word to you. I would not do that, you must believe me! I have been loyal to you sense I was a boy."

"Then why is it reported to me, that just this evening, you promised some whore a month's supply to entice her to your bed?" Serge's body suddenly got extremely tense.

"It's not that way, Mr. Barajas! She said she needed some medicine. I offered a dose in return for her favors. There was never mention of a month's supply. She could not have interpreted my offer as coming from anything but my own small personal stash," Serge anxiously replied.

"Then my source is lying. Is that true?" "Barajas said.

"Maybe not lying, but certainly there was a misunderstanding," Serge pleaded.

"Then let's get the source in here, shall we? Get Crystal."

One of the soldiers left and returned almost immediately with a tall, slender, yet voluptuous woman of about twenty-five. She had auburn hair coming to the middle of her back. If she was the whore, she was dressed to fit the part. She was wearing an extremely low cut tight fitting short black dress barely covering her butt and red high-heeled shoes. Aside from her clothes, she was exceedingly attractive. As she walked into the room, Serge turned as white as new copy paper.

"Serge here tells me that he offered you a simple fix, not a month's supply - and you must have misinterpreted him. Is that possible?" Barajas inquired.

Crystal hung her head, "No, Sir. He said a month."

Sometime during the interrogation, two of the soldiers had moved in behind Serge and Crystal. The movement was almost imperceptible, but there they were. Somehow. I knew what was to come next.

"She's lying!" Serge pleaded, making an attempt to break free of the soldiers restraining him.

From that point, it all went very fast.

Barajas simply nodded his head to the soldier behind Serge, who had already produced a fine wire with handles attached at the ends. Within seconds and without any sound, Serge was *garroted*. Serge's body became immediately ridged with trimmers in his hands and feet. Arterial blood began spurting from his neck. His body went limp. He was dead in little more than thirty seconds.

I fought back an overwhelming desire to vomit. I'm sure, I was as white as Serge

"Call our friends. Tell them we have a delivery for them. In the meantime, get him out of sight," Barajas barked. "Make sure Crystal gets a nice bonus and get her out of Las Vegas. Send her to our people in Atlantic City. She'll do well there."

Crystal started to protest, but evidentially decided to keep quiet. She was escorted from the room. By this time, Serge had been taken elsewhere, and the soldiers had melted away, just as they had at the beginning of the meet. I was alone again with Barajas.

"Sorry you had to witness that, Mr. Butler, but as I'm sure you will agree, swiftness is often the best if not the only guarantee, of self-preservation."

I nodded and tried to collect my thoughts. I thought it best to proceed "My organization feels the political unrest in certain parts of the world is creating enormous opportunities that may never occur again. Time is, very literally, of the essence. You're either in, or you're out. There isn't time for the luxury of a negotiated organizational structure. We're confident the details can be worked out as we each become more aware of the strengths and weaknesses of the other."

Barajas took a long and reflective sip of the scotch he had fixed earlier. "What comes next, if I am interested?" he asked.

"You're interested! After all, it was Serge and not me that was garroted," I said, attempting to sound cocky "The first, shall we say evidence of good faith, will be a sale of refined and uncut cocaine to some newly developed interests in the Middle East. Because you have not, and will not, have time to fully analyze the potential of our partnership, we will pre-pay you for the product. Delivery will either be to one of our ships on the high seas, or directly to a designated port in the Middle East. The price you will charge the partnership will be the rough equivalent of your cost. The customers will pay the partnership a price far exceeding any you have been able to extract from your markets. The money will be paid to my organization. We will account for all of the costs, associated with the opening of a new market, and we will split the profits- sixty percent to us and forty percent to you. You have no exposure to loss. As we progress, and develop a better business relationship, the percentages may become more favorable."

Barajas was about to speak when I continued,

"I can't imagine why you would need it, but I can give you forty-eight hours to determine your place in the world market. I must know your answer before I leave Las Vegas."

Again his mouth opened as though to speak.

"There need not be any further conversation at this time," I said. "I heard you order the disposal of the "package.' I won't be present when your "friends" appear. I have always maintained a policy against becoming involved in the disciplinary actions or love affairs of my competitors or affiliates. 'You know where I can be reached. I expect to hear from you shortly."

I quickly finished the tonic and lime. I had not realized it, but my throat had become parched. I got up, left the suite, and punched the elevator for service to my floor.

The meet had gone exceedingly well!

CHAPTER FIVE

S adie was pacing the floor of the hotel room. Seventy-two hours had passed since Eric left. The surveillance, intent on her every move, was still in place. For the first time since joining the service, she felt utter helplessness. Her abdominal muscles were tense; her stomach acids were churning. Internally she was in a state of panic. This had to end, yet she could do nothing to end it - except wait. Her nervousness, her absolute panic, could not show. Her life, Eric's life, depended on her being able to present to the interested, a picture of serenity. Slight evidence of boredom could be her only visible characteristic.

The evening hours were approaching. Sadie instinctively realized it wouldn't appear normal to stay cooped up in her hotel room any longer. It was three hours later in Bogotá than in Las Vegas, too early for Eric to send for her. She must get out to appear normal. Dinner was a natural reason to be about and be seen outside the hotel. Sadie wasn't sure she could eat, but she had to try. In any event, the excursion would be a diversion from her panic. Having made a decision, any decision, she felt better immediately. She began to prepare herself to leave the hotel room for the first time that day.

Wearing a full flowered skirt of mid-calf length, a simple white blouse and a native style straw hat, Sadie descended the stairway. She hoped her appearance was one of a carefree, almost flirtatious and somewhat bored, woman waiting to join her boyfriend. The lounge was to the left of the staircase. Obviously, the design was meant to attract the weary traveler arriving for dinner. Why not, she thought, act normal. Sadie smiled, and the bartender smiled back. He was obviously uneasy.

"Do you remember the drink you fixed for me a day or so ago?" she asked.

"Yes Senorita," he replied, "but I didn't think that you liked it."

"Of course I liked it! I didn't feel like drinking that evening. Please, fix me another. I may even get drunk tonight!"

The bartender smiled.

Sadie got her drink and took a sip or two. It was one of those sweet fruit drinks, which if served in the States, would've had a little umbrella inserted in the place of a swizzle stick. In Bogotá, at least in this hotel, the drink lacked even the swizzle stick. The drink could be sipped for a long time before one would be expected to order another, its only redeeming feature. Sadie wanted to appear to be drinking but could not get, even slightly impaired. It was imperative she have her wits about her. She nonchalantly swiveled her bar stool, surveying the immediate area around her.

She could see into the lobby. The elderly couple, previously so interested in her, were gone. Had she misread their intent earlier? Was something going down? Had they been pulled off? Was she jumping to unjustified conclusions? Sadie hated the hot feeling in the pit of her stomach. She was getting really uneasy, but knew she was committed to, at least one more drink, before she could leave .

A native couple was in the rear of the lounge. Otherwise, it was empty. They were absorbed with each other, oblivious to the rest of the world, including the immediate lounge. The woman was about eighteen years old and dressed in local fashion. The man was older, maybe thirty, and was dressed indicative of a somewhat higher station in life.

"Why don't they get a room?" Sadie thought. "At least, they could be discrete." The thoughts had come from nowhere. Sadie was irritated she had even noticed them, let alone becoming judgmental, especially given her own situation. She swiveled back to the bar, resigned to completing the charade.

The menu for the hotel restaurant was posted daily and displayed at the entrance to the dining room. Mostly, the food had been better than average, but this evening Sadie didn't want to face the advertised fair - lamb stew and the obligatory wine. She and Eric had chosen this particular hotel because of its low-keyed atmosphere, as well as its proximity to the international airport. There wasn't an abundance of fine dining establishments in the immediate area. Would it be appropriate to leave the hotel at this time to dine elsewhere? What if Eric were to call? – all questions crossing her mind. Yes, she would do it. She would leave the hotel for dinner.

Sadie knew she'd feel much better if she were to get out of the hotel, go somewhere - anywhere. A part of the Midwestern girl, buried somewhere deep within her, giggled at the prospect of seeing the surveillance scramble to cover her and not be obvious.

Sadie called to the bar tender, "I think I'll dine out of the hotel tonight. Can you recommend a bistro not too far away?"

"I thought you were going to get drunk this evening," he said, smiling.
"Maybe, and maybe not." Sadie teased "When I get drunk alone, I always get into trouble. Now where can I go to get a good fish dinner?"

"About two miles south. You can't miss it. It's the only restaurant in the area, but it has very good seafood."

"Thanks."

Sadie finished her drink and went to the hotel desk. The clerk was busy with ledgers, but took a second, or two, to notice her approaching.

"What can I do for you Senorita?" he asked.

"Please get me a cab, and if my boyfriend calls, take any message he cares to leave. Tell him I'll be back after dinner."

The clerk nodded and picked up the telephone. He spoke to someone in Spanish and hung up the phone. "The cab will be here momentarily. You will be able to see him from the lobby. You may prefer to wait there."

"Thank you, I will," Sadie replied.

Less than a minute passed before a six or seven year old Chevrolet appeared. Sadie got in and the driver began to proceed south, being careful not to exceed a safe speed.

"*Wait !* I haven't told you where I want to go."

"I was told that you wanted seafood," the driver replied.

"Well ... I did, but I'm not sure now. Why don't you go right at the next intersection. Let's see what we find."

The driver, though obviously uneasy, obeyed her wishes. The road onto which they had turned was lined with local commercial establishments. None were restaurants.

"Where does this road lead?" Sadie asked.

"It winds around neighborhoods and local businesses and ends up in the central city." the driver responded.

"You speak very good English. Are you from Colombia?"

"Yes, but I was educated in the States. I came back when the money ran out. I have two years remaining before I could graduate in Structural Engineering. Why are you here?"

"Just came along with my boyfriend. We're from the U.S. He's got some sort of business here."

The cab driver fell silent. In an effort to make conversation, Sadie pressed him further.

"When do you expect to get back and finish your studies?"

"Probably never. There are factions in this country that view travel, and certainly education, to be dangerous to their position. Even if I could get enough money together, I would never be allowed to leave. I only came back because your INS would not allow me to stay."

Sadie sensed frustration, even hostility, in the driver's tone and inflections. The service had trained her not to dismiss those feelings, as they may be valuable later, when one needs a friend. The cab rounded a small curve in the road, and on the right, not more than one hundred yards ahead, were the familiar golden arches!

"Just look at that! A sign from home, just when it's needed most," Sadie exclaimed. She felt better now! "I know -- why don't I buy both of us a Big Mac, fries, and a shake, and we'll eat it in the cab!" How does that sound?"

"OK, but I thought you wanted to get a dinner of fish -- or *something* ? "

"Not when I can get *something* from home, and I'll bet this is as close as I can come to home in this part of the world."

"You're right about that," the cabbie replied.

The cab pulled into the take-out drive, and when it was their turn, the driver spoke to the stationary microphone in Spanish and proceeded to the service window.

They got their order. The driver suggested a small park he knew about a short distance away. The evening was mild with just a light breeze. "Why not! "Sadie said. "It's better than eating in the cab."
After a short ride, they reached the park. It was green and clean and had three tables at the far end. The tables were located about fifteen meters apart. A family, enjoying the evening, occupied one. They had three children ranging in age from about five to an infant. The wife was expecting their fourth.

Sadie chose the table, furthermost from the family, and spread the fare. "Before we eat, I need to know your name," she asked, "I rarely buy Big Macs for a gentleman I don't know."

"My given name is Benjamin Chavez. Everyone just calls me Ben."

"OK, Ben, are you uncomfortable with bringing me here? I sensed reluctance when I changed my mind about fish and asked you to go this direction.

"No Senorita, I am not uncomfortable being with you. It's just - well, there are people in this country who want to know your location at all times. I think it has something to do with the reason you and your boyfriend are in Colombia. I'll have to explain our evening to the hotel manager, or he won't send me fares again. He may not anyway. I hope you understand."

Sadie thought for a time and replied carefully ...

"I do understand, Ben - but may I ask you a question? You always refer to *'there are people'* as though you're not one of them. Is that true?"

Ben's eyes instantly narrowed. She sensed his muscles becoming taunt. He hesitated a moment, as if to gain back his self-control. "No, Senorita, I am not one of them, but because of my circumstances, I must live with them."

"If you could leave this country, never coming back, would you?" Sadie asked.

"Yes, without a second thought! You see I have no family – no family *left*. My father was a member of the government's security forces. During an attempt to shut down a drug warehouse, he saved several other soldiers' lives. He became somewhat of a local hero and because of his notoriety, drug interests murdered my entire family. I survived only because I was driving cab that night. I'm sure, if they knew I was the son of my famous father, I also would be dead."

Ben fell silent, but beneath the common appearing exterior, Sadie could sense a deep and abiding hatred of the men who killed his family.

"I don't know why I told you all this. I shouldn't have. Your boyfriend … maybe you, are dealing with the people that murdered my family. I *pray* you will keep our conversation confidential. My life is in jeopardy."

Sadie hesitated. She didn't know what to do. She desperately wanted to put his mind at ease but, to do so, would place an additional risk on a project which already had too many unknowns.

"I'm unable to tell you why my boyfriend and I are here, but you must believe we are not like the people who killed your family," Sadie finally replied. "We must be getting back now, but before we leave, can you give me a way to get in touch with you? I want to be able to contact you later. I may even need to. No one else must know of the arrangement. Also, the arrangement must be usable for a considerable period of time. I know it's a risk to you, as you know very little about me. Ben, as I stated before, neither myself nor my boyfriend are like the people who murdered your family. You must just accept that on faith.

"Ben looked at Sadie. His dark eyes were bottomless pools. "I won't jeopardize any of my friends, but there is a way. There's a place, near your hotel, where I can receive messages. You can leave a note for me there, and I will have it within two hours. About three blocks, north of your hotel, is an open market used by locals. In the center is a message board. If you want to reach me, leave a note in the upper right corner of the board. Mark the note BC and on the inside and put the letter S. Within two hours, I will meet you here at this park. That's the best I can do."

"It will do fine. Now let's get back."

CHAPTER SIX

I went directly to my room The feeling of success was intoxicating. I was elated at not having years of preparation go down the drain. However, the evening was not over. I had to get Sadie out of Colombia and here to the relative safety of Las Vegas. There was also the matter of my old buddy, Jerry Newberry. He could not be allowed to remain in Vegas. First things first, however, and getting Sadie out of Colombia was my first priority. For this, I could use a normal landline. I picked up the telephone located on the marble table in the spacious and well-appointed sitting room. I gave the hotel operator the information to complete the call and asked him to ring me when the connection was made.

The phone rang a few minutes later , I quickly picked it up. "Hello Sadie, our business went fine. What's the earliest you can catch a flight to Las Vegas?"

"Eric, I've been so bored waiting for your call," Sadie replied, keeping in character. "While I was waiting, I checked the flight schedules. I think there's a flight leaving in about ninety minutes. I'll try to catch it. The plane clears customs in El Paso, so it may take a bit longer getting to Vegas. Is that okay?" she inquired?

"That's fine. Do it. I'm staying at Caesar's Palace, Suite 2115. Call me if there are any problems. I will be here for another twenty minutes. By the way, what time will your flight arrive in Las Vegas?"

"I don't know," Sadie replied "Please make whatever arrangements are necessary, so I will be allowed to go directly to your room when I do get there. I should be there sometime early tomorrow."

"OK, just ask for a bellman named Jeb. He'll get you to the room."

"I'll see you soon. I must get hopping now on the arrangements, or I won't be there for a week. Eric, I really miss you." Sadie hung up the phone.

Twenty minutes to determine if everything goes well for Sadie, then the Jerry problem. The solution will require the use of the secure line. It The call can't be placed from the room. I decided to pass the time by catching the local news. Channel surfing produced only sit-coms. Why don't hotels provide television schedules? I always hated hotel promotions and teasers for the pay channels. I just wanted a news report and to relax. A drink would help I went to the well-stocked mini-bar, surveying the choices. The pre-made Martini caught my eye immediately. Martinis had always been my downfall. I'm not sure if it's the Martini I like, or the taste of cold gin. In any event, I knew I had found the solution to the next twenty minutes. I retrieved a short cocktail glass from above the bar, filled it with little ice cubes, and emptied the mini-bottle into the glass. The bar even had a small jar of martini olives. What more could a man want?

I kicked off my shoes and fell into a large overstuffed chair with matching footrest. I was intent on enjoying the next twenty minutes -- well, fifteen minutes now.

I could have easily fallen asleep. I hadn't realized how tired I'd become. It was approaching thirty six hours since leaving Colombia. Except for little catnaps on the airplane, I hadn't slept. For some reason, a lecture from an instructor at Quantico popped into my head. I don't remember the man's name, but the substance of the lecture was that an operative shouldn't relax when there's apparent success in achieving his objective or mission. The instructor presented statistics showing when operatives got into trouble. A high percentage of agents in trouble had recently achieved their objective. The lesson to be learned was clear. This was no time to relax. I had some work to do before I could sleep. The Martini was gone. I looked at my watch.

Thirty minutes had elapsed. Sadie must have been successful in making travel arrangements. I needed to get to where I could use the cell phone and not risk someone eavesdropping. I hadn't eaten for some time, and was famished. I decided to make the call from the busiest and noisiest restaurant in the hotel, eat at the same time, thereby killing two birds with one stone.

As expected, the busiest and nosiest restaurant was the food court. I surveyed the area for the availability of a table, found one in the center of it all, and claimed it. The food court was split up into ethnic specialties, each specialty having its own service line. I chose Italian, not because I was dying for Italian food, but because its line was the shortest. The bonus was, I do like Italian food. It was late. Many of the Italian dishes were gone, and the servers weren't replacing them. The old standard of spaghetti and Italian sausage was available. I took a healthy portion and returned to my table.

It was late in Las Vegas and three hours later on the East Coast. I knew from prior experience Howard Baker was not going to be happy about the timing of my requests. I also knew he would get the job done, and then claim I "owed" him. Everyone I knew owed Howard Baker. As far as I know, he never collected from anyone. I dialed his number. There was a momentary silence, followed by the electronic whine, signaling it was time to insert my security code. I inserted the code and the phone rang. The phone went through four rings with no answer. I was almost in a panic. I had to get Howard.

"Hello, this had better be important!"

"It is," I replied, "and by the way, it's so nice to hear your voice. This is Eric."

"I could've made book on that. What do you want? Do you know what time it is?

"I need a person removed immediately. He's here in Vegas. His name is Jerry Newberry. He's an attorney I worked with before I joined the Company. He recognized me earlier today. He called me by name, across two tables! I don't believe it caused any problems, as of now, but it will if he remains in Las Vegas."

"How do we locate him?" Howard inquired.

"He's staying at Caesar's Palace. I don't know if he's here alone, but he's got to disappear."

"He will, and before morning," was the reply "Any special way you want it to appear?"

"Not really, just not obvious, and in a way allowing me to claim credit if the matter comes up."

"Consider it done. I'll be in touch and, by the way, you owe me one." Before I could reply, the line went dead. I could relax now, because I knew Howard would not fail, and, yes, I did "owe" him one -- another one.

I finished my spaghetti and left the food court. I was finally headed for my room, intent on some much needed sleep. I had only one more task to complete, and I could do it from the room's land line. On reaching the room I used my card key, opened the door, and literally stumbled into the suite.

On the floor, blocking the door, was the tied, gagged, and *garroted* body of Jerry Newberry. I barely made the bathroom before losing the spaghetti.

31

CHAPTER SEVEN

A s Sadie and Ben approached the hotel, it was obvious their return was anxiously anticipated. From a distance, they could see the hotel manager and a local police officer standing in the barrow, looking both ways, in an obvious attempt to locate something. The *something* was them, and they knew it. Ben's rather dark complexion turned, not less than, two shades lighter.

"What shall we do?" he asked nervously.

"Tell them the truth," Sadie replied. "I changed my mind, and we found a McDonald's, where I bought both of us Big Macs. Let me do the talking. You back me up."

Sadie instantly recalled training she had received in her early days with the CIA. A field agent-instructor, who had spent much of his career in the field, cautioned the young, green agents that placed in a position where they must lie, there were rules to follow.

"Lies are of two basic varieties," he said. "The first is the lie where the facts are altered or manufactured to fit the needs of the speaker. The second is much more subtle and, therefore, much more effective; that is - telling the truth about most of the facts, and omitting or modifying only facts the speaker is attempting to cover.

"Never lie, even a little bit, more than you have to," The agent had said. "It's the embellishments to a simple lie that will be discovered. It's the embellishments that may cost you your life." Sadie couldn't remember the rest of the rules, but that one was clear and timely.

As the cab approached the hotel's drive, Sadie could tell from body language the local policeman was about to show the hotel manager how effective his authority was. The cab stopped. Sadie got out immediately, and, with the same flirtatious demeanor she had exhibited earlier, walked directly up to the manager.

"Now, why is it you kept the McDonald's just up the road a secret?" she said "You know, we Americans invented them. I had to take advantage of this young boy; almost beat it out of him, before he would tell me one even existed in this town. I thought I was going to have to cry to get him to take me there." Sadie noticed the policeman had gotten Ben out of the cab and was holding him by the upper arm.

"I'm extremely flattered, by your concern for me in Eric's absence, but really, the driver was a complete gentleman. I'm here now, only because, the young driver insisted we return. He was concerned you were worried," Sadie said, addressing both the officer and the manager.

"I thought you were going for a seafood meal," the manager explained, "so I made a reservation for you. When you didn't show up for the reservation, I got concerned and notified the local police. Please excuse my apparent intrusion. I meant no harm,"

"Apology accepted! Now, if the officer will release my driver, I would like to pay him for his troubles."

The police officer immediately released Ben's arm and politely excused himself. Sadie paid and tipped Ben without even a meaningful glance and was escorted into the hotel by the manager.

"Can the Hotel buy you an after-dinner drink tonight, Senorita?" the manager inquired attempting to establish a lighter atmosphere.

"No, I think I've had quite enough excitement for one night. Thank you for asking. I think I'll go to my room now. Good evening."

As Sadie was entering the hotel from the cab, she noticed the couple was not in the bar, nor was there anyone in the hotel lobby. Sadie knew something had occurred. She wasn't sure if she could remain patient, waiting to get the call from Eric. The call had to come from Eric. If the call came from anyone else, the news would not be good. Back in her room, she paced for several minutes before recalling there had been surveillance in the street outside her window. It was gone also. It was not time to panic as all indications were the meet had gone fine. *Why didn't he call? What was she going to do until he did call.* All were questions with no apparent answers. Sadie sat on the edge of the bed, thinking about what she would do when Eric called. She would pack and leave. Or, if the call, God forbid, was not from Eric, then she would also have to pack and leave. The common element was packing and that's something she could do now.

She began to empty the hotel drawers of her clothing. Eric never put any of his clothes in drawers. He had admonished her that it was a waste of time and, more importantly, could_be a hindrance in the event a quick exit was required. She smiled, recalling her retort, which was always the same, and one of the few that left Eric speechless, "It's a girl thing." Sadie was glad she had put her things in drawers. At least now she had something to do. She was busy folding colorful skirts and pants, when the phone rang. Suddenly, very fearful, she almost didn't want to pick up the receiver. The phone rang again. Her hands were sweating, and she felt like an athlete just before a big event. The phone was ringing a third time. She knew she must answer it. The phone began to ring a fourth time. She picked it up, "Hello."

"I have a call from the United States,." .

"Thank you. Please put it through." Sadie returned the phone to the cradle. Within seconds the phone rang again.

"This is the long distance operator at Caesar's Palace, Las Vegas. I have a call for you from one of our guests. I'll connect you."

Sadie's heart was in her throat.

"Hello Sadie, Our business went fine."

CHAPTER EIGHT

Howard Baker hung up the phone and looked at the clock on the nightstand located on his side of the bed. His wife had stirred slightly when the phone originally rung, but slipped back into the blissful sleep he had so often longed for. The Baker home was a large two-story colonial home on the outskirts of Washington D.C. The home was bought after Howard's incident. Mildred was in full control of the purchase of the home and its furnishings, with the exception of the one room they referred to as the *library*.

The library was furnished by the Company, including the installation of all equipment. The room was a corner room and had windows opening to the outside. It received the morning and early afternoon sun. Under the guise of a slight remodel, the Company replaced the windows with bullet proof windows that did not open and were coated with a substance that rejected all radio and microwave bands. The walls received a lead lining, resulting in the same total blockage. The room had a closet converted to an equipment room. The doorways to the closet, as well as the adjacent wall, were removed. Bookshelves, matching existing shelves, were installed on a new wall and doorway. The disguised doorway was on hinges allowing it to open when an electronic switch was activated. The switch was positioned on the interior frame of the computer desk, located in the main room of the library. It, already well hidden, was further disguised by being placed behind a panel that slid open if pressure was applied to the near end.

The computer and the monitor didn't appear to be anything one couldn't purchase off the shelf of any well-stocked computer store. A printer and printer table sat next to the computer desk. Machines, whose names and functions would escape even the moderately accomplished computer technician, lined the walls of the closet. All the phone lines and computer cables were catalogued on the closet's short wall. It would have been obvious, even to the uninitiated, that this system was far beyond the ordinary home-business setup. What came in here or left from here was not subject to surveillance or interception.

Howard had gone to his library and fired up the computer. He mobilized the modem and dialed the number of his office computer, located at

Company headquarters.. After inserting clearance codes on two levels, he was in. He quickly inserted the name of William Jennings and waited while the computer brought up the requested personnel file. As the file was being down loaded, Howard determined how he was going to approach this problem. The CIA had files on all of the major law firms in the country as well as on many of the lesser firms. If the firm had any one who had CIA clearance, or had worked with the CIA at any time in the past, it would be indicated in the files. If the law firm which had hired William Jennings years ago had any such connections, Howard would evaluate them. If they appeared trustworthy enough, he would attempt to use them to get Jerry Newberry out of Vegas. If there wasn't the connection, or there was one he felt uncomfortable with, he would call a contact in the Las Vegas Metro Police and arrange for the arrest of Mr. Newberry.

The file came up. Howard instructed the computer to indicate the previous employer of the subject. The Computer buzzed. Instantly the name of Peatree, Newman, Brown, and Smyth was on the monitor. Their business address was in a fashionable section of Denver Colorado. The law firm name was typed into the computer and it was asked to locate a roster of the senior partners and indicate if any had ever had CIA affiliations. One name appeared, Brian Snow. According to the computer, Mr. Snow had been affiliated with the CIA in South East Asia. The file showed he was interviewed for an agent position after he graduated from Fordham Law School. The computer indicated, Mr. Snow had seriously considered the offer, but opted for the more mundane life. He was engaged to be married at the time.

The CIA had kept in contact with him, even to the point of having him represent them in minor civil banking litigation, where it was not appropriate to use the U.S. Attorney. Howard asked the computer for the current address and telephone number of Brian Snow, and dialed it. At the same time, he was wondering just what he was going to say when the Snow household answered the phone. The phone had rung three times.

"Hello," a female voice responded. It was clear by the muffled, almost slurred speech, the lady on the other end of the phone had been awakened.

"Hello. is this Mrs. Snow?"

"Yes," the lady responded with a slight bit more irritation evident in her voice.

"Mrs. Snow, my name is Howard Baker. I work for an organization represented by your husband. It's imperative I speak with him. Would you be so kind as to wake him for me?"

"Hold on. I'll wake him and see if he'll speak to you." The phone went silent. Within a minute the sounds of someone approaching the receiver could be heard.

"Hello. This is Brian Snow."

Howard responded, "Mr. Snow, you don't know my name, but you've done work for an organization I work for. About a year ago, you handled a bank fraud litigation at the request of your government. Operatives of the Central Intelligence Agency conducted the underlying investigation. Your firm was paid by funds coming from the CIA budget. I only recite these facts, Mr. Snow; because I want to be sure you and I agree that you have an attorney client relationship with the CIA. Do you agree with the statement I have just made, Mr. Snow?"

"At the risk of offending you, Mr. ... You haven't even told me your name?"

Howard apologized and stated his name.

"OK, Mr. Baker. Assuming all that you have said is correct, how do I know you are who you say you are? I specialize in the banking field so I won't have to deal with late night calls. To be honest with you, I don't handle them very well. It's my suggestion that whatever business we have done in the past, or may do in the future, can wait until morning."

Howard jumped into the conversation quickly, hoping that Mr. Snow would not hang up before he got the full pitch delivered.

"This concerns your partner Jerry Newberry. And No! It can't wait until morning! If you're not willing to speak with me now, I'll solve the problem in a fashion which will be much more uncomfortable and embarrassing for Mr. Newberry."

"Jerry Newberry! He's on a short vacation in Las Vegas. What has this got to do with him? Is he okay?"

"Yes, he's okay but, because of circumstances I'm not at liberty to discuss, he must be out of Las Vegas by early morning. I only called you, because you have some history with the CIA and have the power to take the necessary action in a way which will not, shall we say, overly inconvenience Mr. Newberry."

"Assuming I believe you - and, I don't know who else would make a request like this at this hour, what do you want me to do?" he asked.

"Is there is any plausible reason you could use to call him and get him to leave Las Vegas tonight?

"Well, there's a project in Chicago I'm leaving for early tomorrow. I guess I could have him meet me under the guise that I am desperate for his help."

"Good! Will you do it? I need to know. Now."

"I'll make the call and see if he'll meet me in the morning. What about flight schedules and airline tickets?" he inquired.

"You get him to agree to go, and I'll take care of the flight arrangements. Now, here's what I want you to do. You make the call to him now. He's staying at Caesar's Palace. Don't know the room number, but I'm sure the front desk will help you when you explain you're his senior partner and have a business emergency. I will call and arrange for the next available flight to Denver. I'll call you back in fifteen minutes and exchange information. You can then call him and give him the flight information."

"That will work. I hope he is in his room," he replied. Howard thanked him for his understanding and help and hung up the phone. Howard picked the receiver up again made a call to the travel section and told them what the needs were. Within minutes the arrangements were confirmed. He now had to wait for Mr. Snow to have time to complete the arrangement with Newberry.

Waiting had never been one of Howard's strengths, but one that he had learned to cope with over the years. A glance at the clock on the computer told him the coffee, which had been put on timer the night before, was brewed. The timing couldn't have been better. He had no need to even consider returning to bed. The sun would be up within the hour, and Howard was mentally awake. He turned from the computer desk to go to the kitchen and was startled by the presence of Mildred. She was standing in the doorway to the library, holding a cup of coffee.

"I didn't realize you were awake and up," Howard said.

"How could I not be with all the excitement? They really should pay you more if we're going to continue to have these late night telephone calls, especially at our age."

"You know, Mildred, I am paid very well for what I do and, by the way, you know when I am in here on Company business, you can't be in a position to hear any part of the conversation. We've discussed this many times. It's for your own safety. Now, please, go back to the kitchen, and I'll be out shortly." There was a detectable element of irritation in his voice.

Mildred grumbled something unintelligible, set the coffee on the computer desk, and shuffled off to the kitchen.

Aside from being slightly irritated by Mildred's indiscretions, the coffee was a lifesaver, and Howard was secretly glad she had brought it. All and all, he could not have asked for a better partner than Mildred. She seemed a bit resentful when it came to the requirements of his job, but supported him in all ways that really counted, especially after the incident ending his field career and putting him in the office. She realized early in their marriage that fieldwork was his life. Howard had always thrived on undercover work and the inherent excitement that went along with it. He was good at it and he knew it. Sadly, now it was just a desk and a front line support role for the agents in the field. At least, he was still involved and could feel the field excitement, even if it was vicarious.

It was time to make the call to Mr. Snow. Howard turned to the desk and dialed the appropriate number.

"Hello, this is the Smith residence."

"Howard Baker, Mr. Smith. Did you have any luck reaching Mr. Newberry?"

"No," Smith responded. "In fact, I thought it was the Hotel calling back when you rang. It seems, Jerry may be pulling an all-nighter. He may have gone to a different casino. He's not in his room and hasn't responded to a page. At least, he hasn't to this point."

"How did you leave it with the hotel?" Howard inquired.

"I told them to continue to try the page every few minutes, and to call me if Jerry responded. What are the flight arrangements? Were you able to make any?"

"He could be on a flight that leaves one hour from now, but the arrangements are he is on the next flight out, whenever he shows up. To get him to Chicago may involve a transfer, but at least he'll be out of Vegas. The ticket agents at United, Frontier, and America West are all on alert. If he shows up at their counter, he's as good as on an airplane."

"What if he doesn't get in touch with me? What do we do then?" Smith inquired.

Howard avoided the question. "I think we can give him an hour. If he doesn't show up by that time, I'll have to involve the local authorities. It's best we get off the line now so you can receive incoming calls. I'll touch base with you in one hour." Howard hung up the phone, leaned back in his computer chair, and sipped his coffee, contemplating what the possible moves were, given the rather limited possibilities.

A red light on the computer console indicated he was receiving an incoming call. The call would be connected if the person on the other end inserted an appropriate code. Moments later, the receiver rang with the same tone as any other phone.

CHAPTER NINE

Having lost all the Italian food I had eaten, I turned and surveyed the entryway to my suite. Jerry looked terrible. Garroting must be a terribly traumatic way to die. His facial muscles were contorted, and the eyes were distended to the point they appeared to be on the verge of leaving the socket. The muscles in the arms and legs were ridged, and where possible, given the cords that bonded him, distended. Jerry was dressed in the same clothes he'd been wearing earlier. From the rigidity of the body, it appeared the time of garroting was considerably earlier. I estimated he died before my meet with Barajas.

I really wanted out of the CIA! Jerry Newberry had died, not because he did anything so grievous or bad he deserved it, but simply because he knew and recognized me. For the first time in my career, I truly didn't know what to do or even how to start to find out what to do. I had obviously known of, and even seen, people die before Jerry. After all, Serge had died right in front of me, in the same way, not three hours ago. I was not affected by his death, because I somehow felt Serge deserved to die. Maybe it was he had chosen his lifestyle with his eyes wide open and knew from the start it could end in his death. The weird irony was, I had made the same decision. The teams we were on were different, but the reasons for our decisions were very much alike. How could I rationalize Jerry's death? How could I live with it?

Something had to be done and done soon. I was the only one in the suite to make a decision. What was it going to be? Let the whole sting go up in smoke? I thought not. Sadie's life, not to mention my own, wouldn't be worth a plug nickel. I needed a drink to settle my emotions and collect my thoughts. The mini-bar was still well stocked. I found two mini-bottles of Black Label scotch whisky. They would do fine. I found a glass, filled it with ice, and emptied the scotch over the ice. I couldn't sit and drink in any chair allowing me to see Jerry's body. The couch was positioned so it looked out over the strip. My back would be to the body.

I chose the couch and virtually collapsed into its confines. After about two strong pulls on the scotch, I could feel my rational faculties returning. Regardless of any long-term decision I may make concerning my future with the Company, it was critical my immediate reaction be appropriate. Anything less will cost us our lives. *God, I wished Sadie was here now.* She was flying blind at a time when her life depended on my next move.

I knew Barajas and his organization were expecting me to react. I would not disappoint them. As I sat on the couch, finishing the drink, I realized the probable hit man was the same man who had done Serge. The proximity of the murders was as obvious as the choice of weapons. Logic and anger led me to the same conclusion. I checked my pocket to make sure I had the key to the twenty-second floor. I had to confront Barajas.

Getting from the couch to the door meant I had to step over Jerry. Somehow I accomplished this feat and, reaching the corridor, called for the elevator. It took some time to get to me, but when it did, it was empty. I inserted the card key and pushed the button labeled twenty-two. The door shut. The elevator slowly rose to the next floor. By the time the doors opened, I was ready to do whatever necessary to save Sadie and to survive. The first thing I saw were the two goons which were present earlier. It was the larger one that garroted Serge during my last trip to this floor. I was betting he had also done Jerry. They were expecting me.

Both started toward the elevator door at the same time. One of them uttered, "It's him"

It was clear they were not sure of my intentions and, were prepared to perform services not at all in the best interests of my good health. "I want to see Barajas. Tell him I'm here," I stated, glaring at the thugs. The smaller one turned and entered the suite. The larger one blocked my path. "I'm not a patient man. You should hope your buddy reappears shortly." Within seconds the suite door opened, Barajas and the smaller thug stepped out.

"So soon Mr. Butler? What can I do for you?" Barajas said, as though he didn't know why I was there.

"You have a package to clean up in my suite. I told you before, I don't take part in disciplinary activities of other organizations, nor do I clean up their residue, legal or illegal. I will ask you, only once, to call your friends and have them dispose of Mr. Newberry anyway you see fit."

"My apologies, Mr. Butler, but you did indicate my organization was to be in charge of the security of our venture. I viewed Mr. Newberry to be a threat. I'm sure you understand. We all have a past and people in that *past* we have to deal with, Mr. Butler. The initial risk of those associations is ours, but the final risk, must be theirs or we won't survive in this business."

I was seeing nothing but red. "That may work in Colombia with people you have dealt with in the past, but it doesn't work here. Unless I ask for your help, you are to assume I can take care of my own organization. I will handle any threat to me or mine. *Is that clear?*"

"It is, Mr. Butler, although I'm not accustomed to the tone of this conversation!" On some imperceptible signal from Barajas, the large thug started toward me. I anticipated this event and, to be in position, had worked my way closer to the larger thug. Thankfully, he was as slow as he looked.

I brought the heel of my left hand up as hard as I could into his nose. I could hear the nose break, and better yet, I felt the skull bone forming the nasal ridge, break from the force of my blow. It was driven into the frontal lobe of his brain. He was probably dead, but to make sure, I grabbed his chin in one hand and the back of his head in the other, twisting quickly and firmly. His spine cracked and broke. The man was never going to *garrote* another person. I let him fall to the floor. There was complete silence.

"I count this as one of your disciplinary problems interfering in my business. I suggest you make whatever arrangements, in that regard, you choose. I'm going to go to have a drink now. I'll be back in my suite in one hour and I expect the mess you left to be cleaned up. If you still want to do business, along the lines we discussed earlier, meet me for breakfast at nine-tomorrow morning -- The Emperors Buffet."   The elevator appeared and I left the floor. I could use this time to contact Howard. Given the events, in the interest of humanity, Howard had to be stopped. Given the events, I wondered what humanity, if any, we retained after becoming involved in this business.

CHAPTER TEN

Sadie wanted to get to the airport a full hour ahead of the flight she hoped to board. Eric had made sufficient arrangements so, when the time came, she could just leave the hotel. Leaving was all that remained. After completing packing, Sadie called the hotel desk, informed them she was leaving, and asked a cab be summoned. She also inquired if anyone was around to help her with her luggage. Sadie generally didn't have trouble with handling her own luggage but because the hotel had stairs and because she didn't want to appear to be anything other than a lovesick female, help from the room to the cab seemed, not only welcome, but warranted.

She decided to wear a plain pair of beige slacks with a slightly darker brown blouse. She chose a loose-fitting ivory jacket built to conceal her small thirty-eight caliber snub-nose. The weapon was secure in her luggage for the pending flight. When she reached Las Vegas, she would collect her luggage, find a ladies room, and transfer the weapon to her jacket. There was a knock at the door to the room. "Yes?" Sadie inquired.

"It's the Manager. I'm here to help you with your things," was the reply.

"Good. I was hoping I wouldn't have to lug these down the stairs myself." Sadie responded and opened the door. In the entry way was the hotel manager and, the same police officer whom had been present when she and Ben returned from dinner.

"I really don't have so much luggage that it will take two strong men to get me to the cab," Sadie said.

"You won't have to take a cab," the Manager said. "Officer Gomez was in the hotel having coffee. He has volunteered to take you to the airport. It's his way of apologizing for earlier this evening."

"Isn't that nice of you, Officer Gomez, but I wasn't at all upset by your concerns. I can just as easily take a cab." Sadie did not like the way things were developing, but instinctively knew she had to continue to act the part she was assigned.

"It's no trouble, Senorita. Officer Gomez has already cleared it with his superiors. Shall we start down with the luggage?" the manager insisted.

43

"Well, OK, if it's not too much trouble, but please relax just one moment. I was just getting a scarf I packed by mistake, and I want to freshen up before leaving." Sadie grabbed the smaller of the luggage pieces and proceeded to the suite's bathroom.

After closing the door, she quickly retrieved the snub nose thirty-eight and secured it in her jacket. She closed the piece of luggage, running the water in the sink for effect. Allowing a sufficient amount of time to lapse, Sadie opened the door and reentered the main room of the suite. "I just don't know where I packed the darn scarf. It's the only one that goes with this outfit. I bought it at that cute little shop down the road . You know the one. Oh well, let's just go. It's not important."

Sadie proceeded to the door. The manager and Officer Gomez followed. Upon reaching the hotel entrance, Sadie noticed the police car was parked immediately in front, as though it had just been driven in. The motor was still running. The officer wasn't intending to stay for any length of time. Sadie's fears were solidified. Officer Gomez wasn't there for coffee. The Manager had summoned him after he learned of her departure. What did this mean? Eric said everything was fine. If that was so, why was the officer *"volunteering"* to take her to the airport? Sadie could only come up with two theories: one, Officer Gomez, or his superiors, wanted to be sure she got out of Colombia; two, Officer Gomez, or his superiors, didn't want her to leave Colombia. Sadie wasn't much of a betting person, but she would have wagered her meager savings theory number two was the answer!

Sadie forced herself to approach the police car as though she rode in one every day. "Let's hurry now. I don't like to be late for my flight, and I haven't bought my ticket yet. Where should I sit?"

"You may sit wherever you wish, Senorita. I might suggest, however, we put your baggage in the back seat, and you ride in front with me," the officer said.

"Fine. Now let's get going."

Officer Gomez slipped in behind the steering wheel, quickly glancing at the hotel manager. A knowing look passed between them, one not lost on Sadie. She knew what she might have to do and was ready to perform. The police car pulled onto the road, proceeding toward the airport. Gomez was attempting some small talk in an obvious effort to lull Sadie into a sense of complacency. As long as they were headed for the airport, Sadie was perfectly willing to play along with the charade. She acted light and carefree, talking about seeing Eric again, but all the time watching Gomez's every move. As they approached the outer limits of the airport, Gomez veered off on a perimeter road not leading to the terminal. Sadie didn't know where it ultimately ended, but knew it wasn't a road she wanted to be on.

The play was over. Sadie knew it was time to drop the act. "Where the hell do you think you're going?" Her voice had lost its lyrical quality. The tone was deadly serious.

"I'm taking you to the terminal, Senorita" Gomez responded. His facial expression changed to one of determination. "This is a shortcut only the police can use. You will see."

"I don't want to see. I want you to turn the car around and go on the highway," Sadie ordered.

Gomez smiled but didn't respond. The police car reached the end of the road. Gomez stopped the car, turning in the seat. "Please exit the car," he said in an official sounding tone.

Sadie thought for a moment. She realized she still had the ultimate element of surprise, and she would be better out of the vehicle than in it. Without saying a word, she opened the door, stepping onto the dirt road. The place where Gomez stopped the car appeared to be an old sanitary landfill, probably used and abandoned before the construction of the airport. It was open, graded, yet very uneven, and was located in the bottom of a small gulch. The police car couldn't be seen from anywhere. Sadie knew she must determine his intentions the instant he came around the car. There was no chance for a second opinion. She must act on her first instinct.

Gomez left the car at the same time Sadie did and was rounding the rear of the car. She saw he held what appeared to be a standard police issue revolver in his right hand. It had been in its holster when Sadie left the car. His intentions were clear. Without any further hesitation, Sadie dropped to the ground, rolled to her right, and cleared her weapon from its hidden restraints, all in one smooth movement.

The silence was broken by the sound of a gunshot. Sadie could detect the sulfur smell of burnt gunpowder. One look at Office Gomez, and it was clear he neither heard the gunshot - nor smelled the burnt powder. Sadie's bullet had blown most of the lower part of his face away. He was losing what common sense he had down the front of his police uniform.

It was Sadie's first. She had often wondered what it would be like. In training she heard other agents describe the immediate revulsion of killing another human for the first time. It was not that way for her. She was not sick. If anything, she was energized. It was like a big shot of adrenaline. The endorphins were running, and Sadie was enjoying them.

She could enjoy them later. Now, she had to get to the airport and get out of Colombia. It would be risky, but she had to drive the police car to the terminal. As she got in, a car appeared on the horizon, which because she was in a hole, was only about three or four hundred meters away. *"A second police vehicle?"* she thought. *"It may be over. No! It was not a police vehicle."* As it got closer, Sadie could see it was an older Chevrolet. Could it be Ben? Sadie eased the police car forward, and as the two cars approached each other, it became clear. It was Ben!

Sadie stopped the police car, got out, and waited for Ben to reach her, "God I'm glad to see you!"

"Hurry. Get in! We've got to get out of here!" Ben responded.

Sadie got in quickly as Ben was spinning the Chevrolet around. They were heading down the dirt road at full throttle. After Sadie caught her breath, she looked at Ben. His facial expression was intense. The eyes she was so attracted to earlier were retracted and dark. It was frightening. "How did you know I was out here? I'm sure this is not a chance meeting? What's going on?"

Sadie knew her weapon was in her jacket. If she needed to use it, she could. Sadie seriously hoped she wouldn't have to. She had formed an affinity for Ben in the short time she knew him, and she didn't want it destroyed.

"I heard on my radio, the Hotel Manager notify Gomez you were leaving. There wouldn't have been a reason for the notification if you weren't in trouble. I wasn't sure I could do anything," Ben said.

"I'm sure glad you showed up. I really didn't want to drive this police car to the airport terminal building."

The cab reached the paved road. Ben steered it toward the airport. "You need to get on any plane available and get out of here. Officer Gomez was a very popular man in these circles. His loss will be resented. Revenge is the only remedy they know."

"What about you? Are you in any trouble?" Sadie asked.

"No, I don't think so. Nobody saw me come in here. They wouldn't think Gomez would need help in this assignment, so there won't be back up sent in for several hours. My guess is he was also directed to bury your remains. Time is on your side right now, but it won't be later".

The cab reached the airport terminal. Ben stopped to let Sadie out at the first opportunity. Sadie understood why. He ran less risk of being inadvertently spotted with Sadie, if she walked the remaining distance to the ticket window.

Ben turned and faced Sadie, "I don't know what business you and your boyfriend have in this country, and I'm not asking you to tell me. Anyone they want to erase must be a friend to me - and therefore to my group. I will rest on that assumption for now. Please, don't forget the message board in the market plaza. Now, go and get on the first flight you can going anywhere in the U.S."

Ben put the cab in gear as Sadie exited the vehicle. She leaned in the front passenger window, "Please believe this, you will hear from me. I know people needing structural engineers." Sadie straightened up, turned, and headed for the terminal. Her cab disappeared into traffic.

She scanned the area with a trained eye. It didn't appear they had been followed. Now, she needed to concentrate on getting out of the country. Sadie walked a short distance and approached the American Airlines ticket counter. She was third in line, but the family at the window was finishing up. "Just relax," she told herself. "The line will move quickly." Sadie was developing a knot in her stomach. She knew the feeling well. Every time she faced a crisis in her life, the knot appeared. She knew from experience, nothing she could do would get rid of it. *Live through the crisis, and it would go away.* This was the first time in her life, however, that *"live through the crisis"* could be interpreted literally.

Her luggage! Her clothes! All of her personal effects! They were all back in the police car. The knot in her stomach grew tighter. The authorities wouldn't have a problem identifying her. The luggage had a name tag on it, and the name on the tag was hers. Sadie was beginning to panic. Thankfully, the Company's training programs had not been successful in changing all of her habits and feminine idiosyncrasies. In all of the events of the last forty minutes, she had never let go of her purse; it contained all her cash, credit cards, and, most importantly, her passport. *"Relax,"* she told herself again, *"I can live without the luggage, but I may not live if I don't get out of here."*

"Next," the lady at the ticket window said looking at her. Sadie approached the window attempting to smile, and appear carefree. "I called earlier about flights to Las Vegas Nevada, in the U.S. I was told of a flight through El Paso, Texas, leaving in about twenty minutes. Is that flight still available? I'll take any class, but I prefer First if it's available." Sadie thought about having to justify first class to Howard. He was such a stickler for saving government money.

She decided not to care what he thought. She would pay the difference herself, if necessary.

"You're in luck. There are several seats available, and two of them are in First Class. Would you like to book the flight?"

"Yes, please. Will I have time to make the concourse?" Sadie inquired, handing the ticket agent her American Express credit card.

"Yes, but we must hurry," the agent replied. "Do you have any luggage you would like to check?" the agent asked looking over the counter.

"No, my boyfriend flew out earlier. He took all of the luggage with him."

"That will make it easy. Let me process this ticket, and we'll get you to the airplane."

"Thank you. You'll never know how much I appreciate your help. Could you help me a little further? I need a ladies room badly. Too much coffee, you understand. Where are the closest facilities? I'll go there while you finish the ticketing process." Sadie had to get rid of the thirty-eight secreted in her jacket. If she were forced through the metal detector, she would be detained and probably arrested.

The ticket agent pointed to a restroom sign not more than fifty feet down the terminal.

"Thank you." Sadie left the window and headed directly for the restroom. It was one of those unisex rooms so popular outside the United States. She was in luck, it was empty. Sadie entered and immediately spotted a trash receptacle in the corner, near a row of sinks. It was about half filled with used paper towels and who knew what else. It would do perfectly. She retrieved the gun from her pocket and was about to plunge it deep in the accumulated trash, when the restroom door opened. In walked a man who was in such a hurry, he didn't notice her at first. When he did, he nodded and entered a stall. Sadie turned on the water and proceeded to bury the weapon deep in the nearby trash receptacle. She assumed by his actions the man had not seen the gun. She shut the water off and left the room.

Sadie returned to the ticket window to collect her ticket and got the gate assignment. The agent saw her coming, collected her materials, and handed them to her. "The plane will leave from Concourse B Gate Three. You have ten minutes to make the flight. Concourse B is the first concourse down the hall. You should have plenty of time. I called the flight attendant, and she's expecting you. Have a pleasant flight."

Sadie nodded her appreciation, collected the ticket envelope, her credit card, and ran down the indicated hall. When she reached Gate Three, as promised, the gate attendant was waiting for her. She smiled, handing the attendant her tickets. As they were being reviewed, Sadie felt the need to make small talk. "I hope I haven't held up the departure."

"No, Senorita. The flight will be leaving momentarily. Please board and take your seat."

Relieved at the prospect of leaving immediately, Sadie proceeded down the jet way to the aircraft. She reached her seat uneventfully and prepared for takeoff. In less than a minute she felt the smooth movement of the aircraft being pushed away from the gate. The plane made a large arc as it turned away from the concourse, stopped, and almost immediately proceeded forward to the designated runway.

Sadie's seat was against the window. She sat in a trance, staring out the window. The large jet was traveling down a runway but was not gaining speed. Sadie supposed it was reroute to the assigned take off runway. The plane reached the end of the runway and was beginning to turn to take- off. Sadie noticed a commotion a short distance from the paved area, down in a small draw. Several police cars with their lights on, and at least eight uniformed policemen had converged on the area. The end of the runway was just above the site Officer Gomez had taken her to! She was viewing the site from which she had just fled - the site where she had been forced to take her first human life. As the plane completed its turn, the gully was lost from view. The airplane gained speed rapidly, and within seconds was airborne, on its way to the United States.

A stewardess announced the flight was going to take several hours. Upon arrival in El Paso, Texas, all passengers and their luggage would have to deplane and proceed to the customs area for entry into the United States. The process would take ninety minutes, and passengers continuing on were advised to check with the gate attendants to determine the status of their connecting flight including concourse and gate number. Sadie hardly heard the end of the stewardess's canned presentation. The relief of being in the air, and finally away from the chaos of the last few days without Eric, was the equivalent of a sleeping pill.

Sadie felt her shoulder being gently shaken. At first she wasn't sure whether it was a dream or reality, but as the totally enveloping fog of a wonderful sleep dissipated, she realized, it was real. The stewardess was standing over her, saying they were about ten minutes out of El Paso, requesting that Sadie return the seat to the upright position, and prepare for landing.

"You must have been really beat. I rarely see a passenger sleep the entire flight." the stewardess said, in an obvious attempt to pass the time before landing.

"Yes, I've been rather sickly the past few days. I'm over it now. I think the flight was a way for my body to regain some needed rest," Sadie lied.

The stewardess smiled, "While you were asleep, I took the liberty of checking on your connecting flight. It will be leaving from the same concourse, Gate Seven." Your layover is only about thirty-five minutes.

"Will that give me time to clear customs?" Sadie inquired.

"Yes. Because of your tight flight connections, I was able to arrange for you to be expedited through customs. Your Las Vegas connection currently shows an on time status, and the flight will take just under two hours."

A bell sounded and the pilot came on the intercom, asking all flight personnel to take their seats for landing. The stewardess smiled and excused herself to take her seat for landing. The landing was smooth and uneventful. Sadie's decision to fly first class was confirmed, at least in her mind.

CHAPTER ELEVEN

Howard Baker always had a sick feeling in the pit of his stomach when he knew one of his agents was calling. Even after all the years he'd been a handler, the fear the call would bring bad if not devastating news, was a fear he hadn't been able to deal with. Bad news didn't happen often, but it happened enough to be stressful. Howard answered the call on the third ring. "Hello."

It was Eric's voice, and Howard detected a degree of revulsion in its tone, "Howard, you can cease efforts to get Jerry Newberry out of Las Vegas. Barajas was more observant than I thought. His body was delivered to me late last night." "Good God! How did it happen? Did he have family with him or anyone at all?" Howard responded.

"They *garroted* him while he was tied up. It happened while I was busy with Barajas. I feel like quitting, Howard. If I can get Sadie back in this country safely, we both might quit."

"Don't make any hasty decisions, Eric. Remember, the events of this evening are the very reason you and Sadie have been putting your lives at risk, and judging from the recent events - at extreme risk," Howard cautioned, attempting to guide him to rational thinking

"Howard, how do we rationalize what we do! People die because of us, and we don't even know if they had a family. What should I do now?"

"Try to get some sleep. I don't know how long you've been going, but it's a long time - too long," Howard suggested.

"You're probably right. I've lost track of the last time I slept. If Jerry had a family, would you make a special effort to make sure they're taken care of?"

"You have my word on it, Eric. Now get some sleep. By the way, when does Sadie get into Vegas?"

"I don't know. She's coming in through El Paso. Hopefully, within the next few hours," Eric said, realizing he'd better end this conversation before his cover was blown. "We'll contact you sometime tomorrow." Eric pushed the "end" button on the cell phone.

I glanced at my watch. It had been forty minutes since leaving Barajas's suite. I needed to spend about twenty minutes more before returning to my suite." The last thing I wanted was to deal with Jerry's body. The second-to-last thing I wanted was to play high stakes Blackjack, but it seemed the lesser of two evils. I found a table and summoned the pit boss.

"Marker for three thousand," I said sliding my players card across the table. "I have just enough energy left for ten or twelve hands."

The pit boss picked up the card, looked at the name, and indicated to the dealer to fund my request.

"I'll be back with your marker, Mr. Butler." The dealer funded my request from the tray, smiled and pushed four five hundred dollar and ten one hundred dollar chips across the table to me. "Best of luck, Mr. Baker," the dealer said smiling.

I pushed three black chips into the betting circle, and looked at the dealer, "Luck be a lady tonight." The dealer was smiling. "I'll bet you hear that all the time, don't you?" I inquired, attempting to appear relaxed and tired. The tired part was easy, but relaxed was not in my vocabulary, at least not at that time.

"Yes, there are several lyrics customers use to ease the tension of high stakes gambling. I can almost guess their age by the lyrics they recite," the dealer replied.

"Just how old am I then?" I responded.

"You appear to be approaching the middle age group, but the lyric you used, generally is used by a much older clientele."

"I must have run an older crowd in my younger years," I responded

By this time I had won two hands and lost three. The dealer was reshuffling the deck. A few more hands, and I could safely go to the room. I suddenly remembered, I hadn't made arrangements with Jeb, the bellman, to get Sadie admitted to my room. I slid a five hundred dollar bet into the circle. "Could you get me the pit boss, please?"

"Certainly," the dealer said. He signaled to the man in the center, overseeing eight or ten tables. The man approached with a smile one only finds in Las Vegas.

"How can I be of service?" he inquired.

"I have a friend coming in from South America later tonight, or early tomorrow morning. I told her I would arrange access to my room. She was to ask for Jeb, but he may not be on duty. Would you contact the bell desk, explain this to them, and request she be supplied a card key to my suite? Her name is Sadie Anderson."

"I'll make the call immediately," the pit boss said, turning to the center consoles and picking up a telephone.

I had lost two hands of five hundred each. "I'm going to slow down," I said to the dealer and slid two hundred into the circle. My first card was the king of hearts, and the second card was the ace of diamonds. The dealer was showing an eight.

"Blackjack," I said, laying my cards down.

"It always comes just when you reduce your bet," the dealer said as she paid me three hundred dollars.

I was about to place another bet when the pit boss turned toward the table, hung up the phone, and approached. "You were right, Mr. Butler. Jeb is off duty, but the entire bell staff has been alerted to watch for your friend. Ms. Anderson will be given a key to your suite. Is there anything else?"

"Thank you for your help. As tired as I am, I'm not sure I could have made the trip to the front desk. In fact, I think I will head for the suite now, myself. Will you take care of these chips? Credit them to my line."

"Consider it done, Mr. Butler. Sleep well," the pit boss said as he watched the dealer count my chips.

I slid back from the table and proceeded to the elevator. I was sure the problem had been taken care of, but was still not looking forward to opening the door to my suite. I reached the floor, proceeded to the entrance, used the card key, and swung the door open. The entryway was as though nothing had ever been wrong. Jerry was nowhere to be seen. I felt like a weight had been lifted from my shoulders. I entered the suite and looked around carefully. The mini-bar had been restocked, and the California king bed was turned down. I took a quick shower, and had hardly hit the bed before the oblivion of deep sleep enveloped me. The evening had finally ended.

CHAPTER TWELVE

I don't know what time it is, but who the hell cares. The feeling I'm having is more than I could have ever wished for. The hands are familiar. The scent is light, yet promises adventure. Sadie is in Las Vegas. In fact, Sadie is in my room, and she's giving me a full body massage. I opened my eyes from and to my amazement and delight, Sadie had been there at least long enough to get completely undressed. She was smiling while she worked on my upper thigh. She was on her knees, leaning forward as she rubbed the leg. Her breasts hung down, unrestricted, and swaying from side to side as she moved up and down the leg.

"I hope all the girls in Las Vegas don't get escorted to your suite as freely and easily as I was," she said.

"Not unless they're expected," I replied. "Now, what's your name, young lady? I generally, but not always, am told the name of the bimbo they send up here. By the way, enough on that leg. Work on the other one."

I rolled over catching a wrist in each hand. Her eyes were flashing, and her lips were pursed in that look of feminine determination she knew was so appealing. I pulled her toward me and she collapsed into my arms.

"I have so much to tell you," she whispered. "It's been awful."

"I've had a rather trying time also. We can talk later," I said, holding my finger across my lips, our private signal for probable surveillance. My finger was moved aside by her lips, and the resulting deep kiss stirred everything in my body capable of being stirred. As the passion grew, all I could think of was the fixture camera in the fleabag hotel where it all began yesterday, or was it the day before? I had lost all account of time.

"Wait! We have to talk first! I have an appointment at nine o'clock. What time is it?" I said, felling rushed. Sadie swung around where she could see the wall clock in the suite. Her breasts were silhouetted against the drapes. It took everything I had not to say "to hell with it all" and just enjoy the moment.

"It's seven- thirty in the morning. What's the problem?" she responded with frustration in her voice.

"Believe me, you will understand and will even thank me. Did you rent a car or take a cab to the hotel," I inquired.

"I rented a car, like I always do in the States," she said. "You told me to do that."

"Good, let's go to the car. Get dressed."

I jumped out of the bed and got into a light sweat suit I always packed but rarely used. Sadie finished buttoning the last buttons on her blouse, grabbed her purse, and started toward the door. I wasn't three steps behind her. We reached the elevator and summoned the car.

"This had better be worth it," she said. "I've been dreaming of our reunion for the past two days. Do I have bad breath?" Sadie was acting angry, but I knew she was scared and needed to tell me what had happened to her. We both needed the assurance we were not alone in this charade turned deadly.

"Let's get to the car. We can talk there with some assurance we won't be signing our own death warrant," I whispered.   Sadie nodded and led me to the elevator which had just arrived. We entered, and she punched the button for the main casino floor.

"The car is in the parking garage. We have to cross the casino and take the elevator to the fourth floor of the garage to get it," she said, using a low tone and talking next to my ear. Any observer would think we were just completing a romantic evening and were oblivious to anybody or anything around us. This was normally an adequate cover, but in these circumstances, probably only mildly effective.

We reached the casino floor and proceeded to cross, heading toward the garage elevators. "Mr. Butler, how about a hand or two of Blackjack. Maybe we can win again." The voice was behind me and to the left. I turned and there at a table we had passed was the dealer I had made bets with yesterday. I instinctively clasped Sadie's hand and smiled at the dealer.

"Not right now, maybe later. You're the only dealer I made any money with in the last twenty-four hours. I'll be back." I could tell by the firmness of Sadie's grip on my hand that she was not enjoying my notoriety.

"Like hell you'll be back," were the only words she spoke - but they were uttered through the sweetest smile she could generate.

We reached the garage elevators and took the first one to the fourth floor. Sadie led me to a late model Dodge Intrepid, unlocked the doors, and we both got in. She started the engine, pulled out of the space, and began to exit the parking structure. I thought the exit spirals would never end, but eventually we were in the sunlight, heading toward the most famous street in the world, Las Vegas Boulevard.

"Get on the boulevard, go right, and turn west at the next intersection. Go to the Interstate and take it south." Sadie followed the directions without question. I turned the radio on and found a station I knew would provide sufficient noise. It was an oldie-but-goodie station playing a medley of rock and roll sounds out of the fifties. I turned the volume up and slid over next to Sadie.

"About eight or ten miles south there's a small town, Sloan, Nevada. There's nothing there except high voltage lines and a rock quarry that's taking down a mountain. We'll be shielded from Vegas. It will be safe to talk when we get there," I said. Sadie nodded, and I turned the radio to a more comfortable level.

It took Sadie about fifteen minutes to reach the Sloan turnoff and another five to get to the quarry entrance. The area was as I had remembered. The mountain hadn't been so decimated by the mining process as to allow long distance electronic eavesdropping. I pointed to a dirt road paralleling some railroad tracks. Sadie drove down the road about two hundred feet She cut the engine, and we just looked at each other. She had tears in her eyes. I suddenly realized, I had never seen her cry. She had always been an "agent" and "agents" didn't cry. But there she was, a woman who was scared. A woman I wanted desperately to protect. We must have sat there without saying anything for ten minutes. Sadie was holding me, and I her. There wasn't the need for verbal communication. The essence of her fears, and her thoughts, seemed to flow into my consciousness though the simple act of our embrace.

We both realized, at the same instant, we needed to talk and to get back to Vegas shortly. Sadie began, speaking very quietly. "I had to shoot a policeman before I left Colombia!" she blurted out. "It was awful. He was taking me to the airport. He took a side road near the perimeter of the airport and got out of the car. His actions made it crystal clear what his intentions were. All training and practice paid off during the next few seconds. When it was over, I felt revulsion, and then there was exhilaration I can't describe. It was like I could walk on water, or fly, or do anything I wanted or needed to do. Later on the trip to the States I wanted out. I just wanted to be with you and out of this exercise in futility."

"I've had some of the same experiences," I replied. Since we split up in Colombia, I have had to kill one man with my bare hands. I watched another man be killed, and an old friend from "before the Company" was killed simply because he knew and recognized me. His body was delivered to my suite, evidently as some sort of barbaric warning. I've also had some of the same thoughts you've had. Is what we're doing going to make even a small dent in the bigger picture? Are we just kidding ourselves?"

Sadie was sitting upright now, and there was A look of extreme concern in her eyes. "My God, are you okay? You didn't get injured did you?" .

"No, I'm fine, but we must get out of this situation before we make any decisions affecting us long term. Do you know of any reason the Colombian police officer was going to do you in?" I asked. Was there any indication as to why or who had ordered him to do that?"

"No, I just knew something wasn't right when the national police were offering me a ride to the airport. I was under continual surveillance after you left, but I expected that. There were no other indications. When I got the call from you, I thought the real danger was over. I expected to have problems, possibly severe, but only if things had gone badly for you in Vegas. Have you got any ideas?" she asked.

"None with any substance, other than it is beginning to appear that Barajas is not as much in control of his organization as he would like us to believe. Maybe he's even taking orders from someone else."

"There's two other items you need to be aware of," Sadie said. "I met a young man in Colombia named Ben Chevez. It's a long story, but the important part is this; his family was all killed by The Cartel. It seems his father became somewhat of a local hero after federal police conducted a drug raid. The cartel killed his whole family in retribution. He had been in the United States as an engineering student, but was sent back by the INS when his money ran short. He's now part of the local resistance to The Cartel. He has become a friend, and I have a way to get in touch with him later.

"After I killed the police officer, my only option was to drive the patrol car to the airport. As I started out of the ravine, Ben's cab came down the road. He said he'd heard on the radio the police officer sign himself out from the hotel and become suspicious. He knew I was the officer's official assignment. He followed us at a distance and found me moments after I had killed the officer. We ditched the police car, and he got me to the airport. I don't think I would have made it in the police patrol car." Sadie hesitated.

"Have you considered the possibility he may have been placed there by the cartel to get your confidence?" I asked.

"Yes, I thought about it a lot on the plane back. It just doesn't make any sense for them to order me killed, and then have one of their own men help me get out of the country. I really believe he is who he says he is. Eventually, I would like to help him get out of the country and to the U.S." Sadie replied.

"The second thing we need to discuss is - when I left the police car to get into Ben's cab, I left all my luggage! In all the excitement, I didn't even realize it, until I was in the airport. It won't take an Einstein to determine who killed the police officer. What do you think the ramifications of that screw up will be?" Sadie asked.

"I don't know, but for now it's the Company's problem. We'd better let them know about it, so you don't get arrested on some expedited extradition warrant. Here's my cell phone. As soon as you can get hold of Howard let him know what's happened. He'll know what to do. I've found the best place to make these calls is from the center of the casino, as near the noisiest group as I can find and still use the phone," I responded, noting Sadie's intensity had returned.

I quickly filled Sadie in on the meeting and the death of the soldier, how I had come to run into Jerry Newberry, what happened to him, and the circumstances under which I did in the second soldier. I told her about the upcoming breakfast meeting.

We currently had an opportunity to get out of this business. I knew it and so did she. I could tell Barajas that reviewing the events of the last two or three days left too many questions concerning his organization. I could indicate we had determined to seek our alliances elsewhere. He already knew I was upset with his tactics. Given the size of the proposed partnership, he must expect I was having second thoughts. I knew the events of the last twenty-four hours had put me in the driver seat. Our safety would not be an issue, and my decision would be final.

While I was quickly covering all of these items, I could tell from the look in Sadie's eyes, she was not ready to throw in the towel. In reality, neither was I. If I walked away from the last several years work, it would make a mockery of my entire reason for becoming involved to begin with. It would mean Jerry Newberry had died for nothing.

Sadie turned, looked at me with the determination that was in her eyes when she was first assigned to me, "We haven't come this far to walk the first time the script is not quite as we would like it! Have we?"

"No, I don't think that we have." I agreed completely. "Start the car. I have a breakfast meeting to make, and you have a phone call to make before the Vegas police come calling."

CHAPTER THIRTEEN

I don't know why, but I always eat the same things at breakfast. I don't always eat breakfast, but when I do, I always have the same things. Today was no exception. I arrived at the restaurant a few minutes early and was seated at a somewhat secluded table. The waitress inquired if I was in any hurry, or whether I could enjoy a leisurely breakfast. I told her another gentleman might join me, but I saw no reason to wait to order. I ordered two eggs, sunny-side-up, sausage patties, well done, hash browns, sourdough toast, and black coffee. No sooner had I completed the order when Barajas was escorted to my table.

"Good morning," he said. "I hope you had a good night's sleep."

"Yes, I did," I responded. "I found my suite in good order when I returned, which went a long way toward ensuring I would be well rested for our breakfast conference. Would you like A Menu?" I inquired.

"I'll take a small bowl of oatmeal and an order of Dakota figs. A menu will not be necessary." The waitress smiled and before leaving the table asked about coffee, which he declined.

I've always hated the awkward silences that normally attend the beginning of meetings where the subject matter is either extremely sensitive or somewhat distasteful. To avoid these periods, I always start the discussions without the small talk so irritating to me. Today was no exception. I was in control and was not going to relinquish that position.

"I assume you've considered our conversation of last night," I said. "Before you give me your thoughts, let me clear up what may have been a misunderstanding relative to the business relationship I propose. First, my organization will run the partnership. We will be the managing partners, so to speak. The role you and your people play will be that of an exclusive supplier of product, for which you will be well paid plus you will earn a profit percentage above that. Your organization will also be responsible for the security of the enterprise, but you will act only on my orders except, of course, for the routine day to day matters. I will not allow the enterprise to be jeopardized by the unbridled acts of violence, so prevalent our line of business and specifically in your South American markets. My actions last night should have proven to you that I am capable of a decisive act. I am not opposed to violence, where it is necessary and appropriate. In today's business world, unwarranted and uncontrolled violence are the very acts drawing unwanted, sometimes lethal, attention to our business interests.

I believe you have already determined the growth, if not survival, of your business interests, will best be served by the partnership I have proposed. You would not be here if you believed otherwise. The question now is whether you will relinquish your leadership role in the greater enterprise and become an exclusive, dependable, working partner in a much bigger business. *Leadership is not negotiable!"* I sat back in my chair and awaited his response.

Barajas's eyes were dark and forbidding. I had seen this look once before and hoped his response would be different.

"Mr. Butler, I am continually amazed at your lack of, what we from the old county refer to as, common courtesy or respect. In another setting, certainly in another time, you would not speak to me in that tone, or for that matter, on the subject of leadership."

I responded in an attempt to placate him, but not to back off my position. "I'm sorry you have interpreted my thoughts as being disrespectful, or a discourtesy. I certainly did not mean to impart such an impression."

"Thank you. I will consider that to be your apology. I am not a stupid man, Mr. Butler. I realize all good things must end, and all organizations must be capable of change in order to survive. My organization must develop markets large enough to absorb our production capabilities. I know we don't have the capability to accomplish this alone, especially in the short run. It is for that reason only -- I would even consider an offer such as you present. But, because I am interested in expanding my business, I am willing to do business with your organization."

"I am very happy, and honored, to hear your decision," I interrupted.

"I, also, have some requirements, however," he went on. "First, you and your organization must agree you will not enter, or otherwise interfere in, the South American market. Second, you and your organization will not interfere in the internal controls of my organization, wherever in the world we may be. Third, my other business interests are not subject to your controls, physically or financially. Fourth and finally, the partnership's need for product must be discussed with me, or my designee, sufficiently ahead of the proposed delivery date, so I can adjust my production and warehousing requirements. For reasons, I'm sure you can understand, it is not always intelligent to overproduce product, anticipating future needs, only to create a warehousing problem."

"I don't think any of the issues you raise are a problem or can't be worked out. You can rest assured, we will not be so presumptive as to insert our management objectives into your internal operations. Also, we won't, without your request, attempt to market in any country in South America, or for that matter Central America, or Mexico. It is my opinion, however, after you see our joint successes, you may want us to service the South American markets. The choice will be yours. The request we stay out of your other business interests is also not a problem. In turn, however, you must agree, with regard to those interests, you will never use the partnership facilities to advance those interests. So that I am clear, this includes joint transportation of the two products."

"You have my agreement," he responded. "What is the next step?"

Before I could answer, the waitress approached with breakfast. She set the plates down, smiled, and inquired if there was anything further we needed. Barajas indicated he was okay, I asked for some Tabasco Sauce. She provided it from an oversized front pocket of her uniform. and excused herself. For the first time, I felt the beginnings of an awkward silence.

"I have to find out now ... Before we get into the next step, tell me why my associate was assaulted by a local police officer in Bogotá? And I must stress, Mr. Barajas, your answer may well affect our future business association."

"I'm sorry, but I don't know what you are referring to," Barajas responded.

"Oh, come now! You knew I had a companion in Colombia, and I had left her to meet you here. She was put in a position requiring her to liquidate one of your local police officers. Sadie, my companion, is a very capable woman and one whose veracity I do not question." I stated in a tone slightly elevated.

"You are correct. I knew you had a companion with you in Bogotá. I was not aware she was also an associate. However, I know nothing about her being assaulted. It was not by my orders," he assured me. "I will make a call and will advise you of the circumstance within the hour."

"I believe you," I lied. "Please assure me the problem is solved. I will await your advice"

"It will be done," he said, in a tone of feigned conviction.

"To get on with our business then, Sadie and I will spend a couple of days in Vegas, just being, or attempting to be, regular tourists. Then I will return to my organization and plan our first joint marketing effort. I need a method of getting in touch with you at any time, day or night. I will provide you a cell number to reach me. It is clean - you can rely on it. I require the same considerations from you. I also need a bank, a bank account number, and routing instructions. The account you provide will be the one we use to conduct our business, so choose it with that in mind. When our first sale is designed, I will call you and describe the delivery and the quantities. You will give me your best price for the quantity involved. Remember, the profits are what we split in the end. I don't intend your organization to suffer a loss on sale to the partnership, but, by the same token, I will be very upset should I discover there was an exurbanite profit made on the sale to the partnership.

We will agree on the delivery date, and I will arrange the transportation with the delivery date in mind. Understand, I am prone to transport by freighter, where time will allow, because secretion of the product in that way is much easier and more effective. Also, the regulations are not as tight, and the enforcement officers are generally more approachable. Where possible I will utilize your fleet. This, of course, could change from time to time, depending on the location of the client and the time of delivery. Do you have any questions at this point?"

"No, it appears you have thought the process through, and I would assume have used the plan in the past," he said, more thinking out loud than providing an answer to my question.

"Yes, we've been using and refining the process," I responded, "but no - we've never had a partner supplying product, helping to guarantee delivery dates, and controlling both the quantities and the quality of the product," I responded.

"There's one area you haven't covered," he added, "I had previously understood we are to supply security to the venture. Has there been a change?"

"Good question. I didn't mean to forget security. The particulars of each sale will dictate the unique security for that trip, but in general, each load will be staffed by between four, and at the most eight, of your men. They will be responsible to insure the product is not discovered or offloaded on the high seas. These men should be union seamen with strong allegiances to your organization. High proficiency seaman skills are a must. They should be capable of taking over the ship, if necessary, and delivering it and the product to any port of destination. I will expect more quality in these men than what I experienced in your suite last night."

"You can be sure, your requirements will be more than adequately met, Mr. Butler." he said bristling. "Now, if you will excuse me, I will check on the circumstances surrounding the problems your associate had leaving Colombia."

"Of course!. I will be in my suite or on the casino floor. I'm sure you will have no trouble finding me." I stood to acknowledge his departure. "I assume the other information will be supplied before I leave Vegas."

"It will." Barajas turned and left the restaurant. I resumed my seat and proceeded to finish, what had become, a cold breakfast. All in all, the meet had been more successful than I ever could have dreamed. It was almost scary. Maybe too scary.

CHAPTER FOURTEEN

The next two days were ours, and I was going to be very jealous concerning their use. Sadie and I hadn't had any time to ourselves since this project was conceived. I was mentally planning the next forty-eight hours, when Sadie appeared. She was in the front of the restaurant where lines would form if it were a busier time. I signaled to her to join me. I could tell, even from a distance, something was wrong. Whenever something was bothering Sadie, she set her jaw - and her mouth tightened ever so slightly, resulting in a look unique only to her. She reached the table and, using one of our personal signals, indicated we had to talk. I was reasonably sure we were no longer the subject of surveillance, but knew we could not risk talking there. Our room may be the best place. I nodded, signed the breakfast tab to the room, and we left the restaurant.

We worked our way across the casino to the elevators going to our suite. An elevator car was standing conveniently ready. We entered and proceeded to the floor, then to the suite. I inserted the card key and opened the door. The suite was just as we had left it with one exception; it had received maid service. I walked across the sitting room and turned on the television. The station, which advertises services, at least the legal services of the hotel, was automatically tuned in. I didn't care what was on. I just wanted noise and that station provided noise. I turned and looked at Sadie.

"What's going on?" I inquired.

"I got in touch with Howard and told him of the problems I had in Colombia. He had already heard about them. There's been a request by the government of Colombia to arrest me. The State Department is involved. Officially, the CIA is not acknowledging me, or admitting any complicity in the operation. This matter should be cleared up. Howard believes, with existing joint cooperation agreements to curtail the drug trade, explanations can be made at high levels. I'm to lay low for several hours. He says he'll call on your cell phone." Sadie dropped to the couch in the sitting room.

"Barajas is also going to get things resolved on the Colombian side. He denies any knowledge of the events," I told Sadie. "I don't believe him. He is somehow responsible, even though he had nothing to gain from having you killed. If anything, it would complicate the cartel's objectives. He is also going to call here. My guess is he'll get his dirty laundry cleaned before we can get this matter handled politically." I smiled at Sadie. "We have no excuse now. We are under orders to stay in the room."

Sadie was still serious, "They probably know I'm here with you. After all, I was escorted to your room last night."

"I really don't think so. We didn't check in together, so my guess is they would never put your name on the register without my permission. Remember - Las Vegas was built on the promise of discretion," I added. "After all, the little woman back home might object if she called only to find I had a roommate."

"There'd better not be a little woman back home, because if there is, you'd better hope I get arrested and jailed before I find out! The authorities will have a real reason to jail me!" Sadie responded, her eyes flashing and playful. The seriousness of the last twenty minutes was gone. "Should we at least inquire about the hotel register?" she asked.

I picked up the phone and dialed the main desk.

"Good morning. How can I help you?" an accommodating voice responded.

"This is Mr. Butler. Could you please check and see how this room is registered"

"Certainly. One moment, please." The standard hotel music came on, and within thirty seconds the pleasant voice came back on. "The room is registered in your name, Mr. Butler. Is there a problem?"

"No, no, of course not. I wondered if the suite was registered in the name of another of your guests. I want the registration to be in my name only."

"Well, that's the way it is. Is there anything further I can do for you, Mr. Butler?"

"No, thank you." I hung up the phone, turning to tell Sadie she had nothing to worry about.

I gasped for breath! Sadie was standing on the top on the bed, stark naked. The look in her eyes indicated she was not to be denied. I wasn't in a mood to deny her anything. It was eleven forty in the morning. Ecstasy was just around the corner and the next and the next.

I was in a dead run to get around the first corner.

The phone rang. I looked at the clock in the suite. It registered after three. I picked up the receiver.

"Hello, Eric Butler here"

"Mr. Butler, I reached my organization in Colombia and have been briefed about the circumstances relating to the problems your associate experienced when leaving Colombia," The voice was Barajas.

"That's fine, I'm interested in the circumstances to which you refer," I responded, "but the issues have broadened, and now involve the governments of our respective countries," I   made my voice sound as irritated as possible.

"I understand but those problems should go away soon, if they have not already. The requests have been withdrawn and apologies have been tendered at the diplomatic levels. The Colombian government has determined the requests were premature as the perpetrator is now thought to be a student, turned cab driver, who was seen in the area. The authorities will be arresting him in the near future."

"That's fine, but again the result is the death or imprisonment of some innocent individual to cover the fact your organization got its wires crossed. At least that's what I'm assuming happened."

"Yes, Mr. Butler, that's what happened. I failed to recognize a weakness in one of my employees. As a result, my instructions failed to be carried out. The death or imprisonment of who you referred to as an innocent individual is not true, however. The cabbie is a known leader associated with an enemy to the interests we both support. His eventual arrest and death will be a welcome event in my organization. Remember, Mr. Butler, in forming our partnership, you assured me my internal affairs, as well as activities on the South American continent, won't be interfered with. I must insist you keep your word. I will be in touch with the other information you requested within the next twenty-four hours." The phone went dead.

I really hated to hang up the phone. I knew the "cabbie" was the man Sadie had met, the man who helped her leave the country. When she learned the circumstance, Sadie would move heaven and earth to get him to safety. I knew I had to tell her if our relationship had any chance of success. I placed the phone in the cradle and turned back to the bed. Sadie was on her elbow smirking, because I had called uncle before she had. A long-standing bet had just been settled. One look at my face, however, must have tipped her off. It wasn't all roses in paradise.

"What's the problem?" she asked. "That sounded like Barajas. Did he have an explanation for the problems I had in Colombia?"

"Yes - it was Barajas. He said one of his men was out of control and, as a result, his instructions were not followed. Evidently, the Colombian government has or will shortly withdraw the request for your arrest on the basis a mistake was made in the identity of the criminal."

"That's wonderful! You know, I feel very lucky! We should be hearing from Howard very soon. I'm so glad this mess isn't going to ruin our short vacation." Then, Sadie began to hesitate, as though she had just recalled an unpleasant memory. "Why were you talking about death or imprisonment of an innocent person? What are they doing? I think I know, but tell me now!"

Her voice had escalated in volume. Her tone was suddenly serious. Maybe even angry. The fear returned to her eyes.

"Calm down. Getting angry won't help anyone," I responded. "Barajas indicated the Colombian officials are now convinced the criminal is a student - now cabbie. The cabbie is a member of an organized resistance group, of some type, opposing the activities of his organization. His exact words were 'he was an enemy of the interests we both support.'" As I was talking, Sadie began to dress. "Where are you going?" I asked, "It still may not be safe for you to go out into public areas."

"I really don't know, but I can't lay here on my ass making love to you while the man, that may well have saved my life, dies for his efforts." She was really angry, her voice betraying the urgency she was feeling. "Why aren't you on the phone to Barajas stopping this whole ugly mess!" Sadie's tone was sharp enough to slice steel as though it was butter.

"Because, he just reminded me of the agreement, and insisted I step back! Part of our deal is we have to stay out of the internal affairs of his organization - including South America. We will not be helping your friend, if I push him any further on the issue. In fact, we might even assure his death."

"Well, what can we do? Are you telling me there's nothing we can do to help Ben, and I must live with that fact?" Sadie asked.

Tears were beginning to appear in the corners of her eyes.

"No, I'm not telling you that. I'm saying we can't help through Barajas. We'll find a way to help." I was fishing for some thread of hope to give her. "We'll put Howard on it as soon as he gets in touch with us. Possibly, the same diplomatic channels he was intending to use for you are available for Ben,"

"That's not going to be good enough. He'll be dead by that time."

"Not necessarily. The very process invoked after your return from Colombia may well save his life. Follow this; they can't just execute him, as they have at least part of the international community aware of the circumstance. This means there must be a trial, and trials take time to complete, even in Colombia. That time will be adequate to get him out of the country," I was still trying to think of some scenario, any scenario, that would give Sadie some hope.

"You're right, but something else occurred to me. Exactly what did that Spanish bastard say to you when he told you the authorities weren't looking for me any longer? Do you recall?"

"Yes, I think I do. He said something about diplomatic apologies are being made. They, the Colombian authorities, had determined a cabbie, who had been seen in the area, was the criminal. I think he also said something about the cabbie being a student. What are you searching for?"

"Did he indicate an arrest had been made or whether the 'criminal' had been apprehended? Was there any indication or inference of that fact?"

"Yes, as a matter of fact he did indicate they did not have him in custody, yet. I believe he said the authorities would arrest him shortly, or something along those lines." I hardly got the words out of my mouth, and Sadie was all over me. The tears had turned to joy and the doom and gloom to gleefulness.

"If they haven't got him now, they'll never get him. He's too smart. When I last saw him, he was already being very careful. When he let me off at the airport, he made me walk from the fringe of the passenger drop-off area because of his concern. I thought his concern was for me, but I can now see he was aware he may be connected to the killing, so he was becoming less visible," she said in a very animated manner.

"I don't even know the man, but I must agree with you. From what I am learning about him, this type of situation is not something new to him. In his role, as a leader of the underground, he must have had plans enabling him to drop out of sight. He would be a fool otherwise."

"I can assure you, he's no fool!" Sadie interrupted. "We still must make Howard aware of the situation, so he can do everything possible to extract Ben from Colombia. All we have to do is wait for Howard to call, and we can begin our holiday."

I agreed, walked across the room to the window, and looked through the open drapes. As expected, the sun was blinding. It was late in the afternoon. I turned to say something.

Sadie was still sitting on the bed.

"By opening the drapes, I can only assume you don't want a rematch. You must be really tired." She giggled.

I closed the drapes and charged the bed. Suddenly, I was blind. The change from bright sunlight to almost total darkness had rendered me sightless! I stumbled and fell across the bed, while at the same time attempting to discard the few pieces of clothing I had managed to put on.

"Not only am I not tired, but I have the staying power of an eighteen year old," I blurted breathlessly.

"Oh, you must have been faking a few minutes ago. You know as you get older, the second wind, if you know what I mean, becomes a real asset - but only if you can find it." She giggled again.

By this time we had both gotten our clothes off - ripped them off is more accurate, and the contest had begun.

CHAPTER FIFTEEN

T he phone rang. Sadie was closest to the receiver so she answered it. Having just showered, I was shaving in preparation for the evening. Sadie and I were going to the steakhouse at Circus Circus, and from there, we were going to go wherever our fancies took us. I heard Sadie telling the caller she was glad it was all over for her. There were the usual pauses, while Sadie listened to what she was being told. I assumed it was Howard. Then, Sadie called me into the bedroom and inquired if there was another phone in the suite I could get on so we could have a three-way. I put my hand over Sadie's phone, stopping any transmission of sound, and asked her how secure she thought the lines were. I suggested Howard replace the call on the cell phone.

Sadie nodded and told Howard to call back in fifteen minutes and to use the cell network. She hung up.

"The fifteen minutes will give you time to finish shaving," she said. "Now get to the bathroom. I need to talk to you before Howard calls back."

I obeyed. "What do you want to discuss?" I asked.

"It's just a feeling, at this point, but I don't think Howard is going to be receptive to helping Ben," Sadie said. "You know how he gets rather officious when he knows we want something he doesn't want to give or doesn't think we need."

I nodded, being careful not to scrape my neck with the razor, as Sadie continued. "I just got that feeling when he told me the State Department had learned the suspect was a cabbie who'd been a student here in the U.S. I told him I already knew that and also knew the cabby. Howard went silent for a moment, and then he said in the tone of voice we both know so well,

I certainly hope your acquaintance won't complicate things more than they already are.' At this point you came, and we asked him to call back. What do you think?"

"I think that right now it's really hard to tell," I said. "Let's wait for the call and go from there."

"That's okay, and I agree with you, but if he does resist helping, I want you to support my position. Can you do that?" Sadie said, seeking my further assurances.

"Yes, I can and will. After all, it may be that Ben is the only reason I still have you in service with me. I owe the man a lot." I finished shaving and did all those things men do before going out for the evening. The cell phone rang; it was in my pocket so I answered it. "Hello. This is Eric," fully expecting to hear the voice of Howard.

Instead it was Barajas. "Mr. Butler, now that we are in business, may I call you Eric?

"Most certainly. I was going to suggest it. What can I do for you?"

"Wonderful, Eric. I just wanted to let you know the arrangements you requested will be complete within twenty-four hours. I will also have the information you requested at that time. Is this adequate? Will you still be in Las Vegas?"

"Yes, we plan on staying for two or three days. We'll be around. Even if we're not, the cell number I gave you will reach me anywhere in the world."

"Fine, I'll be in touch." Barajas hung up the phone.

"Who was that?" Sadie inquired.

"Your friend from Spain," I responded. "He wanted to tell me it was going to take a day to get the information for   our partnership put together."

"How did he get your cell number?" she asked with concern.

"I gave it to him. I needed a clean line. The cell was the only one available at the time. I'll switch it out when we get back and have some time."

Sadie smirked, "I'm glad it was you that gave the number out. You know how restrictive Howard is with the use of those lines."

"I know, but I don't have a worry. He won't concern himself with my slight indiscretion. I have chosen the best time possible. He will be too busy reaming you - for losing all your luggage and in a foreign country no less!" Sadie was about to throw a towel my direction, when the phone rang again. I had the phone, but rather than answer it, I tossed it to her. "Here practice being contrite."

She stuck her tongue out and punched the receive button. "Hello. This is Sadie Anderson." There was a short silence. "Yes, Howard, I'm going to get Eric to come close to the phone. I'll turn the volume up and maybe all three of us can talk."

I walked across the room to stand on the opposite side of a table Sadie was using to set up the phone. She put it on speaker and was working the volume control. "Now, I think I've got it. Can you hear me, Howard?"

"Yes, you sound rather distant but clear," Howard responded. I could hear him clearly. "Well, Eric, say something," Sadie pressured me. "Don't just stand there like a bump on a log." I feigned a frown at Sadie. "Howard, this is Eric. Can you hear me also? As I'm sure you heard, I've been given permission to speak on my own phone."

"Yes, Eric, I can hear you quite well. Some things never change. When the two of you became partners, I went on record saying your partnership wouldn't last six months. The two of you have proven me wrong by several years, and even yet I wonder how you're doing it. What is it requiring a clean line?"

I decided to start. "Howard, it's about that cabbie in Colombia. He was instrumental in getting Sadie out of the country when things got really tight for her. We want you to do whatever is possible, short of sending in the Marines, to get him out of the country."

At this point Sadie jumped in. "Howard, forget about what Eric said - if the Marines are necessary, use them." The pregnant silence on the other end of the line was what Sadie had experienced previously.

"Sadie, it's not that easy, and you know it," Howard cautiously began. "We have to respect the legal processes of the lawful government in Colombia. Years of diplomacy would be lost if we simply usurped their civil authority. I will do what I can, but I'm not going to promise you anything. Bad things happen to good people in this business, and we can't fix all of them. Eric look what happened to your friend, Mr. Newman, I'm sure you understand."

"No, I don't understand, Howard. We put people in these situations, and they die or go to prison or get separated from their families, and because of covert concerns or diplomatic immunity or some other governmental crap, we do nothing. What seems worse, is we're told what we just did was patriotic. Sadie and I have already discussed this and have decided, if the government isn't going to take any action overtly or covertly, we will!" The feelings I had when I discovered Jerry dead, with his head nearly severed from his body, were welling up in me. My anger was becoming disproportionate. It was unfortunate Howard had to be the recipient of my frustrations, but there was no other avenue.

"Eric, you know the Company doesn't respond well to threats and ultimatums. You both could be removed from the field and from your positions. You would lose any opportunity to help your friend. Does that make sense to you, either of you?"

I was about to respond when Sadie jumped in.

"Howard, we understand the Company doesn't respond to threats. What it does respond to is economics. This operation has cost the American taxpayer several million dollars. If we walk, all of that is lost. The Company will have to start over from scratch. Next time around, they may not be as successful. They will have doubled their costs, taken twice as much time, and will, in all probability, end up with nothing. The company will not stand for that result, if there is an alternative - and we offer an alternative."

I winked at Sadie. She was beautiful and was a fighter!

"What do you propose?" Howard asked, after another period of silence.

Sadie didn't hesitate. "Howard, consider this, and please don't take it personally. I don't believe the Company will do everything it can to help Ben get back to the states. In fact, I think the Company may well do nothing, regardless of what you promise us. I think Eric and I will be able to get him out of Colombia, and back to the States, better than any operative you have. I, therefore, propose Eric and I take a two or three week leave of absence, or vacation or whatever, and take care of this ourselves. Now, before you say no, please remember what is already invested in our current project. If we do not, or cannot, have your approval, at least give us your blessing because, regardless of what you say, we're gone! The real test, Howard, will be when the three of us show up on the doorsteps of the United States knocking for entry. If the Company has made arrangements for our entry, then Eric and I will resume our efforts in the current project. If entry is denied, the Company can attempt to resurrect the project through other operatives. We wish them luck."

"What will you use for money? These operations are expensive?" was the only response Howard made. It was my turn to jump in.

"I have about fifty thousand on my person and another two hundred and forty-five thousand on deposit with the hotel. Enough for a few weeks." I smiled at Sadie.

"Without the Company's permission, any use of that money would be theft or embezzlement." Howard was grasping at straws.

"Howard, you fail to remember the money was deposited in a Las Vegas casino for a project that doesn't exist. If we are caught in any capacity, the Company denies any knowledge of who we are or what we are doing. How can they claim embezzlement for monies deposited for a project that doesn't exist and with people they cannot acknowledge? I don't think so." I hesitated to make sure the reality of the situation was fully appreciated, "Now do we have your blessing or are we rogues?" There was a long silence, and what sounded like a muffled conversation in the background.

"I really don't have much choice do I?" Howard finally replied. "The two of you have two weeks to accomplish bringing this individual out of Colombia. I can't promise a day more. You realize I'm not going to be able to keep this off your records so you might want to get your resumes ready. I've said all the official things now, so good luck and keep in touch. It will help me at this end if I know when and where you may be coming into the country. Eric -- Sadie be careful. You know these people play for keeps, and, believe it or not, I want you back safe and I want you with the Company."

"Thank you, Howard. Sadie and I both want you to know we realize how you feel and know what your responsibilities are. We will try not to do anything that could complicate the project - or compromise you. By the way, it sounded like there was someone either in your office or on the line a few minutes ago. Isn't this a secure line?"

"Yes, it's secure. It was my wife. She just can't seem to learn to leave me alone when I'm in here on the phone. Let me know what arrangements you make with the cartel concerning your efforts for the next two weeks."

"We will. And while I've got you I want to bring you up to speed on the operation. Barajas should be contacting us within the next twenty-four hours with information I requested, including banking information and pricing. On the first deal we will pay his production costs upon delivery to the partnership. The Company must be prepared to make substantial cash commitments at that time. I know you think banking arrangements can be made, which appear the as though cash has actually transferred where in fact it hasn't, only the accounting entries will be made. We're all for that, but consider the first deal. It must have the appearance of being squeaky clean, or we've lost the project. When he calls, I'm going to tell him the first operation will be in four to six weeks and will require not less than one-half ton of product. He should be too busy meeting the deadline to worry about where we are or what we are doing. In a roundabout way, he told me he tries to keep as little product as possible warehoused. The first order should keep him busy for, at least, several weeks."

"You certainly seem to have it all thought through. I like the plan," Howard responded.

"It's the old plan with an additional two weeks. Everything is virtually the same. That's the beauty of it." I hesitated, "Howard, there's one thing that's different, however. We won't be able to help you plan the first market. We've already talked about the northern coast of Africa because of the unrest there and the connections we have. The actual plans will have to be completed by your group, without our input."

"I thought of that. It's not a problem. My group has already been working on the market. We will have the solution when, as you said, you 'knock on the door.'"

"Good, and remember, Sadie needs to be briefed on the banking arrangements and the contacts, so set some time aside when we return. We'll call you, before we leave, with the banking information. Bye for now."

I disconnected the cell and turned off the speaker phone?_ Sadie was sitting on the edge of the bed, and I could tell she was pleased with the arrangements. "This is not going to be easy," I said. "It wasn't but a few hours ago you were a fugitive in Columbia."

"I know, but we can do it, and I don't think it will take two weeks. We will be successful or we will fail within the first week, counting travel time."

"I agree, but the extra week gives us a bumper, if we need it. Now we have at least twenty-four hours to enjoy this adult paradise, and I don't intend to let the events of the last hour, or so, upset my plans." As I walked by the bed I pushed Sadie over onto her back.

"Who am I to argue with a big strong bully like you?" she said, "but it just now occurred to me that you, or we, if I'm included in the plans, have a slight problem. To this point you have kept me sufficiently naked that the need for a change of clothes has not arisen. It has now, and my luggage is in Colombia. Is there a contingent plan to dress Sadie, or is she to remain naked for the duration? What do you say to that?" Sadie was smirking again. She knew the look teased me more than any other.

"Frankly, keeping you naked holds some appeal, but we may want to stay in this hotel again, so I guess we'll have to take you shopping. The hotel has a mall. It should have everything you need. Put on your only clothes and let's go. It should be open. After all, this town is twenty-four seven."

"This is turning out to be really fun," Sadie said. "I wonder if there's a Victoria's Secret, although I really don't need the allure," she said coyly." I seem to have done just fine naked."

"Only because you were gone so long, and my standards were reduced," I said, dodging the wet washcloth she was using. "Now hurry, I don't want to spend the next twenty-four hours in some damn mall."

PART TWO
THE RESCUE

CHAPTER SIXTEEN

The last twenty-four hours had been heaven. For the first time in years, I just had fun, not worrying who was there or who was not there. I saw a side of Sadie I wasn't aware existed. She was fun-loving and carefree. She acted as if she didn't have a worry in the world and that was not Sadie. She always worried about everything. When events, schedules, or circumstances became tight, she was very directive and authoritative. I complained about that attitude early in our association. She asked me what I wanted - whining and tears? I reconsidered, and let things alone, believing I already had the best of the alternatives.

We ate, gambled, made love, gambled some more, made love again, and ate some more. I think we both realized this was what the normal couple did on vacation; this was the way they live. We both knew, without saying a word to each other, that this lifestyle was never going to be ours, as long as we were in the service. Although the past twenty-four hours had been ours, it was an anomaly, and it was almost over. Barajas had called. He gave us a telephone number that would be good twenty-four hours a day, a bank, a bank account, and routing instructions. I informed him the first delivery would be approximately five weeks away, and we would need one half U.S. ton. Barajas's reaction was surprising. He asked if the first sale could be smaller. He indicated he needed more time to step up his operations. He suggested six hundred pounds. I agreed, giving him the impression I was reluctant.

"The economics and the profit margin will be adversely affected, but we can accommodate you this time," I said, silently realizing the lesser quantity would be easier on Howard's group.

Sadie and I committed the contact number to memory. The bank account was surprising, if not alarming. Barajas had chosen a French Bank with locations worldwide. When Sadie saw the routing number, she was startled. It was for the bank's branch located in New York City. During the oil boom in the seventies and eighties, this particular bank had a reputation, among some government agencies, of making strange loans to foreign interests operating in the United States. However, to my knowledge, the bank had never been linked to any *Mafia* or other drug related organization. Sadie speculated the bank was unaware what the account was to be used for. When proper paperwork is presented most, if not all, major banks open accounts for foreign nationals. The banking problem was to be Howard's. In any event. We passed on the information.

All matters needing our attention had been handled, and it was time to leave for Colombia. Sadie and I elected to exit the States from Atlanta rather than travel the same route Sadie used previously. Not only would the airline personnel be less apt to remember her, we would also run less chance of an unplanned meeting with Barajas or his people.

I checked with the casino cage and arranged to have the remaining deposit withdrawn in cash. The cage indicated the request was somewhat out of the ordinary, but because they had the better part of a banking day to arrange cash availability, it posed no problem. Sadie and I arranged to purchase two personal money belts, each being large enough to hold approximately half of the cash we would be carrying. We inventoried the remaining cash and found, after the purchase of replacement clothing, luggage for Sadie, and the expenses of the last twenty-four hours we had two hundred ninety-five thousand dollars and some change left. Sadie didn't like the matronly look caused by her money belt when filled with half the cash. She, therefore, carried only one hundred thousand in the belt, and ten thousand dollars in her purse. I carried one hundred thousand in the belt and five thousand in my pocket. We disbursed the balance of approximately eighty thousand dollars in our luggage in areas time had proven to be effective. Because Sadie's luggage was new, we modified the pieces to accommodate the cash.

The last item on our list was to replace the weapon Sadie had been forced to leave in the Colombian trash receptacle. I contacted a Las Vegas gun dealer known to sell handguns with few, if any, questions asked. I told him what we wanted. He said he had several. We went to the shop and signed papers, which appeared to be Brady Bill documents, recording a hand gun had been purchased three days earlier. We walked out of the shop with the weapon. Sadie had just acquired a new Smith & Wesson thirty-eight snub nose.

The weapon just purchased, as well as my pistol, were both secreted in the luggage. Years ago, the Company had shown us how to place a weapon in luggage so it wouldn't be detected by x-ray. Because of our previous experience, we knew customs in Colombia would not be interested in our luggage, if they were tipped to clear us though speedily. Once in the country, the weapons could be removed from the luggage and secreted on our person.

Airline connections had been made, and the time of departure was approaching. I looked at Sadie. "Are you sure this is the route you want to take," I asked.

"Yes, I don't think I have ever been surer of anything in my life," Sadie replied.

I had a question, which had been in the back of my mind, ever since Sadie had asked me to back her play and force the Company to allow the extraction of this Ben. However, Sadie's answer wasn't going to affect my participation in this task. The question was one, which I had to ask before we left the country, and before things and events became confusing or complicated.

"Sadie, there's one thing I must know before we leave, and I hope you don't misinterpret the reason for my asking. Please be assured, I am committed to Ben's extraction. It won't be affected by your answer. Obviously, you are very committed to Ben. Is there something I should know about your relationship with him, or possibly, your relationship with me, causing you to feel so strongly?" I waited for an answer. Sadie seemed to be reflecting. Then she began.

"I originally made friends with Ben, because I thought he might be helpful if we ever had to return to Colombia. In my zest to serve the needs of the Company, I unwittingly converted a possible recruit into a victim of the system. If we don't, at least, try to make it possible for him to escape the mess I created, we aren't any better than they are. I -- we -- the Company will all have profited, if only a little, from the mess I created. Now he's paying for it with his misery and maybe his life. If your question is whether he and I were romantically involved, the answer is no. I can see how that might have gone through your mind, but no!. Eric, he's really just a boy, a young man who has the, what do you men say, the piss and vinegar you and I had at one time. We were struggling for mother, apple pie, and country. That vitality, maybe that innocence, was stolen from us. It was insidiously taken one small piece at a time. Oh, we still believe what we are involved in is the right course, and the enemy, whomever he or she is, is evil. The distinctions, however, have become vague for me. I killed a man in Colombia, Eric. I felt exhilarated when it happened. I haven't felt any remorse to this instant. Somehow that doesn't seem to be right or moral." Sadie fell silent. I didn't know what to say to her, but I knew that I had to try.

Sadie, the police officer was going to do you in, bury you in the ravine. Your body would have never been found. You can't, you shouldn't, feel bad because you're the one who lived. You used your training and your God-given instincts to survive. You got back to the States, back to me. You've done nothing wrong, and the feelings you're having – well, I hope they're natural, because I'm having some of the same thoughts."

"What do you think we should do?" Sadie asked.

"I don't know if what you're asking about is the long term, but I do know you and I have committed to help Ben in the short term, and that's what we have to do. I suggest we decide the next step in our lives when we have successfully extracted Ben - and you, I, and Ben are on solid American soil."

"I agree," she said smiling.

The suite entrance bell rang. Jeb, the bellman, was standing in the door. "Mr. Butler, the limousine for the airport is waiting. May I help you with your bags?"

CHAPTER SEVENTEEN

T he trip to Atlanta was uneventful. Sadie and I were mostly silent and introspective during the flight. A lot had occurred in a very short time. I think each of us needed time to think and to mentally prepare ourselves for the extraction that was to come.

We landed in Atlanta at about six-thirty in the evening, their time. We had an hour layover before our flight left for Bogotá. Time for one last meal before the vacation ended. Sadie found an up-scale *Cajun* steak house in the airport. After a sizable tip, the *maitre d'* was able to seat us immediately. We proceeded to make pigs of ourselves, and were just finishing some sort of desert wine, when we heard the first call for our flight. The gate was only a short distance down the concourse, so we leisurely paid the bill and left for the gate. We had walked about half way, when I spotted one of the soldiers I had seen with Barajas. He was on the concourse ahead of us and gave no indication he had spotted us.

I tugged at Sadie's arm in a way she knew something was wrong. She looked at me and I pointed in the direction of the soldier. We moved to the side of the concourse and followed at a safe distance. At a place near the gate, where we could be somewhat secluded, we stopped. Sadie whispered in my ear, "Who is he?"

I responded in a low tone, trying not to be conspicuous, "He was one of the soldiers with Barajas on the first night."

"Do you think he's following us?" she asked.

"No, I don't think so. If he was, we wouldn't have spotted him so easily. I can't imagine worse luck, but I'll bet he's just going home to Colombia. Let's see which class he boards, and if that gives any indication he's looking for us."

The man approached the counter at the gate and presented his credentials. After what appeared to be small talk, he was admitted to the jet-way for boarding. As soon as he disappeared, Sadie and I proceeded to the counter. Sadie smiled at the stewardess, and inquired if our friend, who had just boarded the plane, was flying in first class. The stewardess said his reservations were for coach. She asked if that was a mistake. There was room in first class for him if we upgraded his ticket. Sadie said no, and made some excuse, indicating we didn't want him to know we were on the same plane with him.

"You won't have to worry," the stewardess said. "Just wait and board at the last moment, and I'll make sure the curtain at the end of the first class cabin is drawn. The regulations require the curtain remain drawn for the entire flight unless there's an emergency. He'll never know you're on board."

In an effort to gain some privacy, Sadie and I stepped back from the podium and discussed whether it was worth the risk, "Do you think we should book another flight?" Sadie said, almost talking to herself.

"My gut feeling tells me the problem is not being spotted on the flight, but who, if anybody, will be at the airport in Bogotá to pick this thug up. If he's picked up, I'm not sure we'll know if we've been spotted," I replied.

"You think we should book another flight?" Sadie asked. "No, but we've got to evaluate the risks. Maybe as we exit the aircraft, we can appear to be separate. That way, if anyone recognizes one of us, the other might go unnoticed," I said, thinking out loud.

"We'd better decide now, or the airline will decide for us. The stewardess just made the last call, and disappeared down the jet way. When she returns, she will expect us to board" I could tell Sadie was getting nervous, and the indecision was not helping.

"Let's go," I said. "Whatever happens, I'm sure we'll have time to deal with it." I could tell from the look on Sadie's face, she was in agreement. We grabbed our carry-on luggage and proceeded toward the gate, just as the stewardess reappeared.

"The curtain has been pulled. If the two of you will board we can begin the flight." We assented and proceeded down the jet way. As the stewardess had promised, the curtains were drawn at the rear of the first class cabin. Our two seats were in the second row on the right side of the aircraft. We stowed our carry-on luggage and settled back for a three to four hour flight. As always, the drinks, flowed regularly and easily in the front cabin. We had just gotten settled when we were offered drinks of our choice. Sadie looked at me. I knew she was wondering whether she should have a drink. It might affect her reactions later.

I smiled, "I don't think a drink or two will hurt. After all, we're not going to get sloshed are we?"

"I would hope not," Sadie replied, turning to the stewardess. "I'll have a vodka martini with two olives, and make it a double."

The stewardess turned to me. "I'll have a scotch, neat please and just a single. One of us has to drive," I said playfully. Sadie stuck her tongue out at me and settled back in her seat. I reviewed the cabin as the plane proceeded to the taxiway. Not counting Sadie and myself, there were only six other passengers in the first class cabin. There was an elderly couple, appearing to be of Spanish or Italian decent, seated two rows directly behind us and two businessmen seated in different rows, but each at least one row removed from ours. Both men were engrossed in making reports, or whatever businessmen do while flying. The final two were young ladies, about 25 years of age, who were traveling together and seemed excited about their future prospects. None of the six appeared to pose any special threat or indicated any special interest in us. I was convinced we were safe and undetected. We could enjoy the flight, so I settled in. When the plane became airborne, the drinks were served along with some snacks that consisted of liver pâté, shrimp dip, and cocktail crackers. Having just eaten, I was not interested in the snacks. I did enjoy the scotch, however.

I must have fallen asleep, because the next thing I was aware of was Sadie shaking my shoulder, "Wake up." The Captain announced final approach to the airport. We have to get our act together for deplaning." I shook myself awake. I was not ready to deplane. I had not planned on sleeping the entire trip. "Look, we obviously don't have a lot of time to consider our options. Here's my suggestion. I will get off the aircraft first and will try to get a read on anybody that may have noticed me. You follow at the end of first class. I will watch for any reaction your exit generates. If we don't generate interest, let's get to our luggage. We'll go to customs and make a decision on how to proceed from there. My bet is our friend did not check any luggage. He had a large carry-on appearing full."

Sadie interrupted, "What if he's in the customs area when we get there?"

"If he is ahead of us, we'll hang back until he clears. If he's not ahead of us, we'll get in line and face the front. I doubt if anybody is so familiar with either of us that they will recognize the backs of our heads. I know it's a risk, but we're here, and I don't see other choices. Do you see any alternatives I missed?"

"No, I think it's the only way. Have you got the money ready for the custom agents?" she inquired.

"Yes, it's in my breast pocket. The last time we were here, there were three agents. I assume there'll be the same amount tonight."

The plane was pulling up to the gate. The stewardess was busy readying the aircraft for passenger departure. Those familiar little bells were dinging, and the stewardesses in coach could be heard admonishing the passengers to stay in their seats until the plane was fully parked at the gate. Our stewardess went to the aircraft door and did whatever she does to get it to swing open. I heard her saying something to an agent in the jet way but could not make out what was said. I had gotten our luggage down from the overhead racks, and Sadie was pretending to get something out of her luggage. I stepped to the front of the aircraft saying, "Why don't I help with the congestion. I'll meet you in the terminal." I said it loud enough so the stewardess heard it and gave me a reason to deplane ahead of Sadie.

Sadie smiled, "Go ahead, I know how you hate this part of flying." She looked at the stewardess, "I think, the only reason we fly first class, is so he doesn't get caught in the crush of people getting on and off the airplane."

"I find a lot of our passengers feel the same way. It's amazing how many people have some degree of claustrophobia," the stewardess replied.

I was en route to the door. I had my luggage swung over my shoulder and was intent on discovering anyone who showed even a little bit of extra interest in me or in Sadie. I reached the exit gate, stepping to the rear to get a full view of the small crowd waiting for friends or relatives to deplane. None seemed to have any interest in me. There was one man who seemed impatient. He was wearing a suit and had a smallish briefcase with him. My bet is he was a business associate of one of the men sharing the front cabin with us. The remaining first- class passengers were beginning to appear and pass through the gates. I could see Sadie, exiting at the end of the first class passengers. She handled the matter perfectly. By all appearances, she was simply deplaning, preoccupied with what she was going to do, or where she was going to go. I watched the crowd. No one seemed to notice her.

She passed through the gates and came to where I was observing the crowd. Again, there seemed to be no interest in Sadie or myself. I looked at her as she approached and attempted to appear very concerned. "You interested absolutely no one as you entered the concourse," I said. I knew this was good news to the professional Sadie but, because of the way I said it, a blow to the feminine Sadie.

"Good," she said "Now let's get to the baggage area, before I show you just how much interest I can generate. We turned our back on the exiting passengers, following the signs to the baggage and customs area. As luck would have it, our two pieces of luggage were among the first on the carousel. I collected the pieces, and we proceeded slowly to the customs line.

The international flights into Bogotá must have been relatively light that evening, because very few people were going through the entry process. Just ahead of us, probably three positions in the line, was the soldier I had previously recognized. He was not looking around. He seemed intent on getting through customs, and home to his wife or girlfriend. We stepped back in an effort to be inconspicuous, in the event he did glance back for some reason. Sadie began rummaging through her oversized purse, in what any casual observer would believe was an attempt to locate her passport or travel itinerary. I watched the soldier, while at the same time, appearing to be interested in the search Sadie was engaged in.

Sadie looked up. "Has he progressed?" she inquired.

"Yes, he's next in line to be checked. If he doesn't have any trouble, he'll be through customs within the next few minutes."

"That's good, because I'm running out of things to look for. We certainly don't want to alert the customs agents to anything suspicious. The line looks longer now. You can practice your small talk. God knows you need all the practice you can get." Sadie spoke in that tone of hers that said *take that*, and by the way, *I'm one up on you.*

"Okay, but I think it best if we wait a few seconds more," I said, not showing any indication I had understood the inference she just dropped. "He appears to be leaving the area." At this point, Sadie was shuffling papers, appearing to put order to what was otherwise a complete jumble of material. As the soldier was leaving, he tipped the customs agents, evidently quite generously, because they became animated and divided the tip between them immediately. I felt some relief when I saw their reaction to the tip. I've always been somewhat reluctant to offer bribes - call it what you want - fearing I might be dealing with the one individual who would take offense to the offer.

Sadie and I walked over, entering the line with the other people waiting for customs clearance. We were five away from the agents. At the speed it was going, we would be through in fifteen minutes. "What is it you would like to talk about?" I asked, with all the sincerity I could muster. "I'm sure in the next few minutes we can either solve most of the world's problems, or in the alternative, discuss why most successful whores insist on wearing red shoes. The choice is yours." I got the response I wanted.

"See how you are. Unless it's business, or one of those man subjects, which half the world could care less about, you have no concept of congenial, light, and friendly conversation. If I suggest we discuss shopping for clothing in Colombia, the first thing out of your mouth would be whether the exchange rate was conducive to shopping. You have no concept of light discussion. I don't know why I spend so much time with you," she said teasingly.

I leaned over and whispered in her ear, "It's because you're assigned to me. It's your job. By the way, why are you wearing those red shoes?"

My timing was perfect because the agent nearest us looked directly at me. "Next."

Sadie and I walked up to a long table, serving as place to search baggage if the agent determined it was appropriate. It also acted as a barrier between the agents and the traveling public. "If I could see your passports, please," the agent requested. I handed the agent my passport. It had been supplied by the State Department, and while it depicted my alias name was, in all respects, official U.S. issue. As he was looking at my papers, he asked the purpose of our visit to Colombia. I knew he was looking at the Colombian entrance and exit stamps affixed just days ago.

"We were here very recently on some business. I got called back to the states early, before we could enjoy the beauties of your city, so we came back as tourists," I replied, trying to anticipate his questions. "We're very tired. It feels like we've been traveling for days. These are the same bags we came in with last week. Is there any possibility that we could be cleared quickly?" I handed the most senior agent three one hundred-dollar bills. I did it in a way only the customs agent and I knew what had happened. He glanced at the bills, and indicated to the other agents a search of our bags would be unnecessary. He and his agents were all smiles.

"You are most generous, Mr. Butler. I hope Colombia is as good to you as you are to its servants. If I might see the passport of your associate, I'm sure we can get you on with your trip." Sadie handed her papers to the agent, and he began what appeared to be a cursory review. Abruptly, he looked up, comparing Sadie to the picture on the passport.

"Come now," Sadie said. "It's not that bad a picture is it?"

"No, Senorita. It is a good picture, Please excuse us for just a moment," the agent said, with a forced smile. He motioned for the other agents to join him in a room located behind the customs table. The room was glassed on the wall facing the customs table. We could see him showing the other agents the passport. Then he evidently instructed one of the men to watch us, because one turned to the glass and was intent on our every move. The senior agent was looking at a piece of paper, at the passport, and then at Sadie.

"I think I know what this is about," Sadie said. "I'm still showing up on some fugitive list."

"Hopefully, that's all it is." I responded. "We can get that misunderstanding cleared up with a phone call."

The customs agent picked up a phone, dialed a number, and talked to someone for less than a minute. At what appeared to be the end of the conversation, he wadded up the paper, threw it in the receptacle, and turned toward the doorway leading back to the customs area. He was speaking to the other agents as he approached the door. When the door came open, he emerged and was all smiles.

"There was a small problem I had to get cleared up, Ms. Anderson. A mistake was made resulting in you being included on a list of fugitives from justice. I made a call and it's all cleared up. The two of you may enter Colombia." The agent was handing us our passports, when Sadie asked, "What do you mean, I was listed as a fugitive? How could a mistake such as that be made? I need an explanation!" I could tell from the way Sadie was standing, I wasn't going to get her to move until the agent satisfactorily answered her questions. The act was brilliant. Had she just accepted the agent's statement, without objection or concern, it wouldn't have been a normal reaction. It may even have been indication of guilt in some circles.

The agent stammered and then replied, "Ms. Anderson, it was a mistake. It seems a local police agent was murdered about the same time you left Colombia several days ago. The location of the murder was near the airport and a piece of luggage, bearing your name was found in the police car. The airline records indicated you boarded a flight to the United States and did not check any luggage. The police officials later determined a local cabbie, who has a history of creating problems and stirring up trouble, committed the crime. He's the cabbie that dropped you off at the airport. The police determined, in your haste to make your flight, you left your larger baggage in the cab. The cabbie then murdered the policeman and planted your baggage in the patrol car, so you would be blamed for the incident. In any event, you've been cleared, and I just hadn't been informed. I'm sorry for any concern this caused."

"Apology accepted. Do you know if they caught the cabbie?" Sadie said, continuing to play the role of a wronged defendant.

"No, I don't think they have, but I'm sure they're getting close," the agent assured her.

"I hope so. Now, if we can go, I would like to find a hotel and sleep for a week."

The customs agent nodded and thanked us again. We collected our bags, proceeded out of the customs area, and ultimately out of the airport. I spotted a cab and waived to get the driver's attention. He saw my overtures immediately, squealing tires to get to us in what appeared to be a race with other cabs, had any other cabs been around. We loaded our luggage in the trunk and entered the rear seat. The driver jumped into the front, asking were we wanted to go. "Take us to the finest hotel on this side of the city," I said.

"Okay, but it's expensive," the driver responded. "The fare will involve a small premium, because I have to drive through the bad part of town to get to the hotel."

"The fare will be ten American dollars and will include your tip, so go any route you choose, but get going," I told him, limiting the amount the driver could pad his normal fee.

"Ten American dollars will be fine," the driver said.

The trip to the hotel took seven or eight minutes. The hotel was very nice. We checked in as man and wife and were escorted to our room. It consisted of a combination sitting room and bedroom with an extremely large bathroom, considered a suite in some circles. What I liked was the well-stocked mini-bar. Over the past five or six years, I've found the convenience of the mini-bar to be a sought after asset, if not an absolute necessity.

I motioned to Sadie not to talk until I checked the room for hidden cameras or listening devices. The hidden camera I found in Las Vegas was a lesson I wasn't going to forget. I checked all the fixtures and furniture that could conceal a small device. I was relieved to find nothing out of order. During the entire time I was looking, I was kicking myself. I'd intended to ask Howard to get me one of those small electronic sweepers. They can detect a bug or camera within eighteen inches and look like any ordinary electric shaver. The device has a nationally known label, so it won't raise suspicions in any setting. I vowed not to make another trip without one.

"Okay, the room seems to be clean, but I think we should be somewhat careful," I explained.

"You certainly have become paranoid," Sadie remarked. "I've been traveling with you for three years and I've never seen you take these precautions."

"I know, but things have happened on this assignment that have opened my eyes a little." I told her about the sleazy hotel room, the hidden camera, as well as the listening devices I'd seen in the trunk of Barajas's automobile. "We're playing in their court now. I believe the devices I saw in Las Vegas will, without question, be available and used here in Colombia. We don't believe they are aware we are in Colombia, but we can't be sure. For that reason, we must be more careful. The tourist story may have satisfied the customs agents, but it will not mislead Barajas."

I still say you're overreacting, but you could be right," Sadie said thoughtfully. "We need to plan the extraction. Do you think it's safe to do it here?"

"I think so. Let's do it now - tonight. By tomorrow our presence may be discovered and it will be more difficult."

Sadie nodded her head in agreement. "Let me shower and get more comfortable, then we can decide what to do. I really need to get all this travel dust and grime off my body. You might want to shower also. I know you'll feel better."

I agreed and proceeded to get what I needed out of my luggage. The evening had been long but productive. At the end a good plan was devised. It was time to get some sleep. Once the plan began, it might be days before the opportunity presented itself again. Tonight was not a night for pillow talk, and we both knew it.

CHAPTER EIGHTEEN

Benjamin Chavez had lived in Bogotá, Colombia all his life. Most people called him Ben. The use of his given name, Benjamin, was reserved only for his mother. He attended government schools and had shown extraordinary promise in areas involving mathematics and natural sciences. Because of his exceptional aptitude for the sciences, and because his father had been a loyal civil servant, Ben was offered the opportunity to attend college in the United States on a full government scholarship.

That was before the drug cartels became so successful in infiltrating the government ranks. It was ironic that one of the important factors considered for initially receiving the scholarship was the exemplary service his father had provided the government as a police officer. Except for a short time, early in his college career, when he was having problems with the language, his grades were exceptional. Ben gave the Columbian government no reason to withdraw his scholarship. The only apparent reason for losing the assistance was, paradoxically, the exemplary service his father had provided the Colombian government at a time when the government was not controlled by the cartel. Ben was no longer one of the favored few. In the two years he had been away studying, the cartel influence had gained enough strength to cause withdrawal of his scholarship privileges.

Ben returned to Colombia feeling he had been cheated, that the government had disgraced his family. He began trying to join the police agencies, but even with the service record of his father, he was rejected. His family had a small savings and with it Ben purchased an older model Chevrolet, going into business as a cab driver. As time went by, he became involved with a group of citizens opposing the influence of the cartel on the government, especially the police. With the death of his entire family at the hands of the cartel, Ben became even more involved. He participated in burning fields owned by the cartel or their suppliers. His specialty was the destruction of warehousing structures when they were filled with product ready for shipment.

The cartel knew of Ben and suspected he may be involved in the burnings, but the proof of his activities and his associations wasn't strong enough, even for the cartel. Ben arranged to be relatively low key on the exterior. The legitimate money he made driving a cab gave him a living. He tried never to appear to be living beyond his means, even though his group accumulated cartel monies in the course of their various raids. Ben learned early that many unwanted suspicions, even jealousies, are fostered when the lifestyle does not fit legitimate income. Ben and his associates accumulated the money but lived the simpler life.

Early on, Ben's upstart group thought of themselves as a Colombian version of the fabled Englishman, Robin Hood. They distributed wealth collected from the ill-gotten gains of the cartel to the needy of Bogotá. On one occasion, government officials became suspicious of the amount of money being circulated by needy people with no visible means of support. An investigation into possible sources followed. Several individual recipients were questioned at length. One of the men interrogated, became so fearful for himself and his family, he divulged information leading the authorities to one of Ben's close associates. Ben's friend was arrested. He was later found dead in his cell. From that time forward, any assets the group accumulated were secreted and not distributed. It became a matter of self-preservation.

As a result of the assistance afforded the American girl and the death of the policeman, Ben realized his low-key life style might well change. The facts, as he knew them, led him to believe she, Sadie, was a cartel woman. Yet, something in him signaled she was somehow different from other cartel women he'd known. It might have been her simple approach to dinner; after all, he'd never met a cartel woman who'd turn down a fancy meal for a Big Mac. Whatever the reason, he was sure she was different, and if what she said was true, so was her boyfriend.

Ben's commitment to help, as Sadie was leaving the country, was virtually automatic. When he realized something might be wrong he immediately began following the police car. When the police car turned into a lane leading to nowhere, he knew he was right. The only question was whether he could get there in time. He had followed from a considerable distance. Why was the cartel, or one of the cartel's purchased police officers, going to do in one of their own? The question kept running through his head. It had to be a mistake. Hadn't they allowed her boyfriend to leave, and then allowed her to remain in the country for another two days? There had to be some crossed wires or misunderstood instructions. The unanswered questions didn't matter at the time. He barely had time to act.

When Ben's cab turned into the lane where the police car had just disappeared, the dust had already settled. Unless Sadie could somehow delay the inevitable, his arrival would be too late. As his cab topped a small hill, he heard the sound of a gunshot. He was already late. He slowed the cab, debating whether to continue and become involved for no reason, or to spin the cab around and go on with his business. Ben hated these decisions. He was forced to make them too often. Every single one was painful.

Ben knew he must proceed. Maybe Sadie had just been wounded. Maybe she had evaded the first shot, and they were playing a game of cat and mouse, a game Sadie would not win without his help. Ben's heart jumped to his throat as his cab topped the last small rise. Coming directly at him at high speed was the police cruiser. His only excuse for being in the area, was to claim he was going to take a nap during the slow part of the day. Not a good excuse, but it might work. Cabbies often sought out secluded places to nap when business was slow. As the police car came closer, Ben realized a policeman was not driving. It appeared a woman was driving. It was Sadie – she driving the cruiser! As soon as Sadie saw his cab, the police car skidded to a stop. She jumped out, running toward Ben's approaching cab.

She jumped into the cab. Before the cab had fully turned around, she had relayed the events of the last few minutes. Both realized she had to get to the airport and out of the country. Ben also knew it must be done without being seen, if he was to have any chance of not being involved. The traffic to the main terminal building was reasonably light. Ben maneuvered the cab into appropriate lanes of traffic without a mishap. Approaching the terminal, he decided to have Sadie walk to the entrance from the outer edges of the airport drive. It was his only hope to escape being connected with *that lady* from America. Sadie got out of the cab, and with perfunctory acknowledgments, proceeded down the sidewalk. Ben eased his cab back into the closest lane of traffic. When an opening presented itself, he inserted the cab the lane furthermost to the left. That lane would go through the terminal traffic with the least congestion.

Approaching the end of the airport drive, Ben realized he'd made a serious mistake. The local airport authority had recently imposed a use tax on commercial vehicles picking up or dropping off passengers on airport property. The cabbies were to add the tax to their fare and have it available to deposit upon leaving airport property. Ben had spent what money he had brought with him on gas for the cab. He had no money to deposit. Approaching the tollgate, he feigned anger, then pulled up and stopped. Before the attendant had a chance to say a word, he blurted out, "My fare stiffed me! They got out of the cab and ran into the terminal without paying. They were my first fare. I spent all my money on gas. I don't have money for the tax. What can I do?" Ben said attempting to instill as much sympathy as possible.

"I just wish you cabbies would pay attention to the suggestions we make for you!" the attendant admonished. "You know I can't waive the fee. You should collect the tax up front on any trip to the airport. Pull your cab into that parking space," he said, indicating a small parking stall just to the left of the gate. "You've got some paperwork to complete."

Ben did as he was told, hoping somehow this would not create a record of his trip to the airport. One look at the forms dashed any hope he had of that. He reluctantly filled out the forms, which required a listing of his home address, his cab license number, his full name, and date of birth. To gain passage through the gate, Ben promised he would return within twenty-four hours and pay the tax plus a one hundred percent penalty. Ben knew he would not return. Failure to satisfy his obligation to the tax authority was not the risk that concerned him. Ben left the tollgate, driving directly to his home. On arrival, he accumulated those personal effects necessary to sustain him indefinitely. Ben had always known a time would come when he would be forced to go underground. He wasn't anxious to leave his open lifestyle, and he hated to leave Maria.

Maria Ortega had been a rock for Ben through the years since his return from the States. She was several years younger than Ben, but he was attracted to her from the first. When they met, she was attending a private school designed to prepare the students to enter the work force with some technical training. The school would be classified as a trade school in the United States. Ben arranged to walk her to the school and, after his cab was acquired, made sure she had a ride both to and from school. From the beginning, Maria seemed to enjoy their relationship, and with the passing of time, feelings between them became stronger. They had talked of marriage on several occasions, but because of the lifestyle Ben had chosen, following the murder of his family, he was reluctant to involve her.

Her family middleclass by Colombian standards, and lived in one of the better sections of the city. Ben met Maria at the same time he was trying to get work with the local police department. His father had told him of business associations the Ortega's had with local government. Her father owned a small printing business, specializing in advertising posters, business cards, and preprinted forms. His business was somewhat dependent on the government's need for handbills and other forms of printed material, and Ben's father hoped the well-connected businessman could help with the application process. He arranged to introduce Ben to Mr. Ortega, Ben's father knew he could help his son if he wanted to.

It was because of that same relationship, Ben had always felt distrustful of the Ortega family. Excepting for Maria, he refrained from contact with them, wherever possible. In a general way, Maria was aware of the activities Ben and his associates were engaged in, and on several occasions they discussed the influence of the cartel on the local government and business. Ben even asked her if she felt her father was doing business with the cartel.

Her response was strange. She didn't deny a business association, or the possibility of one occurring, but simply said she hoped her father was smart enough to avoid such relationships. To Ben this response was the same as an admission, which when coupled with the feelings about his deceased family, classed Mr. Ortega as an unfriendly--- a man to watch.

Now Ben was faced with the probability of going underground to avoid arrest and imprisonment. Any further association with Maria was a risk that should be avoided. However, Ben was convinced Maria was sympathetic to the anti-drug cause. He believed she would not jeopardize him or his associates, but his choice was clear. He could not place his associates at risk, because of his love of a woman, no matter how convinced he was of her loyalties. Just disappearing, without giving Maria an explanation, was also not an option. She deserved an explanation. Ben realized time was short before a warrant would be issued for his arrest. If things went according to form, Mr. Ortega would have the order to print wanted posters within hours. If he was going to make any kind of explanation, it must be done quickly. He had to see Maria.

While in his cab and monitoring the radio, Ben hadn't heard any indication the officer's body had been found. He realistically had only two or three hours of safety, but that would be ample time to find Maria and explain. First, he must go to the safe house and deposit his things. He needed to strip the cab of anything connecting it to him. The underground could repaint the vehicle and use it without much fear of being connected to him, so he cleaned it out, leaving only the plates in place. He was still going to drive the vehicle and didn't want to get stopped because of the lack of plates. His associates could destroy them when he delivered the car.

Now it was time to find Maria and try to explain to her why he was going to disappear. It was the early part of the evening, and he knew she would be home. Ben drove to the Ortega residence, unsure how to approach the house. He wanted an escape route, if Mr. Ortega gave any sign of a problem. The front door was the best approach. Ben parked the cab slightly up the street from the house and left it running. He approached the home in as carefree a manner as he could muster; he attempted to see everything without appearing uptight. Mounting the front steps, he knocked on the door. Maria's mother answered and smiled.

"Good evening, Mrs. Ortega. Is Maria available? If I might, I would like to speak with her."

"Yes, Ben, she is here. Please come in and I'll get her."

"Thank you, but I'm real dusty," Ben said, trying to arrange some privacy with Maria, without appearing awkward. "I'll just wait here on the porch if I may."

"That will be fine," Maria's mother said. "I'll get Maria. I'm sure she will be glad to see you." Mrs. Ortega had that look only a mother has, knowing her daughter has romantic notions and approves her daughters choice. Ben had always gotten along well with Mrs. Ortega. He was sure she did not know, nor did she want to know, of the business associations between her husband and the drug-influenced faction of the government. After all, she had an attentive husband, a beautiful daughter, a nice home, and sufficient monies to conduct an uncomplicated lifestyle. What more could an uneducated Colombian woman want!

Ben could hear Maria approaching with her mother. They were talking about the local marketplace and the lack of some vegetable needed for the dish Mrs. Ortega was fixing. Maria was saying she would ask Ben to take her there, pick it up, and be back in time for the dinner preparations.

"Ben, what are you doing on the porch? Didn't mother invite you into the house?" Maria said playfully.

"Yes. I was invited in. I decided to stay out here so I wouldn't get your mother's house dusty," Ben replied, winking at Mrs. Ortega.

"Would you take me the market? Mother needs a vegetable for tonight's dinner. Ben was not too anxious to go to the market, but the trip would give him time with Maria without worrying about Mr. Ortega coming home. The benefits outweighed the risks. He agreed to go. Maria caught Ben's hand and started down the walk to the street.

"What in the world is your cab doing parked way up there? Couldn't you get it stopped?" Maria said accusingly

"I was not speeding. I'll tell you why it's up the street, but you have to let me talk and don't interrupt. Is that a deal?"

"Yes," Maria said. "What's the matter Ben? Have I made you mad? What did I do?"

Ben's tone of voice, his demeanor, or something had alerted her to the fact that a major change was about to be announced.

"Maria, it's nothing you have done. It's what I've done. Even more than what I've done, it's what I stand for. As you know, my entire family was murdered by the people in this country, profiting from the sale of drugs to whomever has the money to buy them. I've been working with an organization pledged to ridding Colombia of these people and the misery they distribute. In the process, I have associated myself with people who aren't the law-abiding citizens you and I would like to be associated with. They are all fanatically against the interests of the drug cartel and have become extremely militant. I'm a part of that organization, Maria, and I've taken part in many of their activities. You need to know. What I'm going to tell you is about what I am."

Maria's eyes were watering. Ben knew she was on the verge of tears. She tried not to indicate what her feelings were with regard to the activities Ben had just described. "Why is it necessary we discuss this at this time? You must think I'm stupid if you think I haven't figured out you're involved in some of the vandalism my father prints posters about. I know why you're involved. I agree with the goals of a drug free country, but do you have to become more involved? My father is also hoping Colombia will someday become drug free, but he is a businessman in Colombia today, and because of that, I can't become actively involved in the activities of your group. If you become any more active than you are now, my father's suspicions will be confirmed. I will be forbidden from seeing you any further so long as I live in his house. Is that what you want?" Tears had begun to run down Maria's cheeks.

"No. It is not what I want, but it's too late. This afternoon I helped an American woman who was here with her boyfriend. For reasons I'm not aware of, the local police had taken her to the road at the end of the airport. They were going to kill her. What they didn't know was, she also was armed. The result was a dead policeman, who I have personal knowledge was on the cartel payroll. I helped this woman get out of the country. The exact facts and circumstances are not as important as the fact that I'll be charged with the death of the policeman, or with aiding the woman responsible for his death to escape the country. Either way, my ability to operate in the open has ended. I must go underground." Ben hesitated to get her reaction to the bomb he had just dropped on her.

"Do you have any idea what you've done to our future?" Maria sobbed. "What am I to tell my family, our friends? Father will have many questions concerning my involvement with your cause. How am I to respond to him?"

"I don't want you to tell your family, or our friends, anything other than the truth. That's why I haven't told you about my involvement before now. I am not going to tell you where I will be, or when I will try to see you next. You won't have to lie to anyone."

"And what about my father?" Maria injected.

"You have nothing to tell but the truth, and if he doesn't believe you, or has reservations, there's nothing you or I can do about that. You are his daughter and he will want to believe you. I don't know him well, but I believe he is a family man first, regardless of anything else he may be. He also knows you would do nothing to injure him or his business. He will believe you, because that's what he wants to do." Ben stopped, looked at Maria. "I know it feels like your whole world just caved in around you, but it hasn't. Not if you don't want it to. If you give me permission, I will be in touch with you. Whatever happens or whatever decision you make regarding us, please believe what I have told you today and not what you hear from government sources."

During the time Ben had been talking to Maria, she had gotten control of her emotions and become somewhat sullen. They had reached the market square, parking in an area designated for patrons. Maria got out of the car before Ben could say anything. "I think I'd better get the vegetable mother wants and get back or she'll get worried." She disappeared into the crowd of shoppers. Ben's only choices were to stay in the cab and wait, or leave the cab and find a place in the crowd where he could be inconspicuous and still see the cab. The cab was most visible and in a place where he could be trapped. The choice was easy; he would meld into the crowd and find a good vantage-point. Ben already hated the secrecy and deception he knew he had to incorporate into his lifestyle. He knew it was only the beginning.

Ben found a small bench where he could see the cab and had a reasonable view of the area surrounding it. It wouldn't appear out of the ordinary for a man to wait for his wife or girlfriend at that spot. He could go virtually unnoticed in the crowd. The crowds were what could be expected at a local market just prior to mealtime. Everyone was bustling, finding the items they needed, and intent on getting home for the evening. Earlier, when he pulled into the parking space, Ben had noticed a local policeman patrolling the marketplace. He had gotten a good enough look at the officer to know he didn't know him, which was a relief. It wasn't at all unusual for the market to be patrolled, but his presence caused Ben to be slightly more vigilant. Ben was getting nervous about Maria. She should've gotten back by this time.

He was surveying the crowds to catch sight of her, when something caught his eye. The police officer he'd seen earlier was in the parking area, looking in the direction of his cab, speaking into his portable radio. Ben could only sit tight and see what unfolded. The officer positioned himself behind and to the left of the cab. It was becoming obvious that word had gotten out on Ben, and the cab had been spotted. Ben began looking frantically at the evening shoppers in an effort to spot Maria. She was nowhere to be seen. Then his stomach jumped into his mouth, as he spotted Maria just to the right of and walking toward the cab in a crowd of people. She had a bundle of vegetables in her hand. Her walk was quick but not a run. She appeared to be just another shopper in a hurry to get home for the evening meal. Ben couldn't reach Maria before she reached the cab without becoming obvious. A police car carrying two more policemen arrived and parked on the perimeter of the market. The two officers positioned themselves directly behind the cab and across the street. They were concealed behind some shrubbery. The trap had been set. Maria was walking right into it.

Ben was moving toward Maria in a desperate attempt to intercept her before she got to the cab. He was almost where he might be able to get her attention when she stopped. She had gotten to a place where she had a clear view of the cab. She was staring at the cab. Ben could see the confusion and fear in her face. She realized Ben was not in the cab and was alerted to possible problems. Maria's hesitation gave Ben just enough time to reach her.

Getting behind her, he spoke in as low a tone as he could and still be heard. "Maria, don't turn around. Act as though you have to stop and rest. I will move around in front of you and turn around. We can talk then, as soon as my back is to the cab."

Ben moved to a position in front of Maria and turned to face her. "The authorities must have gotten the order to arrest me sooner than I thought they would. I don't have much time. I'm not going to be able to take you home. You'll have to walk. I'm really sorry, but it's not that far … I will understand, if you tell me you never want to see me again. I hope you will give me permission to contact you, when things settle down a bit. I need to know now. I'll make sure any contact is risk free for you and your family. You know how I feel about you. I want to marry you. I hope you realize this separation is as hard for me to require as it is for you to accept."

"Ben, I do want to see you, and I want everything to return to the way it was yesterday. What I especially want is for you to be safe. I'm disappointed and hurt you didn't trust me enough to include me in your life. It will take time for those wounds to heal, but they will. Now go, be safe, and get back to me as soon as you can." Maria smiled for the benefit of the crowd, stepped past him, and proceeded to walk in the direction of her home.

It hadn't been exactly the way Ben would have liked the separation to begin, but it was better than it might have been. Now his job was to survive until affairs in Colombia would allow him to walk in the daylight without fear.

CHAPTER NINETEEN

The morning was typical for the Colombian latitudes, cool and still with the promise of steamy heat later in the day. This was the climate so conducive to the crops Barajas had chosen build his empire. The same crops were grown elsewhere in the world, but nowhere else could compare to this region's ability to flood the market with its deadly product. It may have been a political climate that helped foster the early growth of the drug cartels in Colombia, but however they were born, and however they survived their infancy, they were now fully developed industries. The coca plant created more profit for their owners than any other endeavor in the world. Seventy percent of the world's supply of drugs derived from the cocoa plant comes from Colombia.

Sadie and I had risen early. The plan was to arrange for an automobile without going through the standard car rental agency. The evening before we were in disagreement as to whether it was necessary or smart to avoid the traditional renal agency. I was of the opinion the risk of the wrong people learning of our presence in Colombia was relatively minimal, while the reliability of the vehicle would be unquestioned. Sadie argued, because of the problem with customs while entering the country, the wrong people already knew we were here. If we rented from a traditional source, they would not only confirm our presence, but also know what automobile to search for. I had to admit her argument made more sense.

I was to befriend one of the bellmen and utilize his contacts to rent a vehicle for a few days. It should not pose an insurmountable problem; many families in Bogotá had acquired an automobile, but lacked the income to operate or maintain it. An offer to change the oil, leave the car with a full tank of gasoline, and one hundred American dollars per day would be sufficient to secure a reasonably reliable vehicle. I went to the hotel lobby to seek out a likely prospect to approach. The only bellman, other than the bell captain, was a young man about nineteen or twenty. He was busy sorting baggage that just arrived by bus. I could tell it was not a good time for me to be chatty with him. My experience has taught me the bell captain is on everyone's payroll and cannot be trusted with anything but baggage, and sometimes not even that.

At the far end of the lobby was a smallish Colombian woman. She was cleaning the brass fixtures adorning the rather ornate entrance. I approached to see if she spoke English well enough to understand our proposal. I have learned hotel personnel charged with dealing with the hotel's guests almost always speak English quite well. As the duties of the employee remove him, or her, from frequent contact with the guests, the proficient use of the English language also decreases. I felt the chances of her understanding me to be about fifty-fifty. It was worth a try. She was in her late forties or early fifties and was neatly dressed.

"Senora -- I said as I approached her. "Do you speak English?"

She looked up, smiled, and said, "Yes. My children attended the government schools. I learned the language with them. How can I help you? If your room is in need of extra towels or pillows, I'll have the maid service bring some up."

"No, no. The room is fine," I assured her. "I was wondering if you might know someone who has an automobile my wife and I might rent for three or four days? We would make certain the car was serviced and full of gasoline on return. We will pay one hundred dollars per day for the rental."

"The offer is most generous, but why don't you rent one at the airport? They can take your order over the telephone and will deliver the car to the hotel before noon," she suggested.

"We tried. They haven't got an available vehicle until tomorrow. We would like to get one today," I replied, realizing the lady was more than just a member of the cleaning crew. "The agent I spoke with suggested I inquire of the hotel staff concerning the use of their personal automobiles. He said if I told anyone he recommended this he would deny it. He also said the bell staff would not be much help, as they were compensated by the rental agencies for each customer they referred. Can you help or maybe put me in touch with someone who can?"

"Your request is somewhat unusual, but I may be able to help. My sister has a car they don't use often. I will call her. What did you say you would pay?" she asked.

I knew we had just located a vehicle. "We have one hundred dollars per day budgeted for the automobile. Will that be sufficient?"

"I'll make a call. You wait here. I'll be right back." The maintenance lady disappeared through ornate doors behind the counters.

I found a bench not far from where we were talking. It had a small magazine table located on one end. I sat down and reviewed the selection. There were several Spanish publications, one in French, and last month's U.S. News & World Report. I picked the U.S. News & World Report and began to leaf through it. It amazed me how many major world events I missed when on assignment. The U.S. stock market was at a record low, and according to the short blurb I read, experts believed it was going lower. I looked up. The maintenance lady was returning and, as expected, was smiling.

"My sister and her husband can spare their automobile for the next week. I assume you have the appropriate insurance and license?" she inquired, in an attempt to appear businesslike.

"Oh my, yes!" I responded. "A person can't afford to drive anywhere without insurance. I have an international driver's license in good standing."

"Wonderful! I will have them deliver the car within the hour. They require three days rental in advance. Is that a problem?" she asked, acting as though she was embarrassed to discuss the financial arrangements.

"No problem at all. We'll wait in our room - Room 718. Please have them ring when they arrive," I said, reaching into my pocket to compensate her for her trouble.

"Please, Mr. Butler, I will have them ring, but may they come directly to your room for the exchange? If the bell captain becomes suspicious, I will be in trouble."

"By all means, have them come to our room. Do they speak English?" I inquired.

"My sister speaks enough to get by, but her husband doesn't. She will be with him. Now, I must get back to work." She turned to leave.

"Thank you for all your help," I said, putting an American twenty dollar bill in her hand in a way that could not be seen from the bell desk. The first problem was solved. We had transportation without creating a paper trail.

I went back to the room. Sadie was about ready to leave on our next task. We felt it was not smart to simply approach the market bulletin board and post a notice, looking like we had just left the United States. What was required was dress that wouldn't stand out; we needed to go native. Sadie intended to wear a simple dress drawn in at the waist. I was going to pick up a pair of blue jeans and a work shirt. Both of us were going to get sandals. In these clothes we could fit in and move about freely. Sadie would let her hair go straight, which made her look even more native.

Within the hour the owners of our soon-to-be-rented automobile contacted us. We had invited them to the room, not realizing the hotel management wouldn't allow them access to the hotel. I asked if they needed help. The woman said they could get to our floor by a side entrance, for me not to worry. They were Colombian factory workers and were excited about the extra money they anticipated receiving. They arrived without arousing any suspicions. The wife, who spoke English, indicated the vehicle was a 1975 Plymouth Duster. It ran fine, but the tires were worn. She said the spare tire was inflated, and the jack was in the trunk. I was not happy to hear about the tires. I asked where the car was parked, so I could inspect the vehicle. She said it was parked on the street south of the hotel.

I left them with Sadie and went to inspect the automobile, especially the tires. The vehicle wasn't hard to find. The body looked like its owner had a drinking problem. It was a rather nondescript brown color, and the tires were worn. The front left tire was worse than the rest, but tire cords weren't showing. I started it up. It sounded fine. I let it idle for about five minutes, checking to be sure it maintained oil pressure and wasn't over-heating. I drove it around the block. It had a standard transmission, and the gearshift was not easy to operate. Earlier in my life I owned a car with a standard three-speed transmission, which developed the same stiffness in the shifting mechanism. Worn out guides in the steering column had affecting the shifting lever. This automobile felt the same. Within two blocks I learned the path the lever required to make the gear change. The car would suit our purposes just fine.

I returned to our hotel room, and told the lady the automobile would be acceptable. I gave her three American one hundred dollar bills, thanked her and her husband for delivering the automobile to us, and told her we would leave the car at the hotel when we were through with it. If we owed them for any further days, we would leave the money with her sister. The woman indicated the arrangement was acceptable to them, and they left the hotel room.

As soon as they were gone, Sadie and I left the hotel to go on our shopping excursion. We found a small local market, not far from the hotel, where Sadie was able to get a dress which would allow her to pass for a local woman. I was able to find a pair of blue jeans that fit me, but finding a shirt large enough to conceal my weapon was a problem. We finally found a straw colored shirt that had enough material around the arms and shoulders to accomplish what I needed - if I was careful. The sandals were not a problem and neither was Sadie's native- style purse, which was more like a gunnysack then a purse. It was large enough to secrete her weapon. That was the plan.

Our shopping spree complete, we headed back to the hotel to dress, and then spend the rest of the day in the market area. When the time was right we would leave the message. We parked the car in the hotel parking area; I would have rather parked it elsewhere, but the risk of vandals was greater than the risk the car would be connected to us. On reaching the room, we dressed in our new attire preparing to leave for the day. Sadie was happy about our purchases. She said her outfit was "cute". That's obviously important for women, but I've never understood why something has to be "cute" before they'll wear it without complaining. My clothes were adequate. The shirt had ample room for the 9mm and an extra clip. The waist of the jeans was too big. I needed a belt. I intended to wear the belt I wore with my other clothes, but Sadie said it stood out and was not authentic. We decided I would purchase another belt at the market when we arrived. In the meantime, I just had to suffer with pants falling off at the slightest provocation.

We left the room and proceeded to the car. The extraction process was about to begin. I was comfortable in our plan, but I had to get a belt before I could be truly comfortable there wouldn't a circumstance where I stood out and apart from the crowd.

CHAPTER TWENTY

The Duster handled the streets of Bogotá with ease. I was getting more and more proficient in shifting without grinding a gear. En route to the area where the market was located, we gave wide berth to the immediate area around the hotel where we had stayed on the previous trip. Sadie was concerned with the proximity of the hotel to the market. There was a risk of our being recognized without us knowing. The native clothes went a long way toward helping us blend into the crowds, but if someone, such as a cook or maid, was to approach us directly, they would recognize one or both of us. It was a risk we couldn't avoid. We parked the Duster in a parking area designated for the market square. The contrast, between the local market in Colombia and the local market in the United States, was never more evident. Compared to the mega-parking lots in the States, the parking area in this local Colombian market was sufficient for six automobiles at most.

Sadie and I left the vehicle and began to follow the largest crowds we could find in and around the area. The market was designed in a square with an area in the center for community use. The bulletin board was in the center area. We maneuvered close to the board and got a good look at it, and some of the messages posted on it. Many were notices of church services, special religious events such as baptisms and funerals, and whatever else the community deemed important. Most of the postings were in Spanish. Sadie was more conversant in Spanish than I was, but if both of our abilities were combined and measured, we would still be illiterate. From the knowledge we did have it appeared there were notices for lost dogs, *or* they may have been for found dogs. There were things for sale and messages for friends or relatives. The upper right corner was bare. There were no messages, so we moved away from the board not wanting to show an inordinate interest. Sadie wanted to watch the board from a distance, in an attempt to determine if it was under surveillance. I agreed but felt we should split up for a time. I needed to buy a belt anyway.

I spotted a small leather shop on the other side of the market. We agreed to meet in the vicinity of the board in one hour. Sadie moved off to the left, disappearing into the crowd. I milled around the area for several minutes and then worked my way to the leather shop. It was really quite nice, and had about every item one would ever want made from leather. I indicated to the proprietor I was in the market for a belt. He spoke some English, so the task was not a complete exercise in pantomime. The number of belts he had for sale could have satisfied any need or size. I was interested in a very plain belt, the type a working man wore on a daily basis My size was not a problem. I chose a belt, in short order, and indicated to him I would wear it. The price was ridiculously low by American standards. I paid him in U.S. dollars, and the owner was ecstatic with the U.S. currency. I was indelibly etched in his mind.

Sadie and I needed to get some Colombian currency. The U.S. dollars made us stand out, regardless of the local clothing. In my wanderings I noticed a small local bank and headed for it. I wasn't sure it would be equipped to exchange U.S. dollars, but it was worth a try. The teller at the bank, if that's what you'd call him, spoke good English and was able to change a small amount of U.S. currency, enough for the afternoon and evening. We could get more from the hotel exchange counter later. I glanced at my watch, realizing I had used a full hour buying the belt and getting a small amount of currency exchanged. Sadie would be waiting for me. I moved toward the center of the market as fast as I could without creating any attention. Drawing closer to the board, I slowed down, giving the appearance of shopping. I hadn't yet spotted Sadie. Hopefully, she had spotted me and was working my direction. There was a small bench located a short distance from the board, where I could sit and appear to be resting, while Sadie worked her way to me.

I was watching the board out of the corner of my eye, when a young girl, appearing to be about sixteen or seventeen, approached the board pinning what appeared to be a folded message on the upper right corner. She glanced around, as if she had just done something wrong, and quickly left the area. I remained seated, observing the throngs of people pass by. Within fifteen minutes a young man approached the board and studied the messages posted in the center of the board. He glanced around, while at the same time taking the message from the upper right corner. Then, he immediately disappeared into the crowd passing by. I waited to see if anyone was interested in what had just taken place at the message board. I concentrated on the crowd, in the area of the board, to see if any one tried to follow the man who had taken the message. I felt a slight pressure on my shoulder and spun around.

"Did you see what just happened at the board?" Sadie asked

"Yes, I did. You scared me to death. Where did you come from?" I responded.

"From behind you. I couldn't find a good place to sit and watch, so I've been moving around while I watched the board. That girl made three dry runs to the board before she committed to post the note. The boy came out of nowhere. Both were intent to disappear into the crowd. As far as I could tell, they were completely successful."

"You're good at disappearing into the crowd and then reappearing. Possibly you could work for the underground, ferrying messages," I teased. "I didn't spot anyone interested in the young girl or the boy either."

"The crowds are hard to read with people in groups, going different directions. Let's split up, again, and watch the board to see if anything of interest happens." Sadie suggested.

"I agree. Let's meet back here when it starts to get dark, around seven or seven- thirty."

"That's good for me," Sadie said, quickly disappearing into a crowd of especially vocal shoppers. I think Sadie was enjoying the clandestine aspect of this extraction. I hoped this trip to Colombia will be no more exciting than she was already experiencing, but I also had a feeling future events were going to get much more adventurous.

It was time I moved around a bit. I'd been in one place for over a half-hour. I moved to an area directly in front of the board and looked through some housewares for sale. I was amazed. Most of the merchandise was made in the United States, but carried a price less than half what you would pay in the States. I made a mental note to suggest to a friend in the justice department that the manufacturing companies are raping the American public. If they sell something for five dollars in Colombia, why should it cost ten in Cleveland?

My attention was piqued by the appearance of two local policemen strolling toward the center of the market. They seemed to have nothing particular in mind other than to complete their normal patrol. The larger of the officers was engaged in animated conversation with his partner; the subject must have been emotionally loaded, because he was becoming angry. I could hear the conversation clearly. If I had any command of the language, I would've been able to get the gist of it. I kicked myself for not being proficient in Spanish. I think I slept through the Spanish classes in high school and slept with the Spanish tutor in college. It seems my problem with languages always involves sleeping. In any event, I don't understand Spanish.

As I watched the two officers approach the board, I spotted Sadie. She was not more than six or seven feet from the officers, and in front of them. She was also going directly toward the board, She stopped at the board. The police officers came up behind her. She had nowhere to go. They were still talking, while they looked at the board. The smaller of the officers reached up, took a message down, opened it up, and read it. He replaced it, and scanned the board again. They both moved off to the right. Whether the officers were interested in the messages on the board in general, or were looking for specific messages, Sadie and I would never know.

We had learned two things, however. The underground did watch the board, and so did the local police. Sadie moved to where I was standing just to my right and a bit ahead of me. She spoke in a soft voice that wouldn't carry, "The officers appeared very suddenly. I was taken by surprise. All I could do was continue in front of them. I didn't want them to see my face."

"Were you able to understand any of the conversation taking place?" I inquired. "The larger of the officers seemed very excited,"

"What little of their conversation I was able to understand indicated they were angry about the death of a policeman. There was something about the government. That's all I got. I think the larger officer may have been a friend of the dead officer, but I'm not sure of that."

It was not yet dark, but the day had revealed as much as it was going to reveal. "We might as well return to the hotel for the evening," I suggested and Sadie nodded.

"Do you think we should separate? Meet at the car? Or go together?" Sadie asked.

"I think we better go together. If anyone has been interested in us in recent minutes, to split up, and meet at the car would be a mistake. Let' go to the car being just what we are, two lovers strolling through a market place in Bogotá.

We had just begun to stroll hand in hand when we came face to face with the same officers we saw at the message board. They were making rounds though the market, and we were in their route. I smiled at the officers and stepped aside so they could pass, pulling Sadie with me. The larger of the policemen was still emotional and talking. The smaller smiled, with a look of embarrassment for his partner. After they passed, I could tell Sadie felt relieved. She looked at me and whispered, "Well, that answers another question. Evidently we're not on any wanted posters, official or unofficial."

The return to the Duster was uneventful, as was the return trip to the hotel. We entered the hotel though the side entrance to avoid the bellman. The image we created with the clothes we were wearing was none of his concern.

CHAPTER TWENTY-ONE

B en Chavez was well aware the underground had facilities where he could disappear. Ben was hopeful the concerns of the police would blow over, and eventually he could surface with some safety. The authorities must have had suspicions about the American woman. Why were all apparent efforts focused on apprehending him? It didn't make sense. The first order of business was to get to safety. Once safety was achieved, he could ponder the questions plaguing him.

The cab was a lost cause. Ben reasoned the police impounded it as soon as they realized he wasn't going to return. The underground could have used the vehicle, but it wasn't a big loss. Ben wanted to reach a church in the western part of the city. It was run by a Catholic Father who was sympathetic to the anti-drug underground. He had used the facility once before. One of his associates was injured in a field operation and needed a place to recover.

The priest was middle-aged but fanatical when it came to the cartel. The rumor was his family owned and farmed fifteen or twenty acres around Medellin. The cartel wanted the farmland, and made the family an offer to purchase the land. When they refused to sell, the part of the family engaged in farming was rounded up and tortured until the land was transferred. Because the family had resisted, the payment was reduced to a tenth the original offer. The priest's family now lives in virtual poverty. The cartel allowed the facts concerning the ultimate sale and the priest's family to become public. Afterward, the drug lords had no problems in acquiring land. The priest was attending seminary when the events took place. Many believed he felt guilty he wasn't there to help.

The area of the city Ben traditionally spent most of his time was near the international airport. Most of Ben's friends were there. He knew he couldn't stay in that location, but he needed to get a message to the underground; they had to know he was okay and where he would be. The message board in the central market place was the only way he knew to safely get the information to them. He needed someone to post it there. Ben worked his way through the back streets until he reached the home of an associate of his, known only as Tony. Tony had been on several missions, even helping with warehouse projects, when they came up. Tony was married and his wife was sympathetic to their cause. Ben felt they would be able to help without imposing a risk on them they were not prepared for.

Tony's wife's name was Loretta. She was one of those individuals who, at age thirty, could easily be mistaken for a teenager. She was extremely petite and had a fair complexion. A quick brush through her hair, and donning some appropriate clothing kept around for precisely that reason, made her appear fifteen years younger. Loretta was often used to pass messages where others might be recognized. That was the task Ben wanted her to perform for him.

Ben finally reached the block where Tony lived. He was forced to climb several fences to get to their back door. On one occasion, Ben had to hide behind some barrels for several minutes, while the lady of the house took in laundry. He had to pass through her backyard to reach Tony's, and knocked on the door. He could hear noise in the house, and shortly, Loretta's face appeared between red and white curtains covering the window. She recognized Ben immediately, sensing something was wrong. Ben would never use the back door, otherwise. She opened the door hurrying Ben into the house. She said Tony was out but how could she help. He quickly gave her a short version of what happened and asked her if she could get a message on the community message board. Loretta agreed to do the delivery, excusing herself to get ready.

Utilizing a scrap of paper he found in his pocket and using a simple code, Ben indicated he was okay and would be at the church. Loretta reappeared as Ben finished the note. He was always amazed at Loretta's transformation. She took the note and left the house. Ben went back out the back door and worked his way to neighborhoods where he was not well known. Ben hadn't been able to get any money, so his trip to the west side of the city was on foot. He arrived at the church long after midnight. The message must have gotten through, because the Priest, every one called him Father Armando, was waiting for his arrival.

After the usual pleasantries, the priest motioned Ben to meet him in the rectory. Shortly after Ben entered the church, a woman came in, lit a candle, and settled down in a pew. Father Armando felt he should find out if she needed his counsel. The alternative reason was to determine if she was following Ben. Ben entered the rectory through the side door reserved for the church personnel and invited guests. There was a small waiting room just through the door. Ben settled in a threadbare, but serviceable, armchair and began to relax. The adrenaline required on the streets slowly dissipated, and he gradually came to the realization his feet had become tired and sore. Ben was about to untie his shoes and get comfortable, when Father Armando entered.

"I thought you would never get here. I even sent some friends in automobiles out to find you. What did you do? Walk?"

"Yes, and let me tell you, I can feel it now. I didn't realize how far it really was," Ben responded. He proceeded to tell Father Armando about the events leading him to the church. Father Armando listened patiently until the part about not having any money with him and his problems at the airport. The priest became somewhat irritated.

"Haven't I preached over and over again that you men need to carry a little extra cash at all times? It's circumstances just like this that prove my point. You men never know when something is going to happen, causing you to have to disappear. Without money, you're at their mercy. Just what would you have done if they had spotted you? I swear you men listen to me less than my congregation does, and judging from the time that I spend in the confessional, that's not much."

Ben said that he agreed with the priest and finished the story. Father Armando asked what his plans were. Ben indicated he was hoping to use the church as a base, and to continue his operations. The priest looked troubled. Ben was not sure how to proceed.

"What's the matter Father?" he asked.

"Ben, you know I will fight the cartel until my last breath, and you can count on me for anything within my control. What I cannot do is jeopardize the good people of this parish because of my support of underground activities. I am in trouble with the Bishop now, because he feels the congregation, maybe even the physical facilities of the church, are in jeopardy. I will support your efforts, as always, and you can stay a couple of days while you are making other arrangements, but you cannot use this church as a base camp," Father Armando hesitated.

"That's fine, Father. I appreciate the help you are giving me today and have given me in the past. If I might ask, however, what has changed? Has the cartel discovered your involvement? Are you receiving threats?"

"No, Ben, that's not it at all. If that were the case, we would have to move you tonight. What has changed is the nature of what has occurred. In the past we have been at war with the drug lords and their soldiers. Now we have taken the life of a local police officer. It matters little he was on the cartel payroll, or that you did, or did not participate in the killing. What matters now is - the local policemen from all over the city are angry. They feel, for reasons they don't understand, the government has whitewashed the matter, and the murderers of one of their own have gone free. The result is, what can best be described as, vigilante activity within the police force. The underground is not only fighting the drug cartel, but now what's left of the honest God fearing police force. That's the battle I can't be a part of. I hope you understand." Father Armando fell silent.

"I do understand, and I appreciate the information. I was not aware of the extent of division in the police force. It explains some of what has happened. I will be gone by tomorrow. Father, do you still have the capability to get messages to my friends?"

"Yes, I do, and I'm glad you asked. I have a message for you from the people on the coast. Let me get it." Father Armando disappeared into the living quarters, returning in less than a minute. "Here it is. I can't understand a lot of it, but it sounds like there have been considerable movements of drugs to the coastal areas."

He handed the message to Ben. Ben glanced at the paper, noting it was more lengthy than most messages coming from the field.

"May I sit to translate," Ben asked the priest.

"Yes, of course, you may." Ben sat back in the chair and began to study the make-shift code. As nearly as he could determine, the cartel was moving finished product to areas on the Caribbean Sea, specifically Cartagena and the areas around its bay. The message indicated it was the Barajas organization, although that part wasn't real clear. It went on to say his group had accumulated a cache of explosives and wanted Ben to travel to the coast. There was an opportunity for destruction of a large amount of finished product. Ben knew the transportation of product would result in the warehousing of drugs bound for an unknown market. Ben had never been fortunate enough to deal with a warehouse facility storing finished product. His prior excursions were to places where the raw material was housed awaiting production.

Ben's first reaction was to leave immediately for the Caribbean coast. However, logic told him there were arrangements to be made before he could leave for the length of time contemplated by a project of this magnitude. He could leave by cover of darkness tomorrow. That would give him enough time to make the necessary arrangements. Ben told the priest the gist of the message without disclosing any detail. Ben hinted he might go to the coast and help disrupt as many shipments as possible. Father Armando offered to arrange Ben's transportation. Ben anticipated the Father making that offer, and politely refused. He said he wasn't sure where in the city he was going to be, or when it would be a good time to leave. Father Armando accepted the reason given and preceded to offer Ben a small meal of leftovers and coffee. Ben was starved and willingly accepted the hospitality. He had not eaten all day.

Ben knew he had to get out of the church as soon as possible. The good Father had been an important ally when the battle lines of the drug war were clean; now there was some vagueness to the lines. The priest wasn't comfortable. Ben's intuition told him he could no longer be trusted. Ben finished the food and coffee. Father Armando took him to a small room outside the rectory in the back of the church. Inside there was a cot, a blanket, a water basin with pitcher for cleaning up, and some towels.

"I hope you will be comfortable in here," the priest said. "It's the only area I have that will give you any privacy."

"I'm sure I will, Father - and you have a good night sleep also," I said..

"Thank you. I'm sure I will," the priest replied as he disappeared toward the living quarters in the front of the church.

Father Armando had evidently forgotten the time Ben had been at church before. Ben's injured associate was granted sanctuary for the purpose of healing. There was a room in the rectory used for guests, and it had all the privacy one could want. The priest was not being as straightforward as he had been in the past. It appeared the death of the local policeman had created a huge conflict for him. Ben washed off the grime of the day as he contemplated his next move. His intuition told him almost anywhere would be safer than the church. The authorities could come and remove him without even bothering the priest. A night on the streets was not as appealing as the cot, but it might be a lot safer.

He cracked open the door to the room as he toweled his face. He hadn't turned on a light, utilizing only the light coming through a small skylight above the room. The hall leading to his room was dark as expected, and there were no sounds emanating from the church proper, which was located at the end of the hall and to the right. Ben moved quietly down the hall, stopping just short of going through the entry to the church. He could see the prayer rail. A small amount of light existed, probably from lit candles. The balance of the church was in darkness. Ben moved to the entry door and proceeded down the closest sidewall toward the rear of the church, and the door to the street.   The flooring in the old church was hardwood and creaky. Ben was sure his steps could be heard blocks away. The adrenalin was again pumping. Ben could hear his own heart beat

When Ben reached the back of the church, he stopped, hoping his heart would slow down. He also wanted to be sure the priest hadn't heard him. Everything was still. Somewhere toward the front a small rodent could be heard scratching a morsel of food out of a crack in the flooring. Otherwise, all was quiet. Ben eased toward the door, reaching for the lock and deadbolt. Both were unlocked. He eased the door open slightly, scanning the area in front of the church. The night was still. There weren't any vehicles or pedestrians in the front of the church or nearby. He slipped through the door, easing it shut to avoid any unnecessary sounds. As he stepped from the forgiving old wooden flooring to the flagstone walkway, he remembered how sore his feet were. Ben recalled the admonition, from somewhere back in his training, or possibly, it was in an old movie, that an army's effectiveness is directly proportional to the health of its feet. He had learned the truth of that statement.

Reaching the curb of the street in front of the church, Ben heard a faint sound of automobile engines. The mere fact he heard engines wasn't what caught his attention. The engines were running at high rpm, which meant they were traveling at a high rate of speed. Ben crossed to the opposite side of the street. Twenty or thirty meters to his left was property where the owner maintained a hedge about a meter high. It would have to hide Ben in the event the automobiles were coming to the church. Ben had no sooner ducked behind the hedge, when three cars came into view. Two of the cars were obviously police cars. They had all the appropriate lights and trimmings. The third car was void of any markings identifying it as a police car. None of the three vehicles had their headlights on, and they were coasting quietly down the block. They came to a stop at the church. Two uniformed policemen got out of each of the marked cars. One man in plain clothes got out of the unmarked car. They all left their doors open and engines running. It was obvious they were trying to be as quiet as possible.

They conferred at the front of the church, and then three went toward the main front entrance. Two went around the side toward the back of the building. The three remaining in the front waited a short period, evidently, long enough to allow the other two to get in position and then entered the church. The door was quietly shut. Instantly Ben realized this was his chance to arrange a ride across town and a replacement for his cab. He ran from his hiding place, behind the hedge, and slid into the driver's seat of the unmarked car. He held the car door open, as he maneuvered the shifting leaver into drive position, eased the automobile from the curb, and accelerated down the street. He went more than a block before closing the car door. Ben kept watching the rear view mirror for any signs of activity around the church. There was none.

Thanks to the time spent driving a cab, Ben knew how to get across town without using major streets. It would be just a short time before the radio would be filled with officers attempting to locate the stolen police car. No one would expect he would use back roads where it was unnecessary to use headlights. One of the members of the underground owned and operated a small automobile repair shop. In the rear was a large shed where he kept the junk cars used for spare parts. Ben intended to get the automobile there before dawn, so it could be secreted under the cloak of darkness. The trip to the garage was circuitous but uneventful. By the time Ben reached the garage, the local police airwaves were burning with officers reporting possible sightings of the stolen police car and incriminations of the fugitive that had taken it.

The owner of the garage took Ben to the home of Kenneth and Gale Mastis, a couple instrumental in the formation of some of the underground's communication techniques. They were trusted beyond question. The Mastis's welcomed Ben into their home, giving him a room in the attic with a small window overlooking the street. Ben had heard of the Mastis's and they of Ben, but they never had met. They were aware of the message Ben had received through the priest. The time was not right to move into the north coastal area. The cartel's movement of finished product had just begun. Kenneth suggested Ben rest for a few days before traveling north. They would help him pick a time when the trip could be accomplished with relative safety. The prospect of rest wasn't unappealing to Ben. He'd had an eventful twenty-four hours. He'd gone from cabby to fugitive, left his girlfriend, walked in excess of fifteen miles, stolen a police car, and returned to safety. He was desperate for rest. Ben excused himself, headed for the attic, and fell asleep almost before his head hit the bed.

CHAPTER TWENTY-TWO

The day dawned no different from yesterday. In fact all days seemed to be more or less the same as the preceding day. The difference between today and yesterday was: today Sadie and I were going to leave a message on the board for Ben. Sadie had cut the letterhead off a piece of hotel stationery and had marked a large S on one side of the paper. She had folded it so the S was on the inside, not visible to the casual passerby. On the outside of the folded paper she put the initials BC. The plan required I place the message on the top right corner of the board. Sadie would be in the area watching the crowd. I would later join Sadie, and we would watch the board until the message was picked up.

The plan was simple enough. The planned activities promised enough boredom that I was not looking forward to the upcoming hours. I always hated the stakeout. I'm a bit too active or nervous to be comfortable just sitting and watching. I remember a session, while in the training at the farm, where one of the presenters said the female agents were generally much more effective in a stakeout because they were more patient. That prediction was certainly true, when a comparison is made between Sadie and me. Sadie is able to concentrate on crowds or events much longer than I.

Sadie and I had a nice breakfast at the hotel, finishing about eight-thirty in the morning. After paying the check we went to the room to dress in our native motif. The Duster had been left in the hotel parking lot again. Upon reaching the vehicle, I checked several small indicators set to determine if the automobile was drawing any attention. All the indicators were in place, so we got in and headed to the market. I had Sadie drive. I showed her the special shifting requirements, giving her a chance to learn them. She caught on real quick and shortly was shifting just as smoothly as I did. The plan was for Sadie to drop me at the end of the park opposite the parking area. We would then meet in the general area around the message board in a half hour. I would post the message at that time. We weren't sure from the experience of yesterday, whether the underground, the police, or both watched the board closely, or whether it was checked only once or twice daily.

The Duster approached my drop off point. I had the note and a thumbtack taken from the hotel employees' message board. It was now a matter of looking like I belonged in the market, while working my way to the board. Sadie stopped the Duster, letting me out two blocks from the square. She then backtracked, so she could enter the parking area from the appropriate direction. Sadie was going to back the Duster into the parking space. That would ensure, if we had to leave quickly we could, without risking gearshift problems.

I walked the two blocks, reaching the market area about the same time Sadie would be arriving at the parking area. In the area, where I entered, there were shops that specialized in merchandise appealing to men. New and used tools, along with household fixtures occupied most of the space. There was also a vendor displaying a multitude of car parts, motor oil, and related merchandise. I stopped for a second to look at the layout. It seemed obvious that accumulating the variety of items he had would be difficult. My bet was most of the parts were from stolen cars stripped for this purpose.

As I worked my way through the market area, I became aware the crowds, which we experienced yesterday, were not present. There were sufficient people so I didn't stand out, but no one could have gotten lost in the crowd. I've never enjoyed crowds, but in this instance, I would have preferred more people. I approached the center of the market. The community message board was in sight. I scanned the small crowd to find Sadie. She wasn't to be seen. Possibly I was ahead of her. I stopped at a small stall pretending to be interested in the dried flowers being displayed. Sadie finally appeared, walking and shopping her way toward the board. She spotted me and acknowledged my presence in a way only I would pick up. I moved to the small bench I used yesterday. Sitting down, I proceeded to light a cigarette from a pack I had purchased upon arrival in Colombia. The brand was local. The cigarette was awful but it was authentic, making me appear more local. At least that's what I told Sadie when she saw the package.

By the time the cigarette was finished, Sadie had completed a loop around the message board. During her stroll, no one had acted interested in, or appeared to be following her. She was watching my position, also, and would give me some signal, if there was anything or anybody acting suspicious. Sadie reached a position where she could stop and watch the area without standing out. It was now my turn to move around. I got up and proceeded to work my way slowly toward the board. I had the prepared message in my left front pocket. The thumbtack was also there. Reaching the point of no return, I glanced at Sadie. She nodded, virtually imperceptibly, indicating the coast was clear. I walked directly to the board, reached in my pocket for the message, found the tack, and put the message in the upper right corner. As I turned to leave, two men were approaching rapidly. By the way they were walking, I could tell they were not interested in reading the messages on the board. They were interested in me - and very probably, in the message I had just posted.

I allowed the one closest to me to get real close, before I brought my knee up into his groin. As he doubled up, his head came down. I grabbed a handful of hair and slammed his head into my knee. The man fell like a load of bricks. His partner seemed confused for an instant; an instant was all I needed to get into what crowd there was and make an escape. The man was chasing me. The crowd was falling away and some people were screaming. At some point I realized I had escaped the pursuer. I slowed to catch my breath. The shadow of a tent being used to sell children's clothes was a welcome site and I used it. The crowd in the direction I had come was still noisier than normal. My pursuer must still be back there. I moved out of the shade into an area leading directly to the outer edge of the market. There was no need to run at this point. I had caught my breath, I could stroll with the other shoppers out of the market area into the streets of Bogotá.

Sadie hadn't spotted the men until it was too late. They were dressed in the same type of clothing Eric was wearing. In one respect it was good to know the clothing they were wearing was blending in. On the other hand the opposition was using the same tactic and it was just as effective for them. She realized the advantage she and Eric thought they had was an illusion. The playing field was flat, but at the present time, the advantage was with the opposition. When Eric dropped the lead officer, Sadie knew the chances were good Eric would get away without need of her help. The other officer was hesitant and ineffective. Sadie had to force back a giggle when she thought of Eric in a foot race with the smaller, more agile, of the officers.

The message he had posted was still there. Unless someone picked up the message, within the next few minutes, the attempt was going to fail. Sadie considered approaching the board and removing the message in order to deprive the authorities of any evidence. She quickly decided against that course of action because, in the event of trouble, she was without backup. As Sadie watched the area, a man approached the board and with no apparent reluctance, took the message Eric had posted and moved away, without unfolding the paper or reading the message. Sadie followed him until he disappeared into a group of houses on the periphery of the market square. The message having been picked up, Sadie knew, if Ben were able, he would be at the designated park within the next three to four hours. It was time to return to the hotel and hope Eric would get there in time to join her.

Sadie worked her way to the Duster and started it up. She drove the route she felt Eric might have taken to get back to the hotel. Knowing it was a long shot, she still hoped she would spot Eric. While that was her hope, she also knew she had to get back to the hotel and be ready to leave for the park. Eric may have been fortunate enough to get a cab or public bus going toward the hotel. He might already be there waiting for her to arrive.

Sadie drove the Duster slowly, through the side streets just off the main route leading back to the hotel. She thought she spotted Eric several times. It always turned out to be someone about Eric's size, wearing clothes similar to Eric's. As she got closer to the hotel the traffic on the side streets was more congested. She decided to get to the hotel in as direct a route as she could and see if he was there. The remaining drive took three or four minutes. She parked the car in a different space than they had used the previous day. Sadie quickly set the same small traps on the car to determine tampering and entered the hotel through the side entrance.

Arriving in the vicinity of their room, Sadie could tell that either Eric was in the room or uninvited guests had entered it. She approached the door very quietly and pushed it open with the toe of her right shoe. Her hand was positioned inside her large purse and had a firm grip on the handle of her pistol. There in the chair with his feet propped on the bed was Eric. He was sipping a double martini. "When the hell did you get here?" Sadie asked throwing the door open.

"I've been here fifteen minutes," I responded "What took you so long?"

"I've been driving all of the back streets I could find leading back to the hotel. I was trying to give you a ride.

"How did you get here so fast?" Sadie asked, somewhat irritated.

"Your mistake was to use the side streets. I used main routes. I blended in better there than I could have alone on a side street. Within six or seven blocks, I was able to catch a public bus, which dropped me within a block of the hotel. The rest you can see. I took my shoes off, made a huge martini, and was in the process of sipping its silver nectar when you so rudely busted in, your piece in hand ready to blow me away."

"Well don't get too relaxed. We have to go on a picnic in about an hour," she said, waving her pistol. "Don't tell me the underground showed up after the locals tried to arrest me, or whatever they were going to do?"

"Yes, a man just walked up to the board and took the message. I tried to follow him, but he lost me in the housing on the periphery of the market square. I think he suspected I was following him," Sadie replied.

"Are you sure he was from the underground?" I asked, realizing immediately it was a dumb question.

"No, I'm not absolutely sure, but I believe he was. The message you put there was the only one he was interested in. He didn't unfold it or try to read it. He just put it in his pocket and left," she replied. "I can't think of any other person or group that would act like that other than the underground. They knew the message was theirs."

"What's the next step?" I asked, finishing the martini much faster than I had planned.

"You remember, Ben will be at the same park where we had the Big Mac. He said he would be there within two hours. Now, get back into your native clothes and let's get going. The message was picked up thirty or forty minutes ago, meaning we have already lost at least a half hour." Sadie went to the bathroom to quickly freshen up. She was right, we needed to hurry. If Ben could be located through message board, it would make the trip a lot easier and quicker. I slid back on the jeans and the shirt. If we were going to use these clothes much longer, I needed to get them washed. My sprint from the authorities had resulted in my shirt reeking with the smell of a gymnasium. "Are you sure you can find the park again?" I asked.

"If you can get me to the hotel where you left me to go to Las Vegas, I can find the park from there," Sadie said with a certain irony as she emerged from the bathroom. "Let's go!"

We used the side entrance again, going directly to the Duster. I opened the door and quickly slid into the driver's seat. I found myself painfully wedged between the steering wheel and the car seat. As usual Sadie had adjusted the seat as far forward as she could get it when she first entered the car and then just left it there. I couldn't get in without risking my manhood. I had complained about this trait or prank, I don't know which, for at least two years. I grumbled something about not being able to teach old dogs new tricks, and she said something about the number of buffets I had eaten while in Vegas. I suppose I will fight this problem as long as I'm forced to drive cars Sadie also drives.

I drove to the neighborhood where the hotel was located. We entered the street fronting the hotel several blocks north of the property but south of the street Sadie and Ben used that evening to reach the park. Sadie was able to identify the crossing street with little problem, and we proceeded toward the center to the city. Before long, we spotted the golden arches. The park was in the next block. We drove around both the McDonalds and the park before making any decisions regarding the method of approach. We purchased two large Cokes from McDonald's. The Cokes would give us a reason to be sitting in the park. The closest parking area to the picnic tables was the same area Ben had used when he and Sadie used the park several days ago. I parked the Duster and Sadie and I strolled across the grass eventually arriving at the tables. We chose the same table they had previously used, sat down, and began our vigil.

Ben had been resting for two or three days. He was anxious to get to the coast. The news being forwarded indicated the cartel was not yet shipping substantial quantities but was making arrangements for what appeared to be the largest shipment the underground on the coast had encountered. Ben found it much harder to relax and wait than he had anticipated. Finally a message was received, indicating he should move toward the coast within the next twenty-four hours. The wait was over. Kenneth convinced Ben he should wait for at least twelve hours and join a caravan of workers headed for the coast. Ben could masquerade as a farm worker or someone looking for a job on one of the numerous fishing boats, using the area as a homeport. He was not overjoyed with another twelve hours wait, but all in all, it was good to know the waiting was coming to an end. Ben knew he needed a reason to be traveling to the coast, and the caravan seemed to be just what he needed

In the twelve hours left he could make sure he had everything he needed. Ben considered the possibility of getting some word to Maria. He could not tell her where he was going, but if he could notify her he was leaving for a time, she may not feel quite so abandoned. Ben asked Kenneth if he could arrange a message to Maria in a way her family wouldn't be aware a message had been received. Kenneth said the same girl they had been using for the message board might be able to get the job done. Ben knew he was referring to Loretta._He went to the loft and wrote a short message simply telling Maria he was going to be out of the city for a period of time, for her not to worry, and he would get in touch with her when he returned. He took the message to Kenneth.

"Be sure Loretta knows Maria's father may be a cartel sympathizer. He gets a lot of printing business from them. Tell her the message is not important and not to deliver it if there is any chance she will get be identified or apprehended," Ben cautioned.

"Loretta has been doing this a long time. She has an intuition about the deliveries she makes. We won't have to worry about her. She's the best we have," Kenneth said in an attempt to get Ben to relax and not worry.

Loretta arrived within the hour to pick up the message. Ironically she also had a message appearing to be for Ben. She reported that Tony had been in the market when a disturbance erupted. According to Loretta, Tony hadn't been able to see what caused the disturbance. Two of the local police were attempting to apprehend a man who, appearing to be a factory worker, handled himself more like a commando. In any event, after a scuffle, the police chased him away from the board. At that point Tony strolled to the board to see if he could determine what the disturbance was all about discovering a message in the spot. The message appeared to be for Ben as the cover initials were BC. There was no message inside, just the Letter S.

Ben stared at the message. How could this be? He had done everything but physically place Sadie on an airplane. At first he felt anger. She was the cause of his exile, after all. Without this woman feeling the need to shoot a policeman, he would be still driving the cab and having dinner with Maria at least three times a week. There was something about Sadie, however, that made him believe she was not as she appeared: that she was not the girlfriend of a drug boss from the States Why was she back here, and why did she want to meet with him now, when he was about to leave?

Ben had not told Kenneth the full circumstances around his meeting Sadie and the fact they had an early dinner, if you want to call it that, on the day the police officer was killed. It was time all the facts were known by everyone involved. The group would dictate whether Ben would keep his word and meet Sadie within the next two hours. He was willing to accept that decision. Ben spent the next half hour reciting the details of his experience with Sadie and how he felt she was not part of the drug problem. At the conclusion, Ben reassured his friends he would not show up if they determined it was not safe - or in the best interests of the movement. Gale was the first to speak,

"Why do you believe she's not part of the cartel, if not individually then through her boyfriend?" she inquired.

"It was the tone of her voice, and maybe the look in her eyes, the woman said she felt they could someday help me complete my engineering training. It seemed to me if she was with the cartel, or her boyfriend was a drug boss, she would not have promised help at a later time. She also indicated she, and I suppose her boyfriend, may need *my help* in the future. I believed her then, and I believe her today. That's why I made the arrangements for her to leave a message on the board."

"Haven't you already done enough for this lady?" Kenneth asked. "After all your life, as you knew it, is now gone and she's the reason why. How much do you want to give her?"

"I agree, if that was all that it was - but it isn't. I have a feeling, call it an intuition, that when this lady told me she was not as she appeared, she was not lying. I think she may be a real asset to our resistance. The problem is there's only one way to find out and that's to meet with her today," Ben responded. "My vote is to meet with her and find out what she wants. I will be governed by the group's feelings on this matter however." The group was silent for several seconds.

Loretta broke the silence. "Every member of the underground has been chosen or accepted based on someone's feeling, call it intuition, that their motives and feelings were consistent with ours. Ben has said he believes she is okay, because he feels it. That's good enough for me. I vote with Ben."

Gale was next to break the silence, "I don't know if Kenneth agrees with me, and he can certainly vote the way he feels, but I agree with Loretta. I don't believe our movement will ever have the luxury to run a credit check, or whatever, on people seeking to join us or help us. We have always operated by our gut, and we've not been wrong in many instances. I vote with Ben."

The group looked to the only member present who hadn't expressed an opinion. Kenneth had been silent as all the others expressed their opinions. He was looking at Ben. He started to say something, then stopped. He seemed to be trying to decide how to phrase his thoughts. He realized, as did the others, that a bad decision here could set the resistance back years if not kill it all together. He also realized the group, at least his group and the groups they came in contact with, looked up to him to make decisions that were thought through and were well reasoned. Kenneth began by addressing Ben.

"Ben I have known you personally for a long time. I've heard of your work and dedication through other groups. They've said you were a star and the movement is lucky to have you counted among us. I have a lot of faith in the collective wisdom of the groups and truly believe the success of our movement and Colombia's only realistic chance to defeat the drug interests is through collective wisdom. I also realize you are a man. From what I understand, this Sadie is a very attractive woman. It is my hope and prayer you are thinking with the appropriate head, because if you aren't, the entire movement will be in jeopardy."

Kenneth now addressed the group, "Having expressed my only fear, I also vote to support Ben."

The group was momentarily silent, then all began to speak at once. Ben silenced them by holding his hand in the air, "I appreciate the support you have given me, but I don't want to get any of you involved any more than absolutely necessary. It's not an exaggeration to recognize that a great deal of the strength of the resistance, especially in the city of Bogotá, is present in this room. It wouldn't be a sound plan to involve any more of you, than absolutely necessary, to ascertain the intentions of this woman I barely know. I have a plan that will work for us and will test the intent of the woman. We don't have much time, so listen closely."

Ben explained his plan. The group discussed alternatives, and an agreement was reached. The group split up. The next few hours were going to be critical.

CHAPTER TWENTY THREE

S adie and I had been in the park for just over forty-five minutes and nothing had happened. As I mentioned before, Sadie was always the better agent when it came to the stakeout. This time was no exception. I was already beginning to complain about the fact I was bored, I didn't believe anyone was going to show up, and my Coke was gone. Sadie was scowling at me.

"If I give you a dollar so you can have another Coke, can you keep your thoughts to yourself for another hour or so? If they don't show by that time, I will agree with you and we can leave."

I was about to agree with her, when I realized she was treating me like a little kid. I, therefore, did what any red-blooded American man would do; I refused the Coke, remaining totally miserable. I think I felt better, because I had shown her she couldn't treat me like a kid --- maybe.

I was silently mulling over the circumstances leading to my being involved in this aspect of the extraction, when Sadie planted her elbow firmly in my side,

"That old Ford has been around the park twice in the last fifteen minutes," she said, nodding toward a bluish 1958 Ford turning onto the street where the Duster was parked.

"Can you see who's in the car?" I asked.

"No, not now, but I would swear there was a man and a young girl in the car when it went by the last time. I don't believe Ben was in there unless he has altered his appearance."

The old Ford pulled in the parking spot next to where the Duster was parked. After what seemed to be an exorbitant length of time, a man got out the driver's side and a teenage girl exited the passenger's side. They appeared to have no specific destination in mind, strolling lazily toward the area where we were sitting. I could tell from the way they were approaching, they weren't as interested in a table as they were in us. Sadie must have gotten the same impression. She whispered something about being sure they were from Ben's organization.

As they approached, Sadie punched me in the ribs again whispering, "The young girl is the same one that picked up the message in the market square yesterday."

"How do you want to handle it from here?" I inquired.

"What do you think is best?" Sadie replied.

"If it was me, I think the direct approach is the best. I don't like the dancing around that occurs when the ice is not broken."

"I agree. You make the first overture. I will keep watch on the surrounding park. It's obvious, I'm much better at that than you are," Sadie responded.

"Okay, but I think they're expecting to meet with a woman. You might want to reconsider. We don't want to scare them away."

"You're right. I'll do it, but you'd better be alert! Are you fully awake?"

Without waiting for an answer, Sadie got up and walked toward the two approaching the picnic area.

"Please excuse me. Do either of you speak English?" Sadie inquired.

Both indicated they did, "We're here to meet with a man whose initials are BC. I know this man and you are not him, Senor. Do you know of him? Are you his representative?" Sadie was direct.

It caught the man off guard. He became a bit flustered. The young girl was not so easily shaken, "If we do know a man with the initials BC, what would you want with him?" she asked, being just as direct.

"He saved my life approximately a week ago. Because of me, he may be in serious trouble, even danger. I've returned with my boyfriend to help him if I can," Sadie replied in a voice portraying urgency.

"That's all fine and commendable, but how do we know you are who you say you are? We know nothing about your boyfriend. Why should BC, whoever that may be, trust you if he's in trouble or danger?"

"Mostly because he told me how to get a message to him. The reason you're here now is because of a message we left.   Your organization - maybe even you - picked it up," Sadie said "The inside contains only the letter S. That's me. My name is Sadie. My boyfriend's name is Eric. Ben doesn't know Eric but he knows of him. You'll just have to take my word that he's okay. Now if you do know Ben -- BC, and wish to help us get in touch with him, now is the time to say so. If not, let's not waste each other's time." Sadie stopped talking. Her eyes were flashing and her entire demeanor was one of authority and control. The man and the young girl were silent. Finally, the man spoke. "If you're going to help Ben resolve this trouble he's in, how would you do it?"

"I'm prepared to offer him a way to the United States. We will arrange for him to be granted asylum. He will be able to finish his education," Sadie replied, relaxing her body language.

"What if this Ben does not want to leave Colombia? What will you do then?" the young lady asked. It was becoming more and more evident the girl wasn't as young as she appeared.

"That's a decision I'll be able to accept, but I'll have to hear it from Ben and not from two *apparent* representatives. Eric and I have come a long way, disrupted our lifestyles, spent a lot of money, and placed our own careers in jeopardy to say nothing of the danger we face by returning to Colombia. The very least you should do is arrange for us to speak with Ben personally."

"Let's sit down at one of these tables and discuss how you can achieve your objective," the man said. "My name is Tony and this is my wife Loretta. We play a minor role in the same organization in which Ben is involved. The purpose of the organization is to rid Colombia of the drug traffic, the drug lords, and return the countryside to the families that farmed it originally. We grow the best coffee in the world, yet we export more of the product of the coca bean. The children of the world are dying of the disease the coca bean produces. The good people of Colombia bear some responsibility for the lives and deaths of those children, if we do not oppose the cartels and their drug lords. This is our passion, Ben's passion. He will not want to leave."

"We understand Tony and applaud all your efforts, but as Sadie indicated, while we can accept that position, we must hear it from Ben," I said, wanting to become a part of the conversation, so they could get to know me, and hopefully trust me, as they were Sadie. "While we aren't at liberty to tell you what our jobs and careers entail, I will tell you the objectives of your group are also dear to the hearts of both Sadie and myself. When can we meet with Ben?"

"Ben entrusted Loretta and I to make that decision. Ben is very valuable to the resistance organization and his talents were recently needed on the coast. He has asked, in the event you convinced us of your sincerity, that we arrange to guide you to a place near the coast. He will be using it as a base camp. The trip will take about eight hours. You can be back in two days. We leave tomorrow night under the cover of darkness. Hopefully, these arrangements are acceptable, because they are the only arrangements available to you."

"If that's the only option, then it will have to do, won't it?" I replied. "When do we meet you next, and what should we be prepared for?"

Loretta looked at Tony, and thought for a minute, "The two of you should arrange to purchase clothing acceptable for jungle travel. My suggestion is fatigues, a hat, and lots of underclothing. Don't forget a good supply of insect repellant. Tony indicated two days. I'd plan for four. Check your luggage into a storage unit in your hotel. The government doesn't monitor hotel storage. Tell the desk that you are going on a hunting and fishing trip. That will allow you to dress appropriately without raising suspicions. Purchase backpack frames and bags to store your extra clothing. One for each of you, in the event you get separated. Sadie, if you have a weapon, bring it with you. Otherwise, we will supply one to you. Eric, you have a weapon just under your coat. Bring it. Pack no less than one hundred rounds in your personal pack. In the market where you left the message, is a merchant displaying the type of clothing I have described. He's the only one there with that type of display. He'll have all of the clothes and ammunition you need. He'll be discreet. Your guides will meet you in this park at sundown tomorrow. There will be two of them. Their names are Kenneth and Gale. They are loyal to the core. Neither of them will hesitate to shoot one or both of you if they feel you are not what you represent."

Loretta hesitated, looking at Tony, "Have I forgotten anything?"

"No I think you've covered it all. We have to go," Tony said. Loretta nodded, and they left as quickly as they came, leaving us sitting at the table looking at each other.

"She isn't quite the young sweet thing she portrays, is she?" I said for lack of anything else coming to mind.

"No, she's not, and she's not sixteen or seventeen either. Did you see the winkles and crow's feet on her face? I'm probably younger than she is," Sadie responded. Something told me I was glad the guides were not going to be Loretta and Tony.

"Let's get back to the hotel, I, for one, am looking forward to a gourmet meal tonight. It may be the last good meal for several days," I suggested and Sadie agreed.

The trip back to the hotel was uneventful. We parked the car in the area where we always did and entered the hotel through the side entrance. Sadie and I had decided we would leave the Duster in the hotel lot, following tomorrows shopping, and notify the owners we weren't going to need it further. Another two hundred dollars American dollars should cover all the additional use, change the oil, and fill the tank with gas. I needed to remember to find the maintenance lady before we left and ask her to tell her sister and brother-in-law the car was to be available for pick up.

The evening was relaxing. Sadie and I each knew the next few days would be tiring, stressful, and anything but relaxing. Certainly stressful if there was a need to use any part of the ammunition we were instructed to bring with us. Dinner was good. We had a bottle of wine and dessert to put a cap on a meal of local beef marinated in wine, spices, and served in thin slices, much as we would serve brisket in the States. After dinner we strolled through the main lobby in an effort to find an English newspaper to catch up on the world news. We found a Houston, Texas paper three days old. It was good just to read about ordinary American things. We sat in brocaded love seats in the lobby sharing the paper, the stories, and the editorials with each other for the better part of an hour. As we folded the paper, intending to leave it in the lobby for some other traveler, I could tell Sadie was back in the present with all the problems and uncertainty it presented.

"I think we should check in with Howard before we leave. We did tell him we'd keep him up to speed on our progress," Sadie suggested.

"I think you're right. I was thinking the same thing. I've been plugging the cell phone in every night. It has a full charge." I looked at my watch, "It's only nine o'clock. I think we're in the same time zone. Let's go call him right away. Maybe he won't be so cranky."

We went straight to the room. I retrieved the cell phone from the luggage where I had it hidden. Sadie was making herself comfortable. "Don't get too comfortable. I want you available if Howard wants to talk to you," I said.

"And why wouldn't I be available, just because I've gotten comfortable?" she quipped.

"I've tried to get your attention when you're soaking in the bath before. It's like talking to a zombie or a drunk," I joked with her. "In any event, please stay available."

I dialed the appropriate numbers and eventually was put through to Howard's phone. It was ringing. Then a woman answered.

"Hello. Is this Mildred? I was expecting to get Howard. This is Eric. Sadie is here with me. Hopefully, Howard is not ill." I said, not knowing what else to say. "Is Howard available to speak with us?"

"Certainly Eric. He's always available for you. Let me call him. I think he was just getting ready to turn in." Mildred replied. The phone went dead for several seconds. There was the sound of voices in the background. They were unintelligible.

"Is this you Eric?" The voice was Howard's.

"You bet it's me. Since when have you had a secretary?" I responded.

"I tell her she is not to touch anything in this room especially the phone, but she doesn't listen to me. You know that. She never has. Now, that the pleasantries are over, what can I do for the two of you at this ungodly hour of the night? I assume Sadie is there with you." Howard was complaining as always.

"It's slightly after nine o-clock, for Christ's sake. What do you do, sleep your life away? We thought it would be appreciated if we were to check in and let you know we're still alive and kicking, but if you're tired, we'll try to call sometime in the middle of the day, unless of course that's nap time."

"Do you have any idea all the explaining I've had to do over the last three days because of the two of you -the efforts I've made to save your careers, not counting your asses? It's been above and beyond the call of any duty I signed up for. Where are you and when will you be back?"

"We're still in Bogotá, but we're heading for the Caribbean coast tomorrow. We may be down here for an additional three or four days. Are the arrangements in place for Sadie's friend to be admitted to the U.S.?" I asked.

"Yes, the arrangements are in place, but only because I convinced the company he may be useful to us. I don't think he will be able to stay here indefinitely, at least not on the admission status I was able to get for him. If he's truly an asset, I'm sure other arrangements can be made."

"We've received some indications Ben may not want to come back with us, but if he does, how do we get him in."

"The custom and immigration agents at every port-of-entry have received bulletin number 129 which will admit him to your custody. Why the hell doesn't he want to come back? Isn't he a fugitive in Colombia?" There was obvious irritation in Howard's voice.

"I didn't say he didn't want to come back. I said he might not want to come to the States at this time. As strange as it may seem to you, Howard, there are people who find their native country is where they want to live. They find it's worthwhile fighting for that right. In any event we'll be in touch with you soon and hope to be back in your capable grasp within the next week."

"I'm looking forward to your return. It's always a challenge to try to save an agents ass, when they've given the Company every reason to fry them. I may lose this one. Talk to you soon." Howard ended the conversation. The phone went dead.

We went to bed early, almost as soon as I got off the phone with Howard. The conversation continued in bed, however. Sadie was concerned that Howard had not asked to speak to her. I had also noted a change in Howard's general attitude. In the past he'd always wanted to say Hi to her or asked if I was treating her all right. He hadn't even spoken to her through me. I could tell Howard was mad at us, but he had been mad at us before and not acted as he did in this conversation. Sadie was about to get out of bed and call him back. I talked her out of that idea by suggesting it might be better if we just left him alone for now, while we were in Colombia, especially that late at night.

"Howard may feel that we have crossed the line on this one, and maybe we have, from his view point anyway," I said.

"Well, I'd do it again and I hope you would to. It really pisses me off that Howard and the Company can sit there and say we've crossed the line when all we're trying to do is retrieve a man who saved my life. Navy Seals have a principle that when they're on a mission they never leave a man behind.

For them that's brave, gallant, even in the best traditions of the armed services." Sadie was really on a roll. "But for us it's somehow different and we've crossed the line. I don't think so!"

"Firstly, let me say I agree with you, but are you trying to equate Ben with a member of a Seal team? Are you saying the camaraderie is the same? I also believe we owe it to Ben to extract him, if he wants to be extracted, but I doubt you or I will be able to sell the Seal analogy to the Company." I was hoping Sadie would become more reasonable.

"You weren't there when I saw Ben's cab crest the small hill and I realized it was him, and I was going to be able to get to the airport without raising a turmoil by driving in with a police cruiser," Sadie retorted almost crying. "It was like seeing family with water when you were dying of thirst in the heat of some God forsaken desert. Tell me how that's different than the Seals?"

"It may not be in your eyes -- probably not in my eyes, but remember we're dealing with the Company. It has no collective conscience. Both of us have known that reality for years, in fact, we were told that in training. We have accepted it in the past, and we're going to have to accept it now and at least for now move ahead. Now it's time to go to sleep. Now come over here and '*nugger*'," I said. *Nugger* was a word Sadie used all the time to indicate snuggling. Sadie did as I suggested and before long we had both drifted off.

CHAPTER TWENTY-FOUR

The travel alarm, I always carried so I could be independent of hotel switchboards, had gone off at the usual 6 AM I reached over and hit the infamous snooze button, which gave us an additional twelve minutes. I must have repeated the snooze button process at least four times, because it was after 7 AM when I finally gained enough clarity to realize we had to get up and get going. Sadie was awake and was more alert than I was.

"I thought you were never going to quit hitting that damn button," she said

"Why did you let me continue to sleep?" I asked. "You know we have a huge day."

"I know but since when am I your keeper? If I can't be a Seal, I certainly can't be your keeper," she said in a tone reeking of left over irritations from last night's discussion.

"Okay. Let's pretend you're a Seal, if that makes you happy, but if you're a Seal, then I'm a Great White Shark. Now if you don't get out of the sack, I'm going to take a big bite out of your ass. Now, how do you like being a Seal?" I said knowing my taunting would get her out of an irritated state of mind.

"I just love it when you talk tough to me. It turns me on, but I'm always disappointed when the tough talker becomes nothing more than a moaner." She threw a pillow and ran for the bathroom. The mood had been broken, and I knew from experience, Sadie was now ready to tackle the next problem.

I dressed in normal clothes, shaved, and went to the lobby to locate the maintenance woman. As luck would have it, she was in the foyer polishing more brass. I approached her and motioned I needed to talk to her. She moved to the area where I was and where we could talk without everybody hearing our conversation.

"We no longer need your sister's automobile," I said. The woman nodded indicating she had heard and understood. "I have an additional two hundred dollars for them. Your sister indicated we could leave it with you." I slipped the money into her hand so no one saw the transfer. Again she nodded,

126

looked around and whispered, "I got in some difficulty for talking with you before and don't want to get caught again."

"Where can we meet?" I whispered. "I want to tell you where and when your sister can pick up the Duster."

"I have a half hour break in fifteen minutes. I'll meet you at your room." I nodded agreement and went to the desk to make arrangements to check out; the process took about ten minutes. I left immediately for the room, wanting to get there before the maintenance lady. We didn't need the complication of explaining why Sadie answered the door with her thirty-eight in hand.

I reached the room and unlocked the door. As the door swung open, I lost what contents were left in my stomach from last evening. I also lost one hundred percent of my composure. There, in the armchair next to the bed, was Sadie's bullet riddled body. She had six or eight obvious entry wounds beginning in the neck and ending in the upper thigh of her left leg. The room hadn't been disturbed otherwise. I found myself sobbing on the floor of the entryway. For some reason, there was a fantasy- like quality about what I was seeing. I had the feeling this was just a bad dream. I was going to wake up at any time. Sadie and I were going to get dressed and head for the market.

I kept looking at Sadie's body, but it didn't change. The bloodied dressing gown was still draped around her body. It was obvious the intruders had taken her by surprise. Her weapon wasn't anywhere in sight, and her oversized purse was across the room on a dresser with some of her other things. Her eyes had the same stare I had tried to avoid on so many other occasions with so many other bodies. Somehow now, when they belonged to the one person in this whole world I loved I couldn't stop staring at the deadness they portrayed. I don't have a clue how long I was on the entryway floor. At some point, I heard a gasp and short scream. At first it seemed to be miles away and unconnected to anything happening to me. Eventually, however, I became aware that the maintenance lady was standing above and behind me in the doorway and was gasping for air as if someone had punched her in the stomach. I attempted to bring myself to my knees and found that I was unable to do so. All I could do was roll over. I asked the lady to call the authorities. She nodded and started for the phone in the room. The professionalism I had lived with for years was still operating, at least on the surface, because I stopped her and told her to use a different phone in an attempt to preserve whatever evidence may yet be available. As she left the room to locate the nearest house phone, I was able to get up and regain my feet.

I realized I should make every effort not to disturb any potential evidence. There were spent shell casings on the floor of the entryway. Having regained my feet, I picked up one of the cartridges. It appeared to be a forty-five caliber. It had some odd markings. Without thinking, I slipped the spent shell into my pocket. The maintenance lady had just returned, still sobbing. Her speech was virtually unintelligible, but the gist was that the authorities were notified as well as hotel security. Both would be here shortly. As she was speaking I heard the elevator doors open and the sound of several people rapidly approaching the room. The first through the door was the hotel security officer. He paid very little attention to Sadie's body. Much more attention was spent on the room and whether it had been damaged. Before anything could be said he was walking around the room, moving furniture and generally disrupting the crime scene. I finally got enough wits about me to ask him to stop what he was doing until the police arrived. He looked at me like I was an intruder. He said something in Spanish to the maintenance lady and she responded. She told me he did not speak English, but she was sure he was doing things that would help the local police when they arrived. She informed me she was going to have to go back to work.. She would be in touch with me later. She dried her eyes and left the room.

As she was leaving the room, additional hotel management arrived on the floor. They spoke briefly to the security man and then approached me. The manager of the hotel spoke impeccable English. He expressed his personal and the hotel's regrets for my loss, and asked if I had any idea who had murdered Sadie. I indicated that I had none, which was a true statement. I explained I had gone to the lobby of the hotel earlier, and when I came back, Sadie was dead. There was no one around.

"When will the police get here?" I asked. "I'm sure they have been called."

"They will be here soon. The morning is the busy time for them, and they are understaffed to start with," he answered.

My grief was rushing to anger like I have never felt before in my life. Less than an hour ago Sadie was alive. She was a healthy, vibrant, beautiful woman with an entire lifetime ahead of her. Now she was dead. She had been shot gangland-style in a foreign country. The only organization that seemed to give a shit was the hotel, and the hotel seemed to be more concerned with the damage to the hotel room than the death of a human being.

"Get out of this room -- all of you. There isn't one of you who has a vague idea of what in the hell you're doing. Now get out before I throw you out, and if any one doubts my ability to do just that please, please come forward! We're ending this circus now! I will protect the crime scene until someone who knows what the hell they're doing shows up!" There was a flurry of Spanish spoken, none of which I understood, and then they left.

"I'll make another call to the authorities and see if I can speed this process up for you. We can lock the door to the room pending the arrival of the police, and you can wait in an adjoining room if you wish," the manager said, attempting to appear helpful.

"No, thank you. I think I'd like to be here with Sadie until she's moved," I replied and shut the door behind them. As I turned around, I realized the room was closing in on me. It felt like I was being entombed in a closet. I had to leave the door open and hope I would not be bothered until the police arrived. Before I opened the door, there was something that had to be done. I wasn't sure I could do it. I had to close the lids on Sadie's eyes. As I approached her body, the searing pain of grief enveloped me. I knew I shouldn't touch her, but I had to. She looked so uncomfortable. I couldn't leave my Sadie in that position. She was dead and I knew it, but I needed for her to look comfortable. It seemed like the least I could do for not being there to protect her earlier. With that thought, I broke down and sobbed. It was not all out of a sense of grief for losing Sadie. A part of it was sheer anger at what had happened, and I had not been there. With everything she had recently been through, how could I have left her, ever, even for a minute? I felt alone like I had never felt before.

I reached Sadie's body and gently closed her eyes. I lifted her shoulders, setting her body straight in the chair. Her left leg was not straight so I fixed it and, in so doing so, realized the bullet that entered her left leg had broken the thighbone. I put her hands in her lap. She looked as peaceful as she could with six or eight bullet wounds. By this time my mind had reduced the room to the size of a small shower. The door was about five or six steps from the bed. I made the trip in three. With the door open I had the feeling there was breathable air in the room. The walls seemed to move back out to where they had been previously.

My training told me there were things that must be done, but my mind wouldn't focus on the needs. The grief was coming and going in waves, and the waves were paralyzing. I knew I had to get a hold of Howard. Sadly enough, he'd been down this road before and would be able to guide me while I was dysfunctional. The cell phone was still plugged in. It was on the dresser where I had my effects. I crossed the room, got the phone, and dialed the number.

Howard answered on the second ring, "Hello."

"Howard, this is Eric. Please get ready because I need your help. Sadie has been murdered."

"What do you mean Sadie has been murdered? Eric, if this is a joke it isn't funny," Howard responded

"It's no joke; I'd give anything if it was. She was killed this morning. Someone shot her six or eight times while I was down in the hotel lobby, arranging to return a car and checking out.

"Do we know who did it?" Howard asked. "Was it the cartel? Who else would do that to Sadie?"

"I don't think it was the cartel. They have no reason to want either of us dead. I don't know who it was. All I know is they were efficient. The local police have been called and hotel security has been on the scene. The hotel seems more worried about their room than Sadie. I threw them out and am waiting for the local police to show up. They were called at least ninety minutes ago. They don't seem to be interested. I don't know what to do. I need your help."

"Firstly, Eric, do you think they were after you, also, or maybe just after you and Sadie got in the way?"

"I don't know, Howard. How the hell am I supposed to know who they were after? If I were to guess, I think I would guess they were after Sadie. Sadie was the only one who had a history of any significance in Colombia. They hit the room when I was gone, and they haven't been back for me, and they've had the opportunity. Those facts lead me to believe, whoever they are, they were interested only in Sadie."

"Let's hope for now, that's the way it is. Here's what I want you to do. Listen closely. I take it you are still in the room. Is that true?"

"Yes, but I don't know how long I can stay here. What arrangements should I make for Sadie's body? I won't leave it here for the flies."

At this point I broke down again. It was several minutes before I regained my composure and could continue the conversation. Howard was patient. "Sorry, Howard. Where were we?" I said, trying to get control of my emotions.

"You don't have to apologize for what you're feeling." What you have to do is get your weapon and Sadie's weapon. Put them in your luggage where they're not obvious. You know how to do that. Make sure the ammunition is also secreted. Pack your luggage so you can leave on short notice. I know the next task is going to be painful, but pack all Sadie's things in her luggage so they can be shipped back to the States. I want to end this conversation at this time, so you can accomplish what I've told you to do. Call me when you have completed the packing. In the meantime I'll get the attention of the local police. Regardless of what happens, Eric, I will arrange for the return of Sadie's remains. Now disconnect this call and start packing."

I did as I was instructed. It was all I could do. I was thankful Howard was there to issue the orders. I found Sadie's gun in her oversized purse and with it was the only extra cylinder she had. I took both to my luggage and put them in the lining I had created earlier to hide my weapon. My own weapon was around my shoulder in its holster. I was about to pack it also when something told me to wait. I could always throw it in at the last minute.

Sadie had gotten most of her things packed before she was murdered. There were a few items in the bathroom needing to be packed. The native clothes she was going to wear to the market were on a chair near the dresser. I decided the native outfit did not need to be returned to the U.S. I left it where it was. I located Sadie's money belt and the monies she had in her luggage and put them in mine. I was going to need the money more than she was. Next, I packed all my things. The whole operation had taken no more than thirty or forty minutes.

I called Howard. He answered the phone after the normal amount of rings.

"Is this you, Eric?"

"Yes, it's me. I've done everything you told me to do. What's next?" I asked .

"I've made arrangements for Sadie's body to be returned to the U.S. later today. She will be picked up by a Marine detachment assigned to the American Embassy in Bogotá and flown to Langley. I'll notify the family when the body is in the States. Eric, there's something wrong. I approached the local police from the highest diplomatic levels and am not getting any satisfaction. I suggest you trust me to take care of Sadie. You get the Hell out of there as soon as you can. I don't like the feel of it."

"I'm ready to go now but, I don't want to leave Sadie. I'm not even sure I can."

My head was spinning. On one hand, I had learned to trust Howard's judgment and intuition. On the other hand, I didn't want to leave Sadie until I was sure her remains would be respected. I felt I owed her at least that much. Howard interrupted my thoughts,

"Eric, Sadie would not want you to risk your life protecting a body she has already left. You know that better than anyone. Now listen to me! Get your bags and leave the hotel by any way other than the main lobby. If you still have the car, use it. I will assure you the company will make it right with the owner. Work your way, by back roads if possible, to the nearest border and cross it. Contact the American Embassy in that country and we will bring you home." Howard hesitated, waiting for a response.

I knew Howard was right. I knew I should get out of the country. All of the logic and reason in my body told me to listen -- to follow instructions. However, a big part of me was not going to listen to logic and reason so easily. The anger I felt earlier hadn't dissipated and was welling up inside me. I knew I was destined to complete the task Sadie and I had come to Colombia to accomplish. From there, I wasn't really sure what would happen, I wasn't even sure I cared.

"I trust you, Howard, and I'll trust you with Sadie, because I know you are right about the feeling you have. I have the same feeling. I'm not coming home, however. Sadie and I came here to do something. I'm going to finish it." Before I could complete my thought, Howard broke in. He was angry.

"You don't have a stake in saving this man -- this Ben. He evidentially saved Sadie, or so she thought, and as a result, she felt some allegiance to him. You can't have that same allegiance. He didn't save you. Why in God's name would you want to jeopardize your safety, not to mention your career? Howard was almost screaming. I could hear his wife in the background. I assumed she was admonishing him for his loudness.

"I don't give a damn about my career so don't continue to throw it in my face. If the truth were known, Sadie and I would have left the service after this assignment. What you fail to understand, Howard, is that Ben was successful in saving Sadie's life! I was not! I'm not sure why, but I feel I owe it to him to complete the task she felt so strongly about. Without him I wouldn't have had the last two weeks with Sadie. I will call you when I have contacted him and determined what his wishes are relative to returning to the States."

Again Howard interrupted, "That option may not be open to him at that time," he said with a certain restraint in his voice.

"You know, Howard, what you just said really doesn't surprise me. If anything it reinforces a feeling I've had for some time. There's really no difference between the two sides, other than what they sell. Their tactics are the same. The end always justifies the means, doesn't it, Howard? I've lived for many years with the same philosophy, so I probably can't change at this time in my life. What I can do, however, is recognize that neither side is completely right nor completely wrong in the tactics they utilize. I can recognize I was naïve, as was Sadie, to believe we were the champions of good - that justice was on our side We are soldiers just like they are soldiers. We just answer to a different boss.

"Don't *go south* on me, Eric!" Howard said. His voice was as cold and hard as a steel bar.

"I'll call you in a few days," I replied. "We both have a lot to think about." I hit the stop button on the cell phone, breaking the connection.

Howard had given me the ultimate warning, *"Don't go south on me Eric!"* All agents knew the term "going south" meant the agent wasn't to be trusted by anyone. In most instances the agent was relieved of his or her duty and then prosecuted for alleged transgressions against the government of the United States. In a few instances the agent was hunted and eliminated. In either event, the agent was never allowed to publish his grievances. There's an old English saying, which I'm sure was true in old England, and which is definitely true inside the CIA, "You don't slander the King." It was a good possibility I had just slandered the King.

I took one last look at Sadie as I was making sure all my bags were packed and ready. She appeared more comfortable now than she had before my conversation with Howard. I somehow knew she approved of my decisions. I gathered up the luggage and left, shutting the door and a good part of my life behind me.

I went directly to the Duster. There was no one in the lot. I unlocked the car and started the engine. It was close to noon and I had to buy some clothes. I reached the market without any problems and parked the Duster where Sadie and I had always parked. I was dressed in the slacks and sport shirt I had worn to the lobby earlier. I failed to see any reason for wearing the sweaty, smelly clothes I had worn the past few days. We had purchased those clothes so we wouldn't stand out. They evidently didn't work. At least, something didn't work. The market was beginning to get crowded. It was easy to become part of the crowd, even dressed as I was. The shop I was looking for was at the far end of the square. I'd seen it on other occasions. It stood out in my mind because the type of wares it displayed was so different from the common housewares and clothing displayed by the other shops located in the area.

As I was working my way toward the shop, I spotted the two police officers Sadie and I had encountered a day ago. They were walking toward me and were discussing something. As usual, whatever it was they were discussing was taking all of their attention. I was able to avoid them by going to my right with a crowd moving in that direction. The shop was only one hundred meters down the walkway. I could almost see the front of the display area. I was concerned about the police officers. I was sure they hadn't noticed me, but felt I had to be careful. Rather than go directly to the shop, I went around the side of the nearest tent and watched the crowd from there. The individuals in the crowd seemed to be concentrating on whatever it was that had brought them to the market. None seemed to have any interest in me. The police officers would be busy at the other end of the square for a while. That gave me fifteen or twenty minutes to make my purchase and get out of the square.

I proceeded around the end of the tent and walked directly to the shop. The display area was exactly as I remembered. Camouflage clothing was spread out on the tables in front of the tent for all to see. The proprietor was sitting on a small stool watching the crowd for the slightest glimmer of interest. He was ready to jump on any prospect in an effort to make a sale. When I approached directly, it must have taken him by surprise, or more probably, he wasn't expecting someone like me. Rather than jump up to entice a sale, he sat for some time and watched me go through the pants and shirts, seeking an appropriate size and style. Eventually he came to where I was.

"Is there anything specific I can find for you sir?" He said in very good English.

"I'm looking for some fatigues and a shirt that'll fit me. I'm going on a hunting trip later today, and I didn't bring the appropriate clothing with me. I'll also need about one hundred rounds of nine mm ammunition and about fifty rounds of thirty-eight special. Can you help me with these needs?" I said, being as direct as I could.

"Your needs are a bit unusual, but I think I can accommodate you. Why don't we step in the tent and get out of the sun?" I nodded and followed him into the shade of the interior. "I was expecting you. I assume you're Eric," he said as soon as we were out of the mainstream of shoppers.

"Yes, I'm Eric. I was told you could supply me with my needs."

"And that I can do, but I was expecting a young lady to be with you. Have the plans changed? I believe her name was Sadie."

"Sadie is dead. She was murdered this morning. I'll be making the trip alone." I replied, barely able to maintain my composure. I'm sure he sensed the strain in my voice.

"I'm very sorry for your loss," he replied with sincerity in his voice. "It is so sad, and unfair, that we lose so many good human beings. It seems that regardless of how one looks at the cartels and the resistance, it all equates to war. One of the most defining facts is loss of life. It seems the war we have here in Colombia is much like the war your country fought in Viet Nam. The soldiers can't tell who the enemy is until it's too late. I will attempt to let your guides know they will be meeting a party of one rather than the two they are expecting."

"Thank you for your concern and your cooperation. I wasn't sure whether the guides would approach me alone. I was told to get some camouflage fatigues, a pack board or frame with sack, a hat, and extra underwear, as well as the ammunition I mentioned earlier. I assume it's better to have the clothing looser than normal, in which case a forty-inch waist would be good and an extra-large shirt will work. My contacts didn't mention it, but I should also have some comfortable boots, generally size ten and a half. Can you supply the entire order?

"All but the boots. There's a vendor not far from here I know. I'll get word to him and have the boots brought up. In the meantime, let's try on some pants until you find a pair that fits and is comfortable. The sizes in Colombia are not the same as they are in the United States. We'll have to go by feel." He handed me a pair that I could tell by looking was too big.

"Let's try a slightly smaller pair," I suggested, and he handed me another pair that appeared better. I tried it on. It fit loosely but not baggy. We found a shirt that matched the pattern of the pants and a hat of the same basic material. In the corner of the tent was a stack of pack frames, appearing to

134

be of military origin. I chose one having all the necessary straps and buckles. He rummaged through a pile of what appeared to be canvas bags of various sizes and emerged with a packsack that appeared to be almost new. It fit the frame perfectly. There was a supply of khaki colored socks and shorts on a table in the front. We grabbed a generous supply of each and put them in the bag.

"Why don't you sit and relax while I get the ammunition and the boots. It will take about fifteen minutes." He turned and walked to the outside of the tent, to the area where his wares were displayed.

I was not adverse to a short rest so I took his advice. I could hear him giving instructions to a smallish native looking man whom I could see from where I was sitting. The man nodded and went off. A customer came up and he sold him a small camouflage T-shirt. He was rearranging the clothing on the display table when the small native man reappeared. He had a pair of hiking boots in one hand and a heavy looking canvas bag supported by a strap, which went over his shoulder, in the other. They had some conversation in Spanish, following which he took the boots and the bag and came back in the tent.

"Try these boots on. There's nothing worse than having boots that don't fit on a long walk in the jungle," he said, and I agreed with him. The boots were of relatively soft leather, which meant I would not have to break them in if they fit. I took a pair of the military socks from the pack, put them on, and slid the boots on my feet. I could tell, even before I laced them up that they were fitting just fine. The canvas sack was loaded with ammunition. The calibers of the two types of cartridges were correct. The other clothing had already been put in the sack. I put the ammunition in the pack and tied the boots to the outside. After taking a mental inventory of what I had purchased, I was confident I had what I had been told to get. "How much do I owe you for this?" I asked. The shopkeeper looked a little embarrassed.

"If I could, I would like to give it to you. I'm sure that you will be of more value to our cause than the meager amount of merchandise you require. The sad part is, I can't afford even the small cost this entails. Would fifty dollars American be too much?"

I was amazed. The ammunition alone would have cost twice that amount in the United States. "I will not accept fifty dollars American as a fair price. For the goods I have gotten and the service I have received, I insist you accept two hundred American, nothing less." I gave him ten twenty-dollar bills. I'll never forget the look on his face as I counted the money into his hand. It was as though he'd never seen that much money at one time. He was ecstatic. Even I felt a little better. I shouldered the pack and left the shop.

I decided to go to the perimeter of the square and circle around to the Duster. At least then, if I had to move quickly, crowds would not inhibit me. The trip to the Duster was uneventful, although I did see the two police officers patrolling just inside the edge of the Market Square where the sidewalk came close to the adjacent street. Upon reaching the Duster, I left the area. It was almost two o'clock in the afternoon. I had at least four hours to kill before I could expect to meet the so-called guides. It was time for a drink or two, but first I must find a place to store my luggage, preferably close to some small, local bar. I determined the smarter move was to change into my traveling clothes just before I met guides rather than risk being conspicuous in some bar while I got half swacked. It didn't really matter if the authorities found the luggage. There wasn't anything in it I couldn't replace. I decided to rent the first small locker I saw, take what I needed from the luggage, and hope I could remember the location if I came back this way.

I passed a small local bus station. On the hope the station would have a few lockers large enough to handle my luggage, I went around the block and parked in a small parking lot behind the station. The location allowed me enough privacy to transfer what I needed from the luggage to my packsack. I really only wanted Sadie's gun, the extra cylinder, and the money. I first attempted to get the items out of the luggage and into the packsack while inside the Duster. The Dodge interior was too small to accomplish the transfer quickly and smoothly. After struggling for a short time, I ultimately decided to make the transfers in the open. The hood of the car seemed as good a place as any. No one was around and the transfers went smoothly. The thirty-eight fit nicely in one of the pockets of the sack. I had one of those soft velour shoe bags with my extra shoes in the luggage. The shoe bag was perfect for the money. I gathered the extra money we had secreted in the suitcase and, together with the contents of Sadie's money belt, put it all in the bag. The bag went to the bottom of the packsack, covered by the extra clothing I had just purchased.

I locked the packsack in the trunk and took the luggage into the station. Inside was a ticket agent and what appeared to be a station manager. The agent was helping an elderly couple. They were having some difficulty in arranging an itinerary they wanted. The manager was getting irritated with the elderly woman and the inability of the agent OR and his inability to handle the problem. No one was paying attention to me. I had some Colombian money appearing to be in the correct denominations. The locker was large enough for my bag. I put the luggage in the locker, the money in the vending machine, closed the door, turned the key, and extracted it. I must have used the right amount of money because it all worked. I turned and left the station. As I approached the Duster, I noted there weren't people in the area, and it didn't look as if there had been any in my short absence. I realized I was getting careless, as I hadn't set a trap on the Duster that would have allowed me to be sure no one had tampered with the doors.

Somehow I didn't care. The only thing that mattered was finding a small bar with a dark corner. I wanted to pass the next two and one-half hours having several drinks in an attempt to dull the pain in my gut. A bar near the park where I was meeting my "guides" would do just fine. I drove in that direction. As I approached the park, I was beginning to wonder if the Colombian people drank. I hadn't passed one watering hole. All of a sudden, and within two blocks of the Golden Arches was the familiar Coors sign one expects to see regardless where in the world one travels. The building was a small one-story dump. Inside was a bar and approximately twelve or fourteen stools all screwed to the floor. There were eight or ten tables, one of which was at the end of the bar in the back. The table had my name written all over it. I approached the bar.

The bartender came over. He spoke almost no English, however, I was able to communicate enough with him to get a bottle of bourbon It was surprisingly good bourbon, and I managed to get down two quick shots while standing at the bar. I motioned to the bartender, indicating I was going to sit at the table at the end of the bar. He nodded approval. For the next hour and a half I sat there drinking most of the bottle of bourbon.

For the first time in my life, I was unable to get drunk. I couldn't feel any effects from the alcohol. The pain in my gut was just as intense after five or six drinks as it was when I got off the telephone with Howard earlier. I felt a tremendous sense of loss and loneliness, and yet there was very little sorrow associated with Sadie's death. As I drank more, and the time for me to leave for the park drew nearer, I came to realize I was feeling something new to me. I was experiencing pure hate.

A part of me enjoyed the newly found freedom hate had made possible. Howard, the project to bring down an important part of the drug cartel, my career with the Central Intelligence Agency, my friends in and out of the agency, my goals and aspirations for a traditional life, and eventual retirement - all seemed to be unimportant now, in fact, insignificant. I wasn't sure what was important to me, although I somehow knew money was a part of it. I also knew I had to avenge Sadie's death. I wasn't sure how I was going to accomplish that feat. I would probably never know who killed Sadie. I suddenly realized it didn't matter who did it. Both sides were to blame. I wasn't sure what that revelation would mean later in my life. What I did know was I was no longer anyone's soldier. I was operating on my own from now on. Without realizing it, I had just *"gone south."* There was no turning back.

The time was approaching to meet my guides. I left the bar and pulled the Duster around on a secluded side street behind the bar building. I changed clothes in the Duster. I threw the old clothes into a large trash barrel in front of a small bungalow nearby. Discarded with the clothes, was the key to the locker where my luggage was stored. The fact I was not going to return for my luggage seemed very clear to me. I proceeded to the park to meet my "guides".

CHAPTER TWENTY-FIVE

I glanced at my watch as I pulled the Duster into the parking area on the perimeter of the park. I had a good twenty minutes to kill before the sun would set. I sat in the Duster-not really thinking about anything. It was as though my mind had shut down momentarily. I felt like I was alert, yet, there was tranquility, a restfulness I had not felt in days, not since those wonderful days Sadie and I had spent in Las Vegas. I must have been in that state for ten or fifteen minutes. As I became more aware of the immediate surroundings, I realized the sun had just about disappeared over the horizon or at least the part of the horizon which can be seen from the center of a somewhat modern city. I gathered my pack from the trunk and locked the Duster. I kept the keys just in case I might need the car later.

The park benches were only about one hundred meters from the Duster. I covered the distance in less than a minute. I put the pack under the table where it would be less noticeable and settled down to wait for my guides, Kenneth and Gale. There wasn't another soul in the park. I felt I was extremely conspicuous, especially dressed the way I was. The park was completely still. I had been there about five minutes. I was beginning to become skeptical about the chances of them showing, when I heard someone approaching from the side of the park opposite where the cars parked. As I turned, I could see two people approaching. Each appeared to have a gun in their hand. It was too late for me to reach for my weapon, so I just sat and waited for them to arrive. The woman spoke first.

"Dressed as you are and with the pack under the table, we assume you're Eric. We were expecting to meet with two people. Where's the girl? Please don't reach for your weapon. It would be a big mistake."

"Evidently the shopkeeper from the market didn't get in touch with you. The woman, as you refer to her is dead. By the way her name was Sadie. She was shot earlier today. I'm your only passenger. I don't mean to sound ungrateful, but I've had a huge loss today, and I'm not in the mood for any further delay and certainly no bullshit. Either shoot me, let me go my way, or let's begin the trip to the coast. The choice is yours," I said, meaning every word.

"Please, Mr. Eric, it is not our intent to make your loss any more painful than it already is. We must be careful in these matters. Our group suspected the circumstances of your loss earlier today. You may, or may not, be aware that we monitor the police bands. In any event, the reports of an American woman being murdered was a major topic. We heard reports of her traveling companion, an American male, disappearing from the scene before the authorities arrived. At this time, Mr. Eric, the authorities are blaming you for the death of your companion," the man said.

"I apologize if I seemed ungrateful. Was there any other information your group was able to learn from the radio transmissions?" I asked

"No, nothing other than it seems strange the attempts to apprehend you are not what they normally would be in cases of this nature. We believe their only efforts have been limited to watching the airports, thinking sooner or later you will show up in an attempt to escape the country. Normally, in cases such as this there would be a dragnet placed over the city and roads leaving the city, at least for a day or two. None of that has happened," the man replied.

"Don't forget to tell him about the involvement of the American Embassy," the woman said, addressing her companion.

"Oh yes, I almost forgot. The strangest thing happened. It was the subject of many conversations over the radio after the initial reports started coming in. It seems before the local authorities could complete their investigation of the scene a detachment of armed United States Marines from the American Embassy appeared at the hotel and claimed the remains of your companion. The understanding we got from the radio was the authorities, on site when this occurred, objected to the removal, but the marines requested they stand aside as the body was removed. The locals reported they were sure the authorities would have been shot it they had resisted further," he said. He hesitated, looking to me to answer the questions arising as a result of the actions of the Marines.

The last thing I wanted to do at this point was reveal any more information of my involvement with the United States government, and especially the CIA, than was absolutely necessary. I decided to play dumb, at least for now,.

"That is strange. Maybe Sadie's parents were more influential than I was aware. I'm glad her remains were claimed by the United States though. I assume they will be shipped to her relatives." I was truly relieved Howard had kept his word with regard to Sadie. "Shouldn't we be going somewhere? Don't we need to get started?"

"Yes, we should. At least we should get out of this park. We note you have driven the Duster. Do you intend to leave it here?" the woman asked.

"That's my intent. Is there a problem?" I responded.

"No, there's no problem. We will have the resistance pick it up. We can always use additional transportation."

"I would rather the vehicle be left where it is and not picked up. We rented the car from a couple who were good enough to trust us with what I'm sure was their major family asset. Could we get word to a maintenance lady at the hotel of its location so they can reclaim it? It has a shifting problem anyway, and I doubt just anyone could successfully move it."

"We will abide by your wishes. Do you know the maintenance lady's name?" she asked.

"No, I don't remember it, if I ever knew it, but she should show up on a police report. She was the first one on the scene other than myself. The automobile is her sister and brother-in-law's."

"We will do our best. Now let's get out of here." I grabbed my pack and followed my guides toward their car, which was in a parking space at the opposite end of the park.

The woman turned to me as we were walking and said, "By the way my name is Gale and this is my husband, Kenneth."

I nodded and continued to follow them. The vehicle they had was an old, old International Scout. I noted the tires appeared to be new and there was a well-maintained winch on the front with what appeared to be three-eighths cable. The cable appeared to be new also. Kenneth must have noticed I was looking at the vehicle.

"We've found we're better off with a mechanically well maintained vehicle that is not as new and shiny as you Americans are accustomed to. It is not as visible to the authorities. Don't you worry, the Scout will get us anywhere we want to go."

We loaded my packsack in the rear compartment and I got in the back seat. Kenneth and Gale got in the front. We began the trip to the coast. Kenneth headed out of the city, driving north. As we approached the edge of the city, the character of the land was changing from semitropical to what appeared to be absolute jungle or rainforest. The road Kenneth was using was somewhat improved but had not been surfaced with asphalt or concrete so the ride was rough. I was sitting such that it was easy for me to see the road behind the Scout. The dust was so thick that visibility was only a matter of a few feet beyond the back bumper. I noticed the rear compartment, where I had placed my gear, was stocked with enough food to last the three of us at least a week. There were also several ammunition boxes. My previous training was kicking in. I was unconsciously learning as much detail as I could about the vehicle and my companions. From my vantage-point in the rear seat, I could see Kenneth was giving extreme attention to the road ahead. More attention than one would expect and certainly more than necessary to drive the vehicle. Gale also seemed fixated, concentrating on what was ahead. There was no conversation between them, and neither one of them was paying any attention to me.

I was the first to break the silence, "The two of you seem apprehensive about what's ahead. Are we expecting any trouble?"

"Not really expecting trouble. The State Police sometimes set roadblocks on these back roads in an attempt to curb the transportation of illegal consumer goods and firearms into the country. It's best we don't get involved with them if we can help it. We are also transporting some ammunition and other supplies to the coast. The supplies are fine, but we might have a hard time explaining the ammunition. With you along, it's even more important to avoid answering a lot of questions."

"I understand. How long will it take to make the trip, assuming we don't have trouble of course?" I asked. "By the way where are we going?"

"There's a little town on the Caribbean Sea named Cartagena. Ben and a group of our loyal young men are on a small ranch just west of the town waiting for us to arrive. If we are lucky we should arrive in Cartagena mid-morning tomorrow. It will take us about another hour on really bad roads to reach the ranch. There are faster ways but these back roads are the safest."

"Do we have enough gasoline to get us there? It sounds like a long trip."

"This old buggy has been modified and carries slightly more than fifty of your American gallons. Enough to get us to Cartagena. We'll refuel there. The ranch also has a supply, but we like to keep it for the inevitable emergency."

"It sounds as though you've figured it all out. It's obvious you've taken this route before under similar circumstances," I said, more as a question than a statement. I waited for their reply. None was forthcoming. After an awkward moment of silence, I broke the ice again.

"If you need to be spelled at the wheel, you'd find I am an excellent driver. I actually have experience in vehicles such as this one. I was raised with an old Jeep. I took it everywhere in the mountains of Colorado."

"Thank you for offering and we'll keep it in mind. It is a long trip," Gale replied. "You might just sit back and get some rest. We'll let you know if we need relief."

Gale was looking back at me and smiling. I knew what she had just said was a polite way of telling me to relax, get some sleep, and mostly shut my mouth and leave them alone. My background, my training, and my very nature all screamed to be in control. This was one time I was just going to have to relax and let someone else take care of me. I really didn't want to relax for another reason. With the exception of the few minutes I was alone with Sadie's body and the time in the Duster, I had been busy or drinking. I now had to face, to come to grips with, what happened earlier today. I felt alone while I was in the little bar drinking whiskey, but without realizing the alcohol had numbed my senses just enough to make it bearable. I'd thought the alcohol hadn't affected me, but it had and I was learning that now.

I knew I wasn't going to break down in tears. It probably would have been better if I had. I don't think Kenneth and Gale would have thought any less of me if I had shed some tears. They may have even thought it strange. I didn't. In any event, I couldn't, but that didn't affect the feeling of loss, which was almost unbearable. My mind kept playing games with me. I found myself pretending Sadie was still alive and waiting for me in Cartagena. Then I would awake from the daydream. The pain would start all over again.

Sometime during the early evening hours I fell asleep. I must have needed the rest, because the next thing I knew the sun was rising. I know because it woke me. Gale was doing the driving. We were on a road that had been used more and was a bit smoother than the one we were using when I dozed off. Kenneth was sleeping with his head draped over the seat, more on the driver's side than the passenger's. I decided to keep quiet for a while to see what developed. Kenneth was snoring so loudly it would have been hard to carry on a conversation with Gale in any event. I adjusted my body so I could see part of what was ahead from the side window. As I moved, I realized I had slept with my left arm and leg in an awkward position. The resulting stiffness was causing shooting pains to radiate into my shoulder and left hip. In making the move I must have made some sound, because Gale turned around to see if I was waking up.

"It's about time you came around. You've been asleep for the last seven or eight hours."

"I must have needed the rest," I replied. "I don't remember going to sleep. I sure am stiff. I must've slept in an awkward position -- Where are we anyway?"

"We're not more than thirty kilometers outside Cartagena," she answered "I was just about to wake Kenneth. He's been this route before. Like you, this is my first trip. I've been to the city many times, but not since we joined the resistance."

The conversation must have awakened Kenneth. His head jerked up and he mumbled something to Gale. I didn't get in full what was being said but it was something about whether she was having any trouble.

"The last four hours have been fine. Other than the sighting of the troop truck earlier, there's been no traffic on the road. The moon remained high so I didn't have to use the headlights. I think you should take over now as were about thirty kilometers from the city."

"Okay. Let's find a good spot and pull over," Kenneth said. "We all need to stretch our legs. We also could use some food." Kenneth looked around at me and smiled. It was the kind of smile that reeks of superiority and indicates he thinks he is in total command of the situation.

"How long have you been awake?" he said looking directly at me.

"Only a few minutes," I said. "I wasn't much help last night. I evidently needed the rest."

"I'm surprised you got any rest. You seemed to sleep in fits and starts with a lot of thrashing around and mumbling."

"What did I say?" I asked, somewhat concerned, but more to foster the conversation.

"Nothing we could understand, so rest easy. You didn't give away any state secrets. You did mention the name Howard several times, however. You seemed angry when his name came up. Who the hell is Howard, if you don't mind me asking?"

"He's my contact in the states. I can't imagine why I would be angry," I responded, hiding the real truth.

We were passing a few houses, huts would be a better description. The road was becoming progressively better. Gale found a wide spot in the road and pulled in. As soon as the Scout was stopped, we all jumped out. I soon realized that not only was I stiff from the ride and the awkward sleep, but I needed to relieve myself badly. Everyone must have had the same thing on their mind, as Gale excused herself and headed toward the trees. Kenneth headed toward a different stand of trees. I followed him.

As we emerged from the tree line, Kenneth stopped short. I almost ran him down from the rear. I looked over his shoulder and there in the clearing, parked beside our Scout, was another vehicle.

"You stay here until I find out who they are. Let's hope they're tourists looking for directions or potential thieves. We can handle both of those. Are you armed?"

I felt my shoulder holster. It was complete with my weapon. "Yes," I responded.

"Don't get trigger happy but be ready and follow my lead," he said as he walked toward the Scout."

I remained hidden in the trees and bushes. There appeared to be three men in the other vehicle. They all waived at Kenneth and he said something to them in Spanish. He must have been about five meters from them when the taller of them withdrew his hand from his pocket brandishing a weapon. Kenneth stopped, but had no opportunity to draw his gun. He put his hands in the air as much to show me he was in trouble as to indicate submission to the three men. Several minutes passed and there was much conversation in Spanish, passing between Kenneth and the three men. Gale had not shown up. I was sure that she was in hiding -- waiting for the same opportunity I was.

The three men were positioned around Kenneth such that he was surrounded. I didn't have a shot that wouldn't endanger Kenneth or leave one of the men untouched and able to retaliate. From my vantage point it appeared that if Gale had positioned herself somewhere consistent to where she disappeared into the trees, she might be in a better position to shoot, if it became necessary. I didn't know if she was armed, however. She might be ostensibly helpless. The distance from the trees, where I was located to the area where Kenneth was being interrogated was only about twenty meters. Too far to simply surprise them by running out, weapon in hand, and reach them before they had an opportunity to react. I needed a distraction allowing me time to make two or three steps toward the men before my presence was known. I could throw a rock into the bushes near where Gale went in and charge while they were confused as to the source of the noise. It was a risky move but seemed the only viable plan.

I searched the ground around me for a rock big enough to make a distracting noise yet small enough to insure I could throw it far enough. I found a rock slightly smaller than a regulation softball. It seemed made for the task. I picked it up and edged my way to the outer limits of the tree line, choosing a target about thirty meters away. I was about to launch the missile when Gale stepped from the trees acting as though she had not a care in the world. The man with the gun stepped forward, separating himself from the rest by several meters. I dropped the rock and freed my nine mm of its holster. It was now or never. He appeared to be the only one that had a weapon. If I took him out Kenneth could handle the other two.

I aimed at the shoulder of his gun hand. His arm was extended as he walked toward Gale. I wanted to wing him, but I also didn't want to miss. My finger tightened on the trigger, and instantly the area was inundated by the sound of the discharge. The gunman screamed and whirled around in pain. His friends were dumbfounded by the sound and were easily taken by Kenneth.

Gale had also immediately reacted to the shot by charging the gunman. She had him on the ground and he was screaming something in Spanish. She slapped his face with the barrel of the pistol she'd confiscated from him, as she tackled him and screamed something back in Spanish. The gunman was whimpering something that sounded like pleading. Gale hit him again with the gun and got off him, leaving a whimpering pile of foul smelling flesh on the ground. The two men Kenneth had neutralized were pleading in Spanish. Kenneth said something to them and they reacted_immediately, moving to the area where their downed friend was lying on the ground moaning. Gale was already getting the Scout ready to leave.

Kenneth looked at me with a slight smile I took to be gratitude and said, "So much for a nice quiet picnic lunch. We'd better get down the road before someone gets nosey.

We both started toward the Scout at the same time. I got in the rear seat and shut the door just as the Scout lurched forward and regained the pavement, such as it was.

"What the hell was that all about?" I asked.

"They were common variety road agents. They saw the Scout and how it was loaded. Thought it would be an easy mark, They're not as dangerous as they appear. The pistol they had might not have even fired. It appeared older than any one of us. I'm frankly amazed we haven't run into more of them," Kenneth said. "By the way, that was a good shot!_You've evidently used that weapon before."

"I have, but it's always a rush of sorts, and I didn't want to miss. I had to wait until you and Gale were clear," I explained. "Where do we go from here?"

"We'll have to get some gas before we go much further, The station we use in this area is up the road about fifteen or twenty kilometers. From there it's a more primitive road to the ranch."

The next fifteen kilometers were uneventful. It was obvious the city of Cartagena was becoming closer. The countryside was changing from the virtual rain forest, of last evening, to cleared farmland interspersed with dense forest and then to suburban hovels, separated by small stands of trees. Kenneth switched places with Gale without stopping the vehicle and was again driving. The two of them dropped back into the uncommunicative, but totally alert state I had experienced since leaving Bogotá.

Gale suddenly leaned toward Kenneth and said something. I couldn't hear what was said, but Kenneth nodded and slowed the Scout. I looked to the front and saw the road appeared to fork about five hundred meters ahead. It appeared the fork to the right continued to a small hovel type abode, while the fork to the left was more commercialized. There were billboard- type advertising signs, and judging from the large metal cylinder, what appeared to be a small petroleum bulk plant. As we approached Kenneth slowed the car, and I could tell we were going to pull in. I decided this must be where my guides were intending to refuel. There was only one pump, and it looked like ones I had seen in Norman Rockwell drawings, depicting the early fifties or late forties.

Kenneth stopped the Scout but did not pull to the pump. A man came out and they conversed in Spanish for a short time, then turned and walked away. Kenneth followed to the back of an old dilapidated shack, evidently serving as the station office. Gale turned in the seat as Kenneth disappeared.

"There's no trouble if that's what you're wondering. Kenneth is arranging for the petrol. We may be taking on more provisions here also."

"That's a relief," I responded. "Where are we going to put more provisions? The back is packed now."

"There still a little room in the back," she replied. "We don't know how much they've been able to secure, but if necessary, the seat you're sitting in will fold down, and we can load that area. The three of us may have to ride in the front."

"That will be cozy," I said. "I thought the road got primitive from here in."

"It does, as I understand. I've not been to the ranch either, so it will be a new experience for us both," Gale said just as Kenneth reappeared from behind the shack.

He waived for the Scout to follow him and he again disappeared. Gail was already sliding behind the wheel and starting the engine. The area where she drove the vehicle was hardly a road. You'd have to stretch your imagination even to call it a path. As she came around the shack, I could see the petrol tank was about twenty meters away. Kenneth and the man were standing by the tank and motioning us to approach. I noticed a perfectly good road on the other side of the tank. It was obvious the tank was designed for withdrawals to be made from a well-used turnout on that road. Gale maneuvered the Scout around a pile of old car parts and empty drums parking next to the tank.

The man Kenneth had conversed with was removing a small panel from the tank. The panel itself was rusted and discolored. From my vantage point I could see the screws were new and made to look old. The panel fell away. I couldn't see what was behind the panel, as the man was now in my direct line of sight. Kenneth retrieved a hose from somewhere. It was about eight or ten centimeters in thickness. He handed it to the, for lack of a better title, station attendant and he attached it to the tank. Kenneth had placed the end in the fuel spout of the Scout, nodding to the attendant who opened a valve near the end going in the tank. I could hear gasoline gushing into the Scout. With the size of the hose and what appeared to be a straight gravity feed, it took no time at all to fill the tank. Kenneth shut the valve just as the fuel topped the tank and started to spill over.

Gale leaned out the driver's window, got Kenneth's attention, and asked if there were to be more provisions. Kenneth walked to the Scout.

"They've been able to accumulate a few provisions but no ammunition. They have a hindquarter of an old heifer that was hit on the road a day ago. It's all they could salvage. The rest of the meat was too bloodshot to be usable."

"How are we going to carry the meat without it spoiling?" Gale asked.

"We'll just have to put the middle seat down and carry it there. We should be able to get some brown paper from the merchants around here to lay it on. We should be at the ranch by noon, maybe before. They have some refrigeration. It won't be enough, so we'll be eating very well for the next few days."

Kenneth looked at me, and I could tell he was thinking and probably wishing I wasn't along.

"Eric, why don't you and Gale get your seat folded down, and I'll arrange for the paper." Gale was getting out of the Scout, even before he'd finished the sentence, so I immediately opened my door and got out.

The seat was attached to the vehicle by a series of three latches. When the latches were released the entire seat came out, leaving a space that could have accommodated two beef quarters. As we were completing the removal of the seat, Kenneth reappeared with a roll of brown butchers' paper. Between the three of us, we were able to line the compartment left by the removed seat and get enough paper covering the rest of the load to protect it from whatever drainage occurred when the meat was placed in the Scout. We had completed the preparation for the load when the Station attendant came back. He said something to Kenneth in Spanish to which Kenneth agreed, and he immediately left. Kenneth turned to Gale and said, "The meat will be here in about thirty minutes. Why don't we finish what we started before we got interrupted and get something to eat?"

"This is not the ideal picnic area but it will do. I packed the food for the trip near the back of the load. We can get to it from the tail gate," she responded.

Kenneth was already opening the rear of the Scout and had located the sack of provisions. We all were hungrier than we thought, because there was very little conversation as we downed the lunchmeat, cheese and bread the sack produced. We were about half finished, when Gale rummaged in the back and found a second sack, containing eight or ten bottles of warm Colombian beer. I was never a fan of warm beer, but it not only provided the liquid to make the dry bread digestible, it actually tasted good.

We had finished the lunch and were beginning to clean up the empties, when two hefty Spanish looking men together with the station man came around the corner of the station, carrying a full hind quarter of beef. It was wrapped in a cloth, resembling muslin, and was well-stained with blood. It was obvious that the beef had recently been butchered. Kenneth motioned the men to put the meat in the area of the Scout we had just prepared. It took the best efforts of all of the men to get the beef into the Scout, on the paper that had been placed there for that purpose, and situated in a way that it did not leak on the rest of the load. When they were finished, and Kenneth was satisfied with the result, he handed the two helpers several bills. Their eyes lighted up, and they left in a flourish of Spanish clearly meant to express their appreciation for the money.

The station attendant shook Kenneth's hand, said something in Spanish, and walked back to the front of the station shack.

"We should get out of here before we attract more attention." Gale said

"Yes, we should," Kenneth responded, "especially, if we're to get to the ranch before noon."

I took that as my queue to get in the vehicle for the balance of the trip. Gail slid into the Scout and to the middle spot. The Scout front seat was bench style so it accommodated the three of us with reasonable comfort. Kenneth started the Scout and pulled it forward to a spot just past the petrol tank where there was more room and turned it around. As we drove forward and around the shack, the station manager was talking to a well-dressed Spanish looking gentleman. He specifically avoided looking in our direction, and in fact, was drawing the man's attention to something on the petrol tank. It was obvious Kenneth was attempting to get the Scout on the road with as little commotion as he could. Gale was intent on watching the well-dressed man. The Scout reached the roadway, and we proceeded to the north.

"What was that all about?" I asked.

"I wish I knew," Kenneth answered. "I've never seen the man before, but from the cut of his clothes, he's not an ordinary farmer. My contact at the bulk station was clearly trying to draw his attention away from us. I hope we haven't compromised his cover."

"Was the man a government man or a member of the drug cartel?" Gale asked.

"My guess is he's both. The timeliness of his visit doesn't leave much to the imagination." Kenneth responded.

I could tell Kenneth was mentally struggling with something, and I thought I knew what it was. "If the man was one of yours, and you're confident the suit was not there for coffee, why don't we help?" I asked. "We could turn around and come in from the road on the other side of the tank, leave the Scout fifty meters down the road, and gain surveillance of the front of the station without being seen. If he's in trouble, we can help, and if not, we can go back to the Scout. No one will be the wiser. Either way it shouldn't cost us more than twenty or thirty minutes at most."

"Do you know what you're talking about when you say we could help? If our contact is in trouble, we'll have no choice but to extract him from the area and leave no witnesses. Are you ready to become a fugitive in a foreign country?" Kenneth asked me.

"If you'll remember, I'm already a fugitive. You can add to that whatever charges would be levied because I shot and wounded the man you referred to as a road agent. I don't think I have a lot to lose. You know I can handle a gun and every second you continue north we're losing time, and maybe your contact. What're you going to do?"

Kenneth was slowing the Scout, even as I was speaking. He turned it around, stopping the car on the shoulder of the road facing south.

"Eric, you'd better reload your weapon, and, Gale, get yours from the back. Take an extra clip just in case. The suit, as you call him, may have gotten help by now. Again, follow my lead. After that you're on your own. We'll meet back at the Scout. The keys will be in the ash tray, in the event I don't get back." Gale was getting back in the Scout, as Kenneth was finishing. She had a weapon that was the match to mine, plus the extra clip.

"May I congratulate you in your choice of firearms?" I said, attempting to loosen the atmosphere.

"You may," Gail said smiling. "It was the only woman's weapon I could locate at the time." There was a smirk on her face making me realize I had just been had. I felt a smile creeping across my face. It felt weird. I hadn't felt like smiling since Sadie's death.

Kenneth had the Scout moving. He chose a small dirt road going slightly easterly. "This should intersect with the main road to the bulk plant," he said. Within three hundred meters a well-used road appeared that seemed to lead south. Kenneth turned right and stepped on the gas. In less than a minute the cylindrical bulk tank appeared.

The road widened as we neared the tank. Kenneth turned the Scout around and parked it heading north. He put the keys in the front ashtray, looked at Gale, and then at me. "How do you say in your country – "Let's rock and roll'?"

I checked to make sure my gun was secure and the extra magazine was in my left front pocket. I exited the Scout, attempting to shut the door with as little noise as possible. Gale had her weapon and was coming around the end to the vehicle. Kenneth motioned us to come in close. "Eric, you and I will retrace the route we used when we left, until we can get enough of a view of the front to see what's happening. Gale, you hang back but keep us in sight, and I'll signal you where to go. Stay as close to the Scout as you can. If we have to make a quick exit, you get to the vehicle as fast as you can, and get the motor started. Are we ready?" Both Gale and I nodded.

As Kenneth and I made our way around the bulk tank, I could feel the adrenaline rushing to my head and muscles. I was beginning to realize, I had the same feeling every time I had been in situations where I was going to, or at least might be, involved in life and death activities. I remembered Sadie telling me about the rush she had when she shot the cop in Bogotá. She said she thought she liked it. I found myself feeling the same way. It began earlier today with the skirmish on the highway on the way in. What I was feeling now was just an extension of what had begun earlier. Little did I know, this feeling was to become a lifestyle, my lifestyle.

Kenneth and I were almost to a point where we could get a peek of the front of the station. Kenneth reached back and got his weapon. I followed his lead. There were several old oil barrels stacked against the side of the station. A few of them had fallen or been thrown down from the otherwise orderly stacks. They provided us sufficient cover to get a short distance from the side of the building. It was a much better vantage point. Kenneth was ahead of me and slightly to my right. He had the best view of the front of the station. I couldn't quite see the area where we had last seen the station manager and the man in the suit, but I could see there were two late model Fords parked in the area where we had previously driven.

Kenneth looked around and held up four fingers. I could tell from the strain in his face, there was trouble for his friend. Kenneth moved forward to an area where two barrels were standing in close proximity to each other. After he reached the barrels, I moved to the position he had just vacated, and then joined him at the more forward position. As I cautiously peered around the edge of the barrel and gained a view of the front of the station, I saw the manager and four other men. It appeared one of them was engaged, or more accurately had been engaged, in beating Kenneth's friend. They were attempting to get him to his feet. The man we had seen earlier motioned for one of the other men to bring the vehicle closer.

I was thinking that for a short period we would have some separation between the four men. It seemed to me it was time to move.

Kenneth must have been thinking the same thing. "Put your weapon in your front pocket. Let's just walk in," he ordered.

"I never thought you'd ask," I replied. I glanced back to locate Gale and saw her at the rear corner of the building. I held up four fingers. She nodded and disappeared.

Kenneth was already standing and was about to walk forward. I joined him. I kept my hand in my pocket with the nine-millimeter. I noted Kenneth's hand was also in his pocket. None of the men including the manager had seen us as we started forward. Within five or six steps, however, the one getting a vehicle spotted us and yelled something in Spanish. Kenneth waived him off without missing a step.

"You watch him. I'll watch the other three. If he shows a weapon shoot him. We can't leave any witnesses that could describe us or follow us to the ranch," Kenneth said in a low voice.

I grunted my agreement and separated myself from Kenneth, as I walked more toward the lone man who had spotted us. The apparent leader yelled something to Kenneth. By the tone and the gestures I assumed we were being told to leave the area. Kenneth answered and pointed to the station manager. The tone of voices became louder. It was obvious the men were getting angry. Ken didn't slow his pace. Two of the men stepped forward and were in the process of drawing weapons located in shoulder holsters. Kenneth removed his hand from his pocket and shot twice. Both of the men stopped in their tracks. There was a surprised, almost startled, expression on their faces. They both fell to the ground. There was no question. They were dead.

With all the action taking place, I hadn't kept my eye on the third man who was getting the vehicle. As I turned he had his gun drawn and was taking aim at Kenneth. I withdrew my hand quickly and shot. It was a lucky shot as I hit him in the neck. He dropped, never knowing what hit him, or from where. I watched to make sure he was not moving and turned toward Kenneth. He had reached the apparent leader and was in the process of disarming him. The man was struggling. I heard a muffled shot and the man fell to the ground. Kenneth had shot him at point blank range. The man's body and clothing had muffled the shot.

Gale appeared suddenly from the side of the station. She had her weapon out and was obviously ready to use if necessary. I reached the man I had shot and moved him with my toe. He was dead. As I turned around Kenneth was checking to make sure the other three were not going to be able to tell any stories. Gale already had the station manager in tow and was heading around the station toward the Scout. I was caught up in the excitement of the moment, really the ecstasy of the victory, but realized I must get to the Scout. Kenneth was already turning the corner running toward the back of the station and our escape. Just as I turned and started to follow, I noticed an old pickup truck slowly driving by the front of the station on the road we had first used to get to the bulk tanks. The occupants of the vehicle were viewing the scene with obvious astonishment. I didn't take time to do a head count, but my impressions were the pickup had a family of two in the cab and two or three children in the bed of the truck.

I reached the Scout just a few seconds behind Kenneth. Gale was already behind the wheel and the motor had been started. Kenneth pushed the station manager in the back of the vehicle with the meat as I was getting in the front seat and sliding over next to Gale. The Scout was in gear and moving almost before Kenneth was aboard. The door didn't get closed until after the vehicle had left the parking area and gained the primary roadway. I glanced around at the manager. He was lying across the meat, the color in his face completely gone. The contrast between the reddish pink of the recently butchered meat and his colorless face was astonishing. The absolute fear, terror he was showing, was something I didn't understand.

Kenneth was giving directions to Gale as I turned around. She was heading northwest toward what I supposed, was the route to the ranch. "A family drove by the station just as we were leaving. I'm not sure what they were able to see, but they saw the bodies for sure. They also got a good look at me," I said directing the statement at both Kenneth and Gale. Kenneth hesitated for a moment.

"Gale, turn the Scout around. Let's make sure they can't follow us. We'll go east, further into the city, and cut back after we're sure we're not being followed. Do you think they were able to see the Scout?" he said, directing the question at me.

"I don't see how they could but I can't be sure," I responded.

"Better safe than sorry," he said as Gale turned the Scout around. She pulled over and opened the driver's side door.

"I think you'd better drive," she said to Kenneth. "I haven't been here in a while, and if we do have trouble, you're better able to lose them."

Kenneth was already sliding over. Gale had run around the vehicle and was sliding in the passenger side door. "The two of you keep a sharp eye on our tail and let me know if anything looks suspicious" Kenneth instructed us.

I was way ahead of him as I had turned to the rear and adjusted myself to be able to see beyond our new passenger and the meat. Nothing had shown up to that point, in fact, there was no traffic on the road at all. Kenneth took the first intersection to the left that appeared to be anything larger than a private wagon road to one or more hovels. He continued to drive in a more or less northerly direction toward the city. The houses were becoming more prevalent and appeared to be occupied by a slightly more prosperous population. There were several automobiles that came in behind us but each one seemed to veer off on a different road or private entrance. Kenneth had driven about six or seven kilometers without any interference or any suspicious cars appearing.

"Isn't it time we headed for the ranch?" Gale inquired.

"Yes, it's probably as safe now as it'll get," Ken replied. There's a road a short distance from here. We can take it to get back to where we need to be. It intersects with the road to the ranch about ten kilometers west of the bulk station. Kenneth turned in the seat and looked at our new passenger. "Is the road still there and will it be safe?" he inquired of the man. The man nodded, indicating a yes to both of the questions. "By the way, Eric, this is Herman Garcia and, Herman, this is Eric."

I nodded and Herman acknowledged me in a like manor.

"A few minutes ago Herman was a sympathizer with our cause. Now he's a full-fledged member. How do you feel about that Herman?" Kenneth asked.

I could see Kenneth looking in the rear view mirror, evidently to see the expression on Herman's face. Herman was pale as a sheet but that wasn't any different than he'd been since we rescued him from the suits. He was fumbling for words. It was obvious he either didn't want to answer the question or was not proficient in English. By the time he spoke, it was obvious he wanted us to believe it was the latter. "No comprendo, Senior Kenneth," Kenneth spoke to him in Spanish, and he became very excited and animated, at least as animated as one can get while lying on a partially butchered beef.

"He's afraid the authorities will hurt his family and his girl- friend. He wants us to let him out, and he will take his chances in Cartagena," Kenneth said, relaying to us the substance of the conversation he just had with Herman.

Something was wrong, very wrong. While I was watching the rear for suspicious vehicles, I noticed that under the ragged shirt, Herman was wearing a gold necklace that would have done justice to a Vegas high roller. Herman understood Kenneth's question about the route and its safety, as well as the introduction to me. Why couldn't he understand the last question? There could be only one reason. He was not as sympathetic to the anti-drug movement as he wanted us to believe, and in fact, was most probably an informant to either the authorities or the cartels, or both. He wanted out of the Scout, that was for sure. In the meantime he wanted us to speak freely, believing he did not understand what was being said.

"I think the man is old enough to know what he wants to do." I responded to Kenneth. Gale agreed

"Where do you want us to let you off?" Kenneth asked Herman in English. Herman pointed to the side of the road. Kenneth pulled over and Gale and I got out of the Scout. Before leaving the Scout, I released my weapon from its restraints.

As Herman got out of the vehicle, I pulled my nine-mm and shot him in the chest at very close range. His eyes went cloudy almost immediately. He slumped over falling toward me. I stepped aside as he fell to the ground. As he hit the ground, I realized Kenneth's gun was also drawn. He was smiling. "I never thought you'd do it," he said. "Get back in the Scout, and let's get out of here. By the way, what tipped you off he was not one of us?" he asked, as the Scout was speeding down the road.

The road was getting rougher and rougher. We seemed to be relatively safe, as the area had again become quite rural. "It was two things," I said. "He wore a gold necklace worth more money than he could have earned in five years. He was also very selective in his understanding or lack of understanding of the English language. It seemed to me those two facts led to only one conclusion. He's not one of your people. Under the circumstances, if he's not one of your people, he must be one of them. I didn't want him to describe me to the authorities. I had no option."

"You might not make a bad hand after all. I didn't pick up on the jewelry, but I did notice his selective ability to understand English. The tip-off for me was one of the suits, as you call them, was a little more understanding than they'd have been had he been solidly in our camp. That, together with his unwillingness to join us after we eliminated the local officials, if that's what they were, was enough for me," Kenneth said. His mood and tone of voice changed slightly. "What exactly is your agenda here? We could certainly use a man with your obvious training and ability to act on instinct, but I can't understand your involvement. What's in it for you? This isn't your country, and unless there's something I'm not seeing or don't understand, you don't have a financial stake in Colombia's problems. Just what is it you do want?"

"In the past twenty-four hours, I've lost the only person I ever loved. Her name was Sadie. She was gunned down in our hotel room, while I was away for a few minutes attempting to return a rented car to one of your nationals. I'm not even sure who did it, or for that matter why. Approximately two weeks ago, Sadie had befriended the man you refer to as Ben Chavez. As she was traveling to the airport, to join me, one of your local police officers attempted to kill her. She was left with only one option. She had to protect herself. The officer was killed.

Ben Chavez somehow realized Sadie was in trouble and appeared on the scene shortly after the fracas. It was through his efforts Sadie got out of Colombia. She was adamant that we needed to help Ben get to the United States and away from the problems she felt she'd created for him. He had confided some of his involvement to her. We weren't sure he'd want to leave Colombia, but Sadie felt she had to give him the choice. When Sadie was killed, I decided I must continue her efforts to find Ben and give him the choice Sadie died for." I stopped talking as the tears were welling up inside me. There was silence for some time.

"Sadie must have been quite a woman," Gale said. "I don't think Ben will leave Colombia at this time, but Sadie has paid the ultimate price to have the question posed. The price you have both paid is above and beyond any reason. We, here in Colombia, have found the price of honor can be devastating. It is obvious you have learned the same lesson."

I could tell Kenneth had some questions of his own. He chose not to voice them at the time. The balance of the trip to the ranch was uneventful and silent for the most part. The ranch sat in a small valley. There appeared to be only one road in and one road out. The fortifications were complete. The Scout passed through two separate checkpoints, manned by armed guards. As we drove into the ranch yard, a dark complected man of about twenty-eight came out of the ranch house. He was well built, and, by the reactions of the other men in the yard, well respected.

155

He approached the Scout just as I exited the vehicle. He walked up to me and held out his hand.

"You must be Eric. My name is Ben Chavez."

CHAPTER TWENTY-SIX

Howard Baker was in his study with all its surveillance protection and electronic gear. His wife Mildred was in the adjoining room where she always was, doing those things middle-aged women do. Howard had been on the phone all morning. The majority of the calls were from, or to Scott Steel, the only man he considered his boss, and the only one to whom he ever reported. The phone rang again.

"Howard, I've heard from our people in Colombia. Other than Eric's' being sought for the murder of Sadie Anderson, they've not heard a word. I'd thought, under the circumstances, he would've gone straight to the U.S. Embassy for protection. What the hell is going on? He's your agent! Why hasn't he contacted you? That's standard procedure!" Scott railed

"Yes, that's standard procedure, Scott, but we're not dealing with a standard agent. If Eric had been the standard agent, such as you're accustomed to dealing with, he wouldn't have gotten as far inside the cartels as he has. As I told you earlier, we just have to wait and hope we get contacted. You also must consider the possibility he might be dead," Howard replied.

"I've considered the possibility and to be honest, Howard, that might be best for the agency. After all I've learned, it appears his allegiance may have altered."

"That's bullshit and you know it. Eric may be a bit confused, especially with the loss of Sadie, but I don't think we can consider him a liability, at least not yet."

"Well, you might not be able to, but the director is about to classify him as *gone south* and you know what that means," Scott retorted.

"I wasn't aware the director's office had been kept that well informed. What exactly did you tell them, Scott, and don't feed me a bunch of bullshit regulations? We're talking about one of my agents, and one with an exemplary record. What did you tell them?"

"You must know they were involved in retrieving Sadie's body. Not even you can get the Marines to act that fast. The question arose quite normally as to whether the extraction would also involve Eric. I had to tell them he was out of communication and had been for some time. You know how paranoid the director gets when things go wrong and agents disappear," Scott responded.

"What exactly did the director indicate he was going to do?" Howard pressed.

"Well, he didn't exactly say, but I got the impression that if his location and orientation wasn't determined within the week, I would have the authority to sign an order for neutralization. He didn't come right out and say it, but the implication was unmistakable."

"You can't do that. It would, in all probability, spell Eric's death warrant," Howard replied becoming obviously upset.

"You know that, and I know that, but so does the director. Let's just hope Eric calls in the next two or three days and clears all this up," Scott replied.

"Yeah, let's hope, but I know Eric, and he might not check in for weeks. It's happened before."

"Not in circumstances like this, Howard. His friend, fellow agent, and probably lover has been killed, evidently by the very people with whom he's trying to conduct business. My guess is he's either dead or has snapped. Only time will tell. You'll contact me if he contacts you, won't you Howard!" Scott stated in a tone that was obviously meant as a command rather than a question, "The last thing I want to do is put an agent in your house to assure me I'm getting all available information. Promise me, Howard."

"Yes, I promise. You know me better than that. I would never withhold vital information. I, frankly, resent the insinuation. You'd better let me know anything you hear as well. I think we best end this conversation now before either one of us says something we might regret." Howard hung up the phone.

The injuries that had put Howard in the office rather than the field were beginning to bother him. Several years ago a long blade, wielded by a religious fanatic, had severed the large muscles and many of the nerves of his right thigh. The primitive nature of his surroundings, and the fact that he had previously lost communications with his handler, resulted in not getting the kind of medical treatment needed. The wounds healed badly leaving him severely crippled and often in pain. Normally he would take a smallish brown pill and within a few minutes the discomfort would be gone. On this occasion, however, Howard's thoughts were on the immediate problem, not on his discomfort.

Mildred Baker was sitting on a classical loveseat located in the room adjacent to the office. She had head phones on, evidently because she was listening to music or some audiobook from the city library. As Howard was hanging up, she took the head set off.

"You look as though you've lost your best friend," Mildred said as she rose from the loveseat.

"I may have done just that," Howard replied.

"What's the problem?" Mildred asked as she walked to the doorway of the office.

"It's Eric. No one has been able to locate him, and he hasn't contacted anyone, certainly not me," Howard replied, attempting to get more comfortable in the chair that had been specially made for him - the Company's effort to accommodate the residuals of the old injury.

"Mildred, would you get me two of those brown pills. I think I'm going to need all the help I can get for the next two or three days. By the way, the disappearance of Eric is off the record. He's not even supposed to be down there."

"Well, you know Eric. He never was one to take directions. It's probably that trait that made him excel, and why you picked him for the project. Where did you see the pain pills last?" Mildred replied from the kitchen area, as she was rummaged through some drawers and counters.

"I think in the bathroom off the TV room, at least that's where I last remember them."

"Yes, they're here. Are you sure you want two of them? The doctor suggested you taper off the medications," Mildred said, cautioning him, as she approached the study with a small brown plastic bottle in her hand. "By the way, you know everything you and I talk about is off the record. Honestly, how many years have we been doing this, and I haven't made one slip."

"I know, I know, but you shouldn't be involved in any of my business dealings. It's against regulations. Hell, it's probably a crime," Howard replied.

"Well, if it's a crime then I'm a criminal too, and we'll go to jail together." Mildred hesitated, "Where do you think Eric is, Howard? You know the man better than any other human being. If you can't guess where he might be, then no one can."

"I've racked my brain for the last twenty-four hours and really can't come up with anything solid. Eric is not a man who will need, or want for that matter, a period of mourning. They were on a personal mission to save some Colombian they felt had helped or saved Sadie a short time ago. As I look back on my last conversations with Sadie and later with Eric, it appears they considered it to be a matter of honor or trust. I believe if Eric felt that way, Sadie's death did not alter his fervor. My guess is he's still in Colombia and is still on the same mission." Howard got up, proceeded to the wet bar, got water, and washed down the pills.

"Why haven't you told Scott about your theories?" Mildred inquired.

"How do you know I haven't -- but no, I haven't. Eric is one of the best agents the Company has. The run of the mill agent, such as we currently have in Colombia, isn't going to find Eric if he doesn't want to be found. It would also be unnecessarily dangerous for the agents, possibly even Eric, if an all-out hunt were to be called. Scott believes he's in Colombia also, but has not called the hunt, at least not at this time."

"What do you think will happen?" Mildred asked.

"I don't know. All I know is that Eric has two or three days to contact me. After that the hunt may be on. The safeties will be off the weapons. Scott thinks he's *gone south*."

CHAPTER TWENTY-SEVEN

Y ou will have to excuse me. I must stretch my legs and back and yes, I'm Eric Butler. Your road into this fortress leaves something to be desired. I certainly hope you never have to leave here quickly, or if you do, I'm not along," I responded to the greeting Ben Chavez had offered.

"But Mr. Butler if we ever have to leave fast, it will all be over, of course, I can't think of a better place to make our final stand. We could consider it to be our version of what you Americans refer to as the Alamo. Let's go inside and get acquainted. It can be very muggy and humid here as the coast is less than five kilometers to the northwest.

I nodded my agreement and started to follow Ben toward the ranch house. There were eight or ten men busily unloading the Scout, and I could tell from the excitement the beef hindquarter was an unexpected treat. The ranch house was much larger than it appeared from the front. It was one of those buildings where most of the space was situated in the rear of the structure, including a second floor that was not evident as we drove in.

"I'll show you to your quarters. Ben started toward the rear of the ranch house. It's not much but will be comfortable for now. The men will bring your things, after they've unloaded the meat I saw in the rear."

"No offense, but I would just as soon handle my own gear," I replied.

"No offense taken. I'll wait here and you can collect it now," Ben responded.

I nodded agreement and turned to retrace my steps, when a very large Spanish looking man came through the door with my pack board and sack over his shoulder. He smiled as he handed the gear to me.

"I thought you might be needing this."

"Thank you, I was just on my way to get it," I said as I took the pack board by the straps and swung it over my shoulder. As I turned toward Ben he was saying something in Spanish to the big man. I didn't understand any of it, although it involved Gale and Kenneth, as I heard their names. Ben was off to the back of the house. The room that was to be mine was very small, having only a single bed and a smallish table against the opposite wall.

"The shower and the toilet facilities are just down the hall. I assume you would like to clean up a bit. I know I always do after I've negotiated the trip from Bogotá. The water is not hot although a cool shower is often more refreshing in these latitudes."

"Thank you, I think I'll take you up on the offer," I responded. "I must have a private conversation with you immediately afterward. Will that be possible?"

"I don't see why not. I must meet with Kenneth and Gale now, but I should be free in about half-hour. Why don't you get cleaned up and come to the main area when you're done? We can talk then." He had turned and was heading back to the main area as he spoke.

I took a quick shower, which was needed as much as it was enjoyed. The packsack was on my bed in the room. I checked it to make sure the money I had secreted was there. I was relieved to discover my belongings had not been searched. The shower made me feel like a new man. While dressing, I mentally chastised myself for not purchasing extra pants and shirts when I was in the market place in Bogotá. At least I had a change of underwear and socks. They would have to suffice for now.

I was ready to meet with Ben and offer him a way to America, a way to complete his education. A big part of me didn't want to go. I realized when Ben made his decision, whatever it was, everything Sadie and I had come to Columbia for would be complete. I would no longer have a tangible connection to her. I would only have her memory. I wasn't sure it was going to be enough, but then what options did I have?

As I entered the main area of the ranch house, Ben was entering the front door and with him was Kenneth. They saw me at the same time I saw them. Kenneth motioned me to a table which was complete with locally grown fruit and some type of bread that appeared to be covered with an extremely hard crust and was probably soft and very tasteful inside. Colombian beer was on ice at the end of the table.

"Let's have a bite as we talk," Kenneth said

"That's fine with me, but I told you I wanted a private conversation," I said addressing Ben's presence and attempting to keep the frustration from my voice, but knowing I was not being successful.

"You did. Kenneth and I have no secrets, including the offer you are about to make to me." I realized Kenneth had told Ben the purpose of my visit. I felt like I had been robbed. My anger flashed to the surface. "Well, if that's the case, why don't I just have the afternoon snack with Kenneth. I'm sure he can answer the question as well or better than you could. That will free you to pursue more urgent matters," I fired out.

"I'm sorry we've angered you. I realize you've come a long way to see me, and it was unfair to trivialize your purpose. I am somewhat aware of the circumstances that brought you here. I am very sorry about the death of Sadie. She was a unique woman. In the short time I knew her, I sensed she was different. I know my feelings of loss are not nearly what you must be feeling, but I too have a certain emptiness in learning of her death. Please proceed."

Ben had disarmed my anger, while at the same time putting me at ease to discuss the purpose of my coming to the ranch. I didn't know where to start. The answer to the ultimate question of Ben going back to the states had been answered in the totality of the trip to the ranch, the way the Kenneth and Gale spoke of him, and the respect he so obviously had from the men around the ranch. He was a leader, probably the leader, and would continue to be until he was eliminated or his cause was won.

"Sadie believed you saved her life that afternoon she shot the police officer, and when you helped her to the airport so she could leave Bogotá. It was her fear that the risk you took to help her put you in extreme danger. She felt very strongly that you might need help in the same way she needed help. She was prepared to offer you passage to the United States together with an immigration status allowing you to stay as long as you cared to. She died in an effort to reach you-- to give you that choice. I realize now that what we were prepared to offer you is not something a man, such as yourself, in your position, can or would, even consider. I believe I have completed Sadie's mission, our mission, by simply realizing that fact and in meeting you in the process." As I completed the offer I noticed Ben was looking at me intently. I felt his sincerity, his empathy. Sadie had not been wrong to have placed her trust in this man.

"You're right. I cannot consider the offer. In another time, in another place, I would jump at an opportunity such as you present. I think I may have indicated to Sadie I would welcome that opportunity. If so, it was wishful thinking more than reality. Sadie was a very special woman, and you, sir, are very fortunate you had the time with her you did. I realized she was special the first time I met her. Her intensity and dedication to you, and to whatever assignment or duty you had was evident. As a result of the police incident, I also became aware she had considerable training. I understand you also have certain, shall we say, abilities considerably beyond those enjoyed by normal tourists." As Ben finished, his eyes were still intensely focused on me and on my reactions.

"Feeling fortunate isn't a luxury I have enjoyed, at least not to this point. Sadie's death is much too recent for me to have reconciled losing her with the future. I feel only the pain of her loss, and anger toward the individuals that were involved." I intended to ask Ben questions concerning his knowledge of whom might have been responsible when he interrupted me.

"Mr. Butler, may I call you Eric?'

"Yes, of course," I responded.

"May I inquire as to your background and business in Colombia," he asked.

"You may, but I must ask you the relevance of the question. Why is it important to you that you know my business? You have turned my offer down, understandably, but you still turned me down. By tomorrow, I will be out of your life. What need do you have to know my business?" The table had turned. Now I was intently studying Ben's reactions, as well as any response he might give.

"A fair question, but one, Eric, that must be evident. Firstly, you are street savvy enough to have contacted my associates in Bogotá. You display a proficiency with your weapon, and a mental disposition concerning its use that's rare, even for someone with a cause. Yet you aren't one of us from any standpoint. Secondly, you are the first foreigner, the first person not previously proven to be loyal to our cause, to be allowed to know the exact location of this ranch. Finally, and possibly not so evident, we have some operations upcoming in the near future in which a man with your talents and intuitions would be invaluable to us," Ben responded.

One week ago I would have answered the questions posed by Ben in a much different way. I responded directly, however, without any concern of compromising my assigned duties.

"Sadie and I have been working undercover for an agency of the United States government. One of the agency objectives, and our assigned duty, was to stem the importation of illegal drugs from Colombia into the United States. I was in Colombia approximately three weeks ago in an attempt to arrange a meeting with one of your largest drug cartels. We were attempting to set in motion certain events calculated to lead the cartel into a circumstance where their leaders would either be arrested, so hot internationally that no one will deal with them, or bankrupt."

"Which of our glorious citizens are you targeting," Ben interjected.

"That's not important for now. The point is, I've believed since Sadie first told me about you, that we were both on the same side, pursuing different ends maybe, but on the same basic side."

"Based on what you've said, I have to agree. Where do we go from here," Ben inquired.

"I don't know if we go anywhere. Since Sadie died, the way she died, I have reevaluated my priorities, including the basis on which I'm willing to go forward -- with anybody. I know, at least I think I know, I am not willing to put myself in a position to lose, like Sadie lost, without a substantial amount of consideration. That means money. You want my services, or as you put it 'my talents and intuition', then we can negotiate. The United States government has bought and paid for my services, and although they may be suspicious as to my present orientation, probably expect those services in the future. They too may well become a bidder." I hesitated to get a full reading on Ben's reaction.

His intensity and directness had not changed. I could tell he was beginning to speak. I wanted to finish before he spoke. I continued, "It appears we have a common objective although our rewards are substantially different. Now, you have a clarification of who, and what I am, or have become. Are my services of sufficient value to pay for them at the rate of one hundred thousand dollars a day? If they're not, we have nothing further to discuss, and I have completed my moral duty to Sadie's memory. I would ask only for you to get me to a telephone as quickly as possible. I will return to Cartagena on the next available transportation." There was silence for what seemed an eternity. Ben's eyes never left mine.

"Mr. Butler, I think we'll leave it at Mr. Butler. I generally don't make as big a mistake evaluating people as I have in your case. I suspected you were affiliated with the United States government. I naively hoped the United States would join us in our efforts against a common enemy. I hoped you would be the conduit to help accomplish this partnership. I was obviously mistaken. A mistake I hope I never make again." Ben began to rise from the rustic chair he was sitting in.

"If it's the money, I require, causing you to dismiss my offer, consider this. I know the drug lords keep large amounts of cash, generally in U.S. currency, with their transport of the finished product. I've always assumed it was for bribes of local officials and army officers, but whatever its intended use, it will suffice for my fee. My only requirement is you give me an opportunity to locate and acquire their cash before you destroy the product. We'll call this arrangement a contingent fee. I get all the money, if any, and you get my services at no cost to your organization. Ben, you may not like me, or what I now stand for, but I think you know, I can make a significant contribution in any given operation your organization undertakes. Do you need time to consider, or are the conversations and negotiations over?"

While I waited for a response I realized the words and sentences I had just spoken seemed as if they were coming from a source other than myself, and from a considerable distance away. They were barely audible, vague and foreign sounding. Had they really come from me, or was I hearing someone else that sounded like me? Had I become the person I was hearing? Had I become a mercenary?

CHAPTER TWENTY-EIGHT

T he pain pills were beginning to take effect. Howard Baker had remained in the general vicinity of his very special office to ensure he would hear the phone, if it rang. The house was spacious and had ample room for him to roam around yet be in the vicinity of his world, the world of the Central Intelligence Agency.

Mildred had moved to another part of the house. She was using the general telephone line servicing the residence. At one point, he could hear her arguing with someone about the timeliness of a delivery of some sort. Mildred handled all of the normal household accounts and frequently argued with some creditor or another about some contested bill. Howard wondered what it was she ordered that had not been delivered. It seemed Mildred was always purchasing merchandise, of some type or another from catalogue houses or internet companies. When the merchandise was received, it usually set around the house unused, or at least that's how it seemed. Howard often teased her by announcing he was making every attempt to find another man to take her, but he had not found anyone who could afford her addiction to catalogue and internet purchasing. Mildred's standard response was to ask Howard how many meals he had missed over the years because of her spending habits. Howard had to admit he had always eaten very well, in fact too well, according to his doctor.

It had been only a few hours since he last talked to Scott Steel, but it seemed like days. Howard had always realized the personality of successful field agents created a chemistry, resulting in them being susceptible to considerations of entering the business for themselves. It had happened before but always with other field managers. It had never happened to Howard. The fear most paralyzing to Howard was his knowledge of what the Company did when an agent crossed the line. He became a hunted man. The Company didn't care if the man was returned under his own power, or if he was brought back in a body bag, as long as he was returned. Often it was better for the agent if a body bag was necessary. For those returned alive, the *debriefing* often left the man a shell, virtually unable to function. Scott had already alluded to that operation in their last conversation. He had given Howard two or three days before he would order the hunt, but something in Howard told him the hunt could begin anytime, if it hadn't already.

As Howard paced the area, his mind was racing. One moment he was evaluating the possibilities related to Eric's location and activities. The next moment he was muttering to himself about the ultimate unfairness of life and the cards that had been dealt to him. After all, if it hadn't been for one assignment where he ended up on the receiving end of some lucky, knife-wielding fanatic, he well might be sitting in Scott's position. He should be making the life and death decisions, not Scott. He was senior to Scott by at least ten years. He deserved the rank and the respect that came with the title of Assistant Director.

It wasn't the money that bothered him. The Company had always paid enough to allow him to provide a very comfortable living for the two of them. His government retirement would be adequate when combined with the saving and investments they had been able to amass. What really bothered him was he was not able to make the decisions approving, or disapproving, the programs the next level entailed. Howard realized what he really wanted was power - power he would never have because of that one unfortunate assignment.

Out of his mental confusion, Howard heard the sound of a telephone ringing. At first, he couldn't determine if it was his office or residence phone. As he became more aware and mentally focused, he realized it was the office phone. Suddenly all the thoughts of the past moments were gone, and Howard found himself rushing to the office. There was no need to rush. Anyone who used the office number knew that on occasion it would take Howard a bit longer than most to reach the office and answer the call. Howard was rushing anyway. His mind was clearing of the jumbled and confusing thoughts he'd been having. He was hoping, no praying, the call would be from Eric.

"Hello," he said. "State your business."

"Howard, this is Scott. Have you heard anything from our Mr. Butler?"

"No, but it's only been a few hours since we last talked. I told you I would contact you on any message or information I got. Isn't that enough? If you don't believe me, post another agent here. I could care less."

"Hold on, Howard. I'm not calling to question you. If you remember, I was going to call you if I heard anything from this end," Scott reminded him, his voice becoming somewhat sharp.

"I'm sorry, Scott. I guess I was upset you weren't Eric. What information do you have?"

"It's not much. Maybe you can pick something out of it, we can't. One of our agents in Colombia, with good connections in the local Bogotá police department, has reported a local family reported a 1975 Plymouth Duster stolen. It seems they rented the family car to a man and woman staying at a hotel where the sister of one of the car owners worked. As it turns out, the hotel is the same hotel where the Embassy Marines collected the remains of agent Sadie Anderson. The Duster turned up parked on the edge of a public park some distance from the hotel. What do you think?" Scott inquired. "What do I think? I think the car was rented to Sadie and Eric. Have your agents, even attempted to verify who rented the car from the owners?" Howard said, his voice becoming more intense with every passing second.

"Now settle down, Howard! The agent is trying to locate the owners as we speak. You've got to realize, he is also trying not to blow his cover. We have sixteen months invested in this man. That means we can give him some time to give us our answers."

"You're right. I apologize again."

"Apology accepted again. Without verification from the owners, what makes you so sure the automobile was rented by Sadie and Eric?"

"Because given the circumstances Eric and Sadie had in Colombia, Eric would never rent an automobile from an established agency. To do so would leave a paper trail. My understanding is the locals were already seeking Sadie for the death of a police officer. My guess, although I have no proof, is they got new passports before they went down," Howard answered.

"Why would he abandon the car at a public park? If he's down there and moving around, as he must be, it seems he would need transportation?"

Howard could tell Scott was pumping him for information to use later, possibly during the hunt. He decided Scott had gotten enough, at least for now.

"I don't have a clue why he'd do that. Let me think at bit, and I'll call you back if I come up with any ideas. Is that all the info you have at this point?"

"Yes," Scott responded. "Now you be sure to call. Remember you gave your word." The phone went dead.

Something in Howard told him the preparations for the hunt were beginning. He had been given two days to locate Eric, and all he knew was that Bogotá was the last place where Eric left any tracks.

CHAPTER TWENTY–NINE

B en glared at me for what seemed an eternity. When he did speak, his voice was soft and very controlled. "Do you realize what you are asking? You conclude your proposal by offering the contingent fee. You must realize an organization, such as this one, does not run on the donations of a grateful but impoverished population. The *contingent fee,* you require, is the very money we use to operate. Your assumption that this method will relieve the organizations need to come up with cash for your services is correct, but to use the cartel's funds for your fee means we forgo the cash. The end result is the same."

"The choice is yours," I responded, sensing what I had just heard was not a 'no' to my proposal. "The day is young, so consider the benefits of my services on the operations you're currently planning and let me know later. By the way, do you have a phone I could use to contact my family in the States? They haven't heard from me for quite a period. I should let them know I'm okay? I will place the call in such a manner that you'll not be charged toll fees, and it will not be traced. You have my word on that."

"How do you expect me to take the word of a man who will prostitute himself in an arena where the result of the product being marketed is human suffering?" Ben was about to continue when I stopped him.

"You sanctimonious son of a bitch. Your self-professed abilities to judge people must be deteriorating quite rapidly. You certainly couldn't be more wrong about me. What makes you think I would make my services available to the people who murdered Sadie? Exactly what makes you think I am not committed to the same goals you are? The only difference between the two of us is that you need and accept the loyalty and admiration of your people as consideration for your efforts. I simply chose a different form of consideration, and for that, you question my truthfulness," I hesitated to let the effect of my words register. "It may be I don't want to work with someone with as little intuition as you exhibit. It's possible both of us need the afternoon to consider the pros and cons of our further association. Now, I need to take in some of your clean mountain air. We can meet later, possibly after dinner, if you, or I, think there is anything further to discuss,"

I said, as I got up and headed toward the door. "I'll stay in the immediate area, if that's a concern."

I could tell that Ben was studying me as I left the great room. I think, I was truly in hopes that he would see his way clear to accept my offer, although my thought processes were clouded by a sense of duty, maybe even loyalty, owed the Company.

The afternoon was clear and cool. The immediate area around the ranch house was just what you might expect if you walked on a working ranch anywhere in the northern South American continent. There was a smell of animals, and several horses were corralled just to the north of the main house. On the left of the corral was a long bunkhouse, which was obviously used by the hands working on the ranch. Behind and to the north of the bunkhouse was a fenced pasture. Just beyond the pasture on the north was a bluff of what appeared to be the remnants of a larger granite ridge that had existed in the geologic past. The air contained an earthy smell mixed with the more pungent animal smell one might expect on ranch property. The aroma was not unpleasant. In fact the aroma was such that it fostered a feeling of well-being and promoted relaxation.

I headed toward the rocky ridge, anticipating I could do some thinking, and get some needed relaxation, while I enjoyed the views both back toward the ranch house and to the north. The hike across the pasture was further than I had estimated. I wondered if I was causing Bens group any concern because of the distance I was going. A check of the ranch area indicated my travels weren't a concern to anyone, at least to anyone I could see, so I continued. Upon reaching the base of the ridge, I noted a rather well-worn footpath ascending the ridge on an angle, making the climb less steep. In my state, less steep was better so I took advantage of the path. As I crested the ridge, I realized why there was no concern as to my travel. Astride the top of the ridge was a small lean-to, housing a guard, obviously a sentinel, to detect intruders from the north. As I reached the crest, his actions made it clear he had been made aware of my travels and was expecting me.

I waved, and as he acknowledged my presence, he indicated I should go no further to the north. I nodded and headed to a high point that was about seventy-five or one hundred meters to my left. As I reached the spot where I intended to spend some time relaxing, I glanced back, and as expected, he was talking on a radiophone. My location was being monitored at all times.

The high point on the ridge was just what I anticipated it would be. I could see to the north and northeast for miles. It appeared there was more haze in the northeast than in the more northerly areas, meaning the ocean was in a northeasterly direction. The country appeared to be jungle, and I couldn't see any sign of roads or villages, just one vast expanse of jungle. I turned and looked back at the ranch which had taken on a miniaturized appearance. There were men working in various areas of the immediate grounds, but none seemed to be doing anything that could be identified as ranch work. It appeared they were in preparation for moving. Each seemed to have a pack, and they were retrieving something from what appeared to be small potato cellars, located in three or four areas around the ranch house grounds. Suddenly, it occurred to me that what appeared to be potato cellars were powder magazines, or ammunition dumps, or both, and they were getting ready for an impending foray.

Ben's mention of an exercise in the immediate future was going to be more immediate than I had expected. My mind was racing as I tried to determine what effect this newly learned fact might have on Ben's decisions regarding my offer. My initial reaction was he would not have enough time to make a decision, but after some thought, I determined it might have a positive effect. The fact Ben even talked to me about joining them may indicate he was lacking in experienced lieutenants. Somehow that made sense, especially when Ben didn't know me personally. All his knowledge of me had been learned from Kenneth and Gail. If this operation was directed toward Barajas's organization and his buildup of product, I may be able to score for both sides.

The concept was strange, but intriguing. If Ben was going to give me employment, and I was able to appropriate Barajas's traveling money, both the Company and I would benefit. If that were the case then I would need to get to a phone immediately after the excursion. It would be time to play some of my trump cards with the Company.

It was getting late in the afternoon or early in the evening, I wasn't sure which but it didn't matter. It was time to get to the ranch and lobby my cause. I wanted to get hired.

As I passed the guard he acknowledged my departure. I could tell he was making sure I went toward the ranch house and not north into the jungle. I scrambled down the ridge, choosing the more direct route rather than the path. It took about fifteen minutes to cross the pasture and reach the ranch house. As I approached the stables, I could see the activity I had noted from the top of the ridge had slowed considerably or was not happening at all.

I approached the ranch house. The area looked serene in the late afternoon light. There was a smell that was unmistakably beef being cooked over hardwood at one of the many cooking grates in the area. I followed the aroma to the back. There, in the glow of the late afternoon, three men were cooking meat on an open grate. Several of the ranch hands were already sitting on long benches which had been built into the back of the building. A picnic table, doing justice to the Guinness Book of World Records, had been placed in front of the bench, and several smaller benches were being moved into place on the opposite side of the table. The steaks were huge. The feast must be consuming all the beef we had brought in.

I walked toward the area where the steaks were being cooked, with full intentions of getting a plate from the stack located just to the left of the cooking area. As I approached the cook, a man whom I had seen when we arrived stepped forward. He was smiling. It was obvious he was going to approach me. I slowed down, nodding a greeting in his direction.

"Senior Butler, it is the beginning of a beautiful evening. is it not?" His English was very serviceable.

"Yes it is, and the mountain air stimulates the appetite," I responded, leaving the conversation open for him to continue.

"Ben asked me to find you and extend an invitation for you to join him for dinner. He has a table in the ranch house. You'll find it much more comfortable."

"I would be honored. Will we be eating alone?" I inquired.

"I think not," was the only response I got, but the tone was friendly. Somehow, I trusted this man. I learned years ago to trust my intuition in matters such as this. The man led me into the ranch house through a back entrance where several women were filling large bowls with what appeared to be the local variety of corn or maize. We went through a large doorway and entered the dining room. I had previously glimpsed the dining room from the main room in the front of the house but had no idea it was as large as it proved to be. There were six places set at the table. Chairs were placed corresponding to the six places. Around the room were other chairs, obviously ready for use when there were more dinner guests. Ben was already in the room as was Gale. As my escort and I entered the room, Ben turned.

"Welcome, Mr. Butler. I'm honored you choose to join us. Kenneth will be with us shortly, as will another of my trusted associates. Mr. Butler, I see you have met Manuel Estivez. He is one of my most trusted associates and one of this country's leading experts in explosives," he said smiling.

I nodded toward my escort, who smiled and took a place at the table. As I was getting seated, Kenneth entered with a man I had not seen before. Kenneth acknowledged my presence and sat down next to Manuel. Ben moved toward the end of the table as he introduced the man who had come in with Ben.

"Mr. Butler, this is Miguel Barajas. He knows the back county of northern South America better than the original natives. He's invaluable to our cause. His knowledge has allowed us to get in and out of places we never could have without him, at least not without getting caught."

I'm not sure if my facial expression alerted Ben, or whether I instinctively reacted in some fashion with my body, but Ben's face suddenly appeared stern, and his eyes never left my face. "Is there something wrong, Mr. Butler? You look as though you've seen a ghost."

"No, nothing's wrong. I thought for a moment I knew Mr. Barajas from somewhere. I must be wrong." I was struggling to regain my composure and clear thinking. "Are you from around here, Mr. Barajas?" I inquired.

"I have family all over Colombia, but the majority of them are from an area south of Bogotá. That's where I spent my youth. Are you familiar with the area?"

"No, I can't say I am. I'm sure I was wrong." I glanced at Ben and turned to the table. Ben was still studying my face, but his stare was much less intent than it had been just seconds ago.

"Let's all get to the table and enjoy the beef Kenneth and Gale were fortunate enough to bring to the ranch. Miguel, why don't you sit next to Gale, and you, Mr. Butler, take the seat at the end of the table. Following the meal we have much to discuss."

The meal was absolutely amazing. What it lacked in variety and presentation was made up in sheer volume. The beefsteaks were a bit tough, but what you would expect from a country where most of the meat is range fed. During the entire meal, I was mentally debating whether I should come clean with Ben concerning my familiarity with the Barajas family name. Could it be that Ben's organization was being set up by the Barajas's cartel? Was Miguel a rogue in his own family? Most importantly, what did this mean to me, my plans? I decided to get Ben aside before the discussions. I was relatively sure Ben had decided to include me in the upcoming exercise. For that reason alone, he needed to know my concerns. I would have to play it by ear from there. The decision having been made, I relaxed and finished the meal. Miguel was very outgoing. He was not at all hard to talk to and seemed to contribute to most of the conversations that took place. The rest of the men, including Kenneth and Gale, seemed to be very comfortable with him.

At the conclusion of the feast, Ben announced that if anyone wanted to step outside and have a smoke, now was the time to do it as the evening was going to get very busy with plans and final preparations. As I was about to suggest Ben and I remain back, he motioned to me to meet him in the adjoining great room. I gladly accepted the invitation. With my coffee cup brimming with fresh coffee, I skirted the room to the doorway and joined him.

Ben had reached the room slightly before I did and was already sitting in one of the big overstuffed chairs sipping his coffee. I joined him, taking a chair facing his with a rough-hewn coffee table in between. I was hardly seated when Ben began speaking in a low tone.

"My men and I have met and discussed your requirements. Frankly, most were reluctant to consider the proposition, especially the financial part. Kenneth is the only man who has seen you in action and is your best supporter. He is also a good lobbyist. He convinced the others, including myself, that you would be an enormous asset on this mission. The result is the group has agreed to your terms. You're in if you want." Ben sat back and awaited my response.

"The answer is yes, but you must hear me out, and promise me that what I am about to tell you will remain strictly confidential. Not even your most trusted lieutenant can be told what I am about to reveal. Do I have your word?" I hesitated for him to respond.

"Yes, you have my word with one proviso. I will not keep silent if it appears there is any threat to my organization, and I alone will be the judge of that."

"That's fair enough," I said, knowing any fact he may consider threatening could be conveniently left out. "I work for an organization within the United States government. My job was to seal off a large part of the supply of illegal drugs from entering the United States. In that capacity, my partner, Sadie Anderson, and I were working undercover, attempting to make a deal that would close down, or at least slow down, one of the largest of Colombia's cartels - one we knew was getting large quantities of drugs into the States," I was about to continue when Ben interjected.

"Let me make a wild guess. That cartel would be the Barajas Cartel. Am I correct?" Ben inquired.

"Yes, you're correct," I was stunned, and I must have shown it as Ben continued.

"I saw the mystified look on your face when Miguel was introduced to you. You recovered nicely, but your initial reaction was one of shock. Miguel is the nephew of Jose Salvador Barajas. Miguel's mother, whose name was Mary, was the younger sister of Jose Barajas. Mary had given birth to Miguel out of wedlock and, as a result, had been excluded from the affairs of the Barajas family. Miguel's father died from an overdose of cocaine when Miguel was only a child. Several years ago, Miguel's mother learned the nature of her brother's business, including that he intended to employ Miguel in his future plans. At about the same time, she learned her brother, the man you know, had supplied the drugs which killed her son's father. Extremely upset Mary went to the Barajas's estate, where she hadn't been in years, to protest the drafting of her son into the cartel. Mary never left the estate. The rumor was she threatened to disclose some family secrets if Barajas didn't leave her son alone.

Barajas reacted violently, yelling and screaming that she, who had disgraced the family, could not now be judgmental about his business. The long and short of it is, Barajas killed his own sister to insure the secrecy of whatever she knew and was threatening to disclose. Miguel hated his uncle for killing his mother and refused to join the Barajas organization. Evidently, Barajas feared if Miguel was not in the fold, he was not only a danger but also an enemy. He issued an order to eliminate the threat. Miguel lived the balance of his youth in the back country of Colombia. When our organization became somewhat successful and more notorious, he contacted us offering his guide services. He's been with us ever since. Anyone here would trust Miguel with their life. You have nothing to worry about." Ben stopped and looked at me to see if I had any questions.

"I'm glad you told me. It removes just one of the uncertainties one faces in the business I'm in," I said.

"Which brings up a question I have -- just what business are you in?" Ben asked. "You tell me that you're with the U.S. government, and then you make a deal on your own. I doubt this was with the approval of the United States government. Just where do you stand in all this?" Ben's eyes were again intent. He was waiting for my answer.

"I'm not sure where I stand, as you put it. I have never before considered, or even thought, about leaving the agency. When Sadie died, I suddenly realized we were simply negotiable pawns in a war, which, in all probability, could never be won. I suspect the authorities killed Sadie in revenge for the death of a corrupt police officer she had to kill. I doubt the drug bosses even knew she existed or was in Colombia. What does all this say about this war Sadie and I thought we were fighting? What meaning does this give to her death? Who exactly was, or is, the enemy? Where does the United States government stand in all of this?

I know if I don't contact my superiors soon, I will be declared one of the enemies. It's happened before, with other agents, in fact it may have already happened to me. As we sit here, I may be a wanted man in every civilized country in the world. For this - this war - I have given up a mundane but normal life in the United States, lost the only woman I ever loved, and all for a mediocre salary and a small pension. A salary and pension that pales in comparison with the salaries and pensions of corporate leaders and professional men who have done nothing but risk capital and time to gain their successes. I've given my time. I deserve the financial benefits that are commensurate with the risks, losses, and sacrifices that not only I made but also Sadie died for! I now view myself, not only as an employ of the agency, but a businessman. Does this shock you?" I hesitated to get Ben's response.

"No, I don't think it does, but there's one thing I must know," Ben said studying my face intently. "Now that you have determined profit is your motive, at least part of your motive, have your loyalties also changed? The cartels can pay you more money than any organization or government would or could. So, will it be just a matter of time before you're nothing more than a well-paid soldier in the employ of the Barajas' of the world?" He hesitated.

I knew my association with Ben depended more on my answer to this question than anything I had said or done previously. The answer was also very clear to me. "Whether Sadie died as a result of the actions of corrupt authorities or by virtue of some drug lord's order is immaterial with regard to where my efforts, my loyalty will be directed. The simple truth is, except for the illicit drug business, Sadie would be alive today. If I was to accept any money or any other consideration for the furtherance of that business, I would be desecrating the memory of Sadie, making her death even more meaningless. That I cannot do. The answer to your question is no. My goals may now include profit, but my loyalties have not changed. In fact, they have been strengthened," I hesitated so he could reflect on what I had said. "I'm either in or out. I'm done talking. The choice is yours. What will it be?"

As I finished, I realized this was the first time I had forced myself to define what I had become to myself, let alone anyone else. Somehow, I was comfortable with who I was or was becoming. Somehow I knew while Sadie and I had never talked about our feelings and goals, she would have approved of my decisions. If she were alive we would be doing this together.

"Let's join the others. We have a lot of planning to do and a long day ahead of us," Ben responded, as he rose and headed for the dining room.

PART THREE

THE MISSION

CHAPTER THIRTY

I was awakened by subtle activities around the ranch house. I've never been a sound sleeper and this last evening was no exception. The plans made the night before were on my mind. Barajas's people were assembling a large amount of finished product around a small seacoast resort west of Cartagena. The resort had the luxury, or misfortune of having a deeper than usual harbor, a smallish dock, and loading facilities comparable to a commercial port. The intelligence Ben's people had been able to obtain indicated the product was being stored in a warehouse located less than a kilometer from the docking facilities. The loads had been arriving for several days, mostly by air. The cartel was utilizing a small but functional airport located between Cartagena and the resort. The product was shipped by truck from there to the warehouse. The security was reported as intense. The roads into the resort had been virtually sealed. The cartel had taken over the entire resort to house its soldiers and lieutenants. Guards were everywhere. It appeared the warehouse and the immediate area around it were impenetrable.

Miguel knew the area well. It seemed he had spent some time there several years ago and, in fact, had utilized the warehouse as a home base, while avoiding his Uncle's soldiers. The area immediately around the warehouse was described as very thick jungle with only one old road leading to the front of the facility. The warehouse was backed up against a cliff approximately twenty meters high, extending at least a kilometer on either side. According to Miguel, climbing gear was required to get up or down the cliff.

The headquarters of the cartel's operation was located in the resort proper with the bosses being housed in the main lodge. Whatever valuables and money the operation had would almost certainly be located there. The road into the resort was barricaded approximately five kilometers from the resort. It was also heavily guarded. The guard changed three times each twenty four-hour period. Other than the changing of the guard and the transport trucks from the local airport, there was little, if any, movement on the road inside the barricade.

An assault from the front of the resort had been determined to be unattractive. The driving time back to Cartagena and then out to the resort on a small coastal road would involve six or seven hours. The distance, as the crow flies, between the ranch house and the warehouse was only eight kilometers. While on my hike to the granite ridge, I had unknowingly surveyed the jungle in the direction of the warehouse. It appeared to be impassable.

I voiced my misgivings, concerning our ability to get through that forest in less time than it would take to go around. Miguel assured me he knew a route that was, or had been, used by locals to get from the resort into the jungle. According to Miguel, the locals had occasion to guide parties of rich foreigners, having an obsession for hunting South American cats, most of which are on international endangered species designations. The trail could be picked up not far from the top of the ridge, where I had viewed the jungles, and would take us to the top of the cliff just to the west of the warehouse. Miguel estimated it would take no more than three hours to cover the ground and reach the top of the cliff.

The plan was to get to the top of the cliff several hours before the midnight shift-change. One group, I was to be in this group, was to work their way around the cliff top, find a way down where we would not be discovered, and position ourselves at a place where we could see the barricade and the guards stationed there. Our task was to take those guards and their replacements out. Using the vehicles that had brought the replacement guards, we were to get back to the resort.

The theory was we could reach the resort without being noticed or causing any alarm. We then were to work our way to the main lodge in any way we could, quietly disposing of those soldiers with whom we came in contact. Once inside the resort lodge, we were to secret ourselves until the second team had detonated explosives destroying the warehouse and product being stored there. When most or all the personnel had left the lodge to investigate the explosion, I, along with Gale and Miguel, were to locate the money and any other valuables we could carry in our packs and get to the vehicles we used to get into the resort. We were to use any necessary force to accomplish the objective. It was clear Ben did not expect us to leave any cartel soldier alive. Our safe return depended on not being followed while we retreated.

The second team was to wait one hour after Gale, Miguel, and I had left and then scale their way down the cliff with the assistance of a long rope ladder that was to be packed in with us. Ben was to gain the roof of the warehouse from the rope ladder and set up an automatic weapon somewhere, near the front, where he had a full view of the road leading to the warehouse. The balance of the party, which consisted of Manuel, the explosive expert, and two ranch hands hand-picked by Manuel, were to descend the ladder to the ground. They were to set and wire the explosives and signal Ben when this was complete. Ben, Manuel, and the two ranch hands would then leave the roof and go to the top of the cliff via the rope ladder. Ben would set up with his weapon so he could see the warehouse as well as the road. When all hands were accounted for, Manuel would detonate the explosives, bringing down the warehouse and destroying the product.

All security coming up the road to investigate the blast was to be taken out with the automatic weapon. The hope was that any security force remaining alive after we had taken out the guards at the road blockade, their replacements, any guards we encountered at the main lodge, as well as those Ben's team had taken out at the warehouse would come up the road to the warehouse. The success of the raid was dependent on there being no advance warning of our presence until after the explosion.

The quiet elimination of the guards was to be accomplished through the use of knives. I have always considered the knife far down on my list of weapons of choice and therefore, never carried one; a fact I made clear to Ben after last night's meeting. He went to a cabinet, and unlocked its swinging doors, revealing a collection of knives that would interest the most avid collector. The knife he choose for me was a weapon with a blade at least thirty centimeters long and a thick ivory handle darkened by use and sun. The hilt resembled the business end of a medium sized hammer. To anyone viewing the weapon it was obvious either end could be lethal. The knife was housed in a scabbard of soft dark leather and lined with a second layer of leather that had been treated, making it extremely hard and resistant to being cut as the knife was withdrawn or inserted. The soft outside covering of the scabbard continued in a single piece to form a soft belt. The buckle was metal darkened by heat. As long as the knife was sheathed nothing would reflect light. I was now appropriately armed and part of the team.

The plan was to leave the ranch around seven-thirty in the evening and work our way to the warehouse with plenty of time to get in position before the midnight shift-change at the road barricade. I glanced at my watch. It was only seven a.m., more than twelve hours before departure. I knew it would be twenty hours or more before I would be able to sleep again. The logical part of me knew I should try to get as much sleep as possible, however, years of early rising and sleeping very lightly had already won out over logic. I was up for the duration. I dressed in clean clothing provided me by a female ranch employee. She had taken my dirty, and somewhat odoriferous, clothes and washed them while I was sleeping.

I checked all my belongings, making sure that no one had been snooping last evening or while I was sleeping. Everything was as I had left it, including the money. Before leaving the room, I set one of the standard traps Sadie and I used when we were traveling. It would alert me if anyone intruded while I was out of the room. I left the room and headed for the main ranch house area. As I approached I could smell breakfast cooking and could hear the muffled sound of voices. Out of habit more than anything else, I slowed in an effort to hear the substance of the conversation before my presence became known. Before getting much closer, I realized the conversation was taking place in Spanish. Having no further reason to delay my entry, I strolled into the dining area and found Ben and the explosives expert, Manuel, having what appeared to be a light conversation over coffee. It was obvious they had completed their breakfast and were simply enjoying the morning.

"Good morning," Ben said as soon as he saw me enter. "Hopefully you had a good night's sleep. We have a big day ahead."

"Slept like a baby. Is this where a man can get some coffee?" I asked as I sat in a chair opposite Manuel.

As I spoke a woman, whom I recognized as one of the servers at the dinner last night, entered the room with a steaming pot of coffee. She smiled at me as she got a cup, better described as a mug, from a shelf at the end of the room and poured it full.

"Breakfast here is probably more limited than what you are accustomed to, but I will try to get you what you want," she said in broken, but passable, English.

"I'm not hard to please," I said. "You've already supplied me with most of my immediate needs. Give me what Ben and Manuel had. I'm sure it will be fine."

As the woman left the room, I noticed Ben and Manuel smiling at each other in a way I knew that I was the object of their amusement. "What's so funny?" I asked with a light and friendly tone.

"Sometimes it's better to ask what it is you're ordering. Hopefully, you will enjoy cornmeal mush. It's a staple down here. I wouldn't know how to start my day without it."

"I actually like mush. I can think of a lot of breakfasts I've eaten around the world that are a lot worse," I replied. At about that time the woman can back with a large bowl of hot cornmeal mush. It resembled a type of hot cereal and had a mixture of chopped local vegetables mixed with it. She also served butter, a pitcher of cream, and a bowl containing very coarse sugar. I poured a small amount of cream over the mush and sprinkled it with the coarse sugar. It was quite good, and as I ate I realized I was hungrier than I thought I was.

While I was eating, the conversation was light. The upcoming mission wasn't discussed. As I finished and was enjoying a second mug of coffee, Manuel excused himself saying he needed to check on the other two hands he'd chosen for the mission. After he left the dining area, I took the opportunity to talk to Ben alone.

"Ben, I mentioned to you yesterday my need to get to a phone and contact my employers in the United States. We got off on other concerns and you never answered me. Does the ranch have a phone I can use to contact my superiors before they send out teams looking for me?" I hesitated to allow Ben an opportunity to respond.

"We do have a way that can be accomplished but it's very expensive. A five or ten minute call to the United States will cost between two hundred fifty and three hundred U.S. dollars. If the call is important to you, and you are willing to spend the money, I will arrange it."

"Money is not a problem and, yes, it is important to me. When can this be accomplished?" I responded feeling some relief.

"Assuming where you will be calling is not sensitive to time zone differences, we can make it now. I have some requirements, however," Ben said. His eyes became focused on my face with the intensity I had seen so often since arriving on the ranch.

"What might those requirements be?" I asked.

"First, there is not to be any mention of the mission we have scheduled for tonight. Second, there can be no mention of your location other than somewhere in Colombia. Third, do not mention the names of any of the people you have met here, and, finally, I insist on being in the room when the call is placed. I will monitor not only your side of the conversation but also the recipients. If you can agree to these conditions, and the time is right, we can make the call now." Ben hesitated ... his eyes seeming to drill through me.

"I can accept all of the requirements except the last one. It's not because I'm concerned about your learning what was or was not said. The man I'm going to call is my field supervisor in the organization I work for. Because of the sensitive nature of the business, we utilize a sophisticated telephone structure which can detect if anyone is eavesdropping on the conversations. If you are listening, he will know it, and will terminate the call immediately. Within minutes of termination all of the teams in Colombia, in fact the world, will be mobilized, and I will become a hunted man. I ask you to trust me on this one." It was my turn to hesitate.

"If the system is that sophisticated, will he be able to trace the call to this location?" Ben asked.

"I don't know your system so I can't answer that question," I responded.

"Without going into detail I'm not sure I understand. The phone here is a radio phone which will connect to your boss through a series of three separate public phone installations. The final installation is located somewhere in Brazil. We've always felt the system was secure, but then we never called your boss. What are your thoughts?" Ben asked.

"I, like you, am not an expert on phone systems, but I have some familiarity with the one we will be connecting into. There is no doubt it will be able to locate the final connection in Brazil. Given enough time, it would also locate the other two connections wherever they are. The problem they will have even if they locate the first connection or relay is it's receiving a signal from a radiophone, and for them to isolate the location of the radiophone would require a triangulation of some sort. They won't have time for that. I will keep the call extremely short, no more than two or three minutes. The ranch location will be secure," I responded.

"Normally a request like this would be out of the question, but I sense how important it is for you, and I still have a glimmer of hope my organization can someday work with your bosses, so I'm going to allow you to place the call," Ben reassured me. "But, Mr. Butler, rest assured and remember if anything results from this call, causing my people or our organization any injury, you won't have to worry about teams put in the field by your bosses. I will personally arrange to take you out!"

"I understand and accept those conditions. Now where is the phone? I want to get this behind me so I can concentrate on tonight," I rose from the chair as I spoke.

"It's located in the barn that houses the ranches' mechanical equipment. Let me locate the operator, and I'll meet you there in ten minutes. The call may take as long as an hour to complete." Ben left the room and headed toward a bunkhouse. I left the main ranch house and tried to determine which of the barns contained the mechanical equipment. The choice was easy. Only one of the barns had any equipment stored outside which would qualify as mechanical. I headed for the obvious.

CHAPTER THIRTY-ONE

It was somewhere between eight-thirty and nine a.m. Howard Baker was eating the breakfast Mildred had fixed for him. Over the years he had truly learned to hate whole wheat bran flakes, but Mildred insisted he eat them-- something about not being regular without them. The choice was either to argue with Mildred or eat the bran flakes he hated. Daily, Howard made the only choice that made any sense. He was just finishing his bran flakes when he heard the phone in the office ring. Something inside him knew the caller was Eric. In his haste to get to the office phone, he tipped over the bowl, and remnants of the cereal spilled across the table. He didn't notice the mess, maybe he didn't care. He would hear from Mildred about it later, but for now his entire focus was on getting to the office and the ringing phone. As he crossed the family room toward the office, he noticed, with some irritation, that Mildred had already assumed her regular position doing one of those needle things. She said something to him, but in his haste he didn't hear what she had to say.

Howard reached the phone and picked it up. He was breathless but still managed his standard greeting.

"Baker here!" He shouted into the receiver.

"Howard, this is Eric. What the hell took you so long to get to the phone?"

"What the hell do you care how long it takes me to get to the phone! What I want to know is where the hell you are and why haven't you checked in?" Howard was almost shouting. To this point Eric knew Ben could hear the entire conversation without the need of an earpiece.

"Relax, I'm still in Colombia. I can't give you my present location and don't try to trace this call. It'll get you nowhere. I'm in the process of causing Barajas some delivery problems. I will get back to you shortly, hopefully, within the next forty-eight hours. In the meantime, call off the dogs, if they've been called out, and be patient. I'll get in touch with you at my next opportunity. By the way, I lost my cell phone so I'll be using other facilities," Eric hesitated, giving Howard time to respond and tell him the information he needed to know. Had he been declared rogue? Was he a hunted man?

"I'm not sure I can do that, Eric, or if I should even try. It's my guess they want you back in this country. They need to know where your allegiances are. I need to know where you stand," Howard's voice had become very steely and deliberate. He was carefully choosing his words. It was Eric's turn to be irate and raise his voice.

"So that's how it is, Howard. Sadie and I bring one of South America's largest cartels virtually to your doorstep. I lose Sadie, the only person I have ever really cared for, all in the name of the Company and for its cause, and they need to know where I stand! You, of all people, need to know where I stand! The Company can go to hell! You can go to hell!" Eric's voice dropped and as expected Howard jumped right in.

"Eric, settle down. Put yourself in their shoes. You and Sadie disappear for the better part of a week. We get a call and Sadie is dead. We arrange to get her remains brought back to the States and you disappear again for the better part of another week. What the hell are they -- am I -- supposed to think? Yes, they've been talking about sending out the dogs as you called them. I will try to get it stopped, but as you know so well, sometimes that's not possible. Can you give me any information concerning where you are or what you are doing? If I can give them anything it might help stall the current thinking," Howard said, almost pleading.

"No, I can't give you anything further than I have already. Tell them for me that if they don't want several years of work and a lot of money to be wasted, they'll wait for my next call. If they are going to send the dogs, tell them to send their best and don't expect them to return. I have to go now. I'll call in two days." Eric hung up the radiophone.

As the phone went dead, Howard Baker's face turned beat red with rage. How dare Eric call his bluff? But what if it wasn't a bluff and the dogs, as Eric called them, were sent out? It didn't matter to Howard whether they came back or not. He would have lost his best operative, and the Company will have lost years and considerable money.

Mildred must have noticed his reddened face. She removed the ear peace, through which she always listened to her beloved classical music, and approached the office door. "What's wrong, Howard? Was that Eric Butler?" she inquired.

"You know I can't discuss these things with you, Mildred. Now just go back to your knitting, or whatever. I have to make some phone calls," Howard replied sharply, as he returned to the phone and started to enter the number he knew would reach Scott Steel. Mildred dutifully adjusted her earphones and went back to her needlework.

Howard really hated to make the call. He was sure Scott would find fault with the way he had handled Eric. He really hadn't gotten any information other than Eric would call again in two days. The implication was Eric was still on the job, but there were no specifics other than he was doing something that would upset or delay Barajas's delivery plans. The number was dialed and there was a dead ringing sound in the receiver.

"Scott Steel," the voice rang of self-assurance.

"Scott, Howard, our boy has called. I just hung up, or rather he just hung up. In any event, he's in Colombia and, by all appearances, seems to be on the job."

"Where in Colombia and what the hell is he doing?" Scott inquired, his voice becoming tense.

"He wouldn't tell me where he was or exactly what he was doing. He did indicate he's doing something to delay or disrupt the cartel's delivery of drugs. He said he would check back in within forty-eight hours," Howard responded.

"That's not good enough, Howard, you know we need more information. He could be disrupting our operations as we speak. Did you tell him he was on the verge of being classified as 'gone south'?"

"Yes, the subject did come up. He reminded me he and Sadie had been about to put the largest cartel in South America on our door step. He also suggested that he had lost Sadie to the Company's cause and, based on those two facts alone, questioned how could we doubt his allegiance," Scott broke in.

"There's been more than one agent that has 'gone south' for less reason."

"I agree, but none I'm aware of where the Company has invested so much time and money. I think we owe it to the Company, to ourselves, and to Eric to give him the two days he asked for. All remedies available now will be available in two days. That's my opinion. I intend to put it in memo form and give it to the director if necessary," Howard said, playing the ultimate trump card. There was silence on the other end of the phone. Howard could hear Scott breathing so he knew the connection had not been lost.

"Hopefully, you initiated the automatic tracing equipment," Scott said finally.

"No, I did not. Eric told me it wouldn't be effective. You and I both know, if Eric didn't want the call traced, it wouldn't be possible to trace, at least not in the time he gave me." The phone was silent again.

"Howard, you've put me in a very awkward position and placed yourself in the unenviable place of having to be one hundred percent right. Your entire career, or what's left of it, is at stake. I will not mobilize the field, at least not at this time, but I want you to clearly understand, it's not because of any memo you may or may not write. I'm convinced any agents I could have in Colombia in the next forty-eight hours would not be sufficiently trained to successfully apprehend Eric. You can rest assured, however, I will be making preparations for an all-out search and with the appropriate personnel. I will set the search in motion immediately upon the expiration of the forty-eight hour period."

"I will not ask you for more time, Howard promised. "I will contact you immediately when I receive further word from Eric." The phone went dead.

Howard remained seated in his comfortable, overstuffed office chair, staring blankly at the phone and the electrical equipment in the background. What Scott had said was true. He was placing the balance of his career on the line. His future suddenly depended on the loyalty of an agent that had given all the signals of '*going south.*'

Over the years, Howard had seen other field supervisors become so confidant in their operative's decisions and loyalty, they placed themselves in jeopardy of losing their jobs and, in some occasions, their lives. He had sworn he would never get himself in a critical position, the outcome of which depended on the actions of another, especially one of his agents. Almost without realizing what he was doing, Howard had done just that. Eric Butler would determine how and when his career would end, and all he could do was sit and wait for the next forty-eight hours.

Howard rose from his chair and turned to exit the office. It was going to be an eternity. As he walked through the family room, he saw Mildred on the telephone in the corner. She smiled at him and putting her hand over the receiver said, "There's more coffee in the kitchen. I'll be in to join you in a minute."

Howard nodded and headed toward the kitchen. He was hoping Mildred's phone call would end shortly. There weren't many times in his life when he felt the need for companionship but this was one of them. The coffeemaker was on a small counter separated from the rest of the kitchen. On the counter was a vertical stack of coffee mugs held in place by a small dowel attached to the base. The dowel ran through the handles of the cups keeping them in place. Howard took the top mug and poured it full of coffee. He debated pouring one for Mildred but didn't because it could get cold if her phone conversation continued. Howard marveled at Mildred volunteering the coffee. Normally she rebuffed him for the amount of coffee he drank. Once again, Mildred must have sensed something was wrong and knew he needed the coffee and some conversation. Howard wished the phone call would end.

CHAPTER THIRTY-TWO

As I hung up the radiophone, Ben was looking at me. I could tell he had something to say.

"I take it, from your side of the conversation, it did not go well," he said more as a question than a statement.

"It could've gone better. I bought enough time to complete this evening's exercise, however," I replied. "After that, I'm not sure."

"Assuming they do come after you, how will they do it?" Ben asked.

"The Company hates publicity, especially where it involves covert activities, so it will be a quiet hunt, one in which they will place their experienced, but somewhat rogue agents in the field simply to hunt me down. My guess is it will be dead or alive, and when one is in a foreign country, undercover, the easiest, quietest way is dead," I responded. "Let's not worry about that now. We have a job to do requiring all of our individual attention and concentration. I will deal with that issue when we are back here, safe and successful."

Ben nodded, turned, and we left the barn together. I looked down at my watch. It was only nine-thirty a.m., a full ten hours before we were scheduled to leave.

"How does one kill time around here?" I asked, as we strolled back to the ranch house.

"We're not accustomed to having guests here and each of us have our assigned duties that will take up a good part of the day. You might try taking a horseback ride around the valley. That will eat up a few hours. I strongly suggest you also spend some time getting your gear together for tonight. We'll have dinner around five o'clock. If you require a midday snack, just go to the kitchen and they'll fix you up. Consider an hour or two nap before dinner. It's going to be a long night," he cautioned.

"Sounds good. Where can I arrange for the horse?" I inquired.

Ben smiled and pointed at a barn with a corral on one side of it. "Be sure you tell the wrangler how well you ride. We have a few pretty rank horses. You might not want one of those."

I broke away from Ben and worked my way to the corral. I made every attempt to appear like I knew what I was doing. The way I put my leg up on one of the cross rails would have made John Wayne proud. There were several horses in the corral, and I attempted to make eye contact with each of them in an effort to determine which one would be the most docile. It didn't appear any of them cared that I was staring them down. A short Spanish looking man came out of the barn and started toward me. As he approached, he broke out in a huge smile and, in doing so, revealed that he had no teeth or very few of them.

"Buenos dias," he said. "What can I do for you?   Would you like to go for a ride? I have just the pony for you."

Pony sounded good, but I didn't like the look in his eye. "I thought I might, but I haven't ridden for some time." I wasn't lying but I didn't tell him it was more than thirty years.

"I have just the horse, Senor. He's gentle as a lamb and big enough to handle your weight." He had a lead rope with him and went up to the largest horse in the corral. He snapped the lead rope into a halter already on the animal and led him into the barn. I personally wouldn't have termed that animal a "pony" but to each his own. I was more interested in determining which side of the horse to mount. I knew it was on the left, but I wasn't sure if it was the left as you faced the horse or left if you were looking the same way as the horse. I decided to wait and see if he would inadvertently give me some clue. Ultimately he emerged from the barn with the horse, which now bore a saddle and bridle. The saddle was western style with a huge saddle horn that had my privates written all over it. It even had a coiled rope tied to one side. He motioned me into the corral. As I entered the corral he took a tug on the cinch and turned, looking at me.

"Would you like to adjust the stirrups yourself or would you like me to do it for you?" he asked.

"It's been some time. Why don't you do it."

"Si, please mount and I'll see where your feet are." I could tell, by the way he was looking at me, that the moment of decision had arrived. He threw the reins over the neck of the horse and stood waiting for me to mount. I chose the side where he was standing. I put my left foot in the stirrup and, with the help of the saddle horn, swung into the saddle. The horse moved toward me as I got aboard. The wrangler steadied the horse and proceeded to adjust the stirrups. The whole process didn't take more than a minute or so. He stepped aside.

"Looks okay to me. How does it feel?"

"Just fine," I replied. What I really wanted to say was that I felt a long way from the ground. As I was responding, he was leading the horse to the corral gate.

"You'll be fine, senor. If you get off the horse during your ride, try to mount with your weight closer to the horse. If you swing out as you just did, the horse may leave you in the field to walk home. By the way, keep a tight rein on him when you turn toward home. Have a good ride."

With those simple sounding instructions he smiled a large toothless smile and headed to the barn. I was on my own.   He hadn't told me the horse's name and I needed something to call him. I reached down, patted his neck, and said the only thing that came to me, "easy Big Fella." I nudged the horse forward. He responded and we started down the path leading to the field I crossed yesterday. I tapped him with my heels and Big Fella and I were in a trot. I stood slightly in the stirrups. Somewhere I remembered standing took the jolt out of the ride and it worked. I reined him to the left and he responded. The ride was becoming quite fun. I really don't know why I had been so worried.

We rode around the field, sometimes walking, and sometimes trotting. About a half-hour into the ride I decided to see if he would gallop. I nudged him into a trot and then nudged him again. He responded by going into a full gallop. The ride became instantly much smoother. It was exhilarating! Big Fella galloped for about half a mile. I slowed him down to a trot and then to a walk. I felt Big Fella and I were becoming one. We went down the road leading away from the ranch and around some fields. In one of the fields we came across a small stream. I hadn't seen it on the way in but there it was. Evidently Big Fella was thirsty, because he trotted up to it, bounced his head up and down until he had gained enough slack in the reins to get his head down to the water, and began drinking.

I thought it was a good time to take a rest. With the reins in one hand I dismounted on the left side of the horse. Big Fella didn't flinch. I let him get his fill of water, led him to the edge of some trees that were close, tied his reins to a big branch, and went to the stream to drink some water myself. When I returned he was waiting patiently. I untied the reins, throwing them over Big Fella's neck just as the wrangler had done. The wrangler had asked me to mount closer to the horse. I wasn't sure what that meant but would try. I put my foot in the stirrup, and with my hands firmly on the saddle horn, began to swing into the saddle. As I did Big Fella swung toward me. I somehow got into the saddle. I don't know how. It seemed Big Fella was in a gallop instantly. I attempted to rein him in with no effect. Big Fella was galloping much faster than he had before. In an instant we were out of the woods and on the road

It was at least three kilometers to the ranch. Surely he would not keep up this pace all the way in. He did. All I could do was hang on to the saddle horn and hope he did not turn quickly. As we approached the ranch house he veered off on the path toward the corral. It was close, but I was able to stay with him. Ahead was the corral fence and he wasn't slowing down. I was certain he was either going to jump the fence or crash through it. I wasn't sure which I preferred and then it happened. He simply put on the brakes. All four feet were skidding and his butt was lower than his front shoulders. As he stopped I went over the saddle horn and up his neck. I slowly fell off the right side to the ground. As I looked up Big Fella was looking down at me. So was the wrangler.

"He got the bit in his teeth, senor. That's why I told you to keep a tight rein on him when you headed home. Are you okay?"

"Yeah, I'm okay!" I said as I got up off the ground. "Do all of your horses act like that?"

"Yes. Most of them are just hard to ride. Some are downright mean. He's the gentlest one we have." His smile was gone now and replacing it was a look of concern. I somehow realized the look wasn't concern for me. His concern was whether I would cause trouble for him and his job.

"It's not your fault. I haven't ridden for some time," I said as I turned and headed toward the ranch house. I hoped that would put him at ease.

All the excitement had made me a bit hungry. It was not the noon hour yet, but I hoped I could find a snack or something that would take the edge off for a few more hours. We were going to have a full meal late afternoon after which Ben wanted to meet and review the plans for the evening's raid. I wasn't sure I could nap but I wanted to try. I knew it would be a long night.

As I approached the ranch house, I could tell the staff was busy with the preparations for the meal. When I entered, I found Ben and a ranch hand I had not seen before discussing something. Ben looked up, smiled, and waved me over to the table where they were sitting.

"We're just finishing up with some of the ranch business. How was your ride?" he asked.

"Not bad until the end," I replied glaring at him. I could tell it was everything he could do not to bust out laughing. "It seems that 'pony' I rode gets the bit in his teeth when turned toward home. I lost control of him."

"I know. I saw you return and, let me say, you were graceful," Ben replied, losing control and starting to laugh.

Initially, I felt an overwhelming desire to strike out at the levity being enjoyed at my expense. However, something was holding me back. It occurred to me my circumstance was humorous, and that all of the events were of my own making. With that realization, I joined Ben in laughter. "My riding skills were not as I remembered them," I said between gasps for breath made necessary by the continued laughter. "I'm glad the saddle horn had a slight angle as it rose from the saddle. Had it been abrupt, I would be speaking in a much higher pitch."

"At least you weren't injured. That would have jeopardized the mission. Let's get something to eat and try to get a few hours rest. The kitchen is planning a meal for around five today." Ben said, rising and heading toward the back of the ranch house. I followed.

As we approached the room where the main table was located, I saw that the staff had arranged a small meal of fruit, cheese, and some of the bread we had last night. Ben and I sat in silence as we snacked on the small lunch. After a few minutes, he got up and headed toward the back of the ranch house.

"Don't worry about oversleeping. One of the staff will make sure you're awake in plenty of time to eat and finish getting ready." Ben disappeared, leaving me alone at the table.

I finished what I was eating and headed back to my room. Upon reaching the room I checked the traps to see if anyone had investigated my belongings. Everything was in order. I discarded my boots and laid on the bed. To my amazement, the next thing I knew was I was being shaken by the young girl I had met earlier.

"Senor, it's time for you to get up. It's after four o'clock. Dinner will be served around five." She stood over me looking down with concern on her face. "You won't go back to sleep will you?"

"No, I'm fully awake. Thank you for waking me. I probably would have slept all night," I replied smiling at her. She turned and left.

I swung my feet over the side of the small bed. I felt the results of my earlier folly. My back was sore and my left shoulder was a bit tight. Some stretching would do the trick. I performed as many maneuvers as I could recall from the training courses the Company had made us endure. The result was positive. My shoulder loosened up as did my back. My pack was on the floor next to the bed. I emptied it of all its contents, including the money. What extra clothing I had, I put on the bed. I also put Sadie's weapon and ammunition under the clothes, hopefully, out of sight. I checked my pistol to ensure it was fully loaded. I disassembled the holster and shoulder harness I normally used. I wanted to carry the weapon on the belt that incorporated the knife scabbard. The holster fit fine on the belt. I had several clips for the pistol and wanted to take extra ammunition. I didn't want to carry all the extra ammo in my pockets. I reasoned the bulk, if not the weight, would inhibit my movement. I needed the fanny pack Sadie carried in lieu of a purse. I decided to ask Ben if he had anything that would suffice. It seemed stupid to carry the full pack for the few items I would be taking with me.

It was almost five o'clock and I wanted to be ready before dinner. I went to the main room of the ranch house. The room was being used as a depot for items that were designated for the excursion. Manuel was gathering the materials he needed to accomplish his goals. I was amazed at the sophistication of the explosives he was amassing. There was enough C-4 to level a small town. It was arranged in small packages, five in all. Each package was the size of a softball, though more flat than round. The electronic detonation system he was using was in the opposite corner of the room and was comprised of a small transmitting radio containing a built in battery pack and several detonators, any one of which would fit in a man's pocket. In the center of the floor were three small packs that had been lined with a soft cloth, which I assumed was to cushion the contents. I approached Manuel.

"Do you have an extra pack like the ones there?" I asked, pointing at the three packs in the center of the room. "It could be even smaller than those."

"Si, Senor. I'll have one of the men get one for you," he promised and left the room. He returned momentarily.

"The pack will be here shortly," he announced. He went back to work, testing the radio and the receivers. I watched, fascinated by the way Manuel handled the explosives -- as though they were Playdoh.

"Wouldn't it be safer if these were assembled in one of the barns?" I asked.

"Does this bother you?" he asked without answering my question.

"Not really. I understand the explosives, but I probably would assemble the components somewhere other than the main ranch house," I responded.

"So would I, but Ben wants to review the system after dinner. We decided this location was the best place to accomplish both."

As Manuel was finishing his explanation, a small dark man entered the room. He had several smaller packs with him. One was perfect for my needs. I thanked him and went back to the room. The pack was one much like students carry their books, lunch, or whatever to and from school. The differences were it was made of heavier material, was somewhat smaller, was camouflaged, and was lined with some of the same material I had noticed Manual was about to use. I put three of the five extra magazines in the pack along with two boxes of extra cartridges. I adjusted the straps so it fit snugly to my back without restricting my movements. The remaining two magazines were placed one in each of my side pockets. I was ready. After dinner, I would come back to the room and gather the knife, gun belt, as well as the pack. The excitement of the upcoming raid was starting to build.

It was time to join the others for dinner. I left the room and went to the dining area. I was the last one to arrive. Everyone was sitting around the table eating and conversing in both English and Spanish. As I entered the conversation became solely English.

"Better sit down and get to eating before these bandits steal all the food," Ben said in a friendly tone.

I nodded and took my place at the table. The meal was some sort of stew and cornbread. It was bland but tasty and would be filling. I fell to eating like the rest and consumed more than I would have at an ordinary meal. I may need the extra energy. Conversation was light and the meal took about an hour to finish. As we were enjoying coffee, Ben stood.

"As soon as you're finished, I want to go over the plans again. For right now, I would like to have Manuel take me though the explosives and the detail of setting them. I'll be back in a few minutes."

Ben left the room and Manuel followed. The rest of us sat back and enjoyed the coffee and some small pastries the staff had set out. It wasn't more than ten or fifteen minutes and Ben returned alone. As he entered the room, the conversation fell to a hushed minimum. I glanced around the table, and couldn't help but notice the entire tone of the evening, at least the portion of the evening that had been consumed by dinner, had changed. The faces of all the participants had become serious and somewhat steeled. Everyone seemed to waiting for Ben to start the review.

"Let's start with the hike in," Ben began. "Each of you recite what you have put in your packs and what you will be carrying on your person. Let's start with Gale."

"I have extra ammunition in the pack along with some clean rags and a large flash light with new batteries. The rags will act as a sound damper for the ammunition as well as the light and for bandages, if we need them. On my person will be my pistol, a knife and two extra magazines, each in their own leather container fitting on my belt. I will have a second knife contained in a scabbard in the top of my right boot. The scabbard has been built in for that purpose," Gale hesitated, as though thinking if there was anything she had forgotten.

"Does the boot scabbard interfere with walking?" Ben inquired.

"No, I've broken the boots in well and really can't tell it's there," she replied.

"Good. Now what about you and your men, Manuel?"

"I will carry the radio detonators as well as extra manual detonators in the event of a failure of the radio equipment. I too will have a pistol on my belt along with a machete in a full-length scabbard to ensure there's not a reflection from the blade. I will have five extra magazines for the pistol, as well as an extra box of cartridges. They will be in the pack cushioned by soft cloth."

"And what of your men?" Ben interjected.

"One of them will have the radio for detonation and will carry the rope ladder. The other will have the batteries for the radio, the explosives, as well as a second rope long enough to scale the cliff if necessary. Each will have their personal weapons, extra ammunition, and a knife appropriate for the mission." Manuel stopped talking.

"Miguel, you're next," Ben announced, without waiting to see if Manuel was truly finished.

"I will have the ammunition for your assault rifle as well as a length of rope that will suffice if we need it to reach the level of the blockade on the road. I will also have three lengths of wire, each with small handles on the ends. I'll have extra ammunition in the pack, three magazines, and my knife on my belt. Soft cloth will eliminate any sound made by the pack. That's about it," Miguel concluded.

"Eric, tell us what you've packed," Ben said.

"I have the knife and belt you provided me, my personal weapon with two extra magazines which I will carry in my extra pockets, together with two more magazines, and an extra box of cartridges in the pack. That's about all I have." I stopped, waiting for Ben to indicate whether I had forgotten anything.

"Eric, I will arrange to have some cloth brought to your room. Use it to make sure the pack doesn't rattle. I will also get you a small flashlight. It might come in handy for your group. Before we go any further, I -- we need to know if you will have any hesitation using the knife or the wire. I know you're good with your gun, that your instincts are good, but can you use those same instincts at close range when the weapon is a knife or wire?"

"I'm not going to bullshit you and tell you I prefer the knife and wire. What I will tell you is, I am very pragmatic and if a knife or wire is the best way to the objective then a knife and wire it will be. Now, if that doesn't satisfy you or this group, that's tough! It's a little late to change the plan or the participants. Is the equipment I have outlined complete, or is there something else I should include?" I responded, feeling the anger well up. Ben began again, without acknowledging my statement.

"I will have the automatic weapon in my pack. It will be broken down, and I will need a few minutes to assemble it at the site. Because of the weapon, my pack will be the biggest risk of an awkward rattle. For that reason, I will bring up the rear and will rely on you to signal me if we encounter any unexpected resistance. Also, I would like to get this weapon back to the ranch, so I may need help as we depart the area. If all goes well there will be no resistance as we depart, but we must anticipate the worst. Are there any questions concerning the equipment?"

Ben stopped and looked at each of us individually in an unspoken solicitation for questions or comments. No one in the group had anything to say. Evidently, satisfied the equipment was taken care of, Ben launched into the next stage of his briefing. "I will head the group that stays around the warehouse. Gale, you will head the group going to the road barricade. I'm sure every one of you who have been with me on other missions know the group leader's decisions must be followed without question or hesitation. Eric, I realize in the past you have acted based upon your own instincts and not on someone else's command. We have found that when we operate in groups, there must be a leader and the leader's decisions and judgments in matters affecting the group must be followed without question. We will expect no less from you.

Gale, you and your group will leave the rest of us when we reach the cliff in the rear of the warehouse. It's imperative your group makes its way around the cliff without alerting the soldiers. Locate the barricade and then find a way down the cliff. Remember, the trip down the cliff is a one-way trip, so if a rope is necessary, collect it when you're all down. I'd like to attempt to leave the cartel guessing how we got in. It's your call as to whether you take the guards out at that time or wait and get them all together. Just make it silent and final. If they have a radio, leave it intact. Miguel, if necessary, you respond to any transmission from the main camp. Hopefully, that won't be necessary. After you have secured the barricade use their vehicle to get to the resort. Use their coats or jackets to create the illusion you're just returning guards.

Eliminate any and all soldiers you come across and get into the main lodge. Silence is the key if you're going to get in. Eric, find the money and whatever valuables you can and do it quick. For what it's worth, we've found they generally leave their stash in a place where it can be evacuated quickly, which isn't always in the most secure place. Look for a briefcase, or pack, hidden behind the furniture near the door. Eric, it's your responsibility to take as many out, in and around the lodge, as possible. If we can eliminate their leaders, we will create chaos among the troops. That will make it much easier for all of us.

My group will take out the guards in the area around the warehouse and set the explosives. When that's complete we'll use the ladder to get to the top of the cliff. I will set up the assault rifle in a predetermined place where I can use it to eliminate any men coming up the road. We will set off the explosives at precisely twelve-thirty. Gale, your group should leave the lodge area before that time and head for the cliff at the closest point. Work your way along the base of the cliff toward the warehouse. We will leave the ladder down for your group to use. When the last of you have reached the top, pull the ladder up behind you. By the time you reach the top of the cliff, we should be done and can head back. Are there any questions?"

Ben again searched every one of the faces before him. No one spoke. I had a question. I decided it was now or never.

"Why isn't Kenneth included in the group?" I blurted out.

"He would be invaluable." Ben looked at me with intensity in his eyes. I almost wished I hadn't asked the question.

"If Kenneth was included and the mission went very badly, who would be here to carry on the cause? Kenneth and I discussed this problem and I won the trip. Does that answer your question?" Ben responded.

I nodded and sat back in my chair. Based on Ben's answer, it occurred to me the mission might not be as much of a slam-dunk as had been portrayed. It could be I was going to earn my money in ways I had not contemplated.

"If there are no further questions, we'll meet here at the main house in forty- five minutes. Be sure your faces, hands, and arms have been painted and nothing on your body is reflective. Eric, one of the kitchen helpers will assist you with your war paint and sound proofing of your pack. See you all shortly," Ben had finished the briefing.

Everyone got up and disappeared in various directions. I got up and headed toward my room. When I arrived, the young woman I had seen earlier was waiting. Following some limited pleasantries, she pointed to the bed indicating I should sit. She went to the only dresser in the room and produced a jar of something. I knew the jar wasn't in the room when I left. She approached the bed and asked me to take off my shirt. I complied, at which point she reached in the jar with the tips of her fingers and retrieved a batch of dark, stiff appearing salve on her fingers. I couldn't tell if it was black, brown, or green because the light wasn't as good as it might have been. She smeared the goop on my arm and started spreading it with her fingers. Her touch was light and sensuous. I began to think thoughts, which only minutes ago, I would have sworn I would never think again.

My arm was covered from my shoulder to the tips of my fingers. She did the other arm in the same fashion. Even at close range my arms seemed to disappear in the dim light. Next, she started at my hairline and covered my face and neck. The pattern on my face was more striped, leaving my eyes and mouth uncovered. Her hands blended the goop, so it was hard to tell where it was and where it wasn't. The result was amazing. I felt I could disappear given a distance of a few feet and dim light. She stepped back to survey her work and, with a look of satisfaction, went to the pack where she wrapped the ammunition and the extra magazines in soft cloth and packed them tightly in the bottom. On top of the wrapped ammunition she placed a flashlight that had already had its handle wrapped in dark cloth. Again, she stepped back and surveyed her handy work.

"The flashlight has fresh batteries. You may not need it as the moon is almost full. Take care of yourself. I want to serve you breakfast in the morning. You have twenty minutes to collect your thoughts. Some of the men pray. Don't be late." She turned and left.

Twenty minutes. Just the sound of it seemed an eternity. I was not accustomed to the planned mission. Most of my, shall we say, dangerous encounters have been spur of the moment affairs. There had never been time to contemplate. I decided to finish dressing and wait in the main room for the others to arrive. I strapped the knife and gun belt on, then checked that there was nothing shiny that would cause detection. The belt felt good. It was soft yet firm enough to support the weight of the weapons. I swung the pack over one shoulder. It landed soft and silent. There wasn't a rattle. I realized I was ready. I made my way to the main room. To my amazement, the entire group was there. The mission was about to begin.

CHAPTER THIRTY-THREE

Ben arranged for one of the ranch vehicles with a large flatbed to transport us to the edge of the ridge. It was parked in front of the ranch house ready for us to board. As soon as I appeared the group was complete. Ben gave the order to start the journey. We all loaded on the truck. I really don't know who was driving, but both Ben and Gale were on the rear bed with the rest of us. We approached the ridge and parked the truck. Ben announced we were in the silent mode, and any communication must be by whispers and hand signals.

Each of us exited the truck and made last minute adjustments to our gear. I had one pack strap that was a bit tight and adjusted it. As I completed the adjustment and put on the pack, the group began to move out. Miguel was in the lead. Ben was bringing up the rear. The entire group had gone silent and was moving up the ridge at a strong pace, but not so strong as to cause anyone problems keeping up. We reached the top of the ridge at about the same location as I had yesterday. The guard was awake and alert. He waived at us, silently wishing us a safe trip by making the sign of the cross. As we began the downward trek to the jungle below, I noted the moon was almost full, as promised. There weren't any clouds in the sky. The light was soft but bright enough to create shadows. This would make it easier to get to the top of the cliff but harder to surprise the soldiers once we got there. I decided to take one step at a time and enjoy the benefits of the moonlight on the trip in. As we reached the bottom of the ridge and were approaching an imposing wall of jungle, Miguel stopped and whispered in the ear of one of the men Manual had brought. The message was passed back by whisper. Miguel was going ahead to locate the trail leading to the cliff area. We were to take a short rest stop. Each of us found a place to sit. While waiting for Miguel to return, I noticed the group virtually disappeared into the night as soon as they got out of the direct moonlight. The dark camouflage and the grease paint were very effective.

In approximately six or seven minutes he returned, and the group proceeded to follow him into the jungle. Within two hundred meters we came upon a small trail. It was more of a game trail than a trail used by poachers. As the entire group reached the trail, Miguel stopped for the second time. He again whispered in the ear of the man behind him and a message was passed back to the effect that one should not lose sight of the man in front of him as the trail took several forks. With that caution the group started on the trail. Miguel was setting a quick pace but one that was comfortable. It wasn't long before I got my second wind and felt as though I could travel at this pace all night.

The man ahead of me, rather the woman, Gale, was difficult to see at all times. Her camouflage was a bit darker in color than what the rest of us had and seemed to blend into the night more effectively. This was information I wanted to store for use at a later time. The moon was also not effective on the jungle floor. It was impossible to see in many areas. In spite of this, Miguel seemed to know the area well enough to proceed down the path without hesitation. We all followed like sheep. The soft cloth in each of our packs was working well. With the exception of a snapped twig from time to time, or the sound of bushes being pushed aside, there weren't any sounds.

It took us about three hours to reach the vicinity of the warehouse. I, of course, was just following Gale and making every attempt not to lose sight of her. We entered a small clearing in the jungle, at which point Miguel stopped. He turned facing the group, which had come to a stop behind him. Ben worked his way through us to the front joining Miguel. They conferred by whispers. A few minutes later Ben worked his way back to us and with hand signals indicated we should move in tight. We complied immediately, forming a group not unlike a football huddle with Ben in the center.

Ben began in a whisper so low it was hard to get every word even as close as we were. "Miguel says we're about seven hundred and fifty to one thousand meters from the edge of the cliff above the warehouse. We will be traveling slower now, and each of you make every effort to be as silent as possible. We don't expect guards on the top of the cliff but be ready and be careful. We will proceed to within fifty meters of the cliff and set our staging area. Gale and I will proceed to the cliff edge to become more familiar with where each of our groups will be going. We'll be back in short order. It's ten-thirty and I want Gale's team to be underway no later than eleven," The huddle broke and Ben and Gale disappeared into the darkness. The rest of us found a place to sit, remaining behind in complete silence.

Within twenty minutes Ben and Gale reappeared. Their approach was totally silent. I realized they were back only because they suddenly were visible in the group. Gale signaled to Miguel and myself to follow her. Both of us complied immediately. She led us down the trail to a point where the trail seemed to fork in several directions at once. She stopped and signaled us to come close. "The cliff is about thirty meters from here. Ben and I have chosen a location at the back of the warehouse where we can utilize the ladder. I'll show you where it will be so there will be no confusion in the retreat. We will then go to the right, maintaining a safe distance from the cliff edge, until we locate the barricade. Once we have located the barricade, we will drop back from the cliff and determine our assault plans. Until then it's total silence." Without asking if we had any questions, Gale turned and started down one of the forks in the trail. Each of us followed.

My alertness seemed to increase exponentially. I would swear my vision even improved. We reached the top of the cliff, taking cover behind some outcrops standing a bit higher than the surrounding area. Below was the roof of a large building. The distance to the ground was less than I had expected -- only about twenty meters. The warehouse was truly backed up against the cliff wall. There was only a meter to a meter and a half distance between the building and the cliff in most places. I wondered to myself if Manual's group could get the packs with the explosives down such a narrow area without lowering them separately. Before I could answer my own question, Gale pointed to a guard on the ground below. He was not interested in the rear of the warehouse at all, concentrating his efforts on the road leading to the front of the building. Behind him I could make out one, possibly two guards that were further up the road leading to the warehouse.

I estimated there were about twenty or thirty meters of jungle between the road and the cliff at the point where the warehouse entrance was located. The road seemed to lead away from the cliff at an angle of seventy to eighty degrees, which given a kilometer, would place the lodge approximately seven hundred meters from the cliff,   facts I stored in memory for later use.

Gale gave all of us time to absorb the lay of the land around the warehouse. She ultimately retreated from the cliff edge, a distance of about thirty meters, and began a silent trek parallel to the cliff edge and to the right of the warehouse. Miguel and I followed. As we worked our way through the jungle, all I could hear was my own breathing. I attempted to make it as silent as possible. At one point, after we had traveled several hundred meters, Gale veered toward the cliff. I was surprised to find the ledge was only about fifteen meters to our left. As we approached the precipice she motioned we should stop as she proceeded forward. At the cliff edge she hesitated, dropping to the ground. Instinctively Miguel and I followed suit. After what seemed several minutes she backed from the ledge, still on the ground. She was utilizing only her knees and elbows as she bellied her way back to us. With a series of hand signals, she conveyed the fact the barricade was directly under our position. It was obvious we should either back track and find a way down, or go further down the cliff and approach from the road area outside the barricade. I was about to signal that my preference was to go back. The Cartel guards would not be as vigilant to intruders from that direction. Before I was able to get her attention, Gale retreated slightly and proceeded back toward where we had come. She must have been thinking the same way I was.

We retreated approximately fifty meters and reentered the cliff area. As we approached the cliff, Gale went through the same ritual as before. This time she did not fall to the ground. In less than a minute she motioned us to the cliffs edge. Miguel and I joined her to discover we had arrived at a place not more than ten meters from a chimney going all the way to the base of the cliff. If we could reach the chimney, a silent access to the base of the cliff would be easy. The only difficulty was a vertical face of about twelve meters that we would have to negotiate to reach the chimney. The rope Miguel had in his pack would be adequate for the purpose.

We worked ourselves back up the cliff top to the top of the chimney. I was the last to arrive. Miguel had already removed the rope from his pack and was rearranging its remaining contents to insure a silent descent. I noticed a small but substantial tree very near the edge. The rope could be run around the base and still have enough length for us to reach the chimney. I carefully worked my way to the tree, and in the most silent way I could, tested its strength. It seemed adequate. As I turned Gale handed me the rope. I took the rope and, making sure I had a good hold on the end, fed the rope over the edge. When I was sure it had reached the chimney, I ran the rope around the base of the tree and threw the other end down to the chimney below. I pulled on the ropes as a final test and began lowering myself over the edge. In a matter of seconds I was at the top of the chimney.

Miguel followed and Gale brought up the rear. As gale landed, Miguel pulled one of the ropes, causing the rope to slide around the tree, eventually falling to the top of the chimney. When the rope was safely stored in Miguel's pack, we started our descent. The chimney was so steep it approached vertical but had enough rock outcroppings to provide more than enough foot and hand holds. We progressed down the cliff, one person at a time. At one point I lost my footing when a rock I was standing on shifted. It was momentary but a small amount of gravel cascaded down the chimney. The noise was minimal, but to us it sounded like a marching band. We froze. After about a minute, Gale continued moving down. Miguel and I followed. I was more careful where I stepped during the rest of the descent.

We reached the base of the cliff without further difficulty. I took my watch out of my pocket. I had put it there as we left the vehicle back at the ranch. It had a dark leather band, but I was afraid that the crystal would reflect light. It was eleven - fifty. We had ten minutes to get in place. Gale was working her way to the rear of the shack. As we approached we could hear the guards talking in Spanish. While I could not understand the Spanish, I was relieved to note there seemed to be no urgency in their tone.

The three of us approached the shack on our hands and knees. As we got closer we were on our bellies, inching forward, moving only when one of the guards was speaking. Gale was in point, then Miguel, and I brought up the rear. As we got closer I realized we hadn't discussed whether to take out the two guards now and then wait to get their replacements or to take them all out at once. My preference was two and then two, but our leader hadn't given any orders. I was angry that we had not been briefed. If I was to work with a team, I should know what the team was going to do -- and when. As I was enjoying my full-blown indignation, Gale reached the back of the shed.

The soldiers were babbling about something or another, making enough noise to cover our entry had we walked to the shed with no regard for the silent approach. Gale held her hand up indicating we should stop moving. Both of us obeyed immediately. I watched as she slowly worked her way around the shed until she was standing on the side furthermost from the road. At some point, she had taken her knife out of its sheath. I didn't see when she did it, but now she was holding it in her right hand. The blade had to be a full twenty-four or twenty- five centimeters long. I could tell by the way she moved with the knife in her hand, she knew how to use it.

Gale turned slowly and signaled me to go the other side of the shack. I followed her footsteps to the back and then eased my way around the corner until I was on the side of the shack where the road provided a gravelly cushion to my footsteps. The distance to the front corner was only about three meters and I traveled it easily. I got on my knees and slowly peered around the corner. The two guards were sitting in old, dilapidated wooden chairs. They were facing the road approaching the shack and were not paying much attention to anything. The guard on Gale's side of the shack looked at his watch and said something to the guard nearest me. He nodded and the conversation ceased. They simply sat there looking at the dark road in front of them.

What in the hell were we waiting for and where was Miguel? I recalled the admonition Ben had given me about not acting on my own. Were we going to sit in the shadows until the replacement guards came? If so, I was not in a position that would promote my good health and longevity! They could see me as soon the lights from the vehicle illuminated the area. As I made my way around the shack, I drew the knife Ben had provided me. It felt comfortable in my hand. I felt as secure with it as I would have holding my nine- millimeter.

As I peered around the shack wondering how I was to know when to attack, I heard a noise coming from the road in front of the shack. I froze. If it was a third guard or a soldier returning from an errand, I was a perfect target. I was about to get my pistol out when a voice came out of the darkness up the road. It was Miguel's! He was singing. Within seconds the guards were scrambling to reach their rifles. Seconds later Miguel appeared. He was staggering all over the road. The two guards, with their rifles raised, began to approach him.

It was crystal clear to me what the plan was and it was time to act. I rose to my feet quickly and as quietly as I could. I covered the ground between the shed and the guard who was closest to me. He had no idea of my presence. I threw my left arm around his head, pulled back, and with my right hand I slit his throat. Any resistance to the blade as it began cutting was immediately lubricated by blood. It was like cutting warm butter. The man immediately went limp and fell to the ground. I released his head and swung around to take out the second guard. My concern was unnecessary. Gale had virtually severed his head from his body. He was slumping into a pool of dark liquid that already covered the immediate roadway. Both men died without making any sounds other than a muffled gurgling of air escaping from their lungs through a severed esophagus.

We only had a few minutes to get the bodies off the roadway and prepare for the replacements. The tree line was only about ten or fifteen meters from the shack. It provided a perfect place for the departed. Both bodies were safely hidden in the underbrush within seconds. The guard I had killed was short but stocky. His uniform coat didn't fit me well, but it fit well enough for the next few minutes. I stripped it from him and was beginning to put it on when I realized the entire front of the coat was soaked in blood. I must have hesitated.

"Let's not get squeamish now. Just put on the coat and get ready for the next shift," Gale said, as she put on the coat previously worn by her victim. Her borrowed coat was in the same shape as mine if not a bit more blood soaked.

"It's not that I'm squeamish, I just hate the sticky feeling," I replied as I completed putting the coat on.

As Gale and I were returning to the shack, Miguel was brushing away the telltale marks we made dragging the guards to the edge of the forest.

"Isn't that an exercise in futility?" I asked Miguel as we walked up.

"Not unless you're sure we can take out the replacements before they notice the marks," Miguel responded. Without waiting for me to respond, he turned to Gale.

"How do you want to approach the next two?" he asked.

"I think two of us should take the chairs in the front of the shack. The third will be stationed in the shadows at the side and behind the shack. It's late, so we can act as though we are dozing. Hopefully, they'll stop the vehicle along the side of the shack and get out there. If that's the case, whichever of us stationed behind the shack can take out the guard which last exits the vehicle. The remaining two will take out the other guard when he turns to see what's happening to his partner. If they park the vehicle in front, we'll just have to wing it. Either way, remember surprise is our most effective weapon. We have to be fast." As Gale finished outlining the plan, such as it was, the faint sound of a motor could be heard in the distance.

"Eric, you and I have the uniform on so we'll take the chairs. Miguel you better disappear into the shadows," Gale barked the orders like a well-seasoned drill sergeant. Before she was through speaking Miguel had disappeared. The chairs were only a few steps away and Gale and I hurried to them. I took the chair nearest the road, and she took the one next to the door of the shack. I took out my knife and put it between my legs with the sharp edge up. Gail settled in her chair with her knife in her left hand, and her arms folded across her chest. Her right arm hid the knife. She glanced over at me. "Good luck," she said, a slight smile appearing on her lips.

The sound of the motor was close now, so close I could tell one of its cylinders was misfiring. The lights were visible in the tree line. Gale's head fell until her chin was against her chest and her arms at the same time. Her face was effectively hidden. I adjusted myself so I was angled away from the road, yet could still see the area in my peripheral vision. The vehicle arrived at the shack. The driver brought it to a stop in a position where it was half in front of the shack yet a part of it had not left the road. It couldn't have been in a worse position for us. I continued to feign sleep. There was no other movement so I assumed Gale was doing the same. I knew I had to act as though I had heard the vehicle stop and began to stir in a manor they would believe I was waking up. The driver was the first out of the vehicle, which turned out to be an old Ford truck. He said something in Spanish to his partner and walked directly up to me. I allowed him to get within a meter, and as he was starting to say something, brought my knife up from between my legs, striking for the center of his chest. The knife hit just below the breastbone and didn't stop until the hilt was solid against his chest. He let out a small yelp and that was his last sound.

I wasn't sure where the second guard was, but I knew I had to withdraw the knife and find out. I lunged back in an effort to free the blade. It didn't come free. Instinctively I released the handle, pushing the body to the ground with my free hand. As I did so I could see Gale was involved with the other guard. He seemed to be getting the better part of her. At the same time, out of the corner of my eye I saw a flash that proved to be Miguel. Before I could move in Gales direction I saw the blade in Miguel's hand and then it disappeared into the ribs of the guard. The guard's grip on Gale immediately relaxed as he fell to the ground. Gale said something in Spanish which, I'm sure, questioned the guard's heritage. She kicked the fallen guard in the head and turned to see if I was in any difficulty. The first part of our assignment was over. It had been successful.

CHAPTER THIRTY-FOUR

S cott Steel sat in his office, contemplating what he was going to do. He knew that whatever it was in the end, it had to prove to be right. Howard Baker wasn't the poster image of what the modern CIA wanted of its field leaders, but he had been around for a long time. His threat to take the Eric Butler matter to the director could not be ignored. The Company had spent in excess of three and one half million on this project. Without Eric, the project would be a total loss. If that was the only consideration the choice might be easy, but it wasn't. There was the question of Eric's orientation, his allegiance to the Company. If Eric had *gone south* his usefulness would be nil. Scott had the authority to put assets in motion that would stop Eric, but he had to be right.

Scott had been a section head less than a year. In that time he'd never had to make the decision facing him now. Was there a middle road he could take allowing him to deploy the assets at a later time, when the circumstances surrounding Eric were solid? Scott realized that whatever he did, he would be subject to criticism from his superiors if the choice turned out to wrong in the end. What he wouldn't have given for an historical view of this whole problem, but that was fantasy and he was faced with a real world decision. Something in Scott told him all the cards had not been played. Call it intuition, but it was there. Whatever the decision, he had to make it quickly and probably without all the information needed.

Eric had always been an enigma to Scott. Privately he had expressed doubts about Eric's abilities. Scott believed Eric was an arrogant, self-sufficient agent who had engineered himself, with the help of Howard Baker, into a premier assignment. One which, while clandestine, was highly visible within the closed doors of the Agency. Simply, he didn't like him but he had never distrusted him. He wasn't sure he distrusted him now, but now Eric's actions could have a direct and adverse effect on Scott's upward mobility within the agency. Without realizing it he was beginning to hate Eric.

Scott realized he needed to make a decision. If the decision was to do nothing at this time and see what developed that was fine, but if the decision was to mobilize the available assets, it should be started now. Once it began it would be irretrievable. Any change of plan would make him look worse if the result was not acceptable to the director of the agency. Something was happening in Colombia the effect of which would give him at least a day to two days lead-time before Eric would be back in touch. If he decided to mobilize, the lead-time would be invaluable. If he waited and then mobilized, the director might wonder why. He could appear to have wavered in making a critical decision.

As Scott contemplated his options, it became clear the only decision to be made was to mobilize the available assets and hunt Eric down. In cases such as this, the standard order was to find and apprehend the suspect agent with every effort being made to bring him back alive. If that wasn't possible, then he was to be eliminated and left where he fell. Scott secretly hoped Eric would not give the agents any choice. He would be left where he fell. Then he could blame the failure of the project on the leadership of Howard Baker. After all Howard was the field supervisor. He was supposed to monitor Eric Butler. He, not Scott, was the person who should have seen the signs the agent was getting out of control and brought him in. Scott, after all, was doing the only thing he could do, given the facts. The Director would surely see the wisdom of this choice even if it proved wrong.

Having reached a decision, Scott felt better. Now it was time to determine how it was to be accomplished and most importantly, who would he send. The intelligence he had indicated Eric was last known to be in Bogotá. It was there Sadie Anderson was killed. Howard had said Eric was on some sort of mission that would frustrate the efforts of the Barajas cartel. It was Howard's effort to justify the lack of communication between Eric and the Company which supported Scott's conclusion that Howard had lost control.

If Eric was on a mission to frustrate the Barajas cartel, and he began in Bogotá - where would he go? The established intelligence indicated that the fields of raw product Barajas controlled were spread out all over Colombia but were   concentrated in mountains south of Bogotá. Scott reasoned there wasn't much that could be done with the raw product, which would affect the ability of the cartel to complete a current delivery. The efforts must be directed toward either the production centers or some point of distribution. Scott was not aware of any intelligence locating the cartel's centers for production. Scott knew he must ascertain where the major points of distribution were located, or to be located.

He needed Eric's case files. They were classified, only open to those with a need to know. He was the section chief and would have no problem getting access to them. Scott left his office, went down the hall to the central records department. He swiped his I.D. card, waited for the metallic click signaling the door had been electronically unlocked, and entered the room.

The main counter was located at the front of the room. An elderly woman he had known for fifteen years manned it.

"Good day, Ellen. How's everything in your world?" Scott asked.

"If I told you I'd have to kill you," Ellen responded in a playful manner. "We haven't seen you for a while. What brings you to the stacks?"

"I need to see a file on one of the projects in my section. It's the Barajas project. I believe its code named Intrusion. Could you get it for me? I'll wait in Inspection Room five if it's available," Scott said as he headed toward a series of small offices with single digit numbers above the doors.

"I'll locate it and have it for you directly," Ellen responded.

Scott let himself into the small office with the number five above the door. It hadn't changed since the last time he was in central records. The desk was a stark wooden relic that was a holdover from the McCarthy days of the fifties. A vintage nineties chair, designed to be good for the user's posture, had replaced the original. The contrast in furnishings was astounding. There were no telephones or electrical receptacles in the room. Scott knew somewhere there were sensors, which would detect any battery operated recording device. The only electrical device evident to anyone using the room was a small black button in a brass fitting secured to the top left rear corner of the desk. Once in the room, use of the button was the only way to get out. It was against the rules to have a pad and pencil in the area. The room was meant for viewing a file, nothing more.

After a minute or two Ellen brought two files to the room. The first was in a large brown expanding folder. The second was a smaller one of the same type. Both were tied together with a brown cloth string which circled the entire file holding the top flaps closed. The larger file was labeled Intrusion and had a designation code that translated to "need to know only."

"Thank you, Ellen. I won't be more than half hour," Scott said, smiling at the longtime employee.

"Take whatever time you need, Mr. Steel. When you're through just buzz me. You know the drill." Ellen put the files on the desk, smiled back at Scott, and left the room, closing the door behind her. Scott heard her place the *occupied* sign on the door and secure the door so anyone inside would have to have her, or someone at the front desk, release it before leaving. Scott had often wondered what would happen if a fire broke out in the building or even in the room. Anyone using the viewing offices would be trapped inside unless the personnel at the front were thinking clearly enough to release the security, allowing anyone viewing files to escape. In prior visits he had been concerned about that eventuality and had even written a memo about his concerns.

Scott never heard whether the memo reached someone high enough in authority to make a change. He never got a response. He felt slighted by the seeming lack of concern for the problem, and for the disrespect the Company showed him by not responding. In an attempt to shield his ego, Scott rationalized that some minor clerk he had slighted had disposed of the memo and his superiors never saw, or were able to consider it. Today, however, he was not concerned with the politics of the Agency. He had concerns that overshadowed any bruised ego he'd suffered in the past.

Scott opened the larger file and spread it on the desk in front of him. The file contained evidence of how money, previously authorized, had been expended and contained authorization allowing field level approval for requests up to thirty million dollars without any further scrutiny. There were notes transcribed from reports phoned in by Howard Baker and minutes of higher level conferences, involving himself and deputy directors, concerning the progress of the project.

Scott continued to review the contents of the larger folder. From the notes and memos it was clear the plan was to trap the Cartel in drug transactions set up to utilize distribution points in smaller non-industrial Mideastern nations where the local authorities would be less vigilant, regarding shipments into their countries. There were banking arrangements in place in several of the target countries, utilizing banks the United States, through its various agencies controlled. One of the last reports filed by Howard indicated the contract phases of the project had been achieved and the Mideastern phase was about to begin. The final report in the file concerned the death of Sadie Anderson. Several million dollars of U.S. currency had been quietly transferred to the chosen banks with authority to honor any request made by Eric Butler or Sadie Anderson.

The question which kept occurring to Scott was, to what extent the death of Sadie Anderson had altered Eric's plans. Current evidence indicated Eric was now operating on his own. There was no evidence, however, that the agent was not still pursuing the objective. He may now, though, have different motivations. If Eric was of the opinion Sadie was killed by the Cartel, the motive might be revenge. If revenge was now a motivation, the original objective may well be in serious jeopardy. The Agency might not achieve its goals and will have wasted enormous sums of money. Scott smiled. He had just formulated the justification he needed for his intended actions.

Given what Scott learned from the file, where would Eric be if he truly intended to interfere with the Cartels ability to deliver the product? If the product were to be delivered in the Mideast, it would have to be shipped to the delivery point. How would the Cartel ship that much product? Air was a possibility, but with the global surveillance enjoyed by most civilized countries afforded by the satellite system, shipping by air would not stand a chance of going unnoticed. The only way that made sense was to ship by ocean going vessels. If those assumptions were accurate, Eric would be somewhere in northern Colombia.

Scott reviewed the balance of the larger file and carefully replaced the documents back in the folder. After securing the file with its cloth string, he glanced at the second file. The last time he reviewed the project, it had not been there. He opened the file and took out its contents. Most, if not all, of the documents concerned resistance checks on the phone system in Howard Bakers home office. Without studying the readings, Scott went directly to the memo, which summarized them. The gist of the memo was there appeared to be a slight loss of signal power occurring in both the reception and transmission circuits servicing Howard's phone. The memo indicated the loss was not necessarily significant, given the length of time the unit had been in service. It recommended the technical arm of the Agency run a diagnostic check of the system when convenient. It wasn't given a priority status. It was dated over nine months earlier and had not been acted upon.

Scott had seen many of these reports in his years with the Company, and each time the problem ultimately turned out to be moisture in a relay or line or some other small insignificant problem. He closed the folder, secured it, and pushed the button to be let out of the room.

Ellen appeared at the door with the electronic key. There was a metallic click and the door fell open. "Here's the file and, no, I didn't make any notes nor did I take any pictures," Scott said as he exited the small viewing office.

"I know you didn't but you know the drill. I still have to pat you down and see what's in your pockets," Ellen replied.

"Yes, I know but you do know what the current rumor is, don't you?" Scott said as a smirk appeared on his face.

"No, I don't, but I'm guessing it's a whopper and you're going to tell me." Ellen was just starting to pat Scott down.

"I wasn't going to mention it, but the rumor is that you ladies have been taking no less than a half hour to pat down the younger, good- looking agents and are letting us old fogies just about pass through. Is there any truth to that, Ellen?" Scott said with a slight throaty laugh.

"It may be true," she retorted, "but the only reason you seniors don't get the same treatment is that you bruise too easily. Now get back to your office and try to do something other than spreading rumors for a change."

Scott left the records room with a feeling of relief and with the adrenaline rush that comes with discovering that you have something urgent to accomplish. He had determined Eric's most probable location. Now, he needed to choose a team to insert in the area and either extract or eliminate the problem. His mind was already racing over the choices he knew were available. Somehow, he had already decided that three was the optimum number of operatives to send but who was to be the leader. A few of the more recent gung-ho recruits came to mind, but with Eric's experience, that choice would be foolhardy. He needed to find someone with experience comparable to Eric's and who would follow orders without question.

There was one man he knew who might fit the bill. His name was John Sailor. He had been recruited by the Agency before the wimps in Congress determined the CIA among other agencies, could not recruit individuals with unsavory backgrounds. John was a mercenary at the time he was approached and had fallen in disfavor with most governments. It seemed, regardless of what kind of mission he was assigned, most of the objectives ended up dead.

The CIA had recruited him to lead their assassination team. His employment was not publicized, even back then. Only the section leaders who had covert responsibilities, the assistant director covering covert operations, and the director knew of his availability. Scott had learned of him in the mid-eighties, when one of the governments thought to be friendly to the interests of the United States was about to be taken over by local rebels rallying around one charismatic leader. It was the Agency's opinion that if that leader were to be eliminated, the friendly government would survive. John Sailor was placed in field operations led by Scott. John was inserted in the country. The leader turned up dead, in fact decapitated several days later. John was extracted but not before seventy percent of the rebels were eliminated. During the debriefing, Sailor stated he eliminated the rebels so there would be no replacement for their deceased leader. There were none. The CIA has kept the employment of Mr. Sailor classified ever since.

Scott had heard Sailor was in the states and was undercover somewhere in the Northeast. How could he find out John Sailor's availability? Scott didn't want his assistant director to know of his decision until it had been executed. That eliminated the possibility of going to him for help. Scott racked his brain for a way to reach Sailor. He didn't remember his code name, if he ever knew it. He seemed to be at a dead end when he remembered that Sailor had become fond of one of the female agents, also of questionable reputation. Her name was Sally Bennett. She was a field agent currently within the groups supervised by Scott. Her immediate contact was Howard Baker. He would have to contact Howard but could he do it without tipping his hand?

Scott was not in the habit of contacting Howard Baker without some reason related to an ongoing program. He didn't like the way Howard Baker treated him, like the new kid on the block; like someone who had to be instructed on the correct way to accomplish something or how to approach a problem. Scott knew Howard blamed his in-service injury for not being promoted to the position Scott was currently filling. He also knew Howard had the ear of the director. Howard could get things done no one else in the Agency could. He would have to be careful or this matter could be pulled from him with a phone call.

Scott picked up the phone and dialed the number of the phone installed in Howard's home office. The phone rang several times. Scott knew it often took Howard several rings to get to the office so he let it ring. Howard picked it up on the sixth or seventh ring.

"Howard Baker," the voice on the other end finally blurted.

"Howard, Scott here. I have been asked to locate one of your charges, a Sally Bennett. It seems one of the other departments has a need for her talents if you know what I mean," Scott hesitated waiting for a response.

"She's currently working on a project involving the importation of illegal immigrants, mostly female, being sold in the white slave market. She's currently in Texas, I think in the Fort Bliss area. Is it critical we pull her now?" Howard responded in his usual business-like manner.

"I'm not sure, but I was asked to contact her to ascertain whether or not she would be interested in a change, of sorts. Would you give me her contact phone number and any code word the two of you have established?" Scott asked. "I'll give her a call and explain what I know of the assignment. If she's interested I'll get back to you, and we can work out the best way to remove her and provide a substitute. How does that sound?" Scott asked.

"If that's an order it has to work. Her cell number is (713) 555-1212. She will answer to the name of Janna. The code is to introduce yourself as Jim Dunn. If she can't talk right then, she'll take your number and call back at her first opportunity. Be sure to give her your cell so it doesn't go through the Agency switchboard. Let me know the outcome as soon as you can."

"Will do. By the way, you haven't heard anything further from Eric have you?" Scott asked, knowing the answer would be no, but felt the question had to be asked to avoid raising any suspicions.

"No, and I told you that you'll be the first to know, so just relax!" Howard retorted.

"I'm relaxed. You just make sure you do just that. I'll contact you when I have spoken to Sally Bennett," Scott said, smiling to himself as he hung up. As soon as he hung up Scott dialed the cell number Howard had given him. It rang about three times.

"Hello, this is Janna," the voice on the other end said.

"Janna, this is Jim Dunn." Scott waited for the code to register. "Can you talk now or should I give you a number where you can reach me later?" There was hesitation on the other end to the telephone.

"I have a moment. Who did you say you were?" Sally asked.

"I said I was Jim Dunn," Scott replied.

"Okay, go on." The voice on the other end of the phone was hesitant.

"I got your number from Howard. I'm his supervisor. My name is Scott Steel and I need your help." Scott paused.

"Go on," Sally said, being very cautious.

"I have to locate John Sailor, and I don't have time to go through normal channels. Can you help me with an address or telephone number?" Scott asked.

"I could if I was sure you are who you say you are," Sally replied. Scott was not in any mood to play the games Sally was beginning to initiate. He could not go through a mutually known third party because that third party would have been Howard and it would tip him off as to the real reason for the need to contact Sally.

"Look, Sally, I've given you the passwords. Your boss is Howard Baker. He gave me your cell number. What more proof do you need for Christ's sake? I'm in a hurry, and if you want to continue with the liberal expense account and the freedom to do what you do best at a very good wage you had better trust me and give me the information I need." Scott had played his hole card relying on Sally's insecurity and greed.

"Okay, but you can't blame me for being cautious. I know of you but I've never met you." Sally was responding as Scott had hoped. "John is in Boston. He can be reached within twenty four hours by placing an advertisement in the Boston Harold want ads seeking to purchase a nineteen twenty vintage Ford Model T. No name, just leave a phone number. The number will be in code. All numerals of your area code and the first numeral of your phone number will remain the same. Add one to each of the remaining numbers for example if you have a zero in your phone number, it will become a one, one will become two, and so on all the way to nine which will become zero. John will call you within four hours of the time the newspaper hits the streets. He'll only try once so stay close to the phone." Sally stopped talking.

"Thank you Sally. I apologize if I sounded harsh. It's just I'm really under the gun. By the way, this conversation is just between us. I told Howard I needed to contact you to offer you a different assignment. I'll tell him you turned it down, preferring to stay with him. That should help you when he does your next review. Do we understand each other? Scott hesitated just long enough for Sally to acknowledge her instructions and he hung up the phone. He'd call Howard later. He needed to place an ad now.

CHAPTER THIRTY-FIVE

The two replacement guards lay where they fell. There wasn't reason to secret their bodies. Gale motioned Miguel and myself to the shack. When we got there she instructed us to check our gear, make sure that all the equipment was there, and we knew exactly where it was. Miguel opened his pack and retrieved the wires with the small handles. He distributed one each to Gale and to me. Gail took hers and put it around her neck so that the small wooden handles fell on her chest. I noticed Miguel had done the same. I couldn't think of a better way to carry the weapon, so arranged it in the same way.

Miguel went immediately to the truck and started the engine. Gale climbed into the back of the truck and laid down. I got in on the passenger side. As the truck started to move forward, Miguel looked at me.

"Good job," he said without any expression on his face. "I know you've had reservations about me because of my family. Hopefully, any doubts you had have disappeared."

"It is and thank you," I responded. "How are we going to proceed from here?" The back window glass was gone so the question was directed more to Gale than to Miguel.

"I haven't been here so, Miguel, you tell us what you think is the best approach," Gale responded, leaning through the rear opening.

"This road leads directly to the front of the main lodge. The dock area is behind the lodge, and the remaining sleeping facilities are behind and to the left. It's my opinion that we should drop you off, Gale, just before we get to the lodge. You work your way around to the general sleeping quarters. They will undoubtedly have guards in the area so be careful. I will drive to the front of the lodge with Eric. I expect most of the guards will be stationed in that area. I will be able to run interference for Eric because I speak the language. Between the two of us we should be able to handle what we encounter. Eric will enter the main lodge and locate the money.

Eric, it is critical that you take out as many in the lodge as you can. Ben has indicated he would like what few survivors remain to be left without any leadership. As soon as Eric is in the lodge, and what guards remain around the main lodge have been taken care of, I'll work my way toward the sleeping quarters and give Gale a hand. Gale and I will work our way to the warehouse and up the cliff. Eric, as soon as you've accomplished your objectives, head for the base of the cliff, work your way to the warehouse, and up the ladder. Hopefully, this will all come together before the warehouse is blown.

I pulled my watch out of my pocket, checking the time. We had no more than twenty minutes to accomplish our objectives and get to the cliff. As I put the watch back in my pocket the old Ford was entering the cleared area where the lodge was located. The Cartel must not have thought an attack on the area was possible because there was no extra lighting. The guards on duty were anything but vigilant. I tried to count the guards. I reached the number six when Miguel slowed the Ford.

There are eight, I think. Four of them are together at the left corner of the lodge. I will drive directly up to them leaving the lights on. Use your best judgment from there," Miguel stated in a hushed tone.

I glanced back through the broken window of the old pickup. Gale was not to be seen. As I turned back to the front I noted that Miguel's knife was sitting on his lap. I also took my knife out of its scabbard, setting it on the seat beside me. As promised, Miguel drove to within two or three meters of the guards. It appeared they were smoking and conversing. There didn't seem to be any alarm. As Miguel brought the truck to a halt, he said something in Spanish to the group. It was almost a whisper but just loud enough to be heard by the guards. The lights of the truck were obviously blinding the men. They were holding their hands up to their eyes in an effort to block the glare.

One of the men grumbled something and started toward the pickup. He came directly to the driver's side window. I noticed he'd left his weapon leaning against the lodge. As he got to the window and began to lean in, Miguel's right hand shot up and through the window. At the same time, he pulled the man's head inside the cab. The poor man never knew what happened to him. His body just went limp. As Miguel was pulling the blade from the man's throat, he was talking to the others as they started toward the truck. There still was no alarm as the men had also left their weapons leaning against the lodge. There were three of them left. Miguel and Gale would have to deal with them.

I opened the pickup door, easing my way out. While they were approaching Miguel, I slipped into the shadows created by the pickup and some bushes that were lining the front of the lodge. I'm sure they were intended to be decorative and probably were, but for now they provided some cover. There were two guards by the door. The count was now six. I hoped that Miguel's count was wrong and didn't include two more, at least not at this location. My only hope was to take out the closest guard before the other was aware of my presence, and then get him before he could alert the occupants of the lodge. A second knife would have been handy but the wire would have to do. I hadn't heard a sound from the direction of the pickup so Miguel and Gale must have been successful.

I worked my way to the edge of the porch. The guards were sitting on the steps leading to the main door. They were no more than two meters from me. The only way to get them both, silently, was to come from behind. That meant I had to somehow slither to the top of the landing and get to them without them noticing me. The bushes would provide cover until I was on top. Assuming they didn't look around or hear something, I could cross the two meters of porch and take out two men before either one of them could make a sound.

The top landing was about one and a half meters high. It was just high enough to allow me to rest my belly and one leg on the top. As soon as I had achieved getting most of my weight on the landing I moved the second leg. The guards were talking in low tones and were not the least bit interested in what might be behind them. My knife was in my hand -- the wire was around my neck. Before making any move toward the guards, I made sure the wire hadn't tangled in my clothing. It hadn't. I rose to one knee, then the other. The guards were still talking quietly, appearing unconcerned. Their rifles were lying on the landing near where I was kneeling. They must have been sitting on the bottom or next to the bottom stair. I could only see them from the shoulders up. My hope was I could knife the closest guard, roll to my left, while at the same time freeing the wire from around my neck, and garrote the second guard before he had time to react. Success depended on split second timing and inattentive guards.

I crawled toward the front edge of the landing. God I hoped none of these boards were loose or creaky. I was about there when the guard furthermost from me began to turn. It was now or never. I lunged toward the closest guard. He must have heard something because he started to stand. I brought the butt of the knife down with all my weight on the top of his head. I heard bone give way and felt the butt sink into his skull. I didn't know if he was alive but he wasn't going to make noise. As the butt hit his head, I began to roll to the left and as I did I brought the knife up hard into the neck of the other guard. He gasped, began waving his arms, and then collapsed, falling to the ground at the base of the steps. As he fell, I withdrew the blade and spun to finish the first man. It was instantly obvious that any further concern was unnecessary.

Time was running short and I needed to get into the lodge. The door was open with only a screen door keeping out the unwanted flies. I unconsciously wiped the blade on my pants and slipped through the door. The main room consisted of several couches and chairs. There was a large fireplace at one end of the room and a card table near the fireplace. I quickly looked behind the couches and chairs and found nothing. Other than a few empty beer cans and a deck of playing cards spread on the card table, the room had no other items indicating anyone had been there. Was this going to be an exercise in futility? Had Ben encouraged me to join knowing there was no booty? I dismissed the latter -- more because I wanted to than on any logic. I was in this now and any hope of getting out would depend on completing my duties. I would deal with the dilemma later.

The lodge was one story so all the sleeping quarters were on the same floor. I noted a hallway in the rear of the room and a second doorway on the right side of the room. I decided to check the door on the right because if it contained sleeping areas. I wanted to take care of those first. Reaching the door, I opened it slowly. My eyes were adjusted to the dim light in the lodge so peering into the darkened area required little adjustment. It proved to be the kitchen and dining area. I immediately proceeded to the hallway in the rear of the main room.

The hall was semi-dark, lighted only by the light coming from the main room. I could see at least six, maybe seven, separate doors leading off the hall. I quickly went to the end of the hall so I could be sure of the number of doors, and also determine whether there were further rooms off side halls. The number was six and there were no other halls. I decided to start with the rooms closest to the main area. That way, I would not be cut off if discovered. I would have a clear way out. With my knife in one hand and the wire in the other, I slipped in the first room quietly closing the door behind me.

My eyes took just a second to adjust. I could see two beds with a man in each. Approaching the first bed, I tripped over a boot. It made a slight scraping noise as it slid a small distance across the floor. I know it wasn't loud, but it sounded like a freight train to me. The man in the furthermost bed mumbled and turned to his side facing me. The man in the closest bed was lying on his stomach. I quickly plunged the knife into the base of his neck and withdrew it, cutting as much of the front of the throat as possible. I must have made some noise because the other man began to wake. I quickly jerked his forehead back and slit his throat. As I was leaving, I looked for any evidence of a briefcase or anything that could carry large amounts of cash. There was nothing other than the men's clothes. They were spread all over the floor.

The next door stood a slight bit ajar so it was easy to determine there were no occupants, none at that time anyway. The next three proved to be the same. The fourth door had evidence someone was staying in the room. The occupants must have been on duty or away from the resort.

The last room was much different from the rest. As I opened the door, I noted it had thick carpet on the floors. Upon entering I was standing in a parlor, or waiting room, with the bedroom separated and located to the rear. As I looked around the entrance I noted a small table just to the right of an overstuffed chair. It had a smaller secretarial type chair in front of it. On the table was a bag, not unlike the old-fashioned doctor's valise one sees in old movies. I made my way to the table and opened the bag. In it was at least five hundred thousand American dollars. I had hit the bonanza. I quickly moved the bag to a nondescript chair near the entrance.

I moved to the rear of the room and peered in the bedroom. It also was different from the others as it had furniture, other than a bed. The bed was oversized. Two people were sleeping in it. I realized I was face to face with a situation I had not anticipated. The man had his wife, girlfriend, or whatever with him. I hadn't contemplated the need to execute a noncombatant, let alone a noncombatant woman. It occurred to me that Gale, a woman, was a combatant. Sadie was also. I shouldn't jump to the conclusion that this woman was a visitor and not a member of the Cartel. I felt the man would give me the most trouble so he had to go first, then the woman. I approached the bed and slit the man's throat. There must have been some noise, because before I could get the knife free the woman was lunging at me. I quickly stepped to the side and she glanced off my leg. I felt a searing pain in my thigh and saw the flash of a blade. She hit the floor at my feet and slightly behind me. Before she could gain her composure, I had the wire around her neck and jerked upward as hard as I could. The wire virtually severed her head from her body. I let her fall and stood there as though in a daze.

Time was of the essence and I wasn't moving. I made myself locate my knife and got out of the room. The bag with the money was where I had left it. In the planning stages of this foray, I thought I would put the money in my pack, and so I began to take the straps off and loosen the top flap. The amount of money, the sheer size of the money bundled as it was, would not fit in the pack. That was obvious as soon as the pack was opened. My only alternatives were to tie the valise to the top of the pack or hand carry the bag. The second alternative was out.

I would in all probability need both of my hands. What could I tie the bag to the pack with? My mind raced and then it came to me. A length of the cord from the drapes or curtains would do nicely. I ran to the nearest window, cut the cord and stripped it from the drape until I had about two meters. It worked fine. With the bag securely tied to my pack, I retreated down the hall and through the main room to the door. I surveyed the yard in front of the lodge. It was vacant. With the exception of the dead guards, there was no sign of humanity. The old Ford pickup was still there. Its lights were still on. The night was quiet.

I entered the front yard, as it was. My adrenaline was running full. All my senses seemed to be on edge. The jungle between the lodge and the cliff was about seventy meters away. I headed directly toward the nearest tree line. I wasn't running, but I wasn't walking either. I kept spinning around expecting to see guards pursuing me. There were none. In fact there was no one. I reached the tree line and plunged into the jungle. I must've picked the densest spot in the area because I could hardly go forward. Vines kept tangling with my feet, while at the same time the higher brush pushed against my chest and slapped me in the face. My thigh was beginning to burn like a hot poker had seared it. I had the feeling my leg was dragging a bit. I never thought about looking at my watch, but I knew the time must be close. I needed to reach the cliff before the explosion destroyed the warehouse. I wanted to follow the glow to the warehouse.

As I was thrashing forward the explosion occurred. The night sky, which was already bright, became much brighter. In fact the glow was so bright it tended to create vague shadows. I saw the cliff -- I was almost there. Another twenty or thirty meters and I could follow the cliff to the ladder, get up the cliff, and back to the ranch. Thankfully, the cliff hadn't eroded much in the millennium it had existed, because the travel at its base was much easier than expected. There were very few boulders and the jungle was much less dense. Before I had traveled one hundred meters I heard shots from the automatic weapon Ben had brought. There were also many rounds fired from smaller caliber weapons.

I was glad to hear the gunfire because it meant things had probably gone well with the others and I now could use my nine-millimeter. The knife had served me well, but my loyalty would always rest with a reliable service pistol or rifle. I drew my pistol and proceeded forward as fast as I could. Sixty meters from the front of what had been the warehouse, I saw something that made me freeze in my tracks. Gale was engaged in hand to hand combat with one of the solders and was losing the battle. I could not get a clear shot. It became imperative I do something so I screamed at the top of my lungs. The soldier looked up and in that split second Gale made a woman out of him. It was his turn to scream, at which point I put him out of his misery.

Gale was on her feet by the time he hit the ground. Her clothes were in disarray as was her demeanor.

"Thanks for helping," she said as she re-buttoned the camouflage shirt with what few buttons still remained.

"Glad I happened along. Let's go. The rest will be waiting," I replied attempting to get her moving.

"It didn't go well. There were many more soldiers around the warehouse than we had anticipated. I don't know if Miguel made it. He was attempting to deal with three guards when I last saw him. This bastard got hold of my pack as I tried to create some distance so I could deal with him. I let the pack go. It was the only chance I had. All my remaining ammo is in the pack and my weapons are empty," she said breathlessly.

"Do you know where it is now?" I asked.

"It couldn't be too far from here, but the jungle is so thick we'd have to trip over it to find it."

"Why don't we take a slight detour back to the cliff and see if it jumps out at us? It shouldn't take much time," I suggested.

Gale nodded and we started back. I let her lead because she had a better idea where she had been. We had gone about twenty meters when she pointed at an area in front of her that was trampled with the underbrush broken down. The jungle canopy above us blocked out the much needed light. I remembered I had a flashlight with me and took the pack off my back. The bag with the money fell to the side. With the straps loosened it was easy to see the cash inside, even in the dim light. I found the flashlight and handed it to Gale. As I was reaffixing the bag to the pack I noted that Gale's eyes were fixated on the cash.

"You did well didn't you?" she said with some irony in her voice.

"Yes, I was lucky. I found it in the last bedroom. Had there been a problem I would've had to leave it," I replied as I got the pack securely on my back. "Any luck finding your pack?"

"Not yet, but I know it must be here somewhere. Just a few more seconds and we'll start back."

The beam of the flashlight was playing on the underbrush around the area. With the pains that were taken to make sure we would blend into the night, there was almost no chance of finding the pack. Gale must have been thinking the same because she shut off the flashlight, stood erect and motioned we should head back to the cliff. With the light gone it took a moment for our eyes to readjust to the dimness. The base of the cliff proved to be just as easy to travel as it had earlier. It seemed like only a minute or two before we could see the glow of the burning warehouse through the jungle. I had taken the lead, mostly because I had the only weapon with ammunition. Gale was following behind but only by a pace or two.

As we edged along the base of the cliff, I heard something that made me stop in my tracks. It was the sound of a human moaning and it wasn't more than two meters away. I held up my hand and Gale stopped. I motioned her to wait as I eased my way toward the sound. It wasn't more than a step or two and I spotted a man lying on the jungle floor. I couldn't tell whether he was one of theirs or ours. He was on his side with his back to me. I slipped up and quickly turned him over. He let out a sharp yelp from the pain. It was a guard. The reason for his moaning was immediately evident. A piece of rough lumber had been driven into his stomach. By all appearances it had gone all the way through. I had no idea whether it had been placed there by one of us, or was simply the result of the blast. It didn't matter. He wasn't a threat to us. I stepped over him and back to where Gale was waiting.

"He's no threat. Let's go," I said as I started down the base of the cliff. Gail grabbed my arm, stopping me.

"He isn't dead. You remember the instructions. There are to be no survivors. Now get back there and finish the job!" Even though light was virtually nonexistent and I couldn't make out any of her facial features, I could feel her eyes burning through me. It wasn't a job I had anticipated. I wasn't in the habit of killing men who weren't a threat to me, my mission, or someone near me. I started to object, at which point Gale turned around and started toward the guard.

"For Christ's sake, if you can't follow orders then I'll do it myself," she said as she put the poor bastard out of his misery. From where I stood I could see the dull sheen of her blade disappear into the chest of the guard. When she withdrew the blade the sheen was gone. The guard didn't make a sound. He was better off dead but I was glad she had done it. I could tell, by her body language, she was disgusted with my hesitation. At that time, I really didn't care how she felt. My singular goal was to get to the rope ladder and get to the top of the cliff and join the others.

We proceeded along the base of the cliff for some distance without incident. The glow from the warehouse made walking easier the closer we got. As we approached the warehouse, the jungle seemed less dense. At times I could see parts of the burning structure clearly. The cliff angled so sharply toward the warehouse that eventually we were close enough to burning embers that we could feel their heat. I glanced ahead and quickly came to a stop. Gale must have been looking somewhere else because she virtually ran up my back. She made a startled sound and immediately dropped to one knee. Ahead, next to the cliff base was the body of a man. Even in the dim light, we both realized it was one of ours.

The body was draped over an old stump which had been left years before, probably a remnant of the clearing necessary for construction of the warehouse. The man's back was to us. A small camouflaged pack rested on his shoulders. Gail regained her footing, and brushed me to one side in her haste to reach the corpse. As I approached, Gale was already turning the body. It was one of the men Manuel had chosen to help with the explosives. His body was riddled with bullets. I'm sure he died as he fell. Without any show of emotion or ceremony, Gale stripped the man of his pack. As she was adjusting the straps to her own back she looked at me.

"We better get to the ladder. The rest are waiting." Her voice had a quality and tone that made my blood go cold.

My cut leg was becoming more painful. I was also beginning to feel the effects of blood loss, so I also was anxious to make the awkward climb up the ladder. The back of the warehouse was only about five or six meters from where we found the body. We covered the ground in a matter of seconds. I hadn't realized the rear of the building was constructed as close to the cliff as it was. Traversing the rear to locate the ladder, we had to kick through some burning timbers. Glowing embers were everywhere. We hadn't gone two meters when I spotted the ladder, or at least what was left of it. The fire had burned the rope to the extent that what appeared to be the first solid rung was no less than three meters off the ground, just above my reach.

By this time my loss of blood, and resulting weakness were creeping into my thought processes. All I could visualize was a struggle to get up the rope ladder and a long walk back to the ranch. I wasn't sure I could make one of those tasks let alone both of them. The ladder seemed miles in the air. Before I could voice any concerns, Gale was scrambling through the pack she had lifted from our fallen comrade. I stood watching her, not having the mental ability to reconcile what it was she was looking for. For the second time in what seemed just a matter of minutes, she turned and looked at me with coldness and efficiency.

"If I remember correctly you were given a length of rope to carry. Find it and help me rig something so we can get to the ladder," she whispered.

"Why don't we just yell for someone to throw a rope down to us?" I inquired, while at the same time struggling to get the pack off my back.

"Because if we do, and there are still some guards out there alive, it will give away our position, and eliminate the only way we have of getting out of here. Now find the damn rope."

I complied without further comment. The satchel of money was cumbersome, and it took me what seemed like an eternity to get inside the pack. Once inside, the rope was easy to find. As I pulled it from the pack my heart fell. The rope was small in diameter. While strong enough to bear our weight, it wasn't meant for climbing upward where a solid grip on the rope is so necessary. The rope had been intended to aid us in a descent. Gale grabbed the rope, unraveling it in short order. It was about fifteen or twenty meters long. She began to tie loops in the rope about half meter apart. By the time she had created eight or ten of them she'd used up most of the rope.

"Can you bear my weight with that bad leg?" she asked, as she arranged the rope around her neck such that she had a short length on her right and the longer length on her left.

"I think I can." I replied not grasping what it was she was going to do.

"Good, lean up against the cliff and let me climb up your back. I'm going to get to the ladder and tie the rope to the bottom of it. I'll climb the rope and you follow using the loops for hand holds. Hopefully, you still have enough strength to pull yourself up the rope, one loop at a time, until you can use the rungs of the ladder. If you can't, I'll find the group, and we'll lower a second rope, which you can tie to you, and we'll help pull from above. Got it?"

I nodded and leaned against the cliff. Gale started to mount my back, using her knees and the small of my back as a starting place. She pulled herself up with her hands, which were on my shoulders. I felt her boots digging into my back, then on the top of my shoulders. She must have stood because suddenly all her weight was on my shoulders. Within seconds all her weight was gone. I looked up. She had gained enough height to access the rope and had reached the third rung. She was turning to tie the rope off. As she was affixing the rope, I retied the satchel to my pack. I wasn't at all sure the method was going to work. I hoped I had enough arm strength left to negotiate the loops and reach the ladder rungs.

Gale had reached the top. It was now my turn. I passed my hand through one of the lowest loops and began to pull myself up. With the aid of my legs and feet working against the cliff face, I was able to get to the next loop and pass my hand through it in such a way that it formed a loop over the back of my hand and my wrist. Again, I struggled upward toward the next loop. I don't know how many of the loops I had to negotiate before reaching the ladder. It seemed like forever. My hands and arms were just about shot when I reached a point where I could get my good leg into a ladder rung and take the weight off my arms. The rope ladder was swinging wildly. I reached out to the cliff face to steady it as I swung my other leg into the wrung above where I was standing. The trip to the top of the cliff was relatively easy or alternately painful depending on which leg was being used to hoist my weight.

As I clawed my way over the top precipice and rolled away from the cliff's edge, Gale was already pulling up the rope ladder. "It looks like we're the last ones here. Let's get this rope and head for the rendezvous. I hope they've waited for us. You need some attention." Her tone was cold and matter-of-fact.

I didn't have enough energy to argue, so I struggled to my feet and began to work my way toward the place where we had separated earlier. I was sure I was on the right route. My mind was slow, probably from the loss of blood and recent physical exertion, but I didn't think I'd lost my bearings. I hadn't gone six or seven meters when I felt a tug, more of a jerk, on my backpack. It was Gale.

"Where the hell do you think you are going, back to the road block? The meeting place is this way." She led me to my right and within minutes we entered the small clearing where the groups had originally split. Ben was the first individual I spotted. I immediately knew the mission hadn't gone well. Ben, using a small flashlight, was bending over another man to dress a wound that was bleeding through a bandage. The light was too dim to identify the injured man. I glanced around the small clearing. My mind was so foggy I was having trouble seeing, let alone identifying the few that were there. I somehow knew we were several short.

I must have been weaving, or wobbling, because Miguel, whom I had not spotted, grabbed my arm. "I think you had better sit down. Where are you hurt?" he asked, as I collapsed to the ground.

"My leg is cut. I don't think it's too bad but I've lost some blood. I must have gotten a little dizzy. I can't make out who's here. We found one of Manuel's men dead at the base of the cliff. Did everyone else make it?" I said in an effort to be coherent.

"We lost both of Manuel's men and Manuel took a bullet in the shoulder. Ben's trying to get the bleeding stopped. Let me take a look at your leg."

I relaxed while Miguel checked my wound. Gale joined us as Miguel was preparing to bandage my thigh. "You are a lucky man. The main artery has not been touched but it can't be far from the cut. A lot of muscle seems to have been sliced," Miguel said. "Haven't you got some bandages in your pack? We'll need all that Ben doesn't use."

I reached around to get the pack off my back. Gale helped. She got all the bandages in my pack, and Miguel started to wrap the leg from above the wound. "For Christ's sake make it tight. He's got a long way to go tonight and doesn't have much more blood to lose," Gale hissed, as she moved Miguel aside and took over the task of bandaging me.

I somehow wished Miguel had completed the job, because the pain I experienced climbing up the cliff was equaled by what Gale was inflicting with the bandages. The good side of all the pain was that it was evident the blood flow had been curbed.

Finally, Gale stopped tugging at my leg and stood up. "That should do it. Get up and move around a bit and see how it feels." She spun around and headed to where Ben was working on Manuel.

I stood and, surprisingly, my leg didn't hurt nearly as bad as before. The bandages provided some support. In any event, walking was much easier. I hobbled to where Ben and Gale was working on Manuel. I could tell, from the way they were working on Manuel, his injury was more serious than a simple shoulder wound. It appeared Manuel was more unconscious then he was conscious. He wasn't making any sounds but it didn't take a genius to know he was hurting. Ben had stuffed clean strips of cloth into the wound and Gale was attempting to wrap the outer dressing as tightly as possible around his chest and shoulder.

I walked away, not wanting to bother them as they worked, and because I wanted some time to think. We started as a party of seven and now we were down to a party of four with one of the four unable to walk back. I wasn't going to be of much help. I wasn't even sure I was going to be able to make the trip. That left two men and a woman to pack Manual back without much help from me. If I wasn't able to make the entire trip, they would have to do something with me. There just weren't enough healthy bodies to guarantee a successful return trip. If I had packed a day's worth of provisions, I would have considered going a safe distance from the cliff and bedding down to get some rest, giving my body a chance to replace the life giving fluid I had lost. The fact was there weren't any provisions. My father had a saying he used when I would lament about something I wished I had. He would say, wish in one hand and shit in the other and see which one gets full first. For first time in my adult life I felt helpless. I had no clue how we were going to make it back. I knew the hand I was shitting in was getting full.

CHAPTER THIRTY-SIX

John Sailor was sitting in the window of a cheap room near the waterfront in Boston. He was contemplating whether it was time for him to move on. John knew there were people and authorities that wanted him dead or alive. Most would have preferred him dead. They were on both sides of the law, which left him with nowhere to hide. He knew he had to continually move to stay alive. He had rented the room for a week and the week was about up.

John had always been an early riser, probably a habit carried over from his formal military background. Today was no different than any other day. He had risen before sunrise. The regiment of exercises he had enjoyed for so many years was beginning to wear thin, yet he persisted. There had been changes made over the years in the actual exercises he performed. His regimen now contained more intensive stretching rather than the emphasis on strength building prevalent in his youth. The length and rigger were maintained however.

As a creature of habit, he always went to the street and purchased the early newspaper immediately after finishing the morning workout. Today was no exception. By the time the sun was breaking over the watery horizon of Boston Harbor, John was back in his room and began to peruse the paper noting which headlines interested him so he could return to them at his leisure. As always, he went to the classified section, located the used automobile section, and scanned its columns for ads offering classic automobiles for sale. John had always maintained an interest in old automobiles. He fantasized of someday owning several, and having a small restoration shop where he could spend his days tinkering with some old body or engine of vintage quality, slowly and tediously creating a masterpiece.

While he had a more than vague interest in the automobiles advertised there, he had another motive. It had been several months since he had worked. John was anxious to get some assignment, any assignment which would make the days pass easier. John had worked as a special agent for the Central Intelligence Agency for several years. Because of politics, he didn't fully understand, he was only contacted by a special code. The code was one he had chosen so it would fit into his daily routine. It was a specific advertisement in the classic automobile section of the classifieds. It would be under "Automobiles Wanted." The ad would seek a nineteen twenty-nine Ford Model T and have a telephone number. A certain manipulation of the telephone number would put him in touch with the agent seeking his specialty, his expertise.

As John scanned the ads, one jumped out at him with the same effectiveness as if it had been placed in bold print. "Wanted a vintage nineteen twenty-nine Ford Model T. Call (202) 555-4331". John searched for a note pad or anything he could write the phone number on. He found a scrap of paper, actually the receipt that had been placed in the sack when he made his last grocery purchase. The back of the slip would do fine. He wrote the area code down as it had been provided as well as the first digit of the phone number. He systematically added one to each of the other digits. The new telephone number appeared, (202) 566-5442. John was actually sweating. Finally, he would be on assignment again. The area code was a Washington D.C. area code. He recognized it from previous contacts. He had only ninety minutes to make the call. The paper had already been on the streets for over two hours. John reached into his back pocket, located his wallet, and extracted it. Inside was a long distance calling card he had purchased some time ago. It had at least sixty minutes left on it, plenty of time to accomplish everything he needed.

There was a phone in the lobby of the rooming house he was living in, but it was open to anyone in the lobby caring to eavesdrop. John needed a bit more privacy and he knew just where to get it. There was a small bar just down the street from the lobby. It was one of those small neighborhood bars that opened as early as the law allowed. The only patrons in the bar at opening would be regulars who sat on round stools located in the front, said nothing to anybody, and ingested the only medicine that would get them through the day. The phone was in the back of the bar. John would have all the privacy he needed. John went to the closet, collecting a small pad from his scratched and scarred briefcase. The mechanical pencil was still on the table where he had deciphered the coded phone number. He grabbed the pencil and put it in the pocket of his coat along with the small pad.

John looked around the room, knowing there was something he had forgotten. There it was -- the grocery receipt containing the all-important phone number. He crossed the room, picked up the slip, and headed for the door. John never locked the door because locking it only invited thieves, and this neighborhood had no shortage of thieves. John saw no reason to change his habits at this time, so he just closed it behind him and proceeded toward the stairs and the early morning Boston streets.

The walk to the bar took less than two minutes. He slowed his pace as he approached the entrance. The morning was crisp and, while the adrenaline was providing ample body heat, he pulled the collar of his coat up around his neck. He would fit in better this way, more what the bartender would expect. The last thing he wanted was to be noticed.

John entered the bar and it was exactly as he expected it would be. There were three other patrons in the bar. They were sitting in the front, sipping whatever brand of medicine they required, staring at the little rings their drink glasses were making on the bar, and paying attention to no one or anything. John sat at the other end of the bar and motioned to the bartender. He ordered a single shot of rot gut whiskey with a water back. After he was served, he went to the back and lifted the receiver on the phone. It was filthy. It must've been in use when someone got sick and the owner hadn't cleaned it up. Before putting it to his ear, John wiped the receiver as clean as he could with his coat. He didn't mind the bar or the early morning patrons, but John did mind the filth on the phone. Convinced the receiver was as clean as he was going to get it, he dropped a quarter in the slot and dialed the operator.

"May I help you?" a chipper young female voice said.

"Yes, I have a calling card and would like to place a long distance call." Before he could continue, her voice broke in and began to tell him he could place the call himself if he was at a touch tone phone. "Yes, I know I can, but I'm blind and not at a phone I'm familiar with. Would you help me with the call? John responded.

"I'm sorry sir. I didn't realize your problem. Do you know the number on the calling card?"

John gave her both the number on the card, indicating he had memorized it for just this circumstance, and the number he was calling in Washington D.C. There was a short delay before the phone on the other end began to ring. John assumed it was because the company was making the connection in a way that would trace the call. In fact it was the telephone company, verifying and processing the calling card John had given them. John was suspicious of the delay, whatever the reason. The phone rang twice before anyone answered.

"Hello, this is Scott Steel." The voice was unfamiliar but the name rang a bell. John couldn't place where he had heard the name but knew he had.

"You were looking to buy an old Ford?" John said, not wanting to give his name until he had assurances that the phone call was legitimate.

"I could be interested in an old Ford, but right now I'm more interested in talking with the man who has the old Ford for sale," Scott replied, realizing John Sailor was being cautious. "I assume I'm talking to John Sailor."

"You are and who the hell are you? I haven't got much time so make it quick," John said meaning every word of it. He hated these cat and mouse telephone calls. John had always felt intellectually inferior to other agents and these calls didn't boost his confidence.

"As I said before, my name is Scott Steel. I'm a section chief with the Company and you are assigned to one of the field supervisors working for me. His name is Howard Baker. Your girlfriend is Sally Bennett. She also works for Howard Baker and is currently on assignment in Texas. I contacted her and she gave me the process used to get in touch with you. Now, if you have concluded I'm legitimate, you'd better indicate so. If not, this conversation is over," Scott waited for a response. A second or two drug into several seconds. Scott was beginning to believe that he had not been convincing enough.

"Why didn't Howard contact me?" John asked, still feeling edgy about the man on the other end.

"Because I'm his boss and I didn't want him to know I was contacting you. Is that good enough."

"I suppose it will have to be. What do you want?" John was still concerned, but he also wanted to get an assignment. He had sat long enough.

"Not over the phone. You tell me where we can meet, and when, and I'll be there. Consider that I'm in Washington, so give me enough time to get to Boston," Scott replied, not wanting John Sailor to be seen anywhere near headquarters. He also wanted to evaluate him personally.

Several places ran through John's mind but none were handy to his room. Then it occurred to him the bar where he was making the call was as good as anywhere else. He gave the man named Scott Steel the address, told him to be there at seven that evening, and not to dress in fancy clothes. He was to look like a working man. Scott agreed. The phone went dead.

<hr />

Scott sat in his office, his cell phone in his hand, and his mind somewhere else. He suddenly came to life. As he spun around in his chair he summoned his assistant. Her name was Jody. She was pleasant enough but was less dedicated than Scott would have liked. He ordered Jody to get him a ticket to Boston and told her he wanted to arrive in the late afternoon. She acknowledged his instructions, asked if he needed a hotel, and when he would be returning. Scott told her to get a room for him and arrange for a return flight early the next day. As she left, Scott got up and closed the door to his office. Now, he had to plan the team and the insertion. The insertion was going to be easy, but picking the right agents to join John Sailor was not an easy task. Scott needed agents who were psychologically able to eliminate a fellow agent and not question the order. They also had to be able to deal with John Sailor who preferred to go solo.

Scott recalled a briefing approximately nine months earlier that updated the section leaders on the recruiting successes and failures of the last year or so. He went to a file cabinet and searched until he located the file he wanted. Its tab indicated it contained information concerning that meeting. He crossed the office to his desk and opened the file. The first page concerned the agenda for the meeting. He scanned its contents until he located what he was looking for. It was a topic involving reviews of recruits the company viewed as marginal candidates for agents. In most cases the reasons given were that they were too small in stature or were not mentally tough enough. In some cases they had connections in their private life which might interfere with the Company's use of the individual. There were a few that were designated as being a bit unsavory.

These were the names Scott was seeking. There were six identified on the list. Two of the six had been eliminated because they had records of rebelling against authority, any authority. Of the four left, one was a woman. Scott eliminated her from consideration immediately. John Sailor would have trouble teaming with men -- he certainly wouldn't tolerate a woman. Of the remaining three, he needed to know if any were currently agents and if they were assigned. A search on his computer revealed that one of the men was on assignment. A second was being held in a local D.C. jail for assault on a police officer, and the third was assigned to headquarters pending assignment. In the case of the man assigned to headquarters, the file indicated that he was hard to handle, and if he remained unassigned for more than sixty days he was to be debriefed and let go.

The choices were thin. Scott had previously determined the team should consist of three men including John. With the young agents available meeting Scott's criteria, unless he sprung one from jail, he only had one other candidate and John. He picked up the phone and dialed the number of an office that in any other agency would be labeled Personnel. In the Company it was referred to as the Resource Division. A man he had gone through initial training with, Bill Moyle, currently headed it

"Bill, Scott here. How's everything down in recruitment?"

"Slow as usual. These damn kids coming out now not only don't want to get involved in our business but, in most cases, actually hate the CIA. I don't understand it. It's been a good living for us and could be for them," Bill replied

"I guess they just don't make them like you and me anymore, Bill. Whether that's good or bad, only time will tell. In any event, I need your help. I am looking for an agent the computer says is currently here in D.C.

waiting for assignment. His name is Steve Hawkins. Could you arrange for me to meet him?" Scott inquired.

"Sure I can, but do you really want him? He has something less than a spotless record and has only been in about a year. It seems he overreacts and hurts people, sometimes people he shouldn't. The agency is about ready to cut him loose. He could be a real liability, especially to our new image, if you know what I mean."

"Yes, I know and that's why I'm interested in him. Will you arrange the interview for late tomorrow? I'll be out of town but I'll be back by then. Shall we say four o'clock?"

"I'll have him there. I hope you know what you're doing," Bill said as he hung up the phone.

Scott replaced the receiver and for the second time in less than thirty minutes seemed to be staring into space. The Company statistics indicated most undercover missions were more successful with three agents assigned. Scott believed that to be true. He also knew the statistics showed that one of the agents should be a woman. It seemed a single man and two agents, posing as a couple, had fewer problems with entry and exit than when all agents were men traveling singly or in groups. Why couldn't John work with a woman? After all, he had on at least one other occasion. The assignment where Sally Bennett was a part of the team immediately came to mind.

Scott went back to his computer and pulled up the biographical data as well as the agency evaluations of the woman he had previously dismissed as a candidate. Her name was Ronnie Matthews. She was twenty-four and a graduate of the University of Wyoming, where she had been somewhat of a soccer star until she was benched for excessive roughness. She quit the team shortly thereafter. The agency evaluations showed her extremely proficient in the martial arts. The evaluations also showed she was a self- starter who had a tendency to act before she thought. That trait had embarrassed the Agency when she attacked a foreign national for heckling her and her charge. The heckler was later determined to be nothing more than an idealistic college student doing what college students do. Aside from the agency embarrassment, the incident blew her cover and left her charge exposed until she could be replaced. The lady sounded perfect, and, if she was available, John Sailor would just have to adapt to having a woman on his team again.

Scott dialed the number for Bill Moyle again and again Bill answered the phone. "Bill, Scott here, don't you have an assistant. Do you always answer your own phone?"

"Only when one of the section leaders calls," Bill replied. "What the hell do you need from me now. I don't hear from you once a year and now it's twice in one day, actually twice within an hour. What's going on?"

"I've got a sensitive situation involving one of our better field agents. I believe he's gone south. I'm putting a team together to investigate, and retrieve if possible, but they also need to be capable of eliminating the problem. If the appointment tomorrow works out, I'll have two members. I want a third. Is Ronnie Matthews available? By the way, this conversation is classified and, for the time being, no one other than you and I have a need to know. Agreed?"

"Who am I to disagree with a section leader? Of course, it's agreed," Bill replied. "But tell me, Scott, why the hell do you want to put together a team from hell. Without asking, I think I know who your third is, and if I'm correct, the poor bastard they're assigned to locate will not stand a chance of coming out alive. Is that really your intention?" Bill sounded concerned.

"No, that's not my intention. Bill, you know me better than that. Let's just say I'm concerned whether the extraction team will come back alive. This agent may be the best we've got. He isn't going to be easy to extract. Let's leave it at that for now."

"That's good enough for me. Let me pull up Ronnie Mathews and see what her status is. Give me a moment," Bill said, as the phone went silent. Scott sat waiting for Bill to come back on the line as Jody, his assistant, came into the office.

"Your flight to Boston leaves in ninety minutes. You'd better get moving. You know how the lines can be," she said.

Scott nodded and motioned her out of the office. Jody was a reasonably competent employee but had never learned that when doors were closed there was a reason and she should honor that reason. Scott was irritated with her and she knew it. She acknowledged his irritation with a sheepish gesture and exited the office as quickly as she had entered. The phone crackled to life.

"Scott, sorry to take so long, but it seems Ms. Mathews has been transferred to the West Coast office and is awaiting assignment in sunny southern California. The Company has gone to some expense to move her out there. I'd have problems getting her moved back. There'd be a lot of questions. Isn't there anyone else you could use? We have four or five female agents here on the East Coast awaiting assignment. Would you like their files?"

"No, I don't think we'd have to move her back. The assignment I have in mind won't take that long. Who is her section chief? I'll call him direct and see what I can arrange," Scott responded.

"One moment. Her name is Malaise Morgan and I don't know anything about her. She's one of the young ones. Got most of her field experience in the Orient, I believe.

Bill gave Scott the number, wished him luck with the team he had chosen, and the conversation ended. Scott looked at his watch. He had just enough time to make the flight. He would make the call from Boston. Scott grabbed an overnight case that was always ready and left the office. As he passed through the outer office, he asked Jody to have a cab waiting when he reached the front door. She indicated the cab had already been called and was waiting. Scott got in the express elevator departing for the street level.

The trip to the airport as well as the flight to Boston was uneventful. As Scott deplaned, he noted the sky was overcast. It seemed it was always overcast in Boston. He actually didn't like the town. He somehow always found himself more depressed in Boston than in almost any other city he knew. Scott hadn't spent much time in the Pacific Northwest, but he had heard it was somewhat the same, or worse. For that reason Scott considered himself lucky never to have spent much time there, let alone being transferred to the Northwest as a base of operations.

Scott rented a car from Hertz. He had the rank to command a government vehicle and have it delivered to him at the airport, but this was not the time to show up at a small neighborhood bar with U.S. Government plates. It would blow any cover John Sailor had established, as well as bring attention to the meeting. Neither was desirable or necessary. The car rental agency supplied Scott with a map of the city, but as usual the map was of major arteries and tourist attractions and did not have the detail that would allow him to locate the meeting place. A quick stop at a service station close to the airport solved that problem. While there was still light, Scott sat in the car and studied the map. He located the address and, luckily, it wasn't going to be hard to find. Scott looked at his watch. It was slightly after five. If he were lucky, he'd be able to make a dry run by the bar and get a feel for the neighborhood.

He remembered that John had requested he dress like a working man. He hadn't had time to change let alone go home to get different clothes. He'd stop and pick up a pair of work pants and shirt on the way. That would have to do.

Even with the stop for clothes, he was in the neighborhood of the meeting shortly after six. He located the bar and made sure that, in his wanderings, he did not pass it again. There was plenty of parking on the street near the bar so he could time his entrance perfectly. The neighborhood was what he'd expected. At one time in the past it had been a middle class area, probably home for families of the men who worked at or around the harbor. That was some time ago, however, because now it was run down, a neighborhood obviously servicing an itinerant clientele, catering to men and women who rented by the night or by the week.

Scott glanced at his watch again. It was now six forty-seven. There was just time enough for him to drive back to the bar, park his rented car, and make his appearance. As Scott approached the street where the bar was located he noted that the number of parking places, which had been available when he made his first pass, had now been occupied. He was irritated he had not considered the locals might be out for the evening, and the availability of parking near the meeting place would be limited. There was one space available about one-half block from the bar. It was small, but if he could maneuver the rental car it would be adequate. He wasn't sure why, but he wanted to have transportation as close to the bar as possible. Scott pulled the automobile into position to parallel park the vehicle. He hadn't parked in this fashion for some time and was hopeful he could get the vehicle into the spot without causing any undue attention. As luck would have it, the automobile slipped into the parking spot without any problems. Scott was elated. Could this be an omen that the meeting would also go as well?

The bar's front door was a frosted glass affair that didn't allow a prospective patron to view the interior without actually going in. He pushed open the door and entered. The smell of stale beer and cigarette smoke greeted him immediately. The establishment was designed so that little if any space, useable by a patron desiring a drink, would be wasted. Within two steps of the door the main bar began its sweep toward the back of the establishment. Stools, which had been affixed to the floor, were every forty-five or fifty centimeters, and most of them were occupied by men who had probably just come from work. The lighting was dim to darkish with most of the light being supplied by the expected luminous beer and whiskey advertisements located above the back bar.

It took Scott several seconds for his eyes to adjust to the lighting. As he was able to see more of the bar, he realized there was an area of tables located in the rear. They afforded more privacy. He was confident John Sailor would choose to meet in that area. He probably was back there waiting for him already. Scott slowly made his way to the back, taking every precaution not to call any attention to himself. As he neared the rear of the establishment, he noted a single man occupied one of the tables. The rest were filled with groups of men and, in one case, a man and a woman who were more interested in each other than with other patrons.

Scott had never meet John Sailor in person. He had only seen the picture of him contained in his personnel file. Scott knew John's appearance had, in all probability, changed or been changed since the picture was taken several years ago. The single man's stature was approximately the same as

John's had been described in the file. It had to be him. Scott approached the end of the bar and ordered a draft beer. He really didn't like beer, but he needed something in his hand giving him a reason to be in the bar. A beer seemed the best choice. He stood at the end of the bar, sipping the beer, and watching to see if the man would give any indication he was looking for someone. The man gave none. After several minutes, Scott decided to approach him.

"You wouldn't be John Sailor would you?" he asked when he had reached a proximity to the table such that other patrons wouldn't hear his question.

"I am, and I assume your name is Scott," the man responded.

"Can we safely talk here?" Scott inquired, as he casually took a second look around the bar to see if anyone was paying any special attention to them.

"It's as good as I can supply. What's on your mind? I know you didn't come all the way from Washington to sip a beer."

"You're right. I didn't. I have an assignment I'd like to offer you. It involves a potentially very sensitive matter. You would report directly to me and to me only."

"Why me? There must be all kinds of agents just sitting on their asses waiting for something to do." It appeared John was being careful not to jump at the first opportunity coming his direction in several months. Scott hoped that Inwardly John was yearning for something to do -- that he was one of those agents he had just referred to.

"Because you're uniquely qualified for the mission, and you have a record of reliability that is needed in these matters. Now, do I continue, or do I go back to the airport?"

"I'm interested. Go on," John said, seemingly determined not to let this operations supervisor go to the airport and leave him in Boston wondering when his next chance for action, any action, would present itself.

"Good. The details will be covered later. The general nature of the assignment involves the apprehension of an agent currently in the South American arena. He has left all the signals indicating going over the edge. His project is ongoing and he is, or may be, jeopardizing its future success. The Company has spent significant monies on this project, and I don't want to see it all lost if I can help it. Your job will be to insert yourself, locate the agent, and bring him out alive if possible. If that's not possible, eliminate him and extract yourself and your team." Scott was interrupted.

"You said team. If you choose me for this mission you know I prefer to work alone. Why the team?"

"You have been an employee of the Company for some time, and whether you like it or not, you know the Company policy is teams be used whenever and wherever possible. That's why. Your team will consist of another man of lesser qualifications than yourself and a woman, who also lacks the experience you possess, but has shown she is reliable. You will be in charge unless or until you disappear as you've done on previous missions. In which case, the woman will be in charge with instructions to bring you out. If that occurs, and you come out alive, this will be your last mission. Now do you still want to continue?" Scott waited for the answer he knew was coming.

"I think I could live with a team but I'm not sure about a woman. Couldn't you get someone else for the assignment?"

"John, you missed the meaning of what I just told you. The choice is not yours. It's mine. If the woman is available she will be on the team. Now are you in or out?"

"When do I have to let you know?" John said, trying to play just a bit hard to get.

"Within the next four or five minutes," Scott responded, knowing John was going to accept.

"Where do I meet the rest of the team?"

"I want you to be in Washington within forty-eight hours. You have my cell phone number. If you need to reach me, use only that number. I will arrange a hotel room for you. We will discuss the specifics of the mission when you're in Washington and the rest of the team has been assembled. Are there any questions which need an answer tonight?" Scott hesitated to give John a chance to respond.

"I need your cell phone number. Both the code and the number were destroyed shortly after we spoke. Other than that, my only request is the hotel room you arrange for me, for us, be inconspicuous. If you know my file you know I can't stand unnecessary exposure."

John Sailor seemed cautious, but he was alive with the anticipation of the mission. Scott could tell, by his subtle body language, "Let's finish our drinks now and then I'll leave." As he was speaking Scott was writing on a small pad he had retrieved from his shirt pocket. He tore the page off and handed it to John Sailor.

CHAPTER THIRTY-SEVEN

Migael turned toward Gale and said something. The tone was so low I couldn't hear what was being said. Gale nodded and Miguel went to where Manuel was being bandaged. He located something I couldn't immediately recognize, but as he moved away, I could see it was the machete Manual had brought. Miguel disappeared into the bush. Within a minute or so I could hear him hacking on what sounded like a tree or underbrush. I realized he was getting the raw materials for a stretcher. Somehow, we were going to carry or drag Manuel back to the ranch.

Gale was completing Manuel's bandage as Ben stood and looked around the small clearing. He spotted me hobbling around and started toward me.

"How badly were you cut?" he inquired.

"It's not life threatening, but I'm not sure I'll be of much assistance getting Manuel back to the ranch," I replied.

Ben didn't respond. He just disappeared back toward the path leading to the cliff edge. My leg was beginning to throb, so I chose a fallen tree which was lying at the edge of the clearing and sat down with it as a back support. The extra effort of getting to the ground made me dizzy. I knew I didn't want to get stiff, but the comfort of the ground was too enticing. The efforts of the night coupled with the injury had caught up with me. My eyelids were heavy. My body screamed for sleep.

Miguel suddenly appeared and was dragging two large poles with him. He almost ran over me in the darkness. The poles were about the size of a small fence rail and were about two and a half meters long. It occurred to me the rails were nice, but what were we going to use for Manuel to lie on. As I was fighting sleep and contemplating the rails in my muddled mind, Ben called my name and told me to gather all the lengths of rope I could find and cut them into lengths of about one meter. I was in no shape to question his instructions, let alone argue with him. I began the painful task of getting to my feet. Getting up was somehow easier than it had been getting down. I began the search for the small rope we had used to get up the cliff. I hadn't paid attention to where Gale had placed it after I reached the top. After some searching, I found the ladder in the area where Manuel was lying. As I picked it up Ben, who had just rejoined us in the clearing, must have thought

I was going to cut the ladder because he immediately came over to where I was.

"For Christ's sake don't cut the ladder! We need it to get Manuel out of here." The question had been answered. We were going to tie the edges of the ladder to the poles, and use it's cross rungs as a pad for Manuel to lay on for the trip back.

"I wasn't going to cut the ladder. We tied a length of rope to it to get up the cliff. I was trying to locate that rope," I replied. Ben was holding a small radio in his hand. I wasn't even aware he had brought one.

"Where did that come from?" I inquired.

"I always carry a CB radio on missions for this very reason," Ben said, as he toggled the lead wires into the unit. "It's a small one and may not have sufficient range to reach the ranch from here. I'm going to have some horses brought to us. It's the only way we're going to get back. The guard on the ridge we crossed just outside the ranch is listening for us. I'll give it a try." Ben dialed a channel, which had been evidently predetermined, and spoke into the mouthpiece. The unit crackled and sputtered. Nothing recognizable as a human voice was forthcoming. Ben tried again. The result was the same.

"I'm going to have to get closer or higher, probably both," he said more to himself than to me. "How well can you travel?" Ben asked, directing his attention to me.

"I think I can do pretty well but it might be slow. My problem is lack of strength rather than pain. What do you have in mind?" I inquired.

"I'm not sure. I'll try once more with the radio. You get Gale and Miguel over here. Let's see what their thoughts are," Ben instructed. He was speaking into the radio as I turned and hobbled to where Gale and Miguel were working on the makeshift stretcher. Miguel was working on strengthening one of the ends as I approached.

Ben would like us to join him. He's trying to make contact with the radio," I said, noting that Manuel had slipped into a coma. Gale finished making the knot she was working on and left to join Ben without a word. Miguel looked up at me. I could tell by the look in his eyes that Manuel was not in any shape to be moved. We both joined Ben. It was obvious he hadn't been successful in making radio connections. Ben put the radio down and looked at both Gale and Miguel.

"Manuel isn't going to make it is he?" he said, addressing both of them. Miguel's eyes dropped to the ground. There was an awkward silence. Gale was the first to speak.

"He's hurt bad, Ben. I can't tell for sure but I think one of his lungs was hit. Just before he slipped back into the coma he coughed up some frothy blood. It doesn't look good."

"I'm not ready to give up yet!" Miguel inserted with emotion bordering on tears. "I'm Godfather to his child. How could I ever live with myself if I left him here to die alone?"

"No one is suggesting we abandon him at this point, Miguel. I need to get somewhere where I can make contact with the ranch and get some horses out here. We also need to put some country between the edge of the cliff and ourselves. I don't think they'll suspect us using the cliff as an escape route, but if they do, they may assembling to follow us as we sit."

Ben swung his gaze to me. "You had the responsibility to take the men out around the lodge. Were you successful?"

"I don't think there were any left alive around the lodge, and I didn't see any living as I made my way back by the warehouse and to the cliff," I responded, and then remembered the one man Gale had finished off. "There was one man who was hurt badly but alive. Gale sent him to the promised land." I hesitated, and was about to add that there may have been others we didn't see when Gale jumped in.

"That was because you weren't going to finish him off, and there may have been others that were injured and crawled into the bush. We have no way of knowing." Gale's tone was exceedingly sharp. Her antagonism was clearly directed toward me. I was about to ask her what her problem was when Ben jumped in.

"Settle down, Gale. We've a long way to go, and your feelings about Eric are not going to get us there any easier or quicker. What we need to do is to get a kilometer or two down the path and then we can relax. Let's get Manuel on the stretcher. Miguel and I will carry him. Gale, you police the area and make sure we haven't left anything which would indicate to them that any of us are injured. When you're sure there's no sign of our problem catch up with us. Eric, you just try to keep up. If you need rest, take it and catch up later. Now let's get going."

Miguel and Ben lifted Manuel onto the makeshift stretcher and lifted him off the ground. I started to help Gale gather what evidence of our presence existed in the area. Gale indicated, with a dismissing gesture, I was to get the hell out of there. I grabbed my packsack, with its valuable attachment, and began to follow the others. The path seemed to be much narrower than it had just a few hours before. In spots it was hard even to justify it as being a path. Ben was in the lead. It seemed the two of them were able to handle the stretcher with an amazing ease. Manuel was not a big man but he still weighed sixty or seventy kilos and was dead weight. Their strength and agility with the burden was truly amazing.

We had traveled about seven hundred meters when Ben stopped and indicated we would take a short rest. I wasn't going to argue as my dressing had begun to slip down my thigh. I needed the time to bring it back up and retighten it. I didn't want to lose any more blood. Manuel had been unconscious for some time, even through all the jostling he was being subjected to on the stretcher. The bandage around his chest and shoulder were showing signs of fresh blood seepage. I instinctively knew this was not a good sign. Miguel was feverishly trying to tighten the dressings on Manuel. I could tell he needed help, so I went over and held one of the bandage ends as he tightened it. There must have been some pain because, even in his comatose condition, Manuel moaned. I thought for a moment he was going to wake. I wasn't sure whether that would be good or bad. As we were finishing what seemed a feeble attempt to stem Manuel's bleeding, Gale reappeared.

She was carrying not only the pack we had retrieved at the bottom of the cliff but also Manuel's. I could see she had also commandeered Manuel's pistol as it was hanging in the holster she wore low on her hip. Her empty weapon must have been stowed in one of the packs. "You've made good time," she said to the group. Turning to Ben, she asked if he had any idea where he could go that would allow him to contact the ranch.

"There's a hill that just might raise to sufficient height to provide line of sight to the guard on the ridge," Ben told her. "It's about a two kilometers further and will be off to our left. I would feel safer if we made it there before settling down to wait for the horses. I'll climb the hill and, with some luck, make connections."

"We better get moving then," Gale said "Before I left the clearing, I went back to the edge of the cliff to get an idea if anyone had survived. The glow of the embers of the warehouse was all the light I saw, but there was some noise from the direction of the lodge. It could be that not all the soldiers were as heroic as they might have been and hid when the fracas started. In any event, I don't think they suspect we came from the top of the cliff but, if they get reinforcements, they may investigate. The further away we are the safer we will be."

"I agree," Ben said. "Why don't you and Miguel take the head end and I'll take the feet. We may make better time that way. As Gale and Miguel were getting positioned to raise the front of the stretcher, I joined Ben at the rear.

"I don't know how long I'll last but let me help as long as I can." I said as I picked up the pole next to my good leg. Ben looked at me and smiled.

"Not too fast now. The test is getting to the hill. Not how fast we get there," Ben said. I knew he said that for my benefit, a gesture I greatly appreciated.

As we moved down the trail, I was pleasantly surprised my leg did not give me more trouble than it did. The mere fact the extra weight was primarily on my good leg seemed to allow my injured leg to follow with less effort. Miguel and Gale seemed to sense the perfect speed and we made good time. The two kilometers turned into three or better, but we made it with only three rest stops. As we reached the area Ben noted the sky was starting to show evidence dawn was not far ahead. With the extra light, slight as it was, we were able to leave the trail, find a small clearing to set Manuel down, and take him off the stretcher. He hadn't gained consciousness during the entire trip. A small trickle of blood was escaping from the corner of his mouth. He was alive but just barely.

Ben immediately began the climb to the top of the hill. The bottom, where we were located, was jungle but the trees and undergrowth lessened near the top. It was not a huge hill but one that would give Ben sixty or seventy meters more elevation. Hopefully the additional elevation would provide line of sight with the guard station at the top of the ridge. I estimated Ben would be at the top within ten to fifteen minutes and back within half an hour. Those of us remaining at the foot of the hill found a spot to sit or recline. All of us remained alert to any sound which might betray someone following us.

Within thirty to forty minutes Ben was back. It was readily apparent he had been successful. As he approached the small clearing he announced that within two hours we would have help. Evidently the transmission was not as clear as he had hoped, but he did get through, and the guard on the other end confirmed help was on the way. My immediate concern was whether the rescuers would be able to find us. The information I was given in the beginning was that Miguel was the guide and his unique knowledge of the area is what enabled us to take advantage of this route. How were the ranch hands going to find us? I expressed my concerns to Ben and he shrugged them off by indicating most of the hands had lived in the area all of their lives. While they may not know the way to the cliff, they certainly knew the way to the only landmark in the area, the hill where we were waiting. I felt somewhat better, but a feeling of insecurity remained in the pit of my stomach.

The group settled in for the two hour wait. For the first time since we left the ranch house hunger was becoming a factor. Gale and Miguel were attempting to get Manuel arranged in a position where he would be more comfortable. He was beginning to gain some fleeting degree of consciousness. Not enough consciousness to communicate, but periodic moments when he opened his eyes. He seemed to recognize Gale and Miguel but beyond that he was out cold. He still seemed to be going downhill.

Ben decided to backtrack and make sure we hadn't been followed. He was going to go back a kilometer or so, staying off the main trail, and see if there were any pursuers. The decision didn't make much sense to me. I believed we were off the trail where we were, and we should all conserve our strength for the remaining leg of the trip back. However, Ben was our leader and it wasn't up to me to question his decisions. As he left our little clearing I located a spot where I could recline. If I needed to rise quickly there was a small sapling available for support and leverage. I made sure my pistol was available even from the reclining position. I kept telling myself Ben was in a position to know what was best for the group yet the uneasiness in my stomach would not go away.

The remaining four of us waited as the dawn rose over the forest canopy to the East. I'm not sure if the others felt the uneasiness I did, but they also were quieter than they had been. I glanced at Gale. She was sitting with Manuel's pistol in her hand. Miguel was sitting close to his friend Manuel but remained alert to the sounds of the morning. We had been waiting about an hour when Ben reappeared in the clearing. He entered it from the same place he had left. He approached the group casually and announced he couldn't find any evidence anyone was searching for us in the jungle above the cliff. I asked him how far he had gone. He said he covered the trail back to where we had one of our last rest stops and then circled the area before coming back to the clearing.

"The horses will be here in about an hour, so if we could stay out of sight until then, we'll be okay," Ben announced as he chose a place to sit and wait.

I noted Gale had put her weapon away, and Miguel was much more at ease than he had been fifteen minutes earlier. It didn't make any sense that Ben would set us up. He had led the raid on the drug camp, and I assume he killed his share of the cartel solders. Why would he lead them to us now, after we had accomplished our mission? I must be paranoid. Why would a man of his experience leave for an hour when there was no evidence of anyone following us or even knowing we were here.

I couldn't allow the questions I had to go unanswered. If Ben had sold us out, I would just a soon confront him now as keep my silence and regret it later.

"Ben, I need to talk to you. There's something bothering me and I need it answered now!"

Ben looked startled but held his composure. "I'll try. What's the question?"

"First, there was no mention of you bringing a radio during our planning sessions. I'm glad you had it, but why wasn't it part of the detailed inventory we all went through. Second, why the hell did you go out to search for pursuers just now? We have had no reason to suspect we were being followed. The very act of the search may have led them to us if they were out there or, on the other hand, maybe they've been led to us now.

There may be good reasons for all of this but from here it reeks." I waited for a reply.

"You ungrateful son of a bitch," were the first words I heard and they didn't come from Ben. Gale stepped out from behind Ben. There was hate in her eyes. "Ben -- not us -- not the group back at the ranch, brought you along on this mission so you could stock your coffers with cash that will allow you to pick and choose your next cause! *You* have become the mercenary and *you* accuse Ben of selling us out!" Gale had her pistol trained on me and, because she appeared so quickly, mine was in the safety of its holster.

"Give me permission and I'll blow his manhood away," Gale said addressing Ben.

"Hold on, Gale, and put the gun away. Eric's questions deserve an answer. We know the answers. He hasn't enough information to make even a guess at the answers to his questions. His wariness should be our assurance he's been square with us. Put yourself in his shoes and with the information he knows. If you are half the soldier I think you are, you would be asking the same questions he is," Ben said. Gale dropped the gun to her side but the hate still burned in her eyes. I wasn't sure what I'd expected but this chain of events wasn't it.

"If there's something I don't know, now is the time to tell me," I replied not knowing what would happen next.

"Eric, there is evidence someone at the ranch is an informer for the cartel. We haven't a clue as to who it might be, so we have taken some steps to protect ourselves. One of those steps was to carry a citizen band radio on this raid. The man who is stationed at the top of the ridge, and the one to whom I just sent the message is a longtime friend and associate whose loyalty is unquestionable. He will lead the horses to us and he will tell no one where we are located."

"Okay, I might be able to buy that in general, but why the citizen band radio, especially with its limited range, and why the recent trip into the jungle?" I responded, not yet convinced this wasn't a setup.

"The CB radio was chosen because it's not as prevalent in Colombia as it is in the United States. A standard radio would result in the distinct possibility that any transmission we made would be monitored. We would not know who was getting the message. The cartel is sophisticated and may be scanning for any transmission that might lead to our whereabouts. The traitor, or mole as you refer to him, may be in the radio shed at the ranch listening for any information he can pass on. No one at the ranch, other than my friend on the ridge and Kenneth, know of the existence of these radios. The three of you brought them with you when you arrived and we secreted them upon your arrival. I can't give you a good explanation of the scouting trip I just took other than to tell you this; I have the uncomfortable feeling the mole may have discovered our plans, at least in part. If he, or she, disclosed our route to the cartel they may be following us. I believe they would make every effort to approach quietly. It may have been foolish, and if so please accept my apologies, but I felt it necessary to double back and ensure we were alone." Ben stopped talking.

The group was intent on my next move. I could tell Gale was primed to raise her weapon should it become necessary. Miguel was notably more tense than usual, like a cat ready to spring. Rather than immediately address the explanations offered by Ben, I decided to defuse the group by simply turning around, going back to where I had been waiting, and sit back down. As I turned back around the group was still looking at me. It was time to speak up. I knew an offense would be more effective than any defense I could offer.

"What the hell are all of you looking at? I was invited on this mission because I have some of the skills that each of you possess. I put my life on the line with each and every one of you. Granted, I had a motive that may not have been as pure as yours, but I did my job. The result of our joint effort was I got what I wanted and you were successful in your goals. Now because you chose to lead me on this mission without sharing pertinent information, I'm the bad guy? I don't think so. Your organization and mine, if I still have one, have the same objectives. It's painfully obvious that we choose to pursue those objectives using people, allies if you will, in ways that differ."

I stopped talking and glared at the three of them. The moment was obviously awkward for the three and that's what I intended. Ben fidgeted with his hands for several seconds, scratched the stubble that was beginning to show on his chin, and turned back toward where Manuel was laying. "The horses will be here within the next thirty minutes. Let's table this conversation until were all back at the ranch safely," he said.

I wasn't adverse to the suggestion. I needed time to digest the reasons Ben had just given me, explaining his actions. To reinforce my displeasure, I simply turned my back on the group and got as comfortable as I could in preparation for the wait. I used the pack and its valuable cargo as a back and headrest. It was safe for the time being. I didn't think Ben would go back on his word regarding the payment of my fee, and I knew Miguel would do nothing Ben didn't authorize. Gale was another case, however. It had become clear that she resented the fact I was going to keep the money. She was hot headed and impulsive. In short, she was dangerous -- my most immediate threat.

The next half hour stretched into fifty minutes before we heard the faint sounds of horses. They were coming from the right direction. Ben listened to the noise for a bit and then announced he would go and lead them to our little clearing. He hesitated, looked at me, and asked if I would feel better if I went to meet them. His voice had an unmistakable edge to it. I didn't respond, other than to give him the *get screwed look* I'd always been so good at. He got the message and started toward the noise.

As he left the clearing I readjusted my pack and satchel that was tied to it. I think I believed most of what Ben had said earlier, but I hadn't gotten this far in life without protecting against contingencies that were within my power to affect. Today was no exception. I got to my feet, shouldered the pack, and began to head for the jungle on the opposite end of camp from where Ben left. As I moved Gale jumped up and confronted me.

"Why don't you sit back down where you were and wait with the rest of us!" Her voice was low but with an unmistakable acidic quality.

"Why don't you mind your own business?" I replied, as she stepped fully in my path. "Gale, I know you feel you can take care of yourself and, from the evidence I've seen, you can. Rest assured, however, you're no match for me. I don't relish killing women, but I did so less than eight hours ago and I can do so again without feeling much additional remorse. Now, if you make a move I don't like it will cost you your life, or at least your life as you know it. Your move will, in all probability, cost Miguel his life also because I'm sure he'll come to your aid. Ben said we would discuss this back at the ranch and that's what I intend to do. Now, unless you have any misguided ideas otherwise, I would suggest you get out of my way. My leg is beginning to pain me as are you. Now move!" As I finished, to my surprise and relief, Gale stepped aside.

I walked into the jungle about ten meters and started to circle the camp. I wanted to get back to the area where Ben had left the clearing. I was going to make sure, for my sake and for Ben's sake if he was legitimate, that the promise of the pending help would not surprise us. I wanted to make sure the help we were about to receive was in fact the help we were expecting. As I circled the clearing I made special efforts to make sure that none of the others in the group were aware of my passage. It took only a few minutes to get to the area where Ben would have intersected the path. I chose a spot where I could see the path and yet be secure from behind. I settled down to wait.

The sounds of the horses and their wranglers were getting closer. If I understood Spanish I could have understood what they were conversing about. Suddenly I could hear Ben's voice. He must have just reached the procession because, even though I couldn't understand what they were saying, there were obvious greetings taking place. The horses were less than fifty meters from where I was hiding. I waited for them to appear. I checked my weapon and my extra magazine. Whatever the circumstance, I was as ready as I was going to be.

The first horse suddenly appeared on the trail, about fifteen meters from where I was watching. Ben was in the saddle. Behind him was a wrangler I had not seen before. He was leading two horses with full tack. Behind him was the wrangler I had met yesterday on my ill-fated excursion. He also was leading two horses. I suddenly felt wave of relief surge through my body. The rescuers were from the ranch. I let them pass and fell in behind at a discreet distance. The last thing I wanted to do was spook the horses.

As the horses broke into the clearing I could tell Gale and Miguel knew the lead wrangler and that the wrangler was most interested in the condition of Manuel. I joined the group. Ben was talking to the wranglers in Spanish, and they were gesturing toward Manuel and back to a smallish mare that was grazing where she stood. They evidently were deciding how to transport Manuel. I could tell from their gestures that the consensus was to rig a travois and drag him in. It seemed to me the only choice. I doubted, however, that Manuel would reach the ranch alive. The wrangler I knew began to examine the stretcher and to re-tie and reinforce the rope ladder. There were areas where, even with both ends being carried, the connections securing the ladder to the pole were working loose.

I knelt down to help the wrangler reinforce the stretcher, and as I did he looked up and smiled his toothless smile.   "I brought a better horse for you today senor," he said

"I appreciate that. I'm not sure I could survive the big one I had yesterday," I replied smiling back. As we were tightening the rigging on the stretcher Gale walked by.

"I'm glad to see you chose to join us," she said with some irony in her tone. I looked up and my eyes met hers. Her eyes remained sharp and piercing but were somehow softer than they were before.

"As I said before, we will resolve this back at the ranch," I replied and went back to helping the wrangler.

It took no more than thirty minutes for us to ready the travois and get Manuel securely placed on it. One of the horses was brought around so that the lead end of the travois could be tied to the saddle. Manuel didn't regain consciousness during the entire process. Gale had redressed the wound, which was still oozing some blood. For the most part, however, the bleeding had stopped. It was now time to leave. I was brought a horse which had to be several hands smaller than Big Fella. It was so small that I was concerned the horse wouldn't be able to support me for the entire trip. I kept my thoughts to myself. I was unable to get into the saddle without help because my leg wouldn't support my weight while at the same time allowing me to swing my good leg over the saddle. The wrangler gave me some help up and handed me the reins.

The procession started. Ben was in the lead. My wrangler was second and he had the responsibility of leading the horse dragging Manuel. I was next with Gale and Miguel following me. The second wrangler brought up the rear. We gained the trail with little problem and started toward the ranch. I felt discomfort in my leg in spite of the even pace and plodding nature of my mount. I can't imagine the discomfort that Manuel must have been feeling. The travois was bouncing over every small irregularity in the trail. The green saplings, to which the rope ladder was tied, acted like springs accentuating every bump. On several occasions the horse pulling the travois was led off the path and around an area where the path was extremely irregular.

We had been traveling toward the ranch for about an hour when I noticed Manuel, though having gained some consciousness, was becoming more uncomfortable. I alerted the wrangler that I thought we should stop and readjust Manuel on the travois. As the group rained up, I could tell Manuel was in some distress. As he gained some consciousness he was beginning to weakly thrash with his arms. Gale dismounted and was approaching Manuel. He looked up and that low guttural sound, that can't be mistaken for any other sound in the world, welled up from deep in his throat and chest. It was a death rattle. Manuel was dead. A silence fell over the group.

The jungle even seemed to get quieter in reverence to the passing of this man. The mission had just became more costly. We had now lost three men. Gale heard the sounds, turned, and went back to her mount. I glanced back and could tell she was overcome with grief. Ben and the wrangler charged with leading the travois reached the litter and checked Manuel. The look on both of their faces confirmed Manuel was dead. No one spoke. The horses stood quietly. My wrangler began performing last rites over Manuel's body. Everyone was dealing with the loss in their own way. I wanted to get off my horse but the numbness in my leg convinced me otherwise. I simply sat quiet, feeling the loss of a man I hardly knew but one with whom I had endured an expensive mission, a mission which had cost him his life.

The remaining trip back to the ranch house was quiet and uneventful. With Manuel passed the pain where the bumping made any difference, we made good time. When we reached the top of the ridge and the ranch was visible below us, Ben stopped the procession. "Let me go first and give me about ten minutes. I think Manual's family, as well as the families of the other men, should be told of the death of their loved ones rather than having us just ride in unannounced without them.

No one objected. We dismounted as Ben rode down the ridge. We could see from where we were that some of the hands and their families had seen

Ben coming, because they were gathering around the corral. Shortly after he arrived, two of the women had to be helped from the area. My wrangler mounted and without saying a word, we started the trek down the ridge. I fell into line, as did Gale, Miguel, and the other wrangler.

On arrival at the corral one of the ranch hands took the reins of my horse and led it to the rail where he tied it off. I attempted to dismount. As my leg hit the ground and took weight, I fell against the horse. The ranch hand said something to me in Spanish while lowering me to the ground. Several of the women came over and helped me to my feet. They took me to the ranch house. I was placed in the small room where I had slept the evening before, and the women began to untie the dressing around my leg. Fatigue was beginning to set in. I could hardly keep my eyes open. The young girl, who had been assigned to me earlier, was present. When the bandages were removed, she proceeded to cut off the rest of my clothing. I felt warm water as she bathed me and cleaned the damaged leg.

At some point she said something to another lady and the other lady left. Shortly, a third and older lady I hadn't seen before came in and examined my thigh. There was some discussion in Spanish after which the young one turned to me, saying the older lady was experienced in wounds such as mine. She indicated I would need stitches. I was not adverse to stiches, but later realized, while they had the basic needs to apply stitches, they hadn't any way to deaden the area. The procedure would be performed with no anesthetic. I raised up on my elbow to a position where I could see the injury. The view left no question -- stitches were necessary. I gave my permission and lay back to endure my upcoming treatment.

The two ladies discussed something in Spanish and the older one left. The young one prepared several towels around and under the leg. By the time she was finished the other lady had returned with a small medical kit. She laid it out on the bed and prepared a curved needle with a thread that was more like mono-filament fishing line than surgical thread. The injured area of my leg was washed in what smelled like alcohol, a procedure proving to be the most painful of my impending treatment. The needle and the thread were also swabbed. There was conversation in Spanish at which point the younger one began to push the edges of the wound together. The ordeal seemed to last forever. The pain was sharp but not something that was unbearable. I couldn't see what was going on nor did I want to.

Finally, the lady stood up, looked at her handy work, smiled at me, said something in Spanish to the young one, and left the room. I managed to raise myself enough to view the wound. It had been sewed up with the efficiency of a trained surgeon. I fell back on the bed. Without realizing what was happening, I was enveloped in a sleep that had been a long time coming.

CHAPTER THIRTY-EIGHT

Scott Steel finished his drink and without saying anything to John Sailor got up and left the bar. The evening was crisp but, in the last hour or so, the skies seemed to have cleared up a bit. Scott's Hertz rental car was parked where he'd left it and didn't appear to be any worse for the wear. He got into the vehicle and started the motor. As he looked up he noted John Sailor was leaving the bar. Sailor turned, proceeding up the street directly toward Scott's car. There wasn't a possibility Scott could go unnoticed. The temperature had fallen sufficiently to cause the area to be clouded with vapor from his exhaust. As Sailor approached the car there was a slight, yet perceptible, acknowledgment of Scott's presence. Sailor passed the vehicle and momentarily disappeared in the exhaust vapors. When he reappeared he was turning the corner. Shortly, he was out of sight.

Scott put the vehicle in reverse gear and backed up a small distance. He engaged a forward gear and, with the extra room he had acquired by backing up, was able to pull forward into the traffic lane. The route to the hotel Jody had arranged for him was not difficult, at least by Boston standards, and he was able to arrive at his destination in reasonable time, while avoiding those insane roundabouts Boston is so famous for. The reception clerk was affable but not overly friendly. In a short time Scott was in his room.

He glanced at his watch. It was after eight in the evening, Eastern Time. That would make it slightly after five in California. Scott dialed the number he had gotten from Bill Moye. The clicks and buzzes occurred that were common when one called into an agency office, especially one where section leaders maintained offices. He knew his phone call would be recorded, probably never audited, but recorded none the less. After the standard number of rings, generally three, a pert young voice came on the line.

"Central Intelligence Agency, how may I help you?"

"My name is Scott Steel. I'm a section chief in Washington D.C. I need to speak to one of your section chiefs, Malaise Morgan. It's important so if she's not in her office patch me through to her cell."

"One moment please," the pert voice responded.

Scott knew the receptionist was checking to see if there was a Scott Steel on the agency roster and whether he was located in Washington D.C. If he checked out he would be connected to Malaise. If not, he would be shuttled to an internal security person.

"One moment please," the receptionist with the pert voice said. There were more clicks and buzzes and a phone rang.

"Hello," a young sounding voice said.

"Is this Malaise?" Scott asked.

"This is Malaise Morgan." There was a pause. "Who's calling?"

"My name is Scott Steel. I'm a section supervisor in the DC office. I'm interested in temporarily utilizing an agent in your section. Her name is Ronnie Mathews. Is she available?" There was a pause on the line.

"She's available. Would you please hold for a minute?"

"Certainly," Scott replied, realizing he had been much too direct. She was making calls to check out his credentials. Scott kicked himself for the way he handled the phone call. It could have been handled in a much better way - - a way that would have been more predictable and standard, given the agency protocols. Hopefully, she wouldn't do anything that would alert any of the directors to his operation. After four or five minutes she came back on the line.

"I'm sorry Scott, but I need to have your operations code. I'm not at the office and, insofar as I don't know you personally, I must be sure. I hope you understand."

"Not a problem," Scott replied. He gave her his seven-digit code number and waited for her to verify that he was indeed who he said he was.

"Everything checks out. Now, you want to borrow Ronnie. Did I understand you correctly?"

"Yes, I have a special need for someone with her capabilities. I believe you said she was available, but you must understand if I use her it may be for two weeks to a month, possibly longer, before she is sent back to you," Scott said not wanting to mislead the section chief.

"Not a problem. It just surprises me that a special request is made for Ronnie. She's not a model agent. I'm sure you know that. May I ask what type of assignment you're contemplating for her?" Malaise replied.

"It'll take her into the South American theater to extract an agent. Beyond that it's classified."

"I'm beginning to understand why you want her. I can spare her for whatever time you need her. When do you want her and where?"

"Get her to my office in D.C. by tomorrow afternoon. You can call my assistant, her name is Jody, and advise her when Ronnie will be arriving and on which flight. I'll make sure she's picked up at the airport. Tell her to pack light and bring all weapons. By the way, she's not personally encumbered is she?" Scott responded.

"No, I don't believe she is, unless you consider most of the men she meets as being an encumbrance. From what I can gather, she has more of a love life than all of my other agents put together. I'll have her in D.C. as you request. You'll keep me posted as to her return, won't you?"

"Of course I will. Thank you for your assistance. The director here in D.C. will be briefed on your cooperation."

Scott hung up the phone and settled back in a comfortable chair. He had arranged the team. Now, it was a matter of bringing them together and making it work. Scott congratulated himself mentally. In his mind it was his ability to self-start and make things happen that got him ahead of Howard Baker. In his mind he had always perceived Howard, with all his contacts, was his biggest rival within the agency. Howard had seniority and extensive field experience. He had been injured in the line of duty. Yet, with all those attributes, when the opening presented itself it was Scott the Director chose to make a section leader. Scott felt – *no he knew* -- he was destined for higher positions. Even the director's position was not out of the realm of possibility. Scott needed to make a few more political contacts in high places. He saw this operation as a stepping stone to that goal. After all, exposing Eric Butler, one of the agencies premier field agents, was ultimately going to save the Company many dollars. Scott knew one of the biggest assets he had was intelligence he got from an informant that fell into his lap several years ago. Information that could help him achieve the Director's seat.

Scott ordered dinner brought up to his room. The return flight Jody had arranged was mid-morning so he could enjoy the evening and even sleep in past his usual five a.m. He picked up the hotel phone and checked the register of extension numbers for the various hotel services. He dialed a number and requested a wakeup call for eight o'clock in the morning. Scott's dinner arrived and was spread on a portable table room that service provided. He tipped the server generously, settling in for a tasty meal and a solid night's sleep. After all, hadn't he earned it?

The trip to the airport and the flight back to Washington, D.C. were as mundane and uneventful as usual. Scott arrived in time to have lunch with his assistant Jody. She filled him in on the various calls that had been received in his absence and advised him the arrangements for the California agent had been made. The agent would arrive at about three forty-five that afternoon. Scott instructed her to pick up the agent and bring her back to the office. Jody mildly objected, asserting someone from the motor pool might be more appropriate as she had other duties needing her attention. Scott directed her to drop those "other duties", whatever they may be, and follow his direction. He told her this was a sensitive matter, and he wanted her to be involved because she was more reliable and less conspicuous than staff from the motor pool. Jody had joined the Company because she liked the idea of being involved in sensitive and secret matters. She envisioned herself someday becoming an agent. Assignments, like Scott had just given her, played into her fantasy. She even convinced herself there was an element of danger involved. She accepted the direction without further question, a result Scott had counted on.

On arrival back at the office Scott returned the half dozen phone calls that had been received in his absence. He knew he had to maintain the appearance of business as usual. At about two o'clock, Jody buzzed him on the office intercom, saying she was leaving for the airport. He told her to drive carefully as the intercom went dead. Now, he could make the balance of the arrangements without interference. Scott called a hotel the Company used on occasion that was nice but off the beaten path, at least as far as the tourist trade was concerned. He reserved three rooms for his team and a suite for himself. With the arrangements made, there was nothing to do but wait for the agents to arrive.

Steve Hawkins was due in his office at four o'clock, which should dovetail with the arrival of Ronnie Matthews. The only loose end was John Sailor, a loose end Scott wasn't worried about. He knew he would be calling shortly. Scott checked his cell phone, making sure it was fully charged. It was. Scott busied himself with some administrative tasks all section leaders had to do and each hated. The afternoon seemed to pass at a snail's pace. At about ten minutes to three his cell phone rang. Scott immediately reached for it then reconsidered. He didn't want Sailor to think he was sitting by the phone waiting for his call. He let it ring three times before he answered.

"Scott here."

"Scott, this is John Sailor. I'm in D.C. Where do you want me?"

"I've arranged for a room in a hotel where you won't be bothered. The room is reserved in your name. I'll meet you there sometime between six and seven tonight." Scott gave the name and address of the hotel, ending the conversation.

It was all coming together. Steve Hawkins would be in around four o'clock and Ronnie Matthews would be arriving in D.C. shortly. Scott had just enough time to put together a dossier on Eric Butler. It didn't need to be extensive but the team needed to know certain facts about Eric and have a picture of him to work from. Scott went to the outer office and approached a bank of files on the wall adjacent to his office. He fumbled in his pocket retrieving a set of keys, sorted through them, and selected the one he wanted. He scanned the labels on the various drawers and settled on one labeled Bu to Ca.

He was about to insert the key and pull the drawer open when he realized the drawer was unlocked. Jody was responsible for maintaining the files in the office. He was immediately irritated. They were supposed to be locked at all times. She was treating her responsibilities in a cavalier fashion again. He would have to speak to her and this time come down hard. Scott found the latest passport photo of Eric and a short resume of his background with the agency. He pulled both of them and went to a color copier located on Jody's desk. He made three copies of each putting one of each in three separate folders.

He went back in his office and settled in to wait for the arrival of the agents. It was about three fifty- five when he heard the door to the outer office open. It must be Hawkins, as Jody had not had time to collect Ronnie and get back. Scott entered the outer office, and, as expected, a young agent was standing in front of Jody's desk with a bewildered look, wondering what to do. As Scott entered, the young agent extended his hand.

"I'm Steve Hawkins. I was told to be in your office at four o'clock."

"You're right on time Agent Hawkins. If you'll have a seat I'll be right with you," Scott replied and turned back to enter his office. Scott shut the door behind him and went to the desk. He put the folders he had just prepared in a leather valise together with a blank pad. He placed the valise under the desk where it wouldn't be seen and returned to the office doorway.

"If you'll come in now we can get started," Scott said attempting to appear as official as he could.

Steve Hawkins entered the inner office. He was obviously very uneasy at being in the office of a section chief. Scott circled his desk seating himself before motioning the young agent into one of the few chairs available for guests. As the agent seated himself Scott began.

"Steve, I have chosen you to be part of a team that will be inserted in South America with the responsibility of extracting an agent we've had in the field for several years. I have information leading me to conclude that this particular agent has *gone south*. Your team will consist of a leader, whom you will meet later tonight, and a female agent who should arrive shortly. Your team will be responsible to me and to me alone. The operation is classified, meaning there must be a need to know before any discussion of your mission or your activities can be discussed with anyone other than your fellow team members or myself. I'm not going to go into the details of the mission now. I will cover them later tonight when the entire team is assembled. Now, before the other agent arrives do you have any questions concerning what I've just told you?"

"Does this mean we will be hunting one of our own?" Hawkins wanted to know.

"Yes, the Company has found that on occasion agents, for reasons known only to them, go astray. They lose their perspective on why they are with the agency, or what their objective is regarding their current assignment, or both. In any event it is sometimes necessary for us to either physically remove them from the field or if that's not possible neutralize the situation." As Scott stopped talking, he was intent on Hawkins' reaction to his explanation, especially the part about neutralizing.

Steve Hawkins sat thoughtfully in his chair and didn't respond for some time. Scott couldn't read a reaction in him one way or another. "Why did you choose me? I know my record with the agency is less than, shall we say, spotless. I know, without your interest in me, I'd probably be drummed out shortly," Steve finally replied. As he was speaking he was looking directly at Scott. It was obvious both of the men were evaluating the other.

It was now Scott's turn to attempt to give the acceptable answer. Somehow, the tables had been turned and Scott didn't appreciate the circumstance. He responded using the oldest trick in the book- that of pulling rank,

"It doesn't matter why I choose you. I am your section chief. I have the ability, no, the right, to make these decisions without explaining them to anyone, certainly not a wet behind the ears agent. Now, if you feel you want to accept the assignment with the facts you have, do it now. You were right about the being drummed out shortly. This is your last opportunity to show you can make it as an agent. If you don't want it we'll speed up the process a bit, and I'll schedule your debriefing conferences beginning tomorrow. The choice is yours." Scott waited for a response.

"I thought that's what was going to happen when I was told to be in your office. Under the circumstances, I guess it won't hurt to go on the mission. I can make up my mind as to whether the agency is what I want later. You know, Mr. Steel, the choice to begin the debriefing interviews is a two way street. I'll accept the mission."

Scott felt better knowing he had two of the agents committed. He was seething inside, however, because of the attitude of this young agent. Scott mentally committed to see to it that this mission would be his last, regardless of the outcome. As the conversation was coming to a conclusion, Scott heard the door to the outer office open and shut. Shortly after a small red light on the interoffice intercom lit, notifying him Jody was back. Without giving Steve any response or reaction to his last comments, Scott got up from his chair, crossed the room toward to door, and asked him to wait in the outer office.

Jody was seated at her desk conversing with a lady seated across from her. The lady appeared to be approximately twenty-three years old. She was about average height and had brown hair that fell around her shoulders. She was athletic in appearance, yet retaining an aura of femininity. Scott guessed she weighed somewhat more than her appearance betrayed. "You must be Ronnie Matthews," Scott stated, attempting to appear pleasant yet maintaining the decorum of authority.

"I am and you must be Scott Steel," Ronnie replied.

"Please step into my office, Ms. Matthews," Scott requested as he turned toward the door. Ronnie Matthews immediately rose from the chair and started toward the office. She was wearing a green pants suit that brought out the red highlights in her hair. As she entered the office Scott noted the slight bulge on the left side of her suit coat. She was clearly ready for a mission. Scott went through the same scenario he had gone through with Steve Hawkins. In the end he asked her if she had any questions, and waited to judge her response.

"Do you feel this agent will require neutralizing?" she asked.

"That's always a possibility, if not a probability in these cases. If it were not, the agent would simply be called in from the field without the need of an extraction such as I have outlined. If neutralization was to become necessary, do you feel it would cause you any hesitation? Remember neutralization is a last resort. If it's necessary, it will most probably be a situation where it's either you or him. How do you feel about that?"

"I have a very strong instinct for self-preservation, Mr. Steel. I don't believe I would have a problem doing what was required in the circumstance you've described," Ronnie answered.

"Based on that response, Ms. Matthews, I am offering you the opportunity to be on the team. I will need an answer immediately. Unfortunately time is of the essence."

"I was sitting around California getting bored so this opportunity is welcomed. Of course, I will accept. When do we leave?"

"I've arranged a hotel for all of you for tonight. We'll cover all the specifics of the assignment this evening after dinner. Now, I want you to meet one of your team. The third is already at the hotel," Scott said as he buzzed the outer office.

"Jody would you show Mr. Hawkins in, please." The door opened and Steve Hawkins strolled into the room.

"Steve Hawkins, this is Ronnie Matthews. Each of you has accepted the assignment I've offered you. The third member of the team is a man named John Sailor. He's currently in D.C. and will be at the hotel where you'll be staying tonight. I want you to go to the hotel now. Jody will get you a cab. Have dinner and get to know one another. I will be there at about seven o'clock. We'll discuss the mission in detail at that time. There's one thing I want each of you to know about Sailor, however. He's not accustomed to working with a team. In fact, it's fair to say he is what you would term a lone wolf. He prefers solitary assignments. He has accepted this assignment knowing he is to be a part of this team. Don't make any effort to contact him when you arrive at the hotel. I will make the introductions when I get there …"

"By the way, agent Sailor will be team leader meaning once you leave the United States, he's your immediate supervisor. Now, if there are no questions, I'll have Jody get you to the hotel." Scott looked at the two young agents before him. There was no effort to voice a question or concern. He buzzed Jody, telling her to get a cab for the agents and have it deliver them to the hotel. Both agents stood and left the office.

Scott busied himself signing several letters prepared for his signature during his recent absence. Scott always read the correspondence prepared for his signature, so by the time he completed the task, Jody had completed the evening arrangements and the agents had gone. He summoned Jody to come to his office and bring a pad.

"Jody, I want you to arrange a flight into Bogotá, Colombia, for the two agents that were just here and for an agent named John Sailor. They will be traveling under their given names. They've been told to have their passport and travel documents with them. Ronnie and Steve will travel as a couple. John will travel unconnected. Hopefully, there will be enough flights to put him on a different plane. If there aren't they can all travel together, but make sure they appear separate. Get John a seat in a different section of the aircraft. Also, draw one hundred and fifty thousand dollars cash for each of them. Prepare the necessary receipts for me. I'll take the money and the receipts with me tonight. Get the money from my contingency fund in the office safe. It should have enough cash left to accomplish the disbursements. I won't need the actual travel tickets tonight, but it would be helpful if you could have the itinerary for me."

Scott inquired if she had any questions. Jody indicated she didn't and left the office. Scott went over the details of the mission in his mind. He had covered all bases.

The Agency dining room was on the top floor of the building. It was open to section leaders and above, including guests. The food was good, not exceptional, like the dining room available to senior agents with the FBI, but good. Scott decided to take advantage of the opportunity to get dinner while Jody was making the arrangements he required. The special was lamb with mint sauce. He'd never acquired a taste for lamb and so fell back on his old favorite, country meat loaf with mashed potatoes and brown gravy. The meal wasn't fancy but was just what he required. The meal took no longer than a half-hour, so Scott indulged himself with an order of vanilla ice cream. The Company prided itself on providing ice cream, tasting as though it had just been made in one of those old fashioned wooden freezers. Tonight was no different.

It was five forty-five by the time he finished his ice cream. It was time to get back to the office and collect the materials gathered for the evening's meeting. As Scott exited from the executive elevator, he almost ran down a delivery boy from the Agency travel department. They were both going to his office suite. As they entered, Jody was finishing some of the daily paperwork that seemed to be never ending. Scott went directly to his office, gathering the satchel he had prepared earlier. As he was finishing up, Jody came in and asked if he needed her any further that evening. She handed him the tickets that had just been delivered and three envelopes, each with a receipt clipped to the outside.

Scott hesitated a moment, going over the needs of the mission and the materials he was accumulating. "Did you get a weapons waiver attached to the airline tickets for the team members?" he inquired.

"I always do, don't I?. None of the three should have any trouble boarding with their side arms. Travel said Colombia was getting tougher regarding entry however. I hope their exemptions from customs will get them in the country armed."

"If Colombian officials give them any problems, they will be able to replace the weapons easily enough. There's hardly anything in Colombia that's not for sale," Scott replied, thinking more out loud than intentionally answering her question. "Yes, you can go. I have everything I need."

Jody turned and left the inner office gathering her coat as she went through the reception area. Scott emptied the envelopes on the desk and counted the money. There was exactly one hundred fifty thousand in each envelope. The receipts were in order. He glanced at the airline tickets. They were also in order. John Sailor was on a flight that left forty-five minutes after his two partners. Jody was very efficient in many ways. Nothing was left but the final briefing.

CHAPTER THIRTY-NINE

S cott arrived at the hotel, where he had placed the mission team, slightly after seven o'clock. He parked his agency car in an inconspicuous space in the hotel parking lot. By the time he got into the lobby and had located a front desk clerk it was about seven- twenty. He mentally congratulated himself for getting the team together, all materials ready for the final briefing, and arriving at the hotel within the time period he had set. The field team would not have to wait for the briefing. He was on time.

As Scott approached the front desk, he saw Ronnie and Steve in the dining room. He stopped before passing and observed their activities. They appeared to be finishing their dinner. Ronnie was clearly making herself available to Steve. He didn't seem to mind. Scott made a mental note to discuss the Company's policy on fraternization. He knew full well that none of the field agents took the policy seriously but felt compelled to make the effort.

The front desk clerk checked Scott into his suite. He requested the suite numbers for the other team members. The desk clerk initially resisted giving him the information, something about patron confidentiality. Scott flashed his credentials announcing that unless the clerk complied he would make sure the CIA didn't use the hotel again. The clerk, not wanting to be accused of losing a large part of the hotels business, complied.

Scott's suite was on the top floor of the hotel and afforded a view of Washington D.C. that would be hard to beat. The suite consisted of a large bedroom, a separate sitting room, and a large bathroom vanity. The sitting room had a medium to large table with four chairs. The room would serve well. It was obvious the hotel was accustomed to having conferences take place in the suites. Scott went to the phone and dialed the room which had been assigned to John Sailor. The phone rang twice before it was answered.

"Hello." The voice was that of John Sailor.

"John, this is Scott. I'm in room 1025. Please get up here so we can talk before the others arrive."

"I'll be there directly," Sailor replied and the phone went dead.

He's not much for small talk, Scott thought as he replaced the receiver. Scott took the few minutes he had to roam around the suite and become familiar with the amenities it offered. He personally had never used or been in this particular hotel. He was impressed with the accommodations and mentally determined to remember it when the next need arose, business or personal. In less than a minute there was a knock at the door. Scott approached the door, looked through the one-way viewer, and let John Sailor into the suite.

"Hope you didn't have any trouble getting here," Scott said as a way to begin the conversation.

"No, but you knew that. Now what's this mission you brought me here for?" John said as he entered.

"Not so fast, John, and it isn't just you I brought here. The other two members of your team are also in the hotel. I wanted to meet with you first because I know it's not your style to work with a team. It is, however, the style of the Company and it's my style as well. I told you that yesterday in Boston. I'll expect you to act accordingly. The two I've chosen were hand-picked to match with your methods. They're a bit green but you could change all that. You will be the team leader. They know they will be taking their lead from you. Just make sure you give them some direction. Is that understood?" Scott hesitated for a response.

"Yes, it's understood. That doesn't mean I have to like it, does it?"

"No, you don't have to like it, but if you want the continued protection from the agency and the style of living you enjoy, I suggest you learn to at least pretend to enjoy it. In fact you might just humor me and act like it was your idea." Scott was looking directly into John's eyes as he directing a man he knew would have no qualms about eliminating him. "Now, since we're pretending you have requested a team, would you like me to brief you on who they are?"

"That would be nice, and while you're doing it don't forget to tell me what time they're supposed to be in bed at night and whether they sleep with a light on."

"It won't be that bad, John, and you know it. Allow me to continue the briefing on them and I think you'll agree."

Scott spent the better part of the next fifteen minutes going over the files of the two agents. He stressed the shortcomings of each and the fact that both of them were not from the mold the Agency preferred. John listened and when Scott was through indicated, in his offhand manner, that there were aspects of each of them that reminded him of himself not many years ago.

"I thought you might see it that way. By the way, with regard to your concern about their bedtime, I don't think you'll have to worry about it. If I read body language correctly, your main problem may be getting them out of bed. I intend to raise that issue tonight but you know how young agents can be." Without waiting for a response Scott went to the phone to summon the two remaining team members to his suite.

"That's wonderful. I not only have green agents on my hands but agents with raging hormones," John uttered, more to himself than to Scott.

Scott dialed the room assigned to Steve. After only one ring Steve answered the phone.

"Hello, this is Steve Hawkins."

"Steve, this is Scott Steel. Will you come up to suite 1025? We're ready to begin the briefing.

"Be right there. I'll get Ronnie." Steve hesitated, "She's on the same floor as I am."

"I'll bet she is," Scott replied. "The two of you get up here STAT."

John Sailor and Scott relaxed, saying nothing to each other. Within two minutes there was a knock at the door. Scott peered through the security peephole and opened the door for Steve Hawkins and Ronnie Matthews. They entered the suite. Scott could tell by the way they both were looking around, his suite impressed them.

"Steve, Ronnie this is John Sailor. He will complete the team. You will have plenty of time to get to know each other later so let's get down to the mission. Before we start would anyone care for a drink? The mini-bar is located under the sofa table. Feel free to help yourself."

"Don't mind if I do. Ronnie would you like a beer or anything?" Steve said. "How about you, John?" Steve said almost as an afterthought. Ronnie took a beer and John declined, indicating he never drank while on the job. The statement was pointed and directed at the cavalier approach to the meeting Steve was taking.

"Let's get started then." Scott said as he pulled a chair from under the table and placed his valise on the tabletop. The three agents joined him. When everybody was seated, Scott began.

"I know each of you will have questions, but please hold them until I have finished the initial briefing. First, each of you are aware the reason for this mission is the extraction of an agent. What you don't know is that he has been strategically placed to infiltrate the largest drug cartel in Colombia. For reasons, which are not important, we believe he has either changed affiliations or gone into business for himself. Your job is to locate this agent and bring him back to U.S. soil. The preferable extraction is to bring him back alive. If that is not possible, or to do so would place any of the team in harm's way, he is to be eliminated and left where he lies. Each of you knew this was generally the type of mission you had been chosen for, and none of you indicated that carrying out the directive would be an insurmountable problem. This is your last chance. Now that I have given you the directive and laid its option on the table, does anyone want out?"

Scott hesitated, looking primarily at the young agents. Neither of them indicated a problem.

"Good, I'll consider everyone in. I'm handing each of you a file containing the dossier of an agent that goes by the name of Eric Butler. He has been working on this undercover assignment for several years. He may well be the best agent we have, or had. To reach him will be an enormous problem and to convince him to return even larger. Our latest intel indicates he is in Colombia, probably the northern part of the country. That's where he was the last time he contacted his field supervisor. The cartel he infiltrated is the Barajas Cartel. He convinced them he's a competitor and they should combine forces to enlarge joint markets. An initial deal was struck and that's when things started to go sour with Mr. Butler. His field supervisor believes he will be communicating with him within the next twenty-four to thirty hours. By that time, I want you in place, in Colombia. If he does make contact, I'll get all the information I can to you. If he doesn't make contact, your job will be the same, just harder. Now are there any questions from any of you at this point?" Scott surveyed the faces of the agents before him. John Sailor showed no emotion or indication he had any questions. Both Steve and Ronnie were intently studying the folder in front of them. Their beers were untouched.

"If not I'll continue." Scott passed out the envelopes containing the money. "In each of the envelopes you will find one hundred and fifty thousand dollars in U.S. currency. On the outside of the envelope is a receipt for the money. Count it and sign the receipt. You will not be expected to account for every dollar, but you can expect, as part of your debriefing, to generally explain what moneys were spent and why. This should be roughly confirmed by how much you returned with. The Agency does expect you to bring the unused money back.

Each of you were told to be prepared to be on assignment for thirty to sixty days, to bring your personal weapon, and all travel documents. Hopefully, each of you has those materials with you. Your tickets contain a weapons authorization code, which will be honored in this country. We have been advised there have been some problems at your destination, however. In the event you can't get your weapons into Colombia, John will get others for you. You are to rely on John. He is your leader. He alone has the experience to deal with problems as they may arise.

The third packet contains your travel tickets. So that you can enter the country without appearing to be together, you will go at separate times. Ronnie and Steve will be traveling as a couple and John will follow later in the day as a single. Once in the country you will join up and begin your search. Each of you have agency issued cell phones. Keep them with you and well charged at all times. They may be your only safe way of communicating among yourselves or with me here in DC. John, I will contact you tomorrow and let you know who to contact in Bogotá that may be able to give you a place to start. The contact will be safe. It will be an agent we have down there for other reasons.

The last item I want to cover is a review of the company policy against fraternization. The Agency has determined a team is more effective and operates within safer perimeters when the relationships remain on the project level and don't involve social or personal entanglements. Motivations seem to be clearer as do the project objectives. I expect all of you to respect that policy and concentrate your efforts solely on the mission. Have I been clear on this and are there any questions concerning the mission?" There were no questions from the younger contingency.

"How old is this intel you have and where and when are we going to meet this other agent who may have information concerning Mr. Butler? It seems you're not even sure he's in Colombia," John Sailor said with some frustration in his voice.

"We believe he's in Colombia and probably the northern part of the country. John, there are no guarantees in these matters, you especially should recognize this. Just exactly what is your problem?"

"If he is not in Colombia, and I locate a trail indicating where he went, do I have the authority to follow him, wherever he goes?" John inquired, still with an edge to his voice.

"Yes, of course, you have the authority, but make sure the trail, as you put it, is legitimate and that I know about it. I'd hate to have to send a team after you." Scott could tell the last remark infuriated John Sailor because his eyes seemed to turn to bullets, blue and lethal.

"I guess I just found out why I have to babysit on this assignment. The Company really doesn't trust me, even in view of my record. Maybe I do want to opt out of this mission, in fact the entire Company." Scott was about to respond when Steve barged into the conversation.

"Babysit-- You sanctimonious son-of a-bitch, why don't you quit? The two of us can certainly carry your sorry weight. What in the hell makes you think you're so special anyway?" Scott could tell his team was falling apart rapidly. If fact, in a more normal circumstance he would have disbanded the members and chosen another team. Starting all over was not an option in this instance, however.

"Just hold up, both of you! Let me tell you how it really is. Steve, you may think, and for good reason, that you are resourceful and especially tough. Accept this or not, the choice is yours. John Sailor is more experienced, more resourceful, and can have you for lunch any time he wants. John, whether you realize it or not, your skills are not what the Agency is actively seeking any longer. Each of you, including you Ronnie, are on the verge of being disassociated from the Company. There will be no more lone wolves in the field. Each of your futures with us may well be determined on how efficiently you complete this assignment, how well you work together. I'm willing to go to bat for each of you and I believe the Company has a need for the special skills each of you possess. However, I am in the minority. Failure here, either by not completing the mission, or an inability to work together will leave me with my hands tied. John, both Steve and Ronnie have skills and mental abilities exceeding those you had several years ago when you were recruited. I will expect you to recognize those attributes and help each of them to hone those skills such that you can remain as a team after this is over. Do I make myself clear? Do any of you have any doubt as to your options?"

The room was silent. John Sailor was obviously considering whether he wanted to continue, and the other two were sitting with blank expressions on their faces. "I want your answers right now! I mean right NOW!"

Ronnie was the first to speak. "I am in," she said, with a certain amount of concern in her voice.

"Me too," Steve added. His voice had lost that defiant quality it possessed earlier. Everyone was looking at John Sailor.

"Well, John, what's your answer? You in or out?" Scott said, pushing John to a decision.

"I'm in, but I want you to understand this," John stipulated, "we won't be successful on the mission if we're not given the authority and support it requires. I'm concerned, based on what you just said, that this may be my last mission, either by my choice or the choice of the Company. In either event, I'll keep all the money that's left and disappear. Call it my retirement fund if you want but that's my condition for participation in this mission. If that's not acceptable, I will be out of your hair within the hour. Scott, the choice is yours and this time I want the decision NOW! What will it be? Am I in or out?"

Scott glared back at John. The tables had been turned and now John Sailor was dictating the conditions that would determine whether the mission would be a success or a failure. A failure, at this point, would reflect on Scott's career. He had no choice and he knew John Sailor knew he had no choice.

"You'll all leave for Colombia tomorrow. Remember you're a team. Decide among yourselves where to meet when you arrive in Bogotá. Call me on my cell not less than every forty-eight hours. John, the Company's Colombian agents will meet you at the Bogotá airport on your arrival. They will recognize you so don't worry about finding him. Good luck to all of you." Scott got up and left the room. The extraction had begun.

CHAPTER FORTY

The sun was rising. It was partially visible above the eastern horizon, resulting in my room having the morning glow so appealing in the tropical latitudes. My leg and hip felt like they were tied to a board. I threw the bed covers away to be sure I hadn't been splinted sometime during the night. I hadn't, and there seemed to be new dressings on my wound. I was completely nude with the exception of my wristwatch, which didn't cover much. Judging from the fact I felt rested and it was dawn, I knew I had slept at least twenty-four hours. I needed to get to a phone. This was the day I was to contact Howard Baker. I swung my feet over the side of the bed. Other than extreme stiffness, I didn't feel any pain that was unbearable. I hadn't put any weight on my leg yet and was a bit apprehensive about doing so. I got my good leg underneath me and, with the help of the bedpost, was able to get to my feet. Just as I was attempting to put weight on the injured leg the door to my room swung open.

In the doorway was the young Spanish girl along with the older woman. The older one I recognized as the lady who had sewed my wound on our return. Seeing me standing there, in all my glory and nothing else, the young girl began to blush and said something in Spanish I assume was excuse me or its equivalent and turned to exit. The older lady scolded her in Spanish and pushed her through the door. Both entered the room. The older lady motioned for me to sit. I complied making an effort to use some of the bedclothes to cover my glory. She took them away and began to loosen the bandage on my leg. As she did so, I glanced at the younger woman. She was preparing new bandages. As our eyes met I remembered that she was the young Spanish girl who had brought to life certain longings absent since the death of Sadie. She was still blushing.

"I'm sorry, Senor, that we entered without knocking. We thought you were still asleep. Your bandages needed changing."

"That's okay. I woke up without any clothing so you aren't seeing anything you haven't seen before."

"That is true, Senor, but it seems different when you are asleep, not quite so personal."

I tried to smile at her, but the older lady was probing my injury and the sharpness I felt drew my attention to what was happening to my leg. The wound looked as though it was healing. All of the stitches were in place, and there wasn't visible discharge from the wound. The older lady's expression portrayed her satisfaction with the healing process. She said something to the younger girl who smiled and translated for me.

"She says its healing fine and you won't need the heavy bandages any longer. We will place a loose covering on it to allow air to aid in the healing. Do you have any loose pants you could wear? You should not irritate the stitches."

"I remember the only pair of pants I had being cut off me, so probably not. Are there some I could purchase that will get me by?" I inquired.

"I will find you something," she said, turning to leave the room. The older woman was just completing the loose bandage and stood to survey her work. She nodded, mostly to herself, and said something to me in Spanish, which of course I could not understand, turned, and left the room shutting the door behind her.

It occurred to me that I had bought some extra shorts on my shopping excursion in Bogotá. I hobbled to the small dresser and opened the drawer where I had put all of the extra items not required on the mission. In the drawer I found the extra socks and the shorts I remembered. I quickly put on a pair of shorts, and for lack of anything else in which to cloth myself, put on a pair of socks. I was at least somewhat presentable, should anyone else enter the room. I located my packsack. It had its valuable satchel attached just the way I remembered leaving it. Before I counted my profits, I checked to see if the balance of the money I had brought from Bogotá was still where I had left it. It was there, all two hundred fifty thousand dollars. You could say many good things about this vigilante organization, including that they were not thieves. I couldn't say that about most organizations I knew, including the Company.

I approached the satchel and untied it from my pack. Opening it I found several bundles of crisp one hundred-dollar bills, all U.S. currency, and a small amount of local money. It was obvious the cartel had more faith in U.S. dollars than in their own currency. I counted one of the bundles. It totaled one hundred thousand dollars. If all the bundles totaled the same, they appeared to be the same size, I would increase my accounts by four hundred thousand dollars. I put the money I had brought with me in the satchel with the cartel money and fastened it securely to the pack. As I was finishing, there was a knock at the door. I went to the door and opened it just enough the see it was the young girl. She had located some clothes for me.

I swung the door open, motioning for her to come in. She entered and spread a pair of farmers bib overalls on the bed. She also had a shirt that had seen its better days. Both were clean, however, and would serve my purposes fine. I put the overalls on and put the shirt on over them. She laughed out loud. From her reaction, I realized the shirt should be inside the top part of the overalls and made the adjustment. It all fit and frankly didn't look at all bad. I smiled at the girl and went to the satchel to get some of the local currency to pay for the outfit. She realized what I was doing and said no payment was necessary. Rather than argue with her I accepted her charity. I determined this young lady would be compensated later.

As I moved around my leg seemed to loosen up. I could feel the stitches and there was no doubt the leg was injured, but I was able to get around reasonably well. I suddenly realized I was hungry. The cornmeal mush, as Ben had labeled it, sounded like a banquet. I left the room and went down the hall. The dining area was empty, but there were kitchen workers around who, when they saw me, rushed to help me to a chair. One of the workers spoke passable English. I told him I needed some of the mush or anything that would pass as food. He told me to wait, while he got something together. The first course was coffee. I think in two days I had forgotten how good coffee tastes in the morning. Before I completed my first cup of coffee, he brought a large bowl of the mush and some fresh baked bread. I thought I had died and gone to heaven.

As I finished breakfast, Ben came into the dining area. "You're finally awake. We thought you might sleep the week away. How is the leg feeling?"

"A bit stiff. I won't be running any races for a day or two but other than that, I feel fine." I hesitated, "I need to tell you I meant nothing personal about my suspicions out on the trail. I guess I've operated too long, with a team of two, to trust a larger group. I can also understand that you knew very little about me and couldn't tell me everything."

"Don't let it bother you another minute," Ben responded as he sat down across the table from me. "I also was guilty of misjudging your perceptiveness. Had I fully realized the extent of your experience and training, I might have brought you more into my confidence."

"Have you heard anything about how successful the raid was or is there any way to know from here?" I asked

"No, we've received no information other than a few radio transmissions, indicating that the entire contingent was wiped out. They're blaming it on a rival drug faction. It seems Barajas' niece or daughter or some close relative was killed in the fracas. She along with all the residents of the main lodge were brutally killed by unknown assailants. You wouldn't know anything about that now would you?" Ben was smiling as he delivered the information.

"I think she was his niece. When I told Miguel about the girl he asked me to describe her, which I did, as best I could. He thought it was his sister. It obviously bothered him. I'm sorry it had to be her, but she was the only one who gave me trouble. It was either her or me," I responded, attempting to fill Ben in on what I had learned.

"Was she the one who cut your leg?" Ben asked, motioning to my injury."

"Yes, she was a light sleeper. When I took care of the man in bed with her, she must have become aware of my presence, because she came out of the bed covers with a knife and fighting. She dived at me. I was fortunate to have been watching her as I slit her friend's throat. In any event, I was able to move to one side just enough to avoid her main thrust. Unfortunately, her blade caught my thigh. As she went past me I used the wire, virtually severing her head from the rest of her body. Under the circumstances I'm glad Miguel was not with me," I responded.

"I'm glad also but it wouldn't have made a difference. Miguel would have done the same thing. He won't hold a grudge against you.

"Speaking of holding a grudge," I said "what is the problem with Gale? She seems to have taken a large dislike to me. I think it developed on the mission and I don't understand."

"Gale is a very loyal and obedient member of our underground. She also has a very definite opinion of the role everyone should take. She indicated to me, prior to our leaving on the mission, that she thought it was unfair you get all the booty. On the mission she felt you didn't help her enough with locating her lost pack and you disobeyed orders by not finishing off the soldier the two of you found en route back to the cliff. Her resentments run deep. It's probably better you're leaving shortly as she would not be one of your allies."

"Doesn't she realize that I was having trouble with my leg in the first instance, and in the latter, the man was dying, even as she slit his throat," I said, feeling the need to defend myself.

"I believe you and don't think you did anything wrong. Gale, however, believes it was a breach of our security. She's still blaming herself for losing the pack even though we have mentally inventoried the contents, and there was nothing in the pack that would lead them here. It's just the way Gale is, and to some extent what makes her so valuable to me." As Ben was finishing, the man, whom I had seen several days before in the radio shack, crossed the great room and stopped in the doorway of the dining area. He said something to Ben in Spanish which Ben acknowledged by merely nodding his head.

"You indicated at the conclusion of your last communication that you must make a telephone call to your boss upon our return-- that it was very important. I have arranged for you to make the telephone call. I hope I'm not being presumptuous, but the routing of the call must be prearranged and the window for the call has arrived. It is fortunate you're up because I would have awakened you. It seemed important to you and I'm hoping it will be to us also. Can you make it to the radio shack on your own?"

"I'm glad you remembered. I was going to ask you to allow me to make the call. It must be made today. Should I go now? I'm sure I can make it. It will be good for me to exercise my leg," I said, relieved the arrangements had been completed.

Ben was the first to rise, going directly to a corner of the dining room and returning with a cane of sorts. He indicated the cane would make the trek to the radio shack easier for me. I willingly accepted his offering and we left the main ranch house. The path, really more of a trail, to the radio shack was much more uneven then I had remembered. The stiff leg caused me some problems, especially in the uneven spots. I was able to traverse the two or three hundred meters without an enormous problem, however, and we reached the shack in good time.

The operator was busy making some adjustment in several of the dials on the radio. As we entered he quit the adjustment and went to the phone. He entered a number or frequency or whatever and spoke in Spanish to someone. He turned and said something to Ben who translated for me. It would be about fifteen minutes before the call would be completed. Ben requested I give the radioman the number I wanted to contact. He would need it shortly. I complied. As the radioman listened for the proper connection and spoke to unknown intermediaries, Ben and I engaged in small talk ranging from the weather to how long I would be laid up before being able to travel. I heard the operator speak a series of numbers in Spanish into the receiver. He looked at me and motioned I should come closer. As I joined him he said something and handed the receiver to me. When I got the radiophone to my ear, the receiver on the other end was already ringing.

My day of reckoning was fast approaching, at least in the eyes of the Company. I only heard one ring and the call was answered, "Howard Baker here."

"Howard this is Eric." Before I could continue Howard launched into me.

"Where the hell have you been? Since our last conversation I have been getting heat from my boss and you know who that is. I'm under orders to get you back in country ASAP!"

"Howard slow down," I replied. "First I have been on a mission with the Colombian underground that has resulted in the destruction of much of the product I believe was destined for our project. If I leave now it will mean the last two years have been for nothing. Several people will have meaninglessly lost their lives. Is that what your boss wants, because if it is, then I'm out."

"You may be out anyway," Howard responded raising his voice. "I can't be sure but there's a good possibility you have already been targeted for extraction. You're under suspicion as we speak and thanks to you, so am I. Just what are you going to do?"

I could tell by his tone that Howard was not just mad and frustrated but also panicked. "First, I'm going to get well. I was injured two days ago and it will take another two before I can effectively and safely travel. If your boss has called out the dogs, so be it. After I can travel I will finish the project. That's with or without your boss's blessing." I hesitated, "I would, however, like to have your cooperation to complete this project. You and I know you can do that without your boss even knowing. I need to know where you stand. Unfortunately, I need to know now."

"What makes you think that I would even consider risking my pension to protect an agent that has given every signal he's gone south? What kind of fool do you take me for?"

"You're not a fool, Howard. This may be the only way left for you show the directors the value of your experience and intuition." I hesitated again, "This could be the end of Scott and that's who, we both know, you're concerned about."

There was silence on the other end of the phone. Howard was at least considering my proposition. "How and when would you contact me?" he asked.

I felt a wave of relief pass through my body, yet something was still bothering me.   You name the means and I'll be in touch with you every two days. We'll have the project finished within one month if not sooner."

"Get yourself well and contact me on my personal cell phone. It's the only way. Use a public phone and not the Agency cell. I'll expect to hear from you within two days. Is that clear?" As Howard was talking I realized what had been bothering me. The Agency would be listening to this transmission, or at the very least would be able to play back a recording of it. I needed to know where Howard stood in a way the Company would not be tipped off.

I took a long shot. If Howard was as alert as he always had been, he would know how to respond.

"Make the first call three days," I said. "I have to heal and locate a place to call you from. After that it will be every two days." Knowing Sadie's parents had been previously contacted, I inquired. "By the way, have you talked to Sadie's parents? How are they taking her death?"

"Three days will be fine but after that only two. No need for code, I have the recording devices as well as the eavesdropping equipment disabled. I installed a switch long ago allowing me to be selective in what the Company hears. Unless they've found a way to tap direct without my knowledge, the Company is not a party to this conversation."

He could be lying but I believed him. He truly disliked Scott Steel and this would be a way to eliminate him. I had to trust someone and Howard was a better choice than anyone else I knew. I terminated the conversation by promising to call in three days. I learned two valuable things in that telephone call. The first was that the dogs probably had been released to extract me. Second, I probably could trust Howard Baker. With that information I relaxed and concentrated on healing.

PART FOUR

THE VENTURE

CHAPTER FORTY-ONE

The last two days had actually been enjoyable. The sun was warm and the breezes were light, all so indigenous to the area, and the hospitality of my hosts, well, one couldn't ask for more. My leg was rapidly healing. The stitches were removed early this morning, an experience better than I could have expected in an area hospital. The old woman was truly an amazing medic. The younger woman had been an enormous aid to me. I learned her name was Marie and that she was twenty-three. I had become quite attached to Marie. I could see why these women were so valuable to Ben's group. In my convalescence, Marie made me move around more than I wanted in an effort to keep the injured leg from getting stiff. The efforts paid off as the leg felt new, and, except for some tenderness around the immediate area of the wound, felt like it had healed completely.

Ben was sending a small group into Cartagena later in the day to gather intelligence and replenish the supplies that had been depleted in the last four or five days. It was arranged that I would be part of the group which left the ranch, but I would not return. My self-imposed duties to Sadie had been more than fulfilled. During my convalescence, Ben offered me the opportunity to join his group as one of his lieutenants. I felt truly honored, but, while I wasn't sure what the future would bring, I knew it did not include becoming a lieutenant in his group. It wasn't that I didn't empathize, even identify with his objectives, but I knew my sights, and entire life-style, were beyond anything he could offer. It was time I was back on my own, relying on my own abilities and instincts.

My most pressing problem was to get the money I had accumulated deposited in a safe place -- a place where I had exclusive access. Without exclusivity it would be only a matter of time before I lost the money to a corrupt government official, to a simple robber, or to the Company. Colombia had a large supply of the first two, and, in all probability, I was wanted by my employer and my government. I really missed Sadie's help. She would have known exactly what to do. I discussed the problem with Ben, resulting in a decision to place the money in a bank on the Caribbean Island of Aruba. I knew the banks there were independent of U.S. control, and liked to pattern themselves after the total confidentially existing in certain Swiss banks. Ben suggested I arrange passage to the island on a private aircraft and make my deposit before I did anything else. The other opportunity was to go to Brazil and utilize their system. The easiest and safest choice seemed to be the Caribbean.

The group was to leave around noon. I had packed my belongings earlier. With the exception of a few items of business, I was ready to leave. Marie, who had taken such good care of me, as well as the older woman, who had sewed me up, deserved something for their efforts. I also wanted to leave the widows of the men who had died with some means to sustain themselves. I mentioned this to Ben and he arranged for the widows to meet with me in the ranch house just before we left. Marie and the medic were going to give me a last inspection prior to leaving. I could compensate them at that time. I determined that five thousand dollars each was warranted and set the amount aside while packing.

I glanced at my watch. It was about eleven o'clock. It was time to gather my gear and make the disbursements. The group would be leaving within the hour. As I approached the ranch house, I saw Marie and the medic also heading for the house and joined them. Marie asked how my leg was feeling and translated my answer to the older medic. The medic was obviously pleased. We reached my room and the medic indicated I was to drop my pants. I complied. She untied the loose bandage and inspected her handiwork. The wound hadn't separated since the stitches were removed, and what little swelling there was had subsided. The older medic was obviously happy with the results of her efforts because she was smiling and pointing out different areas of the wound to Marie. They spoke in Spanish so I understood little to none of the conversation.

Finally, Marie looked at me and said, "The Senora says your wound is healed. She is very happy there was no infection. The cut was so deep, she was uncertain whether she had gotten it all clean. She says you should keep a light bandage on it for another two or three days and then it will be completely healed." Marie hesitated and then said, "I will miss you, Mr. Butler. I was hoping you would stay with us. I felt we got along fine during your short stay, and, given time, we might become better friends."

"I'm sure we would become better friends. I have business that must be attended to, however, and it's time for me to leave. Who knows, I may be back someday and we can reacquaint ourselves." I took this opportunity to deliver a package of five thousand dollars to the medic and asked she be told it was a token of my appreciation for everything she did for me.

The message was translated to her as I delivered the bundle of bills. Her eyes grew large and her mouth fell open. She began to speak Spanish so quickly and with so much emotion that Marie had to slow her down. She thanked me profusely, gathered her medical kit, and left the room. I could tell as she left there were tears flowing down her wrinkled cheeks.

"The Senora thanks you for your generosity. There's no way you'll ever know how much your gift will mean to her and her family."

"It's the least I can do for her after all she did for me. By the way, you have meant a lot to me also, and I would like to give you a gift." Marie gasped, as I reached into the top of the pack, retrieved a bundle of bills, and handed them to her.

"Senor Butler, I only did my duty." As with the medic there were tears running down her cheeks.

"It may have been your duty, Marie, but to me it was the one aspect of the last days that made my life much easier. I want you and your family to have the money. I know you can use it." As I was finishing a voice from down the hall summoned me to dining area. "I have to go now. Please take care of yourself," I said, trying not to show the emotion I was experiencing.

"Senor Butler, I have one last request. May I kiss you before you leave?" I responded without thinking. She was not referring to a friendly parting kiss. I must have had the same thoughts, because when our lips met the kiss was deep and sustaining. As we parted, I had a strong desire to change my mind and join her in a simpler life, a life-style I would never be able to enjoy. I turned, grabbed my pack, left the room, and proceeded to the dining area. It was entirely possible tears were running down my cheeks. At the very least, tears were filling my eyes to the extent my vision was blurred. I hesitated before entering the dining area and wiped my eyes with the sleeve of my shirt.

As I entered the room Ben and three ladies, all dressed in black, were at the table. There was a feeling of sadness in the room that would have been recognized by the most unfeeling individual. "These ladies are the wives of the three men we lost on the mission," he said and turned to leave the room.

"Ben, please stay, I'm sure I'll need an interpreter. Please tell them I am very sorry for their loss. Ben spoke to the women in Spanish. Each of them nodded an acceptance of my condolences. They were on the verge of tears.

"I know there's nothing I can do that will make your loss any less painful, but I can attempt to help with the material loss each of you will be coping with." I hesitated to allow Ben to convey my words to them in their language. The ladies expressions portrayed their obvious confusion. "I have a gift for each of you and I want to give it to you now." As I was speaking, I took the remaining three packets of money from the top of my pack and handed one to each of them. The expression on each of their faces was worth every dollar in the packets. Each looked to Ben, as he was finishing the translation, and then back at me. Tears were now flowing freely. They were thanking me, each in their own way.

"I told them the gift from you was theirs and while you realized it was not a replacement for what they had lost, it would help ease the burden they would be facing. None of them has ever seen so much cash at one time. It will take time for them to realize the extent of your gift," Ben said.

"I hope you will help them to use the money in a way that best benefits them and their families. I have given a like sum to Marie and the older medic lady. They also may need some guidance from you."

"It's the least I can do. You have been very generous to us. We owe you a great deal. It is my hope we will be working together again. I also know that it is the hope of Marie. She has developed strong feelings toward you in the time you've been here. I have known this girl since she was a teenage child, and I want you to know that she does not give her affections away lightly."

"I have strong feelings for her as well, but, at this time, I must continue with my life and my duties, whatever they may be. As you are aware, I lost a lady I was very much in love with not long ago. The feelings for Maria have come too soon, leaving me with a feeling of guilt only time will cure. I know I will resolve these issues, but I must allow time to take its course. I don't know how much Marie knows of my history, but if you could tell her why I must leave without her I would appreciate it. I can't promise I'll be back either. I don't want her to wait for me. I don't know if I could ever fit into her life here, and I don't know if I would want to take her into my life, with all the problems and dangers it entails." I hesitated.

"Of course, I will convey your message but, Eric, you must know that she will wait. Please get word to me concerning your intentions. Whatever they are, she deserves to know," Ben interjected. "Now, we must get you on the road." The conversation ended, we left the ranch house, and entered the front yard area where I had first begun my association with Ben and his people.

The vehicle we took back to Cartagena was not the one that Kenneth and Gale had used when they brought me to the ranch. It was an older model Chevrolet pickup, one of the first models that had the small back seat, accessible from the passenger side. Kenneth was behind the wheel. There was a dark complected man in the rear seat. I threw my pack into the front seat with Kenneth and got in.

Ben shut the door for me. "Hopefully, we will be hearing from you in the not-too distant future. Have a safe trip to Cartagena and take care of yourself. Our cause can't afford to lose valuable people. We consider you to be one of us, whether you're with us, or operating on your own." As he finished, he tapped the top of the cab of the truck with his hand and Kenneth engaged the transmission. We were on our way.

The trip to Cartagena was uneventful and we made good time. The man in the rear did not speak English so most of the conversation was between Kenneth and me. Our exchange was light and centered around soccer, which was the only sport we had an interest in common. We discussed the success of the mission and the economics of running a ranch as a subterfuge to resisting the drug bosses. As we neared Cartagena, I worked the conversation around to Gale. "Why do you think Gale took such a dislike to me on the mission?" I asked.

"Gale is fiercely loyal to Ben and the cause. She lost most of her family at the hands of the Barajas family and their business affiliates," Kenneth responded. "She saw you as a fly by night soldier with no loyalty to anyone but yourself. She will carry that opinion, and act on it, until you convince her she was wrong. She's not along today because of you. Ben and I both agreed it would be better that she not cause any further concerns for you. You already have a full plate and she's not good at hiding her feelings and opinions."

"How do you feel about me?" I asked bluntly.

Kenneth looked at me form the driver's seat hesitating before he answered. "I think you would have been a valuable lieutenant in our organization had you chosen to stay. Your training and intuition would be an invaluable asset. It may be that you can still help. The choice will be yours and time will tell. I personally think the fact that you came to the ranch in an effort to complete the mission of your deceased lady friend indicates you can be extremely loyal. It's that loyalty I find to be your best asset. I believe you are sincere in your convictions and honest to the people that count. These are qualities I find irresistible. I would like to consider you to be a friend, if not a colleague."

"You may always consider me a friend. The colleague part is still to be determined. You can be assured there is nothing I will do that would adversely affect you or your cause. That's about as far as I can go today. I hope you understand." As I finished, I was looking directly at Kenneth. He looked at me with an understanding smile, that made any verbal response unnecessary.

The experience I had just survived, provided me with romantic feelings for a Colombian girl I didn't understand and wasn't ready to acknowledge, and a friendship with Kenneth and Ben, which might survive the test of time. The friendship was foreign to me. It was a first. The feelings of romance would have to be sorted out. All that would take time.

As we were finishing the conversation, the country was gradually changing from jungle to cleared land and sparsely located farmhouses. We'd be in Cartagena shortly. Kenneth's attitude immediately switched from conversational to business. He instructed the man in the back in Spanish. The man became instantly more alert.

"It's best we drop you in the center of town, in the vicinity of the market. It won't be as noticeable. The local airstrip is located about eight kilometers out of town on the south end. You'll be able to find transportation in the market. We don't expect any trouble, but you should have your weapon handy and out of sight."

Kenneth extended his right hand. "Best of luck. Contact us when you can. Gale and I will be going back to Bogotá shortly. You can reach us there." The truck came to a stop in a parking area abutting what was obviously the marketplace. I opened the door and took his hand.

"You can count on it," I said and exited the pickup.

There was a small crowd of locals heading for the market as I got out. It was easy to melt into their group. I needed a change of clothes, and the market was the place to get them. I followed the crowd until I was certain no one, who hadn't been following us, could connect me to Kenneth. One of the first shops I came across had tourist clothing displayed. Just what I wanted. I chose a pair of shorts and a sport shirt that would not stand out in a crowd. The shirt was loose enough that my weapon would not be obvious even if it were tucked into the belt of the shorts. I had kept the local currency available together with several hundred in U.S. currency. I had more than enough to make the needed purchases.

I told the shopkeeper I wanted to try the clothes on. He directed me to the back of the shop where there were curtains designed to give some privacy. I quickly changed into the clothes. They fit perfectly. I put my old clothes in the pack and wore the new ones out. The shopkeeper was happy he had made a sale and accepted the generous offer I made him for the outfit. Now, I needed shoes that would be consistent with the shorts. He had a stack of sandals that looked like they would fit the bill. I located a pair in my size and paid him for those also. I took off the boots I was wearing and they also went into the pack. With the exception of my pack, I now looked like all the other tourists. The pack was made of camouflage material, and, while I wasn't really worried it would be out of place, I decided to purchase another that was not so obvious.

A shop located several outlets down the walkway had an ample selection. I chose one that was forest green and looked like one a tourist would be carrying. I bought the pack and rejoined the crowds.

What I needed now was a taxi that would take me to the local airstrip. I milled around in the crowds until I reached the end of the market. No cabs were in sight. Rather than wasting time, I stopped at a local bistro. It appeared to be popular with, not only the locals, but also tourists, including a group of young men I had noticed earlier. They appeared to be visitors to the city. One of the times our paths crossed, I thought I heard someone speaking English. I casually approached the apparent leader.

"Do you speak English, by chance?" I inquired.

"You bet. I even teach the language," the young man responded, as the rest of the group gathered around us.

"Good, I need to get to the local airstrip. Would you happen to know where I can arrange for transportation?"

"No, but I'll bet I can get the information for you." He spun around and instructed one of the group to find a cab. The man, who was older than the others, looked to the street, spotted a car sitting at the curb, and approached the driver. After some conversation he returned and in broken, but very passable English, said, "The car over there will take you but it will cost ten dollars American." He was clearly a tour guide of sorts and was obviously embarrassed he couldn't get a better price. "There you are," the young leader said. "The driver is going to make his week's wages all from you. Maybe we can find a cheaper driver."

"No," I said. "I'm in somewhat of a hurry -- ten dollars will be fine." I thanked the man, the tour guide, and went to the car. The driver held out his hand before I even got in. He wanted his money in advance. I gave him ten dollars, and he broke out in smiles, indicating I should get in the front of the car. I complied.

The trip to the airstrip was uneventful if not smooth. The roads were reminiscent of some of the back roads of my youth in Colorado. As we arrived at the strip a small aircraft was taxiing to a stop. Almost before it had quit rolling a man was opening the door and preparing to exit. We were more than one hundred fifty meters from the end of the airstrip, so his facial features were not clearly visible. As we approached, and I was able to get a better look at him, my heart jumped to my throat. The man was one of Barajas' bodyguards. I had seen him in Las Vegas. I motioned for the driver to stop, but he simply pointed to a small metal shack that served as the terminal building and kept driving. He was parking within twenty meters of where the bodyguard was exiting the plane. As the cab pulled to a stop next to the building, the bodyguard, who had been walking directly toward the terminal, veered toward the rear of the cab.

I suddenly realized a Land Rover had come up behind us and was turning to pick him up. I glanced to the rear as he passed by the cab. The Land Rover had come to a stop virtually behind the cab. The rear door was opened allowing the bright sunlight to disclose the occupants. Opening the door was none other than Jose Salvador Barajas. The bodyguard quickened his pace entering the vehicle without ceremony. The Land Rover immediately sped away leaving a cloud of dust as it exited the airstrip.

I struggled to bring my adrenaline level under control. My driver was getting impatient and was gesturing for me to get out of the cab. After a final look to the rear, I got out of the car and approached the terminal building. I didn't know whether the cartel had any other soldiers placed in the building but I had no choice. I entered the building to find two other men. One was the pilot I'd seen leave the plane. The other was an older man who appeared to be the station agent. They were discussing something in Spanish as I approached.

"Do either of you speak English?" I inquired looking at the two men.

"I do," the pilot said. "Need a plane?"

"In fact I do. I want to fly to Aruba and need to get there as soon as possible. Would you be available?"

"Well, I just got in from Bogotá, but if you've got the money, I have the time," he responded with thinly veiled enthusiasm. "You'll have to prepay the trip. It will run three hundred and fifty dollars American, and you'll have to pay the fuel bill here and on the island. If that's agreeable we could leave as soon as I get refueled."

"Good enough. Let me hit the men's room and we can get started." I peeled off two one hundred-dollar bills and handed them to him. "These should get you started with the fueling. Let me know the total cost and I'll make up any difference." I turned and headed to the only bathroom in the place.

The pilot said something to the other man and hollered that he would be at the plane helping with the fuel. I went into the bathroom and shut the door. It didn't lock, but with the pilot and the agent heading toward the plane, I felt safe enough. I transferred the cash and extra magazines to the new pack as well as the boots. I took my shirt off and put on the nine-millimeter and the shoulder holster. I redressed, putting on the new shirt again. It was large enough so the weapon was hardly detectable. The pack needed something to cover the money so I used the old shirt I had worn to Cartagena. It worked perfectly. If the top flap of the pack gapped or fell open, the money would not be visible.

I reentered the station and surveyed the area for a large trash receptacle where I could discard the old pack. There was a large barrel in the corner. It had originally been filled with aviation fuel and was now serving as a trash refuse container. I had previously put my passport in one of the new pack's outer pockets. I stuffed the old pack into the container and used what discarded paper and other rubbish were available to cover the pack. I was ready to board the plane.

I left the station heading toward the small aircraft. It was an older Beechcraft but appeared to have been well maintained. The pilot and the station agent were fueling the plane from a fuel barrel with a hand pump. As I approached the pilot looked up.

"This is the last tank. We'll be airborne in fifteen minutes. Throw your gear in the rear passenger seat"

I stepped up on the trailing edge of the wing and stuck my head in the door. The plane had a relatively new radio. Its electrical equipment was far beyond anything one would expect to find on a plane this size however. As I was attempting identify the equipment, the pilot joined me on the wing. "Let me get in and we'll take off." he said as he brushed by me and entered the aircraft. As soon as he was in I entered the plane and sat in the combination copilot -passenger seat. Buckle up," he said, as he was flipping switches and studying the various dials. "Here we go," he said more to himself than to me.

The propeller began to turn. The motor coughed once or twice before catching. The turning propeller speeded up until it was invisible to the eye. He waived to the station man and we began taxiing to the end of the strip. He checked the windsock for a last time, turned the plane around, and we began to gain speed. The plane lifted off smoothly and gained altitude quickly.

"By the way my name is William but everyone calls me Dan, It's my middle name. What's yours?"

"Eric," I replied, not volunteering my last name. "Been running charters long?"

"Only since getting this plane. My old one was not one you would want to ride in, if you know what I mean," he replied as he swung the aircraft north up the coast. "We'll stay as close to land as we can until we get to a spot where we can slip across the Caribbean."

I didn't respond, realizing that we were going to pass above the resort I had visited several nights before. The coast was isolated, somewhat rugged, and where there weren't cliffs. There was jungle growing to the water's edge. As the plane droned its way north and a bit west, the harbor of the resort came into view.

Dan turned the plane north heading out in the Caribbean. "The people down there don't like visitors, and especially small planes, buzzing their resort. I think I'll head toward Aruba from here."

As he turned the plane, I could see the blackened trees around the warehouse. There were several men in the main area. Other than that, the resort appeared empty. "Why are they so inhospitable?" I asked, fishing for as much information as I could get without making him suspicious.

"I really don't know. The scuttlebutt is that a drug family owns it and uses the port for shipments to the states. I bought this plane from a broker who has connections that are, shall we say, not as legit as they might be. He told me this plane was based out of Cartagena. It made sense because it has electronics I would never have a use for. It's my theory it was used to make runs across the Caribbean carrying a cargo someone didn't want discovered. How else would you explain instruments that will tell me if I'm being tracked on radar? I've had to explain where I got this plane to more than one government agent." He achieved the bearing he desired and was putting the aircraft on autopilot. "At this speed we'll arrive in slightly over an hour. Relax and enjoy the flight."

I took his advice and settled back in the seat closing my eyes. I learned years ago that you don't turn down an opportunity to relax. It may be days before you get another chance. The trip was smooth as was the sea. It was the type of day this part of the world was famous for. As I was relaxing and trying to remain awake, I felt the engines slow and the plane start to loose altitude. I shook myself awake. Ahead, on the horizon, was an island.

"Is that Aruba?" I asked.

"You guessed it pal. We'll be landing in less than ten minutes."

"I have a further request. Could you land anywhere other than the main airfield? I'm here on banking business, and I don't want to create a record of my entry. Dan looked at me with a smirk on his face. "I can, but it'll cost you another hundred, and, by the way, I had to give that blood sucking agent a hundred to fill this bird so you owe me that also." His math didn't add up to what he was asking but I wasn't going to argue. I extracted two more hundred-dollar bills and gave them to him.

He stuck them in his shirt pocket, veered the plane to the right, and began to gain altitude again. "We will land on the other side of the island. It has to be quick because they've had me on radar for the last fifteen minutes. I'll land. You jump out and I'll take off again. Hopefully, they will think that I dropped off the radar because I was behind the island. When I reappear they'll be happy. I have enough fuel to get back to the mainland so I won't even have to explain why I ducked out of sight."

"Will there be transportation to the island's banking district?" I asked, not wanting to be stranded with the cash I was carrying.

"More than you'll be able to use. Now tighten your belt, we're going in." With that warning, Dan banked the plane and we lost altitude fast. By the time my stomach caught up with the rest of me we were lining up on a small landing strip just off the beach. He landed the aircraft without a hitch. We taxied to a stop.

"This is where you get off," he announced. I opened the door, reached around, grabbed my pack, and virtually slid down the plane's wing. Before I could thank him or even wave goodbye, he was turning the plane around and was gaining speed, heading down the runway. I watched him become airborne before I turned around to see where I was.

He was right. Before I had taken fifteen steps toward the small hut serving as a terminal, I had six or eight locals offering anything from a short tour to a week's limousine service. I chose a man who spoke good English and asked him to get me to the center of the island's city. He led me to his car, a newer model Ford, and we headed for the city. I somehow knew I was at the genesis of a new life.

CHAPTER FORTY-TWO

Ronnie and Steve arrived in Bogotá in the late afternoon. The customs agents were anticipating the end of their shift and weren't as vigilant as they might have been earlier. They were the first in line. The plan was to appear as any other couple might that had gotten away for a romantic vacation. Steve smiled at the agent as Ronnie draped herself over his shoulder. He slipped the agent a twenty dollar bill and quietly asked him if this could be quick, "We need to get to our hotel." Ronnie coyly flirted with the agent, giggling as Steve made the request. The agent expertly palmed the twenty. None of the other agents saw the money change hands. His demeanor became even more officious, but the result was as anticipated. He didn't look at the passports while stamping them and passed their luggage through without inspection. The ploy had worked. They were in Colombia without a hitch.

"He doesn't know how true that statement was," Ronnie said, still draped on his arm as they walked away.

"I don't know what you mean. You heard Scott warn us about Company policy," Steve replied in a tone leaving no doubt that he had no intention of giving any consideration to the policy. "But we have to find a bar or something to pass two hours before Sailor arrives".

"I know, but it seems like such a waste," Ronnie said with an impish tone in her voice.

As they worked their way down the concourse and into the main ticketing area, Steve noted that two rather shabbily dressed men seemed to be following them. At least the men were everywhere they were. Steve leaned toward Ronnie, giving every indication of a show of affection. He whispered his suspicions. She kissed his cheek.

"Let's split up for a few minutes and see what they do. I'll meet you back here in ten minutes," she whispered.

Steve nodded his agreement and, after an embrace, they each went separate ways. Steve began walking at a slight angle, enabling him to keep an eye on the reactions of both men. As he and Ronnie split, there was meaningful eye contact between the two men. The one nearest Ronnie jerked his head in her direction. The other nodded assent beginning to follow

Ronnie. The remaining man was intent on Steve and began moving in his direction. Steve watched as Ronnie stepped into a small boutique, specializing in the local styles. She appeared to be doing what women with time on their hands often do in airports, shopping. It all looked very natural.

The man following her found a bench near the door of the shop and sat down, obviously waiting for her to come out. As Steve headed toward a small bar and lunch counter his tail became very sloppy, getting too close. Steve sidestepped into the bar at the last possible minute, causing the tail to have to continue on past. It worked. The tail almost ran him down as Steve came to a sudden stop preparing to step into the entrance. Steve hesitated and looked the man directly in the eye, forcing him to apologize for his clumsiness. Steve had effectively neutralized the tail. The man went on down the concourse. Steve exited the doorway of the bar and headed back to where he and Ronnie had separated. It had only been five minutes. Ronnie had not returned.

Steve stationed himself where he could see the shop where Ronnie had disappeared and still keep an eye on the concourse where he had shaken his tail. Within minutes Ronnie exited the shop with a bag under her arm. She proceeded directly toward the man sitting on the bench. Like any woman shopper, she was stopping to window-shop as she went. The tail stayed on the bench acting as though he wasn't aware of her presence.

From Steve's vantage point he spotted the tail he had neutralized, heading for the area where Ronnie was pretending to be interested in displayed trinkets. The two men spotted each other. Steve's tail, the larger of the two, approached the bench and spoke to his partner. They both looked at Ronnie and then seemed to be scanning the concourse in the immediate area. It occurred to Steve that these men might not have intentions which were in the best interests of either himself or Ronnie. They needed to be convinced to leave the area. When the two tails returned their attentions to Ronnie, he quickly, but without raising any attention to himself, put his hand inside his jacket, unhooked his weapon, and moved in behind the two men. As they turned they came face to face with him.

"Gentleman, we have something we have to discuss, don't we? Why don't you both just sit down on the bench and act as though we're old friends, while telling me why you're following us? By the way, this is not a Pepsi bottle I'm holding in my right hand, if you know what I mean."

As the two men turned around, Ronnie, who had seen the confrontation out of the corner of her eye, approached the bench. Her hand was inside her purse and her expression was anything but friendly.

"As you can see my associate has joined us and she also is not holding a Pepsi bottle. Who are you, and why are you following us?

The two men looked at each other and, after a pause, the bigger of the two spoke. "Just relax, I'm going to reach into my pocket and get my identification."

Steve stepped back to get a clear view of what was being extracted. The man produced a ragged billfold and handed it to Ronnie who took it without taking her eyes off the men. She flipped it open glancing at its contents. She moved to the side handing it to Steve. The billfold contained an identification card and badge indicating he was a DEA agent. His name was Denny Smith.

"I assume that your friend can produce like identification," Steve asked, not relaxing his vigilance.

"Mark, show them your identification," Denny Smith said with frustration in his tone.

The smaller man produced a wallet and handed it to Ronnie. She scanned its contents. "It says he's a DEA agent by the name of Mark Johnson. The picture matches."

"Now, gentleman, we know your names and your employer. Why were you following us?"

"We're on special assignment with the CIA. Your boss asked us to meet a gentleman arriving in about an hour. We were also tasked to locate the two of you and make sure you got into the country. Following the arrival of Mr. Sailor, we are to cooperate with you in any way we can."

"Why did you tail us? Why not just make your presence known? Why all the subterfuge?

"We saw you enter and realized your cover was that of a happy tourist couple. We reasoned if we approached you directly, and someone was watching, we'd blow your cover. We obviously were a bit careless."

Assuming we believe you, what do you suggest we do now? If you're who you say you are, we still need to meet John and you need to brief us on what you know concerning our assignment," Steve said, not removing his hand from inside his jacket.

"I suggest we separate. The two of you head to wherever you've arranged to meet Sailor. We'll meet him at the gate, make sure he gets through customs, and hook back up with you later. We'll need our identification back."

Steve looked at Ronnie. She shrugged her shoulders indicating it was his call. He nodded his head and she returned the identification to Mark Johnson. Steve returned the wallet he had to Smith.

"We're meeting John in the ticketing area. Go do your jobs. We'll discuss this later."

The two agents got up and sheepishly proceeded down the concourse.

"I assume you believed them." Ronnie said, more as a question than a statement.

"I'm not sure. I think we should keep out of sight until after John's plane has landed and then approach only after we're convinced John has accepted them. I found a small bar just up the concourse. We'll be out of sight there."

Ronnie and Steve proceeded to the bar area and chose a table that was a bit out of the way, yet allowed them to see most of the ticketing area. Both ordered a beer and sat sipping the brew without talking.

Ronnie was the first to break the silence.

"You handled that really well. I'm sure I would've been more aggressive and blown, not only our cover, but possibly gotten us in trouble."

"You want to know the truth?" Steve said as Ronnie nodded. "I wasn't sure what to do, and my first instincts were like yours, to make a scene. Something told me that would be a mistake, so I forced myself to be subtle. Maybe I'm starting to get that instinct everyone talks about. You did well also -- so don't sell yourself short. You held back so you could cover me if they went ballistic. That was the right thing to do. I think we both may be getting some of that instinct. We may even make a good team. One that can stay together, that is if you want to," Steve said, hesitating, looking for a reaction in his new partner. Ronnie looked embarrassed, a reaction which was new to their relationship.

"I can't make any promises," she said. "I've done too much of that in the past. Let's just take it one step at a time." She hesitated. "Is that okay with you?"

"Hey, I wasn't trying to put any pressure on you. I just thought we made a good pair on that takedown," Steve responded, realizing Ronnie had some issues she needed to work through." As Steve was speaking, the congestion in the concourse seemed to increase. Steve looked at his watch. "I think the plane John is on may have landed. We'd better keep a sharp eye."

Steve and Ronnie finished their beer and stepped into the oversized hallway which served as a ticketing area. Within minutes they spotted the familiar figure of John Sailor in the customs line. One of the DEA agents was beside him. The other was talking to an official who appeared to be the supervisor in the area. The official nodded to the agent and walked over to the area where his men were screening the travelers who had gotten off the plane. He tapped one of the agents on the shoulder and, leaning very close to his ear, said something to him. The agent looked up the line toward where John was waiting and nodded. It took another five minutes for John to get to the screening table. The DEA agent that had been accompanying John in line had joined the agent who called himself Denny Smith. They continued waiting but more to the rear and side of the line of travelers.

As John approached the table, the agent looked to the supervisor and gave an almost imperceptible nod. The agent took John's passport stamped it and motioned him through. Several people in line, whose luggage was in the process of being searched, complained they weren't getting the special treatment. The complaints fell on deaf ears, however, and John gathered his gear and proceeded toward where the two DEA agents were waiting. Steve and Ronnie watched as they conversed. Within seconds John had spotted them and continued to where they had positioned themselves. As he approached, he tilted his head in a way that signaled they should follow him.

John walked through the airport, out one of the main doors, and signaled for a cab. Steve was the first to reach him. John smiled a noncommittal smile, one which he might use when any tourist with whom he hadn't made acquaintance approached him. He spoke to Steve with all the external trappings of a meaningless conversation at a cabstand. The message, however, was to take a cab, separate from his, to the Hotel Standish, which was located near the airport. He would meet them there. As he was finishing, he nodded a farewell, wished them a pleasant stay in Colombia, and got in a waiting cab.

Steve looked at Ronnie, shrugged his shoulders, and summoned a cab which was waiting for a fare. They got into the cab and instructed the cabby to drive them to the Standish Hotel. He nodded and pulled away from the curb into the moderate traffic leaving the airport property. The trip was uneventful and seemed to skirt the main part of the city, staying on the northwest edge. Upon arrival at the Standish Hotel, Steve and Ronnie exited the cab and were immediately met by an elderly man. He was the hotel's answer to a bellman. The bellman took their bags into the hotel, depositing them in front of the main desk.

Steve approached the desk and inquired if the hotel had a room with a view from the front. The man behind the desk nodded, threw a key across the counter, and at the same time offered a registration slip with an old pen he'd been chewing when they approached. Steve wiped the pen dry and filled out the pertinent information required. He looked at Ronnie, who was gazing into the small bar area next to the registration desk.

"Not quite four star," he said with a smile, "but, I'm sure it will do fine." They picked up their luggage, waived off the bellman, and started up the stairs. The room key said three forty five. By the time they reached the room, both were wishing they had used the bellman. The room was more of a small suite than a single sleeping room. It had a small sitting room just off the main entrance. To the right was a doorway leading to a bedroom with a queen-sized bed. Off the bedroom was a bathroom with shower and vanity.

"Much better than I thought it would be," Ronnie said, as she toured the suite. "I think we can be *more* than comfortable." Ronnie had a sparkle in her eye Steve recognized from the previous evening. The look itself was arousing.

"We'd better get settled and get down to the bar so we can see John when he arrives. He couldn't have been far ahead of us. He should've been in the lobby when we arrived. I hope he hasn't run into trouble."

"I think John can take care of himself," Ronnie said. "Which side of the bed do you want? It doesn't matter to me."

Steve indicated he would take the left side and put his luggage on the small dresser top located on the left. Ronnie was doing the same on the right side. Neither of them unpacked, leaving the drawers provided by the hotel empty. Early in training they had been instructed that an agent should never create a circumstance where he could not gather his belongings and leave on a moment's notice. Even in their brief employment with the Company, the trait had become second nature for both of them.

"I don't think we should leave all the money here in the room," Ronnie said in a whisper which was barely audible. "What do you think?"

"The Company designed this luggage with that problem in mind. I don't think anyone will find it, but we could each carry half on our person for now. Let's remember to ask John what we should do when we see him. You brought a money belt didn't you?" As Steve was talking he was strapping on a belt resembling a corset more than a money belt. As distinguished from a traditional belt, it extended about half way up the stomach, allowing one to carry more cash stored flat against the body. As Steve was finishing, he glanced at Ronnie.

She had taken off the blouse she was wearing and was adjusting the belt to eliminate any wrinkles or bulky areas. Her bra was low-cut in the center, allowing Steve to see her more than ample breasts. The effect was pure eroticism. Ronnie asked him to help her adjust it higher on her abdomen to avoid a thickness around her waistline. Steve went behind her and elevated the back portion as she smoothed the front portion of the apparatus. As he adjusted the belt around her, he allowed his hands to stray until they were covering both breasts. They were soft to the touch, yet firm enough to allow her to go without the bra had she chosen to do so.

"Remember, you're the one who said we had to get to the bar to greet John. You'll just have to save this for later, because I'm not going to get into this straight jacket a second time," Ronnie said. As she turned around, she brushed her lips against his and finished dressing.

"You know you could go without a bra if you wanted to," Steve said, realizing she was not going to undress again to satisfy his prurient interests.

"Now, that would be good. I could call attention to the very area I'm trying to disguise. You'd probably be the only one to notice anyway," she said, knowing it wasn't true. Ronnie finished buttoning her blouse. They inspected each other and left the room for the bar.

They'd only been seated for ten or fifteen minutes when the bellman left his post and was heading for the main entrance. Within seconds he re-entered, empty-handed. He glanced at the man behind the desk and shrugged his shoulders. Seconds later John Sailor entered, carrying his luggage. He hesitated, while his eyes adjusted to the dim light, and then preceded to the desk. The check-in process took only a minute or so and John went up the stairs. Steve and Ronnie were dumb-founded. He hadn't even acknowledged them.

"Do you think we should follow him?" Ronnie said, as much to herself as to Steve.

"No. He knows where we are. Let's wait here for him to come to us. He knows what he's doing."

Steve and Ronnie had been waiting in the bar at least thirty minutes when John Sailor came down the stairs. He went directly to the entrance and exited the hotel. He gave them no sign of recognition, let alone any direction. For the second time in less than an hour he had left them without any indication of what they should do.

"I got the feeling in Washington that he wasn't enthralled with having us along. Do you think he is going off on his own?" Steve asked after the shock of him leaving the hotel had worn off.

"No, if he were going to do that, he wouldn't have come to this hotel at all. I think he's being especially cautious for some reason. I'll wait here. You go back to our hotel room. If he somehow got our room number, maybe he left a message."

Steve got up, headed toward the stairs, and disappeared into the upper reaches of the hotel. Ronnie ordered another beer and sat waiting. There was a man sitting in the outer lobby who hadn't been there before. Ronnie studied his face so she could identify him if he appeared again. In her efforts she became obvious, and he noticed her looking at him. He smiled at her, closed his newspaper, got up, and strolled out the door. Ronnie was mentally kicking herself for being so obvious when Steve descended the stairs. He winked at her as he reached the landing and strolled across to their table. Steve sat down sliding his chair closer to hers. His tone of voice was subdued but audible.

"John slid a note under our door. We're to meet him at another hotel in two hours. He said our room was probably bugged, his was. He said to find any bugs and destroy them. Let's finish our beer and get back to the room."

"I've got a better idea. Let's take the beer to the room," Ronnie responded with a slight giggle. "Maybe we can locate them in less than two hours."

"Good thinking. I'll arrange to have a cab here in ninety minutes. That should give us time to take care of everything," Steve said feeling his hormones kick in.

They casually got up and went to the staircase. Upon reaching the third floor and the entrance to their room, Steve unlocked the door. Before entering they discussed how to canvas the suite. Steve was to take the sitting room, and Ronnie was to canvas beginning in the bathroom. They would meet in the bedroom. Any bugs found were to be noted -- not immediately destroyed. Once all were located, they would destroy them at the same time. They entered the room and began their search. All ceiling fixtures and lamps were checked as well as any knickknacks on tables, dressers, and shelves. The last to be checked were the wall receptacles. Each cover plate was unscrewed, unless the screw had been painted over, and obviously had not been removed recently. Ronnie found one bug in the ceiling fixture of the bathroom. There was also one in the base of the lamp located on a nightstand in the bedroom. A third was located in the sitting room under a coffee table located in the center of the room.

Steve motioned Ronnie to the exterior hallway. "You disconnect the bathroom. I'll get the ones in the sitting room and bedroom. We'll flush them down the toilet at the same time. Ready?"

Ronnie nodded and they reentered the suite. Each systematically went about their assignment. Within thirty seconds the bugs were dislodged from their locations and were in the toilet. One flush and they were gone. As Steve turned around, Ronnie had her blouse and bra off and was working on the money belt. Steve looked at his watch. The cab wouldn't be available for another seventy minutes.

———◆———

Steve and Ronnie exited the hotel and found the cab Steve had ordered waiting. As they entered the cab, Ronnie giggled. "I'll bet if they could have heard us, it would have completely ruined their home life."

Steve put his finger to his lips, signaling she should quit talking and instructed the cabby to take them to the Hotel Bogotá. Without much acknowledgment the cab started moving. The ride took about thirty minutes and skirted several local open markets. Upon arrival at the Hotel Bogotá, Steve paid the cabby and they entered a large ornate lobby. A concierge approached and inquired if he could be of any help. Steve asked where the hotel steakhouse was located. The concierge smiled and directed them to the second floor by pointing to a spiral staircase. As they walked toward the staircase, Ronnie hesitated and grabbed Steve's arm. "Don't you think you should tip the hotel personnel? They probably live on the tips they receive.

We may need help later and they might cooperate more if they know they'll be compensated."

"You're probably right. I'm not use to this kind of assignment." He smiled at her. "I'll do better in the future."

Upon reaching the second level the hotel steakhouse was directly ahead. They entered through massive wooden doors that must have weighed two hundred kilos each. A maître d' met them at a small podium located just inside the doors.

"Do you have reservations?" he asked with that fake smile people, who make their living providing comforts to others display.

"We're with the John Sailor party. The listing may be under the name of Denny Smith or Mark Johnson however," Steve said, pressing a five-dollar bill in the man's outstretched hand.

"Very good," the maître d' said. "If you will follow me, the rest of your party has already arrived." He led them between tables that had been set with sterling silver and crystal.

Ronnie leaned over to Steve and whispered, "I think we may be a bit underdressed." Steve smiled at her, in an effort to put her more at ease, but he felt the same. They were led to a small room the restaurant kept for patrons needing some privacy. Already seated were John Sailor, Denny Smith and Mark Johnson. There were two additional settings at the table, one for each of them. As they approached, the two DEA agents stood and greeted the couple. John remained seated, sipping what appeared to be a martini. He acknowledged them with a nod.

"Just in time for a cocktail. Name your poison," Mark Johnson said, as he summoned a waiter.

"I'll have a Gibson," Ronnie responded, turning to Steve. "Coffee will be fine," Steve indicated.

"Just coffee? You realize being able to drink may be one of the few benefits of the work we do," Denny Smith injected with a smile.

"Oh, I can drink and if I say so myself, do a good job when I want to. Tonight I don't feel like a party. We have business to discuss, and I want to be on a sharp edge. Coffee will do fine." As he finished, he could feel Ronnie's disapproval of his candor. She was going to have to get used to it he thought as he turned to her smiling. Her face gave no evidence of the tightness Steve sensed in her body. A glance toward John gave no indication of his opinion. His expression failed to indicate whether he approved or disapproved. He just sat there sipping his martini.

"In that event, I guess we can start now," Denny said, appearing quite awkward. "Mark, why don't you start? I'll jump in if I have anything to add." Mark looked around, making sure there weren't any waiters hovering close to the table.

"Very well, to begin with let me tell you what we understand your assignment to be," he said directing most of his attention to John Sailor. "You're to extract an agent, specifically an Eric Butler, last known to be in Colombia. You're currently staying in the same hotel Butler and his partner stayed in while in Colombia on their initial trip. They left separately. Both traveled back to the States only to return within seven to ten days. Shortly after their return to Colombia, either the drug cartels or the police killed his partner, a Sadie Anderson. In many instances the police and the cartels are one and the same. We're not privy to the assignment Butler is or was on, but the section chief suspects he's gone south. We're here to give you all the information we have on Butler and any assistance we can provide in the future."

At this point in the conversation Denny jumped back in. "As nearly as we can determine this Sadie Anderson is thought to have killed a local policeman. The scuttlebutt is that he was on two payrolls and probably deserved all he got. Nonetheless, both the police and the cartel were anxious to apprehend her. Butler had left Columbia several days earlier. She got out of the country, and for some unknown reason they both returned approximately a week later. It was during that second entry Ms. Anderson was hit. For your information, it was in this hotel that the deed was done. One of Butler's last communications with the Company was to arrange for return of Anderson's remains. As I understand it, a communication was made several days ago, indicating Butler was involved in something he believed was consistent with his assignment. We also have some vague intelligence, indicating the cartel he was working with had some kind of mishap in one or more of their storage areas. The intel is that they had moved product to a coastal area around Cartagena. It somehow got destroyed. This mishap has put the cartel in a real bind."

"Is that all you have?" John asked, with a certain amount of disdain in his voice.

"Well there is one other fact that may be helpful," Denny said defensively. "The police believe Butler is tied to an automobile rented from a maintenance worker from this hotel. The automobile was later discovered abandoned in a public park not far from here. City sanitation workers also found a cell phone in a trash can behind some businesses in an area not far from the park where the car was found. The cell turned out to be one of yours."

"Look, John, I think we've done pretty well, especially when Butler wasn't our assignment. We were only asked to keep an eye out and report what we could to you," Mark injected defiantly.

John didn't say a word. He just nodded.

The waiter approached, inquiring if the group was ready to order. Each ordered a steak and potato, which was served in short order. The conversation around the dinner table was light, taking place mostly between Ronnie and the DEA agents. At the conclusion, John Sailor stood and announced he was leaving. As he started out, he instructed Ronnie and Steve to meet him back at the hotel, indicating his room was next to theirs. He stopped at the door, thought for a second, turned around, and came back to the table.

"Do either of you have any evidence Butler has gone south? Is there anything you have found that would lead you to believe he is acting in any way that would compromise his assignment?" John asked, addressing the question to both of the DEA agents.

"Well, no we haven't, but the information he was came from your boss and that's good enough for us. Isn't that your job anyway?" Mark said, with a certain edge to his voice.

Being true to form, John didn't respond. He just turned and left the room.

"I sure wouldn't want to be in Butler's shoes and have that man after me," Mark said, watching John work his way through the tables in the main dining room.

Steve noticed, as John passed into the hotel hall that two men got up from a table near the entrance and left the restaurant. He glanced at Ronnie. He could tell she also had noted the same fact. "I hope you, gentleman, will excuse us but as you said, 'it's our job', and we'd better get to work," Steve said, as he and Ronnie rose, thanked their hosts, and left the restaurant, taking basically the same path as John.

As they reached the lobby, Ronnie tugged lightly on Steve's arm. "Someone in there will be following us also. You know that don't you?"

"Yes, let's get back to our hotel. We'll gain nothing by confronting them."

Ronnie nodded and they hailed a cab.

The ride back was made in total silence each realizing the real assignment was about to begin.

CHAPTER FORTY-THREE

The small Catholic Church, which had been allowed to remain on the Barajas Estate, was filled to the last pew. All the families living in the surrounding villages owed their livelihood to the Barajas family. Attendance, on this occasion, was thought to be mandatory. The Rosary for Eva Barajas had been held the evening before and while it was traditional for the casket to be open during the Rosary, on this occasion it was closed. Eva was the niece of the family patriarch, Jose Salvador Barajas. The word in the villages was she had been killed in an automobile accident while in the north on family business, but that was the reason given for all the funerals which had taken place here for some time. Mr. Barajas had raised Eva from a child. Her father died under unusual circumstances, as had her mother. Their survivors were Eva and her brother Miguel.

Miguel had estranged himself from the family several years ago. Eva made every attempt to make up to her uncle for what she viewed was a family dishonor. The efforts were enormously successful. Eva had gained the favor and absolute trust of the patriarch.

It was clear to all in attendance that Jose Barajas had been deeply disturbed by her death. The rumor was Miguel was somehow responsible. Aside from the grief, one only had to look at the face of Jose Barajas to sense an anger that struck fear in the native villagers. The local priest had sensed, or been instructed, not to mention the name of Eva's brother, so efforts to console the immediate family in the eulogy only referred to Jose and his wife. The services were as simple as they could be, given the complexities of the Catholic faith. When they were completed the mourners formed a procession to the family graveyard where Eva was placed in her final resting place. The family withdrew to their estate for mourning.

Jose Barajas, Mr. B, as both his employees and villagers knew him, had summoned his lieutenants to the estate. One of the family's lead positions had been vacated and was to be filled. Business needed to go on. As the lieutenants arrived they were directed to a large rather formal area of the estate mansion designed for events where the attendance list was extensive. The staff laid out the traditional fare expected in circumstances such as these. Those in attendance milled around nervously. Each exhibited apprehension, wondering why they were there and what was in store, not only for them personally, but for the operation that had given them a standard of living far above what they could expect as the simple farm laborers they were.

Barajas made his appearance after the group had been assembled for approximately thirty minutes. After receiving appropriate condolences from the men in attendance, he stepped to the head of the table and motioned the men to take their seats.

"The loss of my niece is a blow to my family and a blow to our business. As all of you know, she was entrusted with the responsibility of directing and, on some occasions, leading the field operations on which our business depends. She will be missed, but her death will not go unavenged. Some of you knew we were amassing product in the North. The product was destined for sale in world markets through a partner who will expand our sales abilities. We will be able to market in areas not previously available to us, through contacts previously unknown to us, and we will become a factor in these markets. The designated product was destroyed by the local organization opposed to our interests. It is my belief that Miguel Barajas is part of that organization. I believe he either killed his sister or was part of the faction that killed her. I am pledging one hundred fifty thousand American dollars as a bounty to anyone who can bring Miguel Barajas to me -- and I want him alive! Each of you will pass that information down the ranks and into the communities. I want both our friends and our enemies to be aware of the price on this man's head."

"Bringing Miguel back alive may not be possible. It is rumored he has many followers. It would be better, safer for us, if he could be brought back dead rather than alive," one of the lead lieutenants said.

"I realize that, and I will accept his head, but I want to be the one who takes it. My preference is that he is brought back alive. It's more difficult but not impossible. I will adjust the reward to be as follows, fifty thousand American dollars for his head and one hundred and fifty thousand dollars for his return alive."

Barajas hesitated. It was clear to all present that the issue was closed. "I have given some thought to Eva's replacement and have chosen Salvador Valencia to lead our field operations. I expect each of you to give Salvador the same efforts and loyalty you had given Eva. Because of the events that have taken place recently we are in danger of losing our partner and, therefore, the opportunity to expand our business. Salvador will need all of your best efforts. If any of you are not able to give him the loyalty you gave my niece, speak now." Barajas hesitated and visually surveyed the room. "Good. Now eat and drink to your fill, but remember we have an enormous task ahead of us, and it will begin at dawn tomorrow. Now, Salvador, I need to speak to you privately.

Barajas stood and left the room in the company of Salvador Valencia. The room was quiet. It was several long seconds before anyone moved toward the waiting food and drink. The mood was solemn. The gathering disbursed within an hour, each wondering what changes were on the horizon.

———◆———

Salvador Valencia was large in stature and powerfully built. He had been with Barajas since he was a teenager, having been recruited from a small village in the south where his family was involved in cultivating product. He acted as a personal bodyguard for the immediate family and, in that position, had gained the trust of Barajas. Salvador approached every assignment with a tireless and relentless attitude. He'd personally terminated many men during the period when the Barajas family was struggling with other cartels for dominance in the local and American marketplace. Barajas's only concern was that he did not have the gift of foresight Eva had possessed. Salvador may lose track of the forest for the trees, but God help the trees. He was the best choice available. With a little stewardship, he would develop into a strong leader.

Barajas led Salvador to his private study where he offered a drink to his new captain. As expected, the drink was declined. Salvador sat in one of the overstuffed chairs Barajas had imported for his office. The office was not like the rest of the mansion, which was decorated in local style, often allowing function to overshadow comfort. It was more what one would expect in the office of an American company's president. Barajas enjoyed the warmth and closeness the decor promoted. Mr. Barajas had taken a seat in a similar chair across from Salvador.

"The family has made arrangements to join an American friend in an attempt to expand our markets. If we are successful, we will not be as dependent on the inefficiencies of the American police units. A problem has arisen however. A small band of locals gained access to our staging area and were successful in burning the entire product which had been relocated there. Many of our people were killed during the raid, one of them Eva. We must gather all the finished product we can get our hands on, and get it to the Cartagena compound for shipment. I don't believe the locals will attempt to hit the same place twice but that's going to be your first assignment. You will make sure the product remains safe after it arrives. The locals burned the barn so you'll have to get a temporary structure erected quickly. I've arranged for you to fly into Cartagena from Bogotá with a private pilot. He's not one of us but, like so many Americans, is willing to shut his eyes if the money's right. I'll have you flown into Bogotá in one of our planes for the connection and our people will pick you up in Cartagena. They will show you around but, remember, you're in charge. They have been so advised." Barajas hesitated.

"Wouldn't I be more valuable to you accumulating and transporting product than in Cartagena? I have a man that would be able to secure the area, and I could meet him later?" Salvador questioned.

"Normally yes, but this time I'm going to personally arrange for the product. I need the assurance it will be safe until shipped. Your plane leaves immediately. Gather your things and go to the airstrip. I will be in touch with you when you arrive in Cartagena. Good luck my friend. We will all be better off when we meet our responsibilities to the venture."

Salvador left the room without further comment. He went to his quarters and gathered what few items he needed for the assignment. He was stowing them in the duffel bag he always carried when traveling, when there was a knock at his door. It was a man he knew to be the family banker. Out of habit he checked to make sure there was nothing visible that would cause concern and opened the door. Without coming in, the banker handed Salvador a small valise. "Mr. Barajas forgot to give you this. If you need more let me know."

"What is it?" Salvador asked.

"Its money you may need to satisfy local officials. The money we previously sent was stolen in the raid." The man turned and left.

Salvador closed the door and opened the valise. Inside was more money than he had ever seen. He'd never been entrusted with use of the family's money before. It was then that the gravity of his new position hit. For the first time since childhood, he felt the clutches of panic.

CHAPTER FORTY-FOUR

The center of the city was what one might expect of a small Caribbean island, with one notable exception. In the center of several open markets, were two or three large modern buildings advertising they were in the banking business. As I stood in the market place trying to determine which of the banks to enter, I suddenly missed Sadie. With her international banking background, the decision would have been easy. At least I wouldn't have had to make the choice. It occurred to me, they probably all had the same basic services and it didn't really matter which one I chose. The closest one was the Aruba Bank of Commerce, which advertised it was affiliated with some bank in Switzerland. I chose that bank and entered the oversized doors. I hadn't gotten into the main lobby before a well-dressed bank official inquired if he could be of any service.

"I am interested in opening an account, if your bank can offer me the services I require," I responded.

"Our bank can offer virtually any arrangement. Let's go to my office and discuss your needs," the banker said, as he led me into a narrower corridor with offices on both sides. "Our discussions will be more discreet back here. Our bank prides itself on the confidences we offer." The banker motioned me to a large upholstered chair, which was across the massive mahogany desk he occupied. "What exactly can we do for you Mr. ....?"

"Butler, Eric Butler. I'm interested in opening an account I can access from any major bank in the world. I will need the bank to vouch for my financial capabilities and will need to deposit from anywhere with a pass-code that's different from the one I use to withdraw funds. Finally I need assurance the account can't be frozen by the actions of any government, including the United States." I hesitated, partially to gauge his reaction to my requirements, but also to determine if I had left anything out.

"And what rate of return will you be requiring, Mr. Butler?

"Rate of return is nice but not a requirement if my confidentially is maintained. Can your bank provide me with those services?"

"But of course, and if you waive a rate of return, not even the local government will know of our relationship. How much will you be depositing with us, and what level of activity might we expect?" he asked, reaching for a sheath of papers that were on the desk when we entered the office. The sheath was obviously placed there to facilitate the opening of a new account.

"I'm not sure. Is there a place where I can have some privacy?"

"Yes, of course. I'll step out of the office. You can take as much time as you want. When you have made your decision, just press the button on the corner of the desk." He smiled and left the room.

Before baring my soul, as it were, I checked the room for video cameras. The walls and woodwork were elegant, but not ornate, so the search was relatively simple. Within minutes I satisfied myself that I was truly alone. I emptied my pack on the oversized desk and counted the money I had accumulated. The total was four hundred and seventy-two thousand in U.S. currency. I decided to keep twenty two thousand with me and deposit the remaining four hundred fifty thousand. I replaced the money I was keeping, leaving the rest on the desk. I pushed the button.

Within a matter of seconds the banker re-entered the office. He walked to the desk and slid into its captain's chair without taking a second look at the cash laid out on its surface. "I assume you've made a decision," he said with an air only a banker could have.

"Yes, I will start with four hundred fifty thousand in cash, American. Before we go any further, I want assurances that I will be able to withdraw from the account and deposit into it from anywhere in the world. Do I have that assurance?"

"Anywhere in the world covers a lot of ground. I can't represent to you that every bank in the world will have the capacity to handle a transaction with us. I can tell you we have a banking treaty with every major country in the world. We, also, have techniques allowing us to utilize banks in countries, where because of unstable governments, treaties don't exist. I think we can satisfy your needs. We will supply you with a list of countries we deal with on a regular basis, including the banks that will honor and fulfill all your needs within hours of your request. Most other, shall we say larger banks, will also be able to access your account, but it may take twenty- four hours to complete a withdrawal or deposit. Shall I arrange to deposit your cash?"

I sat in the banker's office contemplating whether I had covered all my bases. God, I wished Sadie was with me. "Yes, what do I have to sign?"

"It's not much. We can have it concluded within the hour. My assistant will get some information from you, while I'm arranging for the deposit." The banker picked up the cash and left the room. I almost stopped him because he hadn't given me a receipt for the money, he hadn't even counted it. He must have seen my apprehension because he hesitated and asked if I wanted to accompany him while he deposited it with the chief teller.

"Does my naiveté in these matters show so clearly?" I responded, attempting to ease through an awkward situation. "I've never opened an offshore account before."

"A perfectly sane reaction, Mr. Butler, and one which you need not be embarrassed about. The Aruba Bank of Commerce wants you to be as comfortable as possible. A trip to our head teller may help achieve that goal. Follow me."

The banker rose from his station behind the desk and went to the office door. I followed, keeping an eye on the sizable bundle of my cash he was carrying. He led me down the hall to a large door, which he pushed open and held it while I passed through. The room we entered was well-lighted and made up of several cubicles, very much like you would expect to find in middle management areas of a large American corporation. He proceeded to a cubicle where a middle-aged man was seated. The desk was covered with ledger cards and sheaths of paper requiring the man's attention.

"Mr. Butler, this is our chief teller, Mr. Goldstrum. He will count your deposit and give you a receipt." As he was introducing us the banker placed my money on the desktop.

Mr. Goldstrum nodded, more to him than to me, and started to count the pile of cash placed on his desk. He had one of those machines that can count paper money while at the same time checking for counterfeit bills. Within minutes the teller announced the total was four hundred fifty thousand one hundred dollars. I had miscounted by one hundred dollars. I reached down, retrieved a one hundred-dollar bill, smiled, and said four hundred fifty thousand. Mr. Goldstrum nodded while entering the withdrawal of the one hundred dollars. He pressed a button on the machine and it spit out a receipt for my deposit.

With my receipt in hand, I followed the banker back to his office where I completed the paperwork contained in the deposit packet, previously supplied to me. The information was basic for the normal depositor but for me it raised questions I had no answers for. I had no address, and I had no next of kin, at least none I wanted identified. After some thought, I designated Sadie's parents as next of kin. My address was more difficult. The banker must have noticed I was struggling because asked if he could be of assistance.

"What do I list as an address if I don't currently have one? I inquired.

"Not a problem," he said. "Why don't you just list the bank? We will provide a mail box very much like a safe-deposit box for your use. Any correspondence we receive, as well as your bank statements, will be placed in it. We will forward its contents to you on request. It's a service we make available to all our customers."

The bank was perfect. I listed it as my address and handed the papers to the banker. He reviewed them and, when he was satisfied they were complete, clipped them together.

"Now we can conclude our business by assigning you an account number so you can access the account as you require. The bank uses an eleven-digit number. You can choose your own if you like, but our advice is you allow us to use our computer to select a random series of numbers for you. This will avoid the use of numbers that might be later identified to you. We find, even the most careful of businessmen, will use numbers having meaning in their life, which therefore, can be traced to them. The choice is yours."

"Your computer will be fine," I responded, somewhat relieved I would not have to choose the series.

The banker nodded his approval and turned to a computer located on a side bar. He entered some of the information from my packet and watched the screen. Numbers began to appear and shortly the screen contained eleven numbers. I looked at them asking if they were my account numbers. The banker nodded and wrote them on my deposit packet. He also wrote them on a rather formal looking form and handed it to me.

"You are now a depositor in The Aruba Bank of Commerce," he announced. "The number on the deposit confirmation is your account number. You should commit it to memory, as it is also your access code. Your address is now officially the bank address, and your mail will be kept in a deposit box that will have a number equal to your deposit number plus one. You may access your account by providing a corresponding bank, our bank's name, and the access number. You will not have to supply any proof of identity. A withdrawal request will be honored within two hours. If you require a separate number for deposit we can accommodate you but I suggest it will not be necessary. All transactions can be managed with the one number. Do you have any questions?"

"Only your name and may I consider you to be my banker?" I inquired, realizing this whole process was much simpler than I had expected.

"Of course, I will act as your banker. I must apologize for not formally introducing myself earlier. My name is Philip Reinholdt. I'm executive vice-president of this bank. You may call me Philip."

"Thank you, Philip, and I have no further questions but I will need two numbers. I hope that will not be an enormous problem."

"It's not. I will get you the deposit code immediately." Philip returned to the computer and a second number appeared in short order. He made notations in the account file and handed me the deposit code number.

"If there are no further questions, then our business is concluded. Will you be staying on the island long?

"No, I'll be leaving tomorrow," I said as I got up to leave. Philip nodded and escorted me to the entrance of the bank.

I had completed what I had come to do. I looked around for a hotel for the night. I needed to make some phone calls. I wanted to know if I was still on the Company payroll and, for that matter, on assignment. I felt compelled to complete my final obligations to the Company, whether they wanted me to or not, and, if everything went well, to make a deposit or two in my new account.

CHAPTER FORTY-FIVE

It was seven in the evening in Washington, D.C. Howard and Mildred had finished their evening dinner and were settling into the regular routine. Mildred would read or do one of those needlepoint things she was always working on. Howard generally worked on the crossword in the evening paper. He never finished it and always felt frustrated when he couldn't. Over the years, however, he'd convinced himself it was relaxing.

Howard hadn't slept well the past few nights. The Butler matter weighed heavily on his mind. Eric had always been a superb operative even if he was a bit unconventional and at times even flaunted the Company protocols. Howard understood this as protocols were designed by men in the office and by accountants who had no clue of the realities a field agent faces every day. Eric, however, had never been as evasive as he had been in past several weeks. His phone, turning up in a trash barrel in Bogotá, was unexplainable.

Maybe Scott Steel was correct after all. Maybe Eric had *gone south*. Maybe the death of Sadie tipped him over. Lesser things had sent other agents south. All of these considerations were weighing on Howard as he struggled with a six-letter word beginning with k and completing the phrase "out of _____." As Howard was pondering, becoming more and more frustrated, the house phone rang. Howard didn't think much about it as Mildred frequently received calls from her friends in the evening.

"Howard, this call's for you. I think you'd better take it." Mildred's voice sounded strained. There was a quality of urgency in her tone.

"Who the hell would call me at this time of night?" he blurted out as he started to the phone, which was located across the kitchen from where he always worked the crossword puzzles. As he passed the door to the kitchen he caught a glimpse of Mildred. Howard only needed a glimpse to tell she was either very concerned, confused, or both.

"Hello. This is Howard."

"Howard, Eric here. Am I a fugitive yet?" There was a light quality to Eric's voice.

"Eric, what in the hell are you doing calling me on this phone. You know it's not secure and where the hell are you?"

"One thing at a time, Howard. First am I a fugitive? I need to know the answer."

"I haven't been told that you've been recalled," Howard's voice trailed off, "but I'm not sure I am in the loop on this one. Why are you calling me on this phone?"

"Because if I am, as you say recalled, I don't want them to have the benefit of this call. If I'm not recalled then it really won't matter. What I want is the ability to complete the Barajas arrangement. Now, am I in or out?"

"I really don't know. Steel has threatened putting dogs in the field. I think I may have talked him out of it for now, but you know the Company. I can't be sure."

"Let's assume, for now, he hasn't. I'll just have to be careful. Now what I need to know is whether I am still assigned to bring the Barajas Cartel down. If I am, I need the money we discussed previously transferred to me. If that isn't possible tell me now and I'll cease my operations." Eric made his voice sound as authoritative and urgent as he could. The line seemed dead for a moment. "Howard, are you still with me?"

"Yes, I'm still with you. I can't answer the question right now. You know I don't have that level of authority. I'll have to go to Scott and he'll probably have to go to the Directors' level. It could take some time."

"I haven't got time. Why don't you call Scott tonight and get a feel for where we are. The funds have been approved and the only thing that could have changed would be my status. Scott should be able to make that decision on his own. I'll call you back in an hour and, Howard, please don't try to locate me. I'll tell you where I am if the project is a go. If not I may be on my own anyway and you won't want to be involved."

"Call me in an hour." Howard hung up the phone.

As he put the receiver in the cradle it occurred to him that Eric was correct, the funds had already been appropriated and transferred to his operating account. Unless Scott had placed a hold on his account, they were ready for transfer on a 24/7 basis. Howard was not a betting man but, if he were, he would bet Scott would not have thought to rescind the authorization or that he would suspect Howard would act on the Butler matter without discussing it with him.

As usual, Mildred was full of questions as to why Mr. Butler was calling him that late at night and why on the family line. Howard had always been quite adept at avoiding her questions but, tonight, he was not prepared to deal with her, especially with the decision facing him. He became very direct.

"Damn it, Mildred, you know these matters are not for your ears. Forget Mr. Butler called and you ever talked to him. Is that clear? By the way, how did you even know it was Mr. Butler?"

"I guess he must have given me his name. Why the hell does it matter anyway? I've just been told he never called and I didn't talk to him. Things never change around here. I'm getting my fill of being second class to everyone in that beloved Company of yours. I'm going upstairs. Someone might call in an hour and I wouldn't want to be in the way!"

Howard was left alone with his dilemma. This wasn't new to him. As an operative his movements, assignments, and even his thoughts had always been his and his alone. Most of his life's work was something he couldn't share with Mildred. They had discussed this problem early in their marriage and, until recently, the nature of his employment hadn't caused an enormous problem. However, recently Mildred was beginning to resent his job and the people in it. Howard didn't blame her. Life with someone in the Company was trying, to say the least, but he didn't need her interference now. Not now, when he was contemplating taking an action that might even cost him his job.

Howard knew, at least he felt strongly, Eric would not place him in a position which would put his job in jeopardy. He had worked with Eric and Sadie for several years and had gotten to know them better than most handlers get to know their operatives. Sadie's death may have tipped Eric over slightly, but his allegiances to Howard and the Company would keep him within bounds. What Howard really saw was an opportunity to humiliate Scott Steel. He may even be able to get the promotion he had always wanted and deserved, but felt his injury and its corresponding disability had kept from him.

Howard went into the office and reviewed all the codes and passwords necessary to transfer up to thirty million American dollars anywhere in the world. If the authorization wasn't revoked, one phone call to a Treasury Department number and the transfer would be made within minutes. Once made, the transfer would be irrevocable. The question was, did he trust Eric enough to take the gamble? As he sat in his special chair, gazing at the equipment in front of him, he knew the answer to his question. It scared him. It scared him to death and he wished he could discuss this decision with Mildred. In his mind he convinced himself she would agree with his reasoning. It would be much more comforting if she could be involved, however. As Howard sat immersed in his thoughts and dilemma, the phone rang. It was the house phone again and he knew who it was.

"Hello, Howard Baker here."

"Howard, have you been able to reach Scott?"

"No, but I didn't try. The approval for the money was obtained weeks ago and unless Scott has revoked it, I still have it." There was a slight metallic click and the volume of the transmission dropped slightly.

"Is anyone on your end listening to us?" Howard asked.

"No, not that I'm aware of, but I am using a hotel phone and you know how those are. Let's be quick. Do I continue with the assignment or not?" Eric Asked.

Howard hesitated, "Where do you want the money?" The decision had been made.

"I will give exact details to you tomorrow, but it will be in Brazil, probably Rio de Janeiro

"The transfer should be as soon as possible. Scott is bound to think of the authorization sooner or later and my guess is it will be sooner."

Eric hesitated, "I do have an account we could use tonight if you feel it's essential the transfer be made tonight."

"I do feel that way. Now, where do I send it?" Howard responded, as he got a pad of paper from the desk drawer.

"I'll need the entire amount. Deposit it in the Aruba Bank of Commerce. The account code is as follows 64924057183. If you transfer it now, it'll be confirmed tomorrow morning before I leave for Brazil." Eric hesitated. "I won't call you back until arrangements for the shipping have been confirmed. We can then make plans to execute the sting and the arrest. By the way, I don't have the use of a cell phone. I discarded it in a moment of confusion, so all calls will be to your home phone and will be from public facilities. I know you don't like that but it's the best I can do."

"How long do you think it will be before your next call?"

"If I'm lucky, inside a week. Hopefully, no more than three days. Barajas has been dealt a temporary blow to his ability to deliver product. I intend using his dilemma to my advantage. I'll call when everything has been arranged."

"If that's the best you can do, it will have to be soon enough. Just realize, I'm way out on a limb. The sooner I have results the better it will be for me and frankly for you also. I need to make some calls now so let's end this. Good luck." Without hesitation, Howard hung up the phone.

As Howard hung up the phone, he heard Mildred stir in their upstairs bedroom. He thought about going up and consoling her. She'd always been understanding. As far as Agency marriages were concerned, their marriage had beaten the odds by lasting significantly longer than the average two years. It had been almost thirty. She deserved some kind of explanation for what was happening but that would have to come later, after the operation was a success and he was a hero of sorts.

A telephone call to a special number in the Treasury Department together with a code would enable Howard to activate the transfer immediately. Several years earlier an agent lost his life because he was unable to deliver a sum of money to a rebel faction the United States was backing in an effort to eliminate an unfriendly political leader. Because of that occurrence the agency had initiated procedures allowing the field supervisors to react to the needs of agents in the field any time day or night. The appropriation had been approved and the procedures were in place to allow the immediate transfer. Howard picked up the phone in his office and dialed the number at treasury. After several rings a man, whose voice sounded more like a boy of sixteen than a responsible treasury agent, answered the line.

"Treasury Agent Moore," the young sounding voice on the other end said.

"I'm Howard Baker, CIA. I need an immediate transfer of the funds being held for a project, code Alpha Epsilon 59773Q. I want the entire amount transferred to the Aruba Bank of Commerce account number 64924057183. I want the transfer to be immediate and I want confirmation. Use my telephone number in your file. Are there any questions?"

"One moment Mr. Baker." The treasury agent was checking to see if Howard was authorized to transfer the money and if the project code was proper. In less than a minute the young man was back on the line. "Everything is in order, Mr. Baker. If you will hang up I will confirm the telephone number by calling you back. Simply answer by stating the code word 'Jessica'. With that confirmation the transfer will be made within ten minutes. I will confirm completion at that time."

"Thank you," Howard said, as he replaced the receiver in its cradle, feeling relieved that the funds were still available. Within seconds the phone rang. Howard picked up immediately and said the code word Jessica. The line went dead. The transfer was in progress. He should have confirmation of completion within a few minutes.

Howard knew the Directors would be alerted of the transfer in their morning briefing and Scott would be aware of it shortly thereafter. The gamble was now irretrievable. It would be either Scott or himself that would come out of this unscathed. The other would be placed in the unenviable position of having to explain himself to the local Assistant Director or worse, to the Director himself.

As Howard sat in his plush office chair staring at the room with all of its electronics, the gravity of his decision was fast becoming a reality in his mind. His gamble was not only on the integrity of Eric, but also on the, almost pathological, ambitions of Scott Steel. The longer he sat there the more comfortable he felt. The pleasure of exposing Scott for the inept fraud he was, and showing the Company the mistake they made in not promoting him -- Howard Baker, would be a highlight of his career.

The phone on the desk rang.

"Howard Baker here."

"The transfer has been made and receipt confirmed," the young treasury agent said.

"Thank you and have a good evening."

Howard hung the phone up. He felt twenty years younger. For the first time in many years he had some semblance of control of his destiny. If only he could tell Mildred. He knew she would be proud of his decisiveness. She may even regain some of the respect for him she had in the early years of their marriage, respect that had been slowly eroded since the incident that kept him from the field and, more importantly, from advancement in the agency.

Howard knew there would be hard questions he would have to handle in the morning but, if he were correct, they would only come from Scott. There would be nothing Scott could do.

CHAPTER FORTY-SIX

Jose Salvador Barajas was arriving in Bogotá in one of the family's private planes when his cell phone went off. Its seemingly louder than usual ring startled him as well as the entourage of bodyguards accompanying him wherever he went.

Within the security corps was the replacement for Valencia. The young man was from the mountains of Colombia. It was the first trip he'd ever made outside the small towns surrounding his birthplace. It certainly was the first time he had ever flown and it showed. His name was Michael Brown which was most assuredly not his given name but one which he had chosen at an early age to seem worldlier, possibly more American. In any event it had stuck and, as he grew older, the name struck fear in the minds of those who opposed the Barajas family interests. His fierce loyalty and unrelenting cruelty served him well. He had progressed through the ranks, culminating in being chosen for the current assignment. His maiden flight proved to be more taxing than he had suspected. At first he was paralyzed with fear and shortly became violently airsick. All in all, it was not the image he hoped to portray in his first big assignment.

After fumbling for the cell phone and locating it in his jacket pocket, Barajas answered with his customary greeting,

"Salvador Barajas."

"Eric Butler here. Can we talk?"

"Of course we can talk. I had hoped I would have heard from you before this. Is everything going as planned?" Barajas responded, making a weak attempt to put the American on the defensive, and avoid the explanations he knew would be demanded concerning his own abilities to perform.

"That question is more appropriately answered by you, Sir. My organization tells me you have encountered a supply problem. We are, quite frankly, nervous about your ability to perform."

"What have you heard that causes you concern?" Barajas asked cautiously.

"Only that a large part of your supply has gone up in smoke. We are concerned not only that your ability to satisfy your obligations under our current agreement may be compromised but, also, that your inability to control the elements in your own country may jeopardize our operations."

"Your concerns are not unfounded," Barajas responded, realizing that to minimize the events of recent days would work to ultimately undermine his credibility with the Americans. "We have had a problem with a small, but well-organized, faction of our people, and the result was the destruction of a considerable amount of product. I assure you this will not seriously impact our mutual operations. I have a contingency of loyal employees, working around the clock to rectify both of your concerns. However, I must advise you that my first shipment may be a bit light, as you Americans say. I hope this will not be a problem."

"That depends on how light and what you accomplish to stabilize your internal problems. I've made commitments in the Middle East that will have to be met if we're to establish a foothold in that market."

"I assure you everything that can be done is being done. I have confidence we will be able to meet our responsibilities. I do need to know the exact time table for the first shipment." Barajas's entire demeanor had shifted from what Eric had dealt with in previous negotiations. Eric's instincts told him he was now in the driver's seat. Barajas would do almost anything to salvage the venture. He would become more reckless in his operations. He could be guided into mistakes, which would ultimately create a shambles of his empire.

"I agree, we need to meet and work out the details but in person, not on the phone. I will be in Rio tomorrow. I suggest you get there and arrange a suite for yourself and one for me. I won't arrive until mid-afternoon or early evening. I'll call when I arrive for directions to our hotel and where to meet. Is that agreeable?" Eric asked, making an attempt to have his directives appear a bit more palatable to a man who had never taken an order in his life.

There was a noticeable moment of silence on the other end of the line, possibly hesitation to digest the instructions, more probably seething anger resulting from receiving orders and the realization that he must take them. "Those arrangements will be acceptable. I will await your call." The line went dead.

As Salvador Barajas replaced the phone in his jacket pocket his face had turned a crimson red. His entourage knew it wasn't the time for small talk. There wasn't one of them that didn't wish they were somewhere else, anywhere else. The family plane was taxiing to a tie down in the Bogotá airport before Barajas said anything to anybody.

"It seems our plans have changed a bit," Barajas said, in an effort to mask his internal rage. "I have to meet our partner in Rio de Janeiro tomorrow. I will be taking Michael with me. The rest of you know what your responsibilities are, and I expect them to be carried out without a hitch. I need not tell you that it is imperative the arrangements I have made for additional product to reach our shipping point in the north are successful.

The authorities between here and the coast have been taken care of. There should be no problems, at least from them. You all know the real threat is from Miguel and his group. I would enjoy nothing more than to deliver the reward to one of you. I will be back within two days. Each of you know how to reach me if necessary."

The group of lieutenants acknowledged the acceptance of their responsibilities with silence as Barajas exited the family plane. Michael was next off, following his charge closely. It was the first time in years Barajas wasn't accompanied by Valencia. He felt naked. Salvador Valencia was in Cartagena, assuring that crucial arrangements were completed. It was more important he remain there and complete his assignment. Michael was certainly capable of ensuring the safety of Barajas, but he lacked experience and his intuition had not been tested, let alone honed. Circumstances, as critical as they were, dictated that he would have to do, however.

Upon exiting the aircraft, Barajas headed directly to the one area where he felt comfortable in the Bogotá airport. The government, which ran the airport facilities, had provided a special lounge where people of political importance and those of means could spend a few minutes or even hours in the privacy to which they had become accustomed. Barajas had been a member of that elite group for many years, and over time, had spent many hours enjoying the lounges seclusion. Upon arrival he was greeted by airport personnel, who knew him by name, and welcomed him into its confines. Barajas registered Michael as his assistant to insure his ability to come and go as need be. The lounge had several cubicles with access to telephones, which were available for its clientele. After ordering a drink, he instructed the hostess to arrange a flight for himself and Michael to Rio later in the afternoon. He also asked that hotel accommodations be made for himself and Michael in one suite, with another made available for a business associate, Eric Butler.

The hostess was a very attractive woman about forty years of age. She was able to satisfy most of her customers' needs by being mature and experienced. This installed a confidence, making the patrons of the lounge comfortable. In the past, Barajas had considered making overtures to her in an attempt to bring her into his organization. Something about her demeanor, however, had told him while she was willing and able to protect the privacy of her customers, she would not be a candidate to join them in their business, especially, when the business was not one sanctioned by her personal concepts of ethics and morals.

As the hostess left to make the arrangements for the requested travel, Barajas found a cubicle not next to one in use and dialed Salvador Valencia's cell phone.

Salvador arrived in Cartagena in good time. The connection to Cartagena, via the somewhat expatriated American pilot, was like changing automobiles. He simply went from one plane to the other. The Barajas family and business interests had utilized the services of this, rather obscure, charter pilot for some time. Salvador only knew him by the name of Dan. He was reliable and his equipment was more than adequate for the needs of their business. Dan's only requirement was that his services be paid in cash, U.S. dollars, and payment was due at the time the service was rendered. No questions were ever asked. Conversation was therefore light, centering mostly on the weather and the news headlines of the day. With Salvador as his only passenger, the conversation was even less than usual. The flight took a little less than two hours. Upon arrival, they circled the field, checking the wind direction, and making sure there weren't domestic animals grazing on the runway area.

As they circled, Salvador spotted two automobiles approaching the airstrip. The lead vehicle was obviously a private car, probably a citizen who supplemented his family's income by providing taxi service to tourists. The second car was a newer sedan. It was probably the vehicle which was to meet him and transport him to the family's shipping point. The plane landed smoothly and taxied to a tie down area in proximity to the shack serving as a terminal. Salvador was exiting the plane as the first vehicle pulled up to the terminal. Salvador was deep in thought, considering what he was going to find and how he was going to handle the problems he was sure to encounter. Otherwise, he would have noticed the cabs passenger did not exit the vehicle as one would expect upon arrival. The sole passenger in the vehicle, other than the driver, remained in the cab as Salvador hurried to his arriving transportation and left the airport area.

The trip to the family's shipping facilities took several hours. During the drive Salvador was briefed regarding the raid and its consequences. It appeared the small airstrip and the bunkhouse had not been touched, but the main lodge had been broken into, the bosses killed, and a significant amount of money stolen. The warehouse was totally destroyed along with all the product stored there awaiting shipment. Salvador questioned the men concerning their activities since the raid. As expected, none had assumed the reins and begun to build a shelter area for the replacement product. While he was sure the surviving men were not lazy, without leadership they could not function in what was clearly their employer's best interests.

CHAPTER FORTY-SEVEN

The cab ride was short, and when Steve and Ronnie arrived at their hotel, the lobby was dark. The only luminescence was from the dimly lit, lantern-style fixtures in the bar and lounge. As with the lobby, it also was empty with the exception of the bartender who was busy dusting and cleaning the various bottles of liquor displayed above the bar. Steve and Ronnie went directly to the staircase that led to the upper floors of the hotel. The bartender looked up from what was obviously a boring task, recognized them, and waived with the anticipation they would relieve him of his boredom by joining him. Ronnie smiled and waved back as they proceeded to the stairs.

On reaching the third level their training surfaced and each entered the hallway with some caution. The hall was dimly lit, only having small lights by the stairwell and at the end of the hall. The lighting was sufficient to disclose the hall was empty. Steve proceeded first, keeping the wall opposite the entrance to their suite to his back. The door to their suite was about halfway down the short hall. The time expended to get there was only a matter of seconds. A glance at the entrance indicated their rooms had been entered in their absence. Steve nodded to Ronnie and she inserted her key into the lock and quickly opened the door, entering the room simultaneously. As Ronnie entered, she began talking as though she was in conversation with Steve concerning the meal they had just finished. As she cleared the doorway, Steve entered with his weapon drawn and in a crouched position. His head was below the level of her waist. If anyone were in the room, they would not have expected Steve to be in that position. He enjoyed whatever element of surprise was possible.

Lounging in a chair was John Sailor. He immediately put his finger to his lips indicating they should be silent. John pointed at the small table beside the love seat. He took the drawer all the way out and there, on the outside of the back, was a small electronic mike and battery. He disconnected the battery. As he turned to face the two, each knew, by his facial expression, he wasn't happy.

"I thought I told you to check the room for bugs," he said as he went back to the chair.

"We did and found several. We must have missed that one," Ronnie replied, with a tone of indignation in her voice. "By the way, who invited you into our room anyway? What gives you the right to simply go anywhere you please regardless of whose privacy you violate?"

"Ronnie, let it drop!" Steve said, in an attempt to smooth out tempers, an effort he already knew was destined to fail.

"Stuff it up your ass! This son of a bitch has acted like he is the chosen one ever since we met and I'm tired of it," Ronnie replied. "We didn't exactly apply to be assigned to this extraction. I'm not even sure I like the idea of hunting down one of our own. We, at least I, accepted the assignment because it's probably the last chance I have to continue with the Company. I have a feeling I'm not alone in that circumstance. I for one am not going to let this self-centered lone wolf ruin my chances," Ronnie hesitated, but continued to pace back and forth.

For the first time since they'd met John Sailor, Steve could sense a crack, maybe even a crevice, in the infamous agent's personal armor. He was about to speak when Ronnie continued.

"If you want to go it alone just say the word and we'll, at least I'll, leave you to your solitude. If Steve joins me, we'll do our best to complete the assignment and will face the consequences of that action, whatever they may be. I, and I think I speak for Steve, am tired of pussy footing around you. The choice is yours. Now what will it be?"

John remained seated in the chair. He looked at Ronnie in a way that made her more uncomfortable than ever. It was obvious he was not accustomed to being addressed in that manner, or being forced to make a decision regarding his "partners" by announcing his intentions related to the use of their services. He had contemplated leaving them in Bogotá and proceeding on his own. "Solo" had been his *modus operandi* on numerous other missions. However, John sensed a pleading underneath Ronnie's obvious anger. He knew, from some comments Scott Steel had made, that what Ronnie said regarding their last chance was true. They both were on the chopping block, and the results of this assignment would either release the ax or give them a reprieve. John could understand the anxieties they both must have had because he had felt the same most of his career.

He also realized that Ronnie, and probably Steve, were different from the other agents with whom he'd been assigned. There was a recklessness, a devil-may-care attitude, that Ronnie exhibited, perhaps both the young agents exhibited, that rebelled against the veneer of Company policy and procedure. John didn't know how to respond to the tirade he just witnessed, but he realized, at least on this occasion, he would not dump his partners.

"In the morning we need to check the airport and any small landing strips used by charter services, to determine if anyone matching the description of

Butler has chartered an aircraft headed for the coast in the last week. Unless either of you have a better idea or theory, I doubt he is anywhere near Bogotá." Having said all he was going to, John got up and left the suite.

"I think that was an apology," Steve said after several seconds of silence, during which both of them tried to digest the events of the last few minutes.

"I think you're right," Ronnie replied. "I think we may be a part of this assignment for the first time. By the way, you certainly didn't help me with Sailor. Maybe John and I don't need you." Ronnie had a smirk on her face intended to betray the fact she was pulling his chain. Inside, however, she was beginning to have doubts about Steve's actions, maybe his intestinal fortitude. She pushed the doubts to the back of her mind and unbuttoned her blouse, exposing the fullness of her breasts, an act she knew Steve could not resist.

"If you think John Sailor can perform even half as well as me, he's yours. By the way I'll bet the ears at the other end of that mike we missed fully enjoyed your ecstasy this afternoon, but then they probably didn't need the mike. You really should try to control yourself," Steve retorted in an effort to regain some dignity from what had developed into an embarrassing circumstance.

Steve woke up, as he always did, just as the sun was beginning to break the horizon. He looked over and Ronnie was not stirring. Ronnie appeared to be in a deep sleep. John hadn't informed them what time he was planning on getting started, but Steve was sure he wasn't talking about mid-morning. He shook Ronnie to get her going, and she erupted to exhibit a trait Steve hadn't seen before. Within seconds she was, by all appearances, awake and had assumed a defensive position. She would have startled even the most seasoned intruder.

"Hold on! Hold on! I was just getting you up so we wouldn't appear as inept when John's ready to leave. What's wrong with you?" Steve said, fearing her next move.

"Don't ever wake me like that again," Ronnie said with a tremor in her voice.

"How the hell am I supposed to wake you, or maybe you want to sleep until you awaken naturally? We have to get ready." Steve's voice sounded of the confusion he was feeling. It was bordering on anger bred by fear.

"I'm sorry. I can't explain it now, but I will someday. Just accept my apology. If you want me awake whisper in my ear. Shoot your gun. Throw cold water on me. Do anything you want. Just don't shake me." Ronnie had calmed down, was off the bed, and heading to the bathroom. "I'll be ready in a few minutes"

Steve was still confused and somewhat muddled by recent events but was willing to accept the explanation or lack of explanation she had offered. "I'll go down to the bar and get coffee. You join me a soon as possible. Steve left the room, locking the door after him, and proceeded to the stairway.

Reaching ground level he noted John was already at the bar sipping coffee. "Good morning, I hope you haven't been waiting long," he said in an effort to start the day off right with the one man who was their only hope of a successful mission.

"No, just got here myself," John replied, without looking up.

Steve noted John looked like he'd slept in the clothes he was wearing. As he got closer he realized that they were indeed the same clothes John had been wearing the evening before. "You haven't been to bed yet have you?"

John looked up. For the first time since meeting John Sailor, his expression was bordering on friendly. "No, but we needed some information I could only get by calling in old favors. The good part is I was successful. I believe we have a place to start. Where's Ronnie?"

"She'll be down directly," Steve replied, indicating to the bartender he wanted coffee also. "She's finishing doing those things women do." Steve wanted to ask what John had been doing but knew this was not the time or the place. Out of the corner of his eye Steve caught sight of Ronnie descending the last two or three stairs before reaching the hardwood landing. "Here she is now." There was the distinct sound of relief in his voice.

"Good. Let's move to one of those tables where we can have a bit more privacy," John said as he stood and started moving away from the bar and toward one of the back tables.

Steve grasped his cup, motioning to the barkeep that he needed another, and went to the table. Ronnie had just arrived looking refreshed and ready for whatever the day might bring. Steve noted her waist was a bit thicker than normal and realized she had put on her money belt. A part of him wished he'd stayed behind to watch her get into it. As they got seated, Ronnie's coffee arrived. John watched the barkeep closely as he placed the cup and saucer on the edge of the table. Before they could start talking, John motioned for silence and ran his hand on the underside of the table in the vicinity of where the coffee had been set. In one smooth motion he produced a small electronic bug. The barkeep had placed it when he delivered the coffee. As the barkeep reached the bar, he glanced at the table. John was holding the bug in his fingers, showing the man he had been found out. The barkeep's face turned an ashen gray. He immediately left the lounge.

"We'd better have our conversation elsewhere and quickly. That man's bosses will be here shortly and I'm sure none of us can pass a close inspection," John said, as he took his weapon out and checked the magazine and chamber, ensuring its readiness. "Neither of you left anything in your room you couldn't live without have you?"

"No," both Steve and Ronnie answered simultaneously.

"Now be alert. Remember not every policeman you see is a policeman, and not every policeman who is a policeman is interested in promoting our longevity." As John finished talking he was already strolling across the room. Upon entering the lobby he spotted the barkeep behind a desk on the telephone. In two or three swift strides John reached the desk and had hold of the man's head by his hair. The look on the man's face was one of pain and fear of death. John ripped the phone out of his hand and in the same motion tore the phone from the wall. John didn't have to say anything. The barkeep lost control of his bodily functions and was crying, something about his family. John simply dropped him. He landed on the floor in a pool of his own urine.

John proceeded out the door. Ronnie followed with Steve bringing up the rear and backing out in an effort to ensure there were no other telephone calls being placed that could jeopardize their assignment. As soon as Steve satisfied himself it was safe to leave, he turned and followed his partners to a late model Ford. He scrambled into the front seat as John started the car. Above the sound of the motor, the sound of a siren could be heard, and a black car with police markings was pulling off the road into the hotel parking area. It was coming directly toward them.

"Hang on!" John said as he punched the accelerator to the floor, creating a massive cloud of dust as the Ford's driving wheels struggled to gain traction on the dirt surface. The police car veered to the right, passing by Steve's closed window. Steve detected three occupants in the police car before his side window exploded into his lap. By that time John had increased the vehicle's speed and the police car disappeared in the dust cloud they had created.

Without realizing it, Steve had drawn his weapon. His hands were shaking. A glance at Ronnie confirmed she had done the same. She was concentrating on locating the police car through the rear window. Her head was low and on the left side of the car. The Company training paid off as the back window exploded all over the back seat. Ronnie appeared to be unhurt. Now that the rear window glass wasn't inhibiting her, she fired three times. At least one of them must have hit its mark, because the police car veered to the right skidding to a stop. The thickest part of the dust cloud caught up to the police car and enveloped it, making it impossible to learn what damage Ronnie had done.

John had a smirk on his face, "Is everyone okay?" he asked, knowing the answer. "I think we all need something to eat. How's that sound?"

"Sounds good to me," Steve answered in an effort to hide the fear that had just taken over from the adrenaline rush of the past four or five minutes. Ronnie, looking out the back window, did not respond. Steve could see enough of her face, however, to know she was far from being as terrified as he felt. He hoped they would drive far enough for him to get control of his emotions, at least so he could stop his hands from shaking.

"Do you think I hit him? Did I kill that man?" Ronnie said with a quality to her voice which betrayed the mixture of excitement and revulsion she was feeling.

"What do you care? He was trying to kill you. Now, just relax and reload. We might not be out of it yet. Keep a sharp eye," John said, as he wove in and out of what little traffic there was on the narrow road. He was monitoring the rear view mirror with the same intensity with which he was viewing the road ahead.

The fact that the passenger side window was gone and the back window was missing didn't make the vehicle stand out as being unusual. There were many cars in the city missing windows among other body parts. The only giveaway was the broken glass spread throughout the interior of the vehicle, and it couldn't be seen from the outside. John chose the first available intersection, turned left, and drove the Ford onto what could only be described as a lane. There was little or no traffic and few houses. At a wide spot in the road he pulled over stopping the car.

"We need to clean out the glass," he said as he exited the driver's side door and began brushing the broken glass from the seat. Steve and Ronnie followed his lead. The vehicle was reasonably presentable in short order. During the cleaning process Ronnie saw John's right pant leg was blood stained between the knee and the hip.

"You've been hit!" she said with alarm in her voice.

"It's only a scratch, but I'll have to find something else to wear," John responded, looking at his leg. "The bullet that took out the passenger window must have grazed me. Let's find a shop where one of you can get me a new pair of pants and then let's get something to eat. I was hungry before this whole thing started and I'm still hungry."

They got back in the vehicle. John turned the car around, and proceeded back to the narrow two-lane road they had been traveling previously. As John approached the intersection he slowed the Ford to a crawl, watching the traffic for any sign of a problem. Steve concentrated on the occupants of vehicles that passed. They were single drivers or families. It was what one would expect to find on a somewhat rural road on the edge of Bogotá. John eased the Ford into the roadway and accelerated consistent with the traffic.

Within a few kilometers Steve spotted a small market.

"We may be able to find you some pants there," he said, "We'll need some sort of bandage also."

As they approached the market it appeared to be as advertised. There were several families shopping in a plaza, which contained ten or twelve small open-air vendors. "It will do fine," John replied as he steered the car into a parking area dominated by vintage pickups and older automobiles. "Ronnie, get me something that will not stand out in a crowd. Steve and I will stay here and watch for problems. If you hear the horn, drop everything and get back to the car."

Ronnie exited the car, taking an extended look at John in an obvious effort to determine his size. She entered the market place. One of the first venders had clothing, most of which were work clothes, designed for use by the locals. There were, however, several pairs of imported pants. Among those she found a pair of tan pants that carried an American label, purporting to be a thirty-six inch waist. After some attempt to communicate with the shopkeeper, she bought them, paying much more than they were worth. A quick survey of the remaining vendors resulted in Ronnie purchasing a remnant of cloth that could be used for bandage material and a small bottle of alcohol. With her purchases in hand, she returned to the Ford.

John and Steve were watching for her and when she appeared, Steve, who was now the driver, started the car. Ronnie slid into the front seat next to Steve, passing the purchases to John in the back seat. He had already taken off his pants. The wound was just as he had described it. The bullet had just creased the skin, leaving a clean wound that had already stopped bleeding. Leaning over the seat, Ronnie helped John clean the wound with a piece of the newly purchased cloth and tore a strip for him to bind the leg with. The pants fit reasonably well. They were large enough that the bandage didn't show. As she finished and was returning to face the front of the vehicle, Steve was turning onto a much larger and well-traveled highway.

"Where are we going?"

"John wants to eat. There should be a roadside inn within a few kilometers where we can eat and still watch the traffic in and out. I could use some food myself. How about you?"

"It's okay with me but I think we need to know what the plan is. We've had problems since we started this morning, and I think all three of us should have all the information available. So far we are in the dark and, John, you're the only one that seems to be aware of what's going on," she said as she turned in the seat to look at John. "We need an explanation."

"You're right. I intended to do that this morning but we left the hotel faster than I anticipated. Steve, why don't you look for a side road we can use to get off this highway? Find a place in the shade to park. I'll bring you up to speed."

An opportunity presented itself almost immediately. Steve pulled the vehicle onto a small farming road that led into a grove of fruit trees. When sufficiently away from the highway Steve stopped the car and turned in the seat.

"First, I met with some men last night I've known for several years. My initial reason for contacting them was to ascertain if they had any information concerning Butler which would help us locate him. What I learned was one of the major cocaine producing families, if not the largest producer, made a significant change in their marketing operations and were warehousing large amounts of the finished product in the North. It seems the local resistance to the drug trade was able to destroy most of the store. A massive effort has been mounted in the South to replace the product. The local police are being bought off at prices that will allow them to retire. As a result, the shipments are arriving in the North unmolested. I was told the family patriarch was spotted in Bogotá recently and he booked a flight to Rio de Janeiro.

Based on what I understand Butler's assignment to have been and what I was able to learn last night, my gut tells me Butler is the reason for the change in marketing. If that's true, I believe Butler is also, or will soon be, in Rio. I don't think Butler is in the North as was indicated by those lackeys who met us at the airport."

"Then shouldn't we be heading for Brazil?" Steve interrupted. "What are we doing driving around out here?"

"Have you forgotten, we had no choice but leave the hotel this morning? The reason we've been driving around out here is to make certain we haven't been followed. Remember Butler's partner, Sadie Anderson, was forced to shoot a cop. Now, he was either not a cop or a corrupt cop. In any event they got her. Butler's partner was a pro, along with whatever else she may have been, and she's lost. I don't want the same result for any of us. We have to be more careful now because they obviously know we're here and probably think we're here to avenge Anderson."

Ronnie's face showed concern. She seemed speechless, at least very confused. "Do you think I killed that man this morning?" she said somewhat hesitantly.

"I don't know if you killed him, if he died in the crash, or if he's even dead. The fact is they knew we were here and now they're pissed. I, for one, am not comfortable with either of those circumstances," John said without any show of emotion. "The real question is how did they know we were here and why do they want us out of the picture? The only answer I can come up with is someone is feeding information to them. The information must be coming from within our own organization. We've been sent down here to extract a supposed rogue agent, and we end up being hunted ourselves. Have either of you got any other ideas because if you have, let's get them on the table."

The automobile was silent. Finally Ronnie asked, "Why would anyone in the Company want us to fail so badly they would have us killed?"

"Who the hell knows why the Company does a lot of what they do. They just do it and without any overview from anyone."

"What do we do about our assignment now?" Steve said, thinking out loud.

"It seems obvious to me we still have to find Butler. The decision whether to bring him in can be made later. If the Company has put a number on us, and we're supposed to be doing their bidding, then maybe the extraction order on Butler is just as bogus," Ronnie said, looking for some reaction from John Sailor.

"I agree and, if my hunch is right, we have to get to Brazil," Sailor replied.

"And how the hell are we going to do that?" Steve blurted out. "We may be making the biggest mistake of our lives based on assumptions and unanswered questions. I, for one, think we ought to contact Steel and get his take on this whole thing."

"That's fine," Ronnie said her eyes blazing, "Can you tell me he's not part of the problem and if he is, where are we? I agree with John. Let's get to Butler and Brazil seems to be the only lead we have."

As Ronnie was speaking she was looking directly at Steve. Even a person who didn't know Ronnie would have realized she was confused with his conservatism -- with his seeming mental confusion. A glance at John Sailor and Ronnie knew he had the same thoughts and reservations.

"I just think we're making decisions not based on solid facts. I think we should let the Company know our concerns before we leap off to Brazil," Steve said, almost pleading, his voice evidencing the fear he was feeling.

"That may be what you think, but it isn't going to happen. You need to decide now whether you're with us, because if you're not, you may as well be against us. I view your present viewpoint to be life threatening. The last thing we need is to have any interest intent on taking our lives knowing what we're doing and where." John stopped talking. The stillness was deafening. The implications of his words were clear and unnerving, but the look on his face expressed an intensity that would have brought a chill to the bravest of men. The result was the most telling of all of Steve's actions. He simply sat and hung his head, not unlike a frightened schoolboy in the principal's office. Ronnie and John came to the same conclusion at the same time. Steve could not be counted on to carry his weight. More importantly, he couldn't be trusted.

John motioned to Ronnie to get out of the car. "Ronnie and I need to confer. You stay in the car or so help me I'll shoot you where you sit."

Ronnie was out of the car by the time John had completed his warning. They both went to the front of the car where they could see Steve yet not be heard.

"He's your lover. What do you want to do?"

"That's an unfair statement but I'll let it go for now. It's obvious we can't count on him even for moral support, let alone, count on him to watch our backs. We also can't send him home for the same reasons we can't let him call Steel. It seems we have no choice but to bring him with us. I really hate to babysit. Do you have any thoughts?"

"I could shoot him and we could claim they got him in the foray this morning," John said, knowing Ronnie would not accept that course, at least not yet. One look at Ronnie told him his assessment was correct. "I have another thought however. We could leave him with some friends here in Bogotá until this is over and send him back later. His stay won't be the most comfortable but he won't be hurt."

"I opt for the second choice but can we make those arrangements quickly?" Ronnie responded with some relief in her voice.

"I will make a call now. You go back to the car and tell him I am making arrangements to get to Brazil. Watch him closely. He still has a gun. If he suspects we're going to abandon him he may decide to use it on us or use it to get away. We might not be able to live, emphasis on live, with either of those possibilities. Can you shoot him if you have to?"

"I've never shot a man before -- unless I hit the man this morning, and certainly not one who I made love to just a matter of hours ago. Yes, if I have to I can, but only because I am convinced he constitutes a present danger to us," Ronnie said in an effort to justify, at least to herself, what she might have to do. Ronnie turned toward the car ultimately entering the front passenger side. John smiled noting Ronnie adjusted her weapon for easy access as she entered the vehicle. Sailor moved several paces down the road and dialed. After several minutes of conversation he started back to the vehicle. Only then did Steve break the silence.

"What's going to happen?" he asked. His face was pale. He had the clammy look of someone terrified.

"John is making arrangements for us to get to Brazil," Ronnie lied, watching every move Steve made, anticipating the move he might make.

John approached the Ford indicating with his hands that Steve should get in the back seat. Steve complied immediately. As Steve exited the driver's side of the car, Ronnie noticed that his weapon was not in its holster. He obviously had moved it to a more accessible location. Ronnie reasoned that would be in his belt, against his belly and under his shirt. When she saw him enter the back seat she knew she was correct, because the shirt in front indicated a stiff object lying just underneath.

Sailor drove to the highway they had been on previously and headed the Ford back toward the city. Ronnie was intent on watching Steve. She had removed her weapon from its holster and placed it beside her in the front seat out of Steve's view. If she needed to she could eliminate Steve by simply shooting through the seat. An act she mentally was ready to do, but one, she desperately hoped, would not be necessary.

"Where are we going?" Steve asked, as the Ford headed down the road they had just traveled. "I know a small airport that might have the capacity to handle a charter to Brazil," John responded in a matter of fact tone.

After traveling ten or twelve kilometers, John made a right turn and then an almost immediate left into a farmyard. It looked like any other farmyard with the exception the barn appeared to be converted into an automobile repair shop. It contained several vehicles of various makes and vintages. The Ford was brought to a stop next to the barn. At the same time it was stopping, three men appeared from the barn, each with an automatic pistol in their hand. Before Steve had any time to react Ronnie made her weapon visible.

"Please, don't make a move to your weapon. We've decided to leave you in the care of these nice gentlemen. You will be made reasonably comfortable and will not be harmed if you act appropriately. Now, get out of the car but before you do place your weapon on the seat. You might also leave your money belt. I doubt you'll be needing it."

Steve's expression was fear and disbelief as he complied with her requests, and, after a struggle getting the money belt loose, eventually exited the vehicle. John was out of the car conversing with the largest of the three locals. He gave him some money. The man appeared to be happy about the deal he'd made and instructed the other two to take Steve to the barn. John and the larger man then disappeared into the barn and moments later John drove out in an older Ford but one with all the windows intact. He motioned for Ronnie to join him. Within what seemed seconds, the vehicle had disappeared in a cloud of dust. Steve had just acquired some well-paid baby sitters and their disciplinary methods weren't restricted by any regulations or government agencies.

When John reached the highway he glanced at Ronnie, who was visibly struggling with the recent decisions they had made. "You should be proud of yourself. Not too many days ago I would have shot him and not thought twice about it. You couldn't have lived with that so he will live and, if he uses his head, he will die an old man. We'll have to deal with him later. Just remember, you saved his life."

"I can't believe you would shoot a man because he's suddenly not useful. I can't -- No I won't believe that!" Ronnie responded, with the same fire in her eyes John had seen earlier. "Just so you will know, had you made a move to shoot him, I would have shot you. I was ready."

"I know that and, no, you wouldn't have shot me because it would have been done long before you realized he was a problem. It would have surprised you almost as much as it would have surprised him. Now, let's drop it, concentrate on getting to Brazil and staying alive."

The fire had not left Ronnie but she had to admit they had more immediate problems needing attention. "How do you suggest we get there?"

"The only way I know is the same way the drug boss got there, by commercial air."

"Aren't we taking a big risk? Won't they be looking for us at airports and private landing strips?" Ronnie asked, showing her confusion and frustration.

"Maybe, but they'll be looking for three and we'll travel as singles, if possible by different flights, even different airlines. We'll regroup at the airport in Rio."

Ronnie wasn't anxious to travel alone but had no better plan. She was willing to accept the uncertainty she felt. When they reached the airport, John parked the old Ford in a remote area in the back of one of the free parking lots. Without a word they separated, each finding a different route to the ticketing area.

In spite of all their planning, the flights to Brazil were not plentiful. They ended up on the same airplane. Ronnie had booked first class. John Sailor had taken a tourist seat. Ronnie took some pleasure in that fact, smirking, as she passed John on her way to the first class waiting lounge.

Having located the lounge, Ronnie sat in one of the overstuffed chairs and relaxed for the first time in several hours. In less than a minute an attractive airline service representative approached and asked her if she would like a drink. Why not, Ronnie thought to herself. She had earned one, after all it wasn't everyday a women kills her first man -- probably kills her first man. Ronnie suddenly realized she wasn't ready to accept taking a life. The feeling of revulsion swept over her again. It must have shown in her face because the hostess asked if she was okay.

"Yes, I'm just tired. I'll have a martini, with lots of olives." As the hostess left to get the drink it occurred to Ronnie that she might have some information which would help them locate Butler and the drug boss. When the hostess returned she smiled and asked if the hostess could recommend a good four-star hotel in Rio de Janeiro.

"Yes, of course, I can. As a matter of fact, I just recently arranged for one of our other guests to be accommodated at the Brazilian Star. The hotel is beautiful. I think you would enjoy your stay there. Would you like me arrange for reservations for you?" The hostess said, hoping she could earn the second generous commission in as many days.

"That would be nice. Could you arrange for two rooms? I'd like them to be adjoining, if possible, but at least on the same floor. I'm meeting my brother there."

"I'll see what I can do. Could I have your ticket, please? It will have all the information I need to make the reservations." The hostess was holding out her hand for the ticket folder. Ronnie realized she might have just made a big mistake. It was too late. To decline now might cause attention and confirm her identify to anyone in the lounge watching for her and John.

Ronnie smiled and handed the folder to the hostess, while at the same time watching the other customers in the lounge. None seemed to be interested in her transaction. Several minutes later the hostess reappeared with her ticket and a reservation slip for the Brazilian Star. Ronnie relaxed. She convinced herself she was being paranoid. The situation wasn't as bad as she'd built in her mind. As she sipped the martini, the hostess approached and announced her flight was ready to board and she should go to the gate. Ronnie took a last sip of the martini, sat the drink down, and left the lounge still feeling she'd made a mistake but realizing it turned out okay.

At the gate, she caught sight of John Sailor patiently waiting in the tourist class line while she and the other first class passengers boarded. She saw him once again as he passed her seat, disappearing behind the curtain separating first class from the rest of the cabin. The takeoff was uneventful. She and John were safely on a plane heading for Rio de Janeiro.

CHAPTER FORTY- EIGHT

S cott Steel was in his office early. It had been over twenty-four hours since he'd dispatched the extraction team. He was hopeful the secure line would bear some fruit as to their progress. In the time since making the decision to send the team, he had a feeling of elation, of euphoria. He was going to discredit Howard Baker for a final time. He was going to show the director that he, Scott Steel, really did deserve the promotion over Baker. Scott had always suspected the Director, while he promoted Scott, still valued the opinion of Howard Baker over his own. Scott was convinced that even though he supervised Howard Baker, Baker was his only hurdle to the next level. Having to extract Howard's premiere agent would show the Directors the instability of the man's judgment. It would show that friendship, albeit professional, had blinded the field supervisor from seeing that his agent had *gone south.*

The secure line held no messages from Sailor or any of his group. Scott wasn't really upset as they had only been out of country slightly more than twenty-four hours, and Sailor was not one to feel he had to check in at regular intervals, or for that matter at all. Scott convinced himself that the old adage, no news is good news, was definitely true in this instance. Scott returned to his office and greeted his assistant, whom he always thought of as just another secretary and treated accordingly, a trait not only his assistant resented but also the entire staff. He gathered the daily reports of the activities that were within his section and began to skim through them. One of the reports stood out. It was from Howard Baker.

It was hidden among the mundane descriptions of what had taken place with regard to Howard's three or four other assignments, mostly agents doing surveillance work in the Middle East. One sentence caught his eye. "Transferred authorized funds to Colombian project." Scott couldn't believe his eyes. Howard knew the project was in jeopardy. Why would he risk, no, squander the Company funds without consulting him? It was unthinkable. Scott read the report again. This time the feelings of amazement and bewilderment were replaced with anger. It was an outrage. A deliberate attempt to undermine his authority! Scott knew the funds were, in all probability gone, lost in the international banking channels. Even if his handpicked team was successful the money would still be lost. He would have to explain why it happened on his watch.

Scott's first instinct was to have his assistant get Baker on the line and force the semi-invalid to explain his actions. Deep down he knew that would be a mistake though, because he hadn't disclosed his concerns regarding Butler to his superiors. It would come down to his word against Howard's. Scott couldn't live with that situation. He would be the loser. The best course would be to contact Howard, let him know he had mobilized the extraction team, and see how Howard reacted. Having reached that decision, Scott summoned his assistant and asked her to contact Howard Baker and let him know when he was on the line.

In less than a minute Scott was summoned to pick up his phone. "Howard, Scott Steel here. What have you heard from Butler?" There was a slight, but noticeable, period of silence on the other end of the line.

"I heard from him a day ago. He says he's ready to drop the net. I gave him authority to proceed," Howard answered, expecting the phone to blow apart with Scott's reaction.

"I thought we had an agreement! You were to contact me the moment he contacted you!"

"An agreement? No, Scott, I was ordered by you to do that. I didn't agree. In any event, given the circumstances, I didn't have time and thought better of it. You don't believe he's still in the fold and I do. The funds had been authorized to be disbursed on my discretion, and I exercised that discretion. The order authorizing the funds hadn't been remanded, so I acted in what I felt, and frankly still feel, was in the best interest of the project and the Company." This time the slight, but perceptible, silence came from Steel's end of the conversation.

"Your 'exercise of discretion' may well have cost the Company thirty million dollars, Howard. I've sent an extraction team to collect Butler and, if possible, bring him back to this county for debriefing. The team I chose is very good and, hear me, they've saved the Company the cost of debriefing on most previous occasions!" Scott hesitated, letting the message sink in. "Know this and rely on it, if you want to save your career, you get in touch with your Mr. Butler and tell him to come home with the money! Do I make myself clear?"

"Oh, you've made yourself clear all right, but consider this Scott. I will deny under oath I was ever warned about your concerns regarding Butler and certainly about any extraction team. It appears you did all of that on your own initiative. You know the procedure. It's very clear. You must notify the handler, the field supervisor, of any extraction effort. As you know well, the rationale behind that procedure is to avoid the very circumstance you have created. It's to insure the Company isn't competing against itself. I did nothing wrong Scott, not anything you can prove anyway. You, and you alone, violated the clear policy and it may cost the Company thirty million dollars. In any event, I think the director will see it that way. What do you think, Scott?"

Howard waited for a reply. He had played all his cards.

To the extent Scott's anger, now mind numbing rage, would allow, he contemplated his options. He wanted to discharge Howard on the spot, but with the lack of any reasonable and provable cause, he knew he couldn't do that. Howard had him over a barrel and he knew it. He would get his revenge but now was not the time. Scott simply hung up the phone.

When the phone went dead Howard knew his gamble had paid off. Now all he could hope for was that the faith he had placed in Eric wasn't in vain. For the first time in years he felt the old adrenaline rush that in another age had signaled confrontation and combat. He felt alive again and he was enjoying it. As he replaced the receiver he could hear Mildred stirring in the sitting room just off his office. Howard struggled out of the chair and strolled, to the extent he could stroll, out of his office. Mildred was fluffing some pillows on one of the loveseats. She turned as Howard entered. "You look like the cat that swallowed the canary," she said. "I assume you just received good news."

"You might say that," Howard replied, as he went to the kitchen to replenish his coffee. On reaching the kitchen, he heard the house phone ring and Mildred answer it. He hesitated in the event it was Eric, but not hearing Mildred summon him to the phone, determined it was one of Mildred's friends calling for some damn thing. Women seemed to spend an enormous time on the phone for no apparent reason and Mildred was no exception.

CHAPTER FORTY-NINE

S alvador Valencia surveyed the family shipping facility, beginning with the gate where two guards had been found dead. The warehouse was totally destroyed. Salvador went to the dock and found it untouched, including the hoists and small cranes that were standing ready to load any ship needing hoisting equipment. Normally the product the family shipped was loaded by hand, but, on occasion, it was hidden in other merchandise which required the hoists and cranes.

The quick survey confirmed what Salvador feared. The weather was going to be a huge risk and protecting the product from the weather was his first priority. Everything else was untouched by the raid. A quick glance at the sky indicated the weather problem was immediate. Clouds were building up in the north and that generally meant rain in the afternoon or evening.

Replacement product was already arriving from the sources closest to the shipping point. The void in leadership resulted in it being unloaded in the front of the main lodge and abandoned there. Luckily, there hadn't been rain since its arrival. Salvador decided to move the product into the bunkhouse. It would displace what workers remained, approximately eight, but they could sleep on the floor in the main lodge.

Salvador sent two of the men to the bunkhouse to gather all remaining personal effects of the dead and the living and place them under the nearby trees. He would find a tarp or something to cover them later. He further instructed the workers to push all bunks and other furniture to the back and to pile it up so maximum space would be available for storage of product. As the laborers began to carry out his orders, he went to the main lodge to survey the damage there.

The door to the main lodge stood ajar. Salvador pushed it open with the toe of his boot as though he was expecting the raiders to be inside waiting for him. The real reason for his apparent cautious behavior was very personal. He had known each of the men who had died there. He felt especially close to Eva Barajas and was not looking forward to viewing the evidence of her demise. The main room was empty and quite dark. All the windows had been covered by curtains designed to block any light from getting to the outside. The curtains worked well in reverse. Rather than turn on the overhead light, Salvador went to the nearest window and opened the curtain.

The resulting light illuminated most of the great room. With the exception of a towel here and a chair upset there, the room didn't appear much different than he remembered it from the last time he was at the family shipping docks. Salvador knew, however, that the horrors had not taken place in the great room but in the bedrooms in the back of the lodge. He could have sent one of the men in to clean the place before he entered, but something drove him to view the rooms himself before they were cleaned. The rooms that had been occupied by the men -- men he had known -- were not as hard to stomach as he had thought. It was easy to tell who was using which room, because the clothing remained as it had been left the night of the raid.

When Salvador reached the room occupied by Eva, he immediately noticed that along with the bloodstains the bedclothes had been torn up. She had given a good account of herself Salvador thought to himself as he was choking down tears. He realized, for the first time, that Eva meant more to him than just a good friend. The fact that she died in bed, with another man, began to override his tears and infuriate him.

As he was standing in the room, surveying the wreckage with mixed feelings of grieving and anger, he noticed a slight trail of blood leading to the door. It might have been from the body removal process but that didn't make a lot of sense. Bodies that were dead as long as they had been don't bleed. Salvador traced the blood to the door and eventually to the outside where it was lost in the dust. Whoever killed Eva was injured himself. By the extent of the blood trail, he may have been hurt seriously. Salvador mentally stored the information. It may be the only lead to the man that killed Eva.

Filled with anger and hurt, Salvador turned and left the main lodge. The men could sleep in there, but he would sleep in the dust and mud before he would again darken the doors of the lodge. As Salvador was walking in the direction of the bunkhouse, he became aware of the sound of a motor. It was barely audible but definitely coming from the direction of the lodge. With one loud whistle he got the attention of the seven or eight men working to ready the bunkhouse for use as a storage facility. He motioned them to come to him, and the way he did it imparted the urgency to hurry.

"Gather your weapons and get to the trees," Salvador ordered. "We're going to have company."

The men complied immediately, leaving him in the road with no evidence he was other than alone on the property. Salvador began walking toward the sound of the motor. He hadn't gone more than fifty meters when he realized the sound was not of one vehicle but of two, maybe more. He slowed his pace, not wanting to get too far from the hidden protection the men provided.

He checked his weapon to ensure its readiness and waited to see who was coming. It took no more than three or four minutes before a large covered truck appeared in the roadway leading to the lodge and bunkhouse. A fleeting feeling of relief swept over him as he realized it was, in all probability, a vehicle delivering product for shipment. The feeling of apprehension returned as he realized a newer model Dodge was immediately behind the truck. Salvador stepped to the side, and, as the truck went by, he knew his instincts were justified. The look on the driver's face gave notice. Something was not right.

As the Dodge pulled up beside him, he noted that two men occupied the vehicle. An older man was in the passenger seat and a younger man was driving. They were in local police uniforms. The vehicle proceeded about thirty kilometers and stopped. The older of the men got out and approached Salvador from the rear.

"Are you in charge here?" the officer asked in a tone imparting the aura of authority.

"Yes, I am. What can I do for you?"

"Your boss has been transporting a lot of – shall we say merchandise. We've been assuring its safe passage. It's customary we should get paid for that service. A lot could have happened en route that would not have been in your boss's best interests. A lot could still happen. Do you understand what I'm saying?"

"Yes, I understand what you are saying, but I was told that you'd already been paid for your services. Is that not correct?" Salvador tried to appear as accommodating as he could.

"Yes, we've been paid some moneys but the volume of traffic we had to supervise well -- let's just say it was much more than anticipated. An additional twenty five thousand American will be sufficient and will insure the merchandise is safe. Now, that's fair isn't it?"

"It seems fair and my boss wants, above all, to be fair. I have some money at the bunkhouse. If you'll follow me, we can get this matter cleared up now," Salvador said and turned toward the bunkhouse. As he turned, he saw the older man smile and nod to the driver. As soon as Salvador had his back to the officer he freed his pistol from his belt. With the deliberateness of one who was accustomed to the act he was about to perform, he turned and in one motion brought the pistol up firing when it reached the level of the officer's head.

The bullet struck the officer in the face and exited the back of the skull, taking a good portion of it with it. The windshield of the police car was splattered with bone chips and what soft matter traveled the two meters between the dead man and the automobile. The young driver was paralyzed with fear. Salvador's weapon was now trained on him. "Go back to your boss and tell him what happened here. Tell him the Barajas family does not pay twice for the same services. Now, gather your friend and get out of here before I change my mind about you"

The fear in the eyes of the young police officer was all the assurance Salvador needed to holster his weapon, turn, and walk toward the waiting transport truck. The driver had just exited the cab, the fear and confusion evident in his eyes.

"Hopefully your entire trip wasn't as eventful as its conclusion," Salvador said as he approached the man. The man could only nod. As Salvador got closer to the cab the man regained his composure.

"I was told to let you know that this is the last load. The supply has been exhausted," he said in a tone indicating he half expected to be reprimanded for carrying the message.

"You've done your job. Now, go back to your family. I'll take it from here."

Salvador's men had begun to filter out of the trees. As the first of the men reached him, Salvador knew he had gained their trust and respect. Men who, not more than a few days ago, were fiercely loyal to Eva.

"Miss Barajas would have done the same thing, Boss, although she might have cut his throat," one of the men said.

"Well, she was better with a knife than I am," Salvador replied. "Now, let's get this product unloaded, and, together with the product previously delivered, get it all in the bunkhouse."

Salvador reached into his pocket, extracted a small cell phone, and began to dial the number he knew to be the personal line of his boss.

Salvador looked to the sky. The afternoon storm was less than an hour away. The men would have to hurry to save the product that was available.

CHAPTER FIFTY

Having made the arrangements to meet Barajas in Brazil, I decided to book my flight and then enjoy some of the pleasures offered by the vacation paradise. The hotel had a concierge able to make my travel arrangements. I went to the front lobby and located the desk. A beautiful dark skinned woman in a very tasteful hotel uniform was busy on the phone but smiled as I walked up. She motioned that it would be only a short time until she would be off the phone, and that I should sit. I wasn't in any hurry so I took one of the two available seats and waited for her to finish. Within minutes she concluded her conversation and swiveled her desk chair to face the front of the desk.

"What is it I can do to make your vacation stay here more enjoyable?" she said in a tone that made you feel she was there for you and you alone.

I was about to tell her I was not there on vacation but on business when I decided she didn't have to have that information. I just smiled. "I want to get to Rio de Janeiro by midday tomorrow. Is that going to be a problem?"

She smiled as she reached under her desk and retrieved what I assumed was a book of the various airlines and their schedules. After thumbing through the book, she rested on a page and studied it for several seconds.

"There are several flights that seem to fit your request, for that matter several airlines. I have one on Pan American Airlines leaving here tomorrow morning and arriving in Rio slightly before noon. There's also one leaving here a bit earlier in the morning but arriving slightly after noon. It is a small commuter airline-- carries about twelve passengers. I've never flown it but it has an excellent safety record. The pilots that fly the route say it's much more scenic, if you would enjoy that. The only drawback is it lands at a smaller airport outside Rio. According to the information I have, it's approximately fifteen kilometers from the city."

"How early does it leave?" I inquired.

"It says here, it leaves the island airport at seven forty-five a.m. The Pan Am flight leaves at nine a.m. If you're considering the shuttle I will confirm its departure time and make the reservation," she said, waiting for my decision.

"Let's try the shuttle, but if it arrives in Rio after, shall we say, two in the afternoon, then book me on the Pan Am flight."

"Fine, I'll need your name and how you will be paying."

"Eric Butler, and I'll be paying cash. I can pay you now or at the airport if I have to pick the tickets up there."

"You can pay me when you stop back for the tickets. They will be here after four this evening."

Having arranged for the trip to Brazil, I began to consider what I was going to do with the rest of the day and evening. I knew from reading the tourist literature that the island offered a lot of daily excursions, but I figured none of the trips would be available in the time I had left. Gambling was available, but I didn't feel like sitting in a darkened casino, matching wits with the house and the loaded odds they offered. I remembered seeing brochures advertising motor scooter tours one could take not involving a tour guide. That seemed an activity I would enjoy. Sadie would have liked that, and she generally was able to pick something we both enjoyed.

One of the tourist brochures in the hotel lobby advertised the scooters and a local map indicating the points of interest which were accessible from the hotel. I again approached the concierge.

"I would like to arrange for one of those motor scooters and the map. The hotel advertises them. Would that be possible?"

"Yes, certainly. You will find it very enjoyable, some say relaxing. I'll have one brought to the front entrance for you. Do you know how to operate the scooter or may I arrange for a short instruction?

"No, I owned one as a boy. I assume they're all about the same. I'm sure I can figure it out, but thank you anyway," I responded, lying about owning one but confident it was no different than others I had operated over the years.

"Shall I add this to your hotel bill, Mr. Butler?" she inquired as she picked up the phone to summon the scooter.

I nodded and turned toward the entrance. I was thinking about the excursion when it occurred to me that I should arrange for a cell phone. It was stupid of me to disregard the secure line, especially the way I had. I decided a stop at the first shop selling cell phones that I ran across was in order. I realized a phone account would be costly, mostly because of my requirements, but also because of my lack of permanency anywhere.

I arrived at the entrance just as the scooter arrived. It was a newer model than I had operated previously but the basic controls were the same. I tipped the man generously, accepted the map, and started my mini-tour of the area. I hadn't gone four blocks before I spotted a shop that was selling communications services and devices. I parked the scooter, being careful to extract the ignition key. Upon entering the shop, I was amazed at the wares for sale. Except for the quaint, shop-like appearance of the exterior, the shop was one which would have done justice to any communications outlet in the United States. There were at least six choices of cell phone systems for sale and all the accessories one could imagine. The shop manager or owner, appearing to be a local, was a pleasant sort of fellow. I explained I was on sensitive business and had lost my cell phone into the sea while leaning over the rail on a sight-seeing excursion. I needed a replacement and preferred it have some security with it. The man hesitated for an instant before indicating he could supply a phone that was state of the art and virtually untraceable if connected to the right system. It would be expensive, however. My experience and training kicked in and I noticed his eyes had narrowed and a slight film of perspiration was evident on his forehead.

My first reaction was to leave and find another shop, but something told me his concern must have origins in something other than concern over me or knowledge of me, probably the prospect of making a very profitable sale. I asked how the security worked and he explained, as best he could, how the phone blocked the normal paths utilized in tracing or eavesdropping operations. It was obviously nothing the whiz kids at the Company couldn't get through but it was better than nothing. I had one final request which was whether the cell could be connected through an exchange in Argentina or Brazil. He thought for a moment and ultimately said it could be done, but, again, it would be expensive. I assured him price wasn't an area with which he needed to be concerned and he should proceed to set the system up.

The manager looked at me, a slight smile forming on his otherwise somber face. He excused himself, disappearing into what appeared to be a back room office. He was gone for several minutes, and I was beginning to feel that my first inclination to find another shop would have been smart. He reappeared, however, just as I was becoming uneasy to the point of leaving. He had a small cell phone in his hand and a rift of papers. I approached the counter, having positioned myself closer to the door in his absence.

"This phone will do you fine," he announced. "Your exchange will run through Argentina, but the phone will work anywhere in the world that can be seen from a stationary satellite. The cost, sir, is two thousand dollars American. One thousand of it will be a deposit on cellular time, and the other thousand is for the phone and the connections through Argentina. The phone number, together with the International area code, is contained in the papers. The line will be activated when I call and verify I have received the deposit. Do you have any questions?"

"No, I don't think so, but I'd like to stay here until I have a dial tone. You understand I hope," I said giving him twenty-one hundred American dollar bills. After counting them a second time, he excused himself and disappeared into the same office. In less than five minutes he reappeared asking me to check the cellular unit. I had a dial tone. I thanked the man and left the shop. I was now back in communication with the world.

A glance at my watch confirmed I had little time to tour before dark. The map indicated a short loop through the downtown area of the island. It seemed to fit with the available light and my need for some fresh air and relaxation. I started the scooter and pulled into what traffic was present at that time of the afternoon. The tourist attractions on the loop consisted of an old church and an open air market that, according to the guide booklet, had been around for centuries. The church was similar to other old churches in this part of the world. The market, while interesting, was just like others I'd known. Both were just as one would expect. The air, however, was clean and invigorating. The wind in my face cleaned out the cobwebs of the day and revitalized my entire body.

As the day waned to dusk I completed the loop, finding myself back at the hotel. I parked the scooter and delivered the key to the front desk. I had just enough time to pick up my tickets and shower for what I hoped would be a leisurely dinner at the hotel followed by an early evening. As I approached the concierge she was arranging her desk to leave for the evening. She looked up and I could tell she was relieved I was there to collect my tickets. She smiled.

"I thought I was going to miss you," she said. "All arrangements are made. Your flight will be leaving at seven-thirty tomorrow morning. Here are your tickets. I've taken the liberty of ordering a cab for you. The flight will be four hundred dollars one way. The cab will be available around six-fifteen, which will give you time to get to the airport. Is there anything further the hotel can do for you tonight?"

"No, thank you for your troubles," I said, as I handed her five one hundred dollar bills. She was very pleased with the one hundred-dollar tip. It was probably more than she made in a week at the hotel.

I turned and walked down the marble entry to the elevators, proceeding to my room. Upon entering the room, I noted the traps, I'd set earlier, hadn't been disturbed. My luggage was intact as were the hidden weapons it carried. I fell into the overstuffed chair in the anteroom, debating whether to go directly to the shower. The day had been busy but successful on all fronts. I was ready to set the trap for Barajas and his cartel. With the supply problems he must be having, I would be in the driver's seat.

CHAPTER FIFTY-ONE

John Sailor had patiently waited his turn to exit the aircraft at the Rio de Janeiro airport. He shuffled his way down the aisle behind a throng of businessman and tourists, some who had brought their children for some sort of holiday. It was hard to know which holiday because the holidays in this part of the world seem to run together. He hoped as soon as he entered the concourse he would spot Ronnie. She would have her patented smug look, betraying the fact that she had booked the more comfortable reservation. Normally he would have resented the rebuke, but, in this case, he found himself looking forward to finding her there. There was something about Ronnie he was attracted to. There was a difference in how he felt toward her when compared to other women he had known.

During the flight he considered his attraction to Ronnie, trying to rationalize his attitude toward her as being protective of a green agent. These concerns, as well as the feelings, were new to him. In his career he'd had his share of women, by some standards more than his share, but he'd never allowed himself an attachment to any of them. He prided himself on being able to leave them crying. Somehow, Ronnie was different. His feelings were foreign to him. He was confused, even frightened, by his own emotions.

As he reached the concourse, he saw Ronnie waiting at the rear of the exiting crowd. She didn't have the smirk he'd expected but the look of a young woman traveling abroad for the first time, a look of defiance. He knew she was dependent on his abilities to get her safely to where she was going and he liked that. For the first time in his recollection, he was looking forward to working with another individual. John nodded to her, almost imperceptibly, but sufficiently to signal her to walk in the direction of the exit and baggage claim. They had separated on the flight for a reason and that reason may still exist. His face showed no sign of recognition as he passed her en route to the exit, knowing she would follow at a discrete distance.

On reaching the outside of the airport, Ronnie approached John under the guise of looking for a cab. As she got within whisper distance, she quietly advised him she had gotten them rooms at the Brazilian Star Hotel. The expression on her face begged the question -- how were they going to get there, separately or together? The look on his face provided her with the answer. They would go separately for now. Ronnie summoned a cab and as it pulled up she announced her destination as the Brazilian Star. John, changing his mind as to their travel strategy, stepped forward, and announced he also was staying at the hotel.

"Why don't we share a cab?" he asked. Ronnie nodded politely and slid into the back seat. John slid in beside her and closed the door. The cab had a Plexiglas division between the driver and the back seat. It wasn't soundproof but it did provide some degree of privacy as well as a degree of safety for the driver.

"I've arranged for you and me to be on the same floor, possibly even adjoining rooms. They're being held under my name," Ronnie said in a low voice while looking out the side window. As she finished she glanced at John. She had an impish expression on her face.

John nodded his understanding, ignoring the expression and telling himself she was not flirting. It was just her way.

"How am I supposed to present myself?" John inquired in a low voice.

"As my brother. I think it will be okay to go in together, don't you?"

"It seems there's no choice in the matter," John replied, glancing at Ronnie with a look that told her he was not upset. She smiled and relaxed for the balance of the ride.

The cab arrived at the hotel entrance in good time. John exited the cab and began to act as if he was a brother, making small talk about their parents and home. They both had carry-on luggage so overtures from the bellhops were politely declined. As Ronnie approached the hotel desk, John nudged her arm and imperceptibly nodded toward a man who was in the lounge area discussing something with one of the hotel officials. Around him were several men appearing to be locals. Ronnie looked toward the man, making every effort to appear as a guest merely surveying the hotel lobby. As her gaze returned to the desk, John whispered to her.

"Don't forget that face and don't ever trust it."

Ronnie tried not to look back but could not help herself. The man was large. He was well dressed, but there was something about him alerting her to an uneasiness he seemed to have. His clothes fit beautifully, but appeared out of place on his body, and the lobby seemed to make the man nervous. He kept glancing around, not at people, but at the opulence of his surroundings. Ronnie got a good look at his face and made an attempt to etch it into her memory.

"May I help you?" a young Brazilian man behind the desk asked with the same fraudulent friendliness one finds at most establishments making a living from wealthy tourists. The question brought Ronnie's attention back to the task of registering.

"Yes, my name is Ronnie Matthews and this is my brother John Sailor. We have confirmed reservations." Ronnie handed the desk-clerk the reservation slip provided to her at the Bogotá airport lounge.

"Yes, Miss Matthews, I have it here and you requested adjoining rooms. Is that correct?" the desk-clerk said with a tone reeking of disbelief that they were in fact brother and sister.

"That's correct. I assume there will be no problems with the request," Ronnie responded, making clear that she didn't care what the man thought. "We will be paying cash."

"Very good," the clerk said, becoming more professional, "and how long will you be with us, Miss Matthews?"

"I don't know, at least three days. I will pay you for three now and if we can't conclude our business by then, I will let you know.

"That will be fine. Two adjoining rooms for three days will be seven hundred and fifty dollars. I assume you will be paying in American dollars?"

Ronnie took out ten one hundred-dollar bills and put them on the counter. Put two hundred to our credit, we may want room service. The fifty is for you. The desk clerk nodded appreciatively, sliding two keys across the desk. Ronnie gathered the keys and she and John headed for the elevators.

Their accommodations were adjoining rooms on the twelfth floor. Each of them entered their own room. Ronnie remembered the drill from the hotel in Bogotá and immediately began to search her room for bugs. She was sure not to omit any drawer that could be pulled out. Having convinced herself she had done a thorough job, she began to place her toiletries in the bathroom. Her travel bag was placed on a bench, provided for that purpose. As she was about to lie down, hoping for a few minutes of rest, she heard a small knock on the door adjoining the two rooms. She immediately opened it, finding John clad in pants and an undershirt. His weapon was hanging from his shoulder and strapped to his waist.

"We need to talk about what we're going to do from here," he said, strolling into her room. "The man I pointed out to you is, or was, hired muscle for one of the local drug czars. What is your understanding of the mission Butler and his partner were on? Wasn't he undercover to bring down a drug cartel?"

Ronnie hesitated a moment. "Yes, that's what we were told. Do you think that man or his boss is who Butler is after? It could be a coincidence." I know we're looking for Butler and he's supposedly meeting a drug boss, but how do we know this is the right one? South America is lousy with drug bosses."

"We don't, but it's the only lead we have so I vote we follow it until it proves to be wrong -- any better ideas? By the way, get your weapon on. That's the first thing you should do when circumstances require you to carry it in your luggage."

Ronnie went to her carry-on and released her weapon and its holster from the lining of the bag. As she was strapping it on, she was reflecting on what John had just said. "If you're right, then, at some point, Butler will be coming to this hotel, won't he?"

"Maybe, unless they've arranged to meet elsewhere. We'll know that also if we can locate the boss and follow him. The man I pointed out is a killer, a very dangerous man. I have run into him before although somewhat indirectly. He may not have remembered yet but he will. If he had remembered, we would already be in trouble. His boss, a man named Barajas, is one of the biggest and most ruthless of the lot. Makes his money not only in drugs but also in white slavery.   Not a nice organization. I was undercover several years ago, attempting to discover how the slave trade operated so freely in some areas of the world. Needless to say, I ran into his organization. I was posing as a trader and was offered an opportunity to join it as a major supplier. This man was one of the men I remember, although he wasn't, at least at that time, one of the inner circle. He was muscle and as such was always on the perimeter. I had eliminated one of their major competitors and gained their confidence. The Company pulled me out just when I had the opportunity to break the ring. They had some theory that, if I was found out, they would be implicated and they didn't want that - not in that trade. I've always sensed I was close to finding connections they didn't want found. It was then I decided to go it alone, contacting the handler only when the job was done. As a result I've been branded as a rogue, of sorts, and given only assignments involving terminations or extractions. Most times they're one and the same. The point is that you are not to trust the man and, if necessary, kill him and justify it later."

"You feel the Company is behind our problems down here also, don't you? You said as much earlier," Ronnie said, still mentally digesting the information she had just been given.

"Yes, don't you? Who knew we were here except the Company, and how do you explain the events of this morning. It has to be the Company or someone in it, acting in his own interest. I can't believe Scott Steel is bright enough or, for that matter, ruthless enough to orchestrate what's been happening. You may not like it but I believe we've been marked, and its been done by somebody inside."

"What do we do from here?" Ronnie asked, realizing much, if not all, of what John was saying must be true. It seemed there was no other explanation.

"We need to find Butler and make a decision about him. In the meantime, we should be making every effort to stay alive. I think we're relatively safe here because no one knows where we are, but that could change."

"How exactly do you propose we accomplish both those objectives? And John- believe me when I say staying alive is way ahead of finding Butler."

"We continue to act under the guise you've set up as brother and sister, man and wife, or lovers for that matter. The hotel desk believes we're not brother and sister anyway. We hang around -- see what happens. If I know Barajas, he will have someone in the lobby at all times. It may be local muscle, but it will be there. When Butler comes in, or when they leave, we follow and try to get to Butler before they do. If Butler has gone south it may be for good reason. That may make him a friend. Even if he hasn't gone south he may be a friend anyway. We need to get to him and let him know why we are down here."

"We'd better get dressed and get down to the lobby. That's where we'll have the best chance of finding Butler," Ronnie replied, as she pulled off the light blouse she was wearing, intending to put on a fresh flowered blouse and a light jacket that would conceal her weapon.

The suddenness of Ronnie's actions caught John by surprise. He was not used to women undressing in front of him. His reaction must have shown because Ronnie, realizing he was uncomfortable, finished dressing in the bathroom, a move totally unnecessary because John left the room, announcing in a meek voice uncharacteristic of John, that he was going to get his shirt. Ronnie felt a twinge of embarrassment. Something in her told her she liked this man -- that he was somehow different than other men she had known.

John closed the door between their rooms as he went into his. When Ronnie was fully dressed, she knocked on the door and got no response. For an instant she was paralyzed by a fear that she had been abandoned. She instantly realized she was, whether she liked it or not, dependent on the man she had just embarrassed, a man who had a significant history of leaving his partners to fend for themselves. The anxious feeling passed just as quickly when John knocked at the front door to her room. He was waiting for her in the hallway. At first, he couldn't look at her directly. He looked past her, through her, but not at her. Because of John's reaction to her partial disrobing in his presence, Ronnie felt uneasy for the first time in many years. She knew, if they were going to be successful at the charade of being lovers, something had to change quickly.

"John, I'm sorry I embarrassed you. It won't happen again, unless you want it to. I was so absorbed in the plan that I wasn't thinking about what I was doing." As she was speaking she turned slightly to look at him, realizing at the same time she had virtually asked him if he was interested in her. He was smiling and not in a way that offended Ronnie. It was a smile she had not seen before. She doubted many had. John touched Ronnie's elbow and stopped. Coming to a stop beside him, she realized she made the statement, not by mistake, but because she was beginning to have feelings for John, feelings she was just beginning to recognize.

"I wasn't embarrassed," John said. "I was trying to decide how to tell you that you are the most beautiful woman I have ever seen. Now, we have work to do."

"So now we can act as lovers and a small part of it may be true?" Ronnie said, more as question than a statement.

"We can discuss that later but for now we need to be alert. We need to live and that may be a full time job. I have a feeling we stumbled into the middle of something I would have preferred to approach from the perimeter." As John was speaking, he turned and they resumed their short walk to the elevator. Ronnie had her arm around John's arm. He wasn't rejecting it.

As the elevator reached the lobby level both were in full control of their faculties, acting as lovers who had stolen a day or two from whatever lives they had temporarily left behind. John was the first out of the elevator. He presented the appearance of being completely enamored with his girlfriend while he scanned the lobby. It took no more than a quick look to spot the sentries stationed by the entrance. There were two and, by the cut of their clothes, they were obviously local. Their obsession with the entrance was a dead giveaway. It was clear, to even the casual guest, that they were expecting someone. A glance at Ronnie indicated she had also spotted the men.

John leaned close to her ear. "I'm sure the meeting has not yet occurred."

Ronnie nodded, giving him a peck on the cheek. "Let's get a drink. The lounge looks nice," Ronnie said in a normal tone of voice, smiling at an elderly couple heading for the elevator car they had just vacated.

John glanced at the lounge area and nodded with a smile. The lounge was dark but had tables positioned where the entrance and, therefore the two men, could be watched. It was unnecessary to watch the entire lobby. The reaction of the men would be all the notice they would need.

After entering the bar and choosing a table allowing them to keep the two men in sight, they were approached by a waiter who asked if they might be more comfortable at one of the inner tables -- more secluded from the lobby. John waived the man off after ordering a local brand of beer for both Ronnie and himself. "Lazy bastard, he just doesn't want to come all the way over here to wait on us."

Ronnie agreed, but with more compassion for the man, remembering the days when she waited tables in a small tavern in mid- America, the sore feet and swelling ankles.

"How long do you think we will have to wait?" she said, reaching across and grabbing John's hand, more in fulfilling the role they were playing than as a gesture of affection.

"I hope it will be soon but it could be anytime, maybe even tomorrow."

"We can't sit here and drink until tomorrow. I won't be able to walk let alone act if the situation presented itself," Ronnie said with a worried look only John could discern.

"We'll have two or three beers and if nothing has happened by that time, we'll go for a stroll. If no one shows by the time we get back, we'll leave and take up the surveillance again in the morning."

"You might have two or three beers, but I am going to have to have something to eat or I'll waste away. You don't want a starving drunk woman as a partner do you," Ronnie joked in a lighthearted voice. John laughed and his laugh was genuine. "Sorry, I am used to working alone. I'll get the waiter." John was summoning the man as he finished.

Ronnie ordered a light dinner made up mostly of finger food, the only food served in the lounge. It was adequate for the time being but she realized she and John had not eaten anything since before getting on the airplane.

"John, you have to have something to eat. I'll bet they didn't serve anything more than peanuts in tourist," she said with a giggle.

"And I didn't eat those," John said smiling, all the while keeping an eye on the men stationed near the door. "I hate peanuts."

"That's good to know. I'll try to remember that and not have any in my room," Ronnie said, making small talk but making sure her invitation was not wasted.

Dinner, if that's what one would call it, came. What it lacked in the traditional American meat and potatoes it made up in volume. Ronnie started with the chicken wings and found them to be a bit too spicy for her taste. John, however, evidently didn't mind the bite and devoured most of them in a short period of time. The cheese, served with what appeared to be local bread, appealed most to Ronnie. She devoured it as she sipped on her beer. She knew it might be a long night and attempted to make the food last. The local beer was strong and high in alcohol content. She did not want to get tipsy. If something happened she would need all her wits intact.

After several hours of watching and small talk, John stood up ostensibly to stretch his legs. "We've used up all the small talk I have in me. If he were coming tonight, he would have been here by now. We might as well try to get some sleep. It may be a while before we get another chance."

Ronnie nodded, feeling relieved that the evening's stakeout was drawing to a close. She took John's hand as they headed for the elevator. Ronnie was about to push the call button when the elevator door opened. Before them was the man John had pointed out to her earlier. Without hesitating Ronnie slumped and fell toward the man. Instinctively he reached out to Ronnie in an effort to prevent her from falling to the floor. As he got hold of her upper arms, she shifted her weight, causing him to turn inward toward the interior of the elevator and away from John.

"Thank you very much," she said, her voice slurred in an effort to feign the effects of alcohol. "I think I can make it from here if you please. Come, darling, the bed awaits."

John timed his move into the elevator to coincide with the bodyguard's exit and just as the doors were shutting. The man seemed intent on watching the drunken woman he had just saved from the floor. John attempted to keep his face shielded from the direct view of the bodyguard. Just as the doors came to a close, however, the man looked back at John, catching a clear view of his face.

With the elevator door closed Ronnie was no longer the drunken woman she had been an instant before. "Did he get a good look at you? Do you think he recognized you?"

"I don't know but go to any floor other than ours. If he did, we can at least confuse him."

Ronnie pushed the button for the tenth floor. The elevator began to rise. It wasn't the high-speed variety one becomes accustomed to in the States but it eventually got there. John exited as soon as the elevator stopped. The hallway was empty and somewhat dim. The lights must have been on a timer with a rheostat switch so they dimmed in the late evening. He motioned for Ronnie to follow and headed to the stairs.

"I hope the doors are not locked from the inside," he said, as he waited for Ronnie to catch up.

"Go into the stairwell and I'll remain here. You try to get back. If you can't, I'll let you in and we'll have to use the elevator."

John nodded and entered the stairwell. The door shut making an unexpected loud sound. In an instant John had reopened the door. It wasn't locked from the inside. Ronnie entered the stairwell and they both started the climb toward the twelfth floor. By the time they reached it, Ronnie was drenched in perspiration. She was feeling the effects of the two beers. John reached inside his shirt and released the strap securing his weapon. He opened the door slowly and when it was open just enough, stepped into the hall. His gun was drawn. The hall was empty. They each went directly to their individual rooms and entered without a word passing between them.

Ronnie fell on her bed feeling exhausted from the effects of the booze and the excitement of the last few minutes. After several minutes, she showered and prepared herself for bed. She was feeling somewhat alone and a bit disappointed John had not taken the initiative to go to her room rather than directly to his. She opened the window, a luxury she rarely found in hotels in the United States, and lay down to sleep. Just as she was about to drift off, she heard a light knock on the door that adjoined the two rooms. She could see a slit of light where the door had been opened allowing light from John's room to reach her. As the door opened wider and the light became more available, she could see John. He had taken the initiative and accepted her invitation.

CHAPTER FIFTY-TWO

Barajas had always been an early riser. It stemmed from early childhood when his family would rise before dawn and prepare to go to the fields. They had a small farm of their own, but, to make ends meet, the family would hire out to larger farms during the busy season. One or, at most, two of the members would remain performing tasks needing attention at the home farm. The rest would work for wages. It was in the mountains of France or Spain, whichever applied from year to year, that Jose Salvador Barajas first heard rumors of immense wealth being realized from products of the coca plant. He worked hard and his family did well by local standards, so well he was able to save a portion of each week's earnings. In his early teens he emancipated himself and left for the profits that could be made far to the west.

The heritage of his youth, especially his early raising, followed him to his new country and was still the rule much more than the exception. The early dawn found Barajas comfortably seated on his hotel balcony, enjoying his third or fourth cup of coffee. Barajas had always liked Rio, not only for its sanctuary in the event trouble erupted in his own Colombia, but also for the pure beauty of the city. The nightlife and festivities the city was so famous for had, years ago, ceased being of major interest. They had been replaced by an appreciation of a city that must have been created where the esthetics of light and form were the primary objectives.

As Barajas was admiring the dawn between sips of coffee, remembering the Rio of his younger years, he was interrupted by Michael Brown, his new lead security guard. "Mr. Barajas, I hate to interrupt your morning, but I have some information. I thought you should be advised."

"Not at all, Michael. Come sit with me. Have some of the best coffee in the world. What's on your mind?"

"It may be nothing but with what we have at stake, I thought everything, even information just a bit out of the ordinary, should be reported. I went to the lobby last night to check and make sure the locals we hired were not asleep. As I got off the elevator I encountered a couple going to their room. She was sloppy drunk and almost fell on me as the doors opened. Her companion seemed unconcerned with the struggle she was having and slipped into the elevator car as I was untangling myself from her. I didn't get a real good look at him but, from what I did see, I believe I've seen him before. It took most of the night for me to put it together. I think he's a flesh broker we dealt with several years ago. It was the trip we made to negotiate new sources. I was just a minor part of your security force at the time and wasn't close to him, but if he's not the same man he looks enough like him to be his brother."

Barajas was listening intently. "If it's the man I think you're describing, he disappeared just as we were getting a deal put together. After it was all over, I had the feeling he wasn't what he professed to be. Were you able to tell where he got off the elevator?"

"The lobby dial indicated the tenth. I checked it out by taking the next available car but, by the time I reach the tenth floor, no one was in the hall. I even walked the corridors thinking I might hear them through the doors. His female companion was real drunk and I hoped she might be talking loudly enough for me to locate their room. I couldn't hear a thing so I went back to the lobby and approached the hotel staff. They initially told me they didn't remember the couple and then said they couldn't divulge the information. An American twenty improved their memories and sense of duty. The man's name is John Sailor and the woman's is Ronnie Matthews. They have adjoining suites on the twelfth floor."

"Did you check the twelfth floor out?" Barajas inquired

"Yes, but by the time I got there, I couldn't hear any sounds or conversation. I left shortly, not wanting to be seen by the hotel staff or another guest."

"You did well, Michael. I can already predict my choice in appointing you to take Salvador's place will be justified. You were right in bringing this to me. I can't risk an intruder wherever he has come from or whomever he works for. We'll have to neutralize him before Butler arrives. I assume he hasn't arrived. Have you checked?" Barajas was deep in thought as he finished the question.

"No one's in his room. I haven't checked with the desk," Michael responded.

"I really didn't expect him until this evening. If my feeling from before is right and this Sailor is not who he seems, we have today to get the problem solved. How are the men you hired? Are they up to the job? We can't afford a mistake."

"They're local hoods -- nothing more, nothing less. It wouldn't be the first time they've eliminated a problem. I'll round them up and get a better feel."

As Michael was standing to leave, Barajas got up and went to the interior of his suite. Michael let himself out, gathered the two men in the corridor, and went directly to the lobby. The remaining two hired guards were there. He approached the men who attempted to look alert, having been up all night. He gathered all the men in a small alcove on the outside of the hotel near the main entrance. As he was talking to them, he failed to notice a couple having breakfast in the outdoor veranda of the hotel dining room. Both the man and the woman were partially obscured by a plethora of vines and flowers, separating the dining area from the rest of the hotel grounds. His discussions were low- keyed and without any meaningful gesturing. Following approximately five minutes of conversation, he and the four men left the area and returned to the hotel lobby. The couple, having finished their breakfast, departed the dining area.

The only safe route to the lobby was through the darkened bar. John and Ronnie utilized the dimness to mask what would otherwise have been an obvious attempt to follow the men. As they approached the bright sun light of the lobby, John reached out holding Ronnie back. Both had released their weapons for an eventuality both hoped would not materialize, at least not at this time. The men got on the elevator and the doors closed. Ronnie was about to rush to the lobby when John's hand stopped her. As she turned around, with full intentions of chastising him for holding her up and blowing any chance they had to see where the elevator was going, the elevator door reopened.   The man John had pointed out the previous night stepped out and surveyed the lobby.

They both froze. The dimness of the bar's interior combined with the brightness of the lobby was sufficient to mask their presence. The man, being satisfied no one was interested in his activities or destination, reentered the elevator and the doors closed. Only then did John move into the light of the lobby. Ronnie looked at John with awe, the meaning of which needed no words. She had learned a valuable lesson and she wasn't going to forget it.

The elevator went directly to the fifteenth floor. There were no higher floors and that floor contained five suites, suites only a few of the guests ever saw. If this drug boss was the man Butler was to meet, they had at least located the floor and potentially the suite of the meeting.

"We need to get back to our rooms and quick. If I was recognized last night they may well be looking for us now."

"Then why would we go back to the rooms? If they want us that's the first place they'll look -- isn't it?" Ronnie asked with some alarm in her voice.

"I'm counting on that. Now, trust me and let's move," John replied as he took her arm and moved quickly but unobtrusively toward the elevators.

"I really don't have a choice-- do I!" Ronnie responded with a slight irritation in her voice as John ushered her forward.

John was already pushing the call button. One of the adjoining elevators sounded the customary melodic ping as the door opened. They entered the car and he immediately pushed twelve. The car started its assent. The trip to the twelfth floor was silent. Ronnie was feeling all the indignation of a woman being forced to go somewhere against her will. As the doors slid open, Ronnie noted John's weapon was out and ready. Her indignation dissolved into concern. The corridor was vacant and they made it to their rooms without incident. They entered Ronnie's room, closing the door firmly, but quietly, behind them.

"Insofar as my life is also at stake, I think it would be nice if you would tell me what is going on, or what you think is going on, and what your plan is," Ronnie blurted out as soon as she got her voice back.

All John's prior experience indicated that he should get rid of this lady so he could handle the problems his instincts screamed were about to present themselves. As he swung around to demand she leave, he was confronted by a woman whose lips were pursed and whose body language told him she was here for the duration. John also felt a twinge of loyalty to this woman, a feeling that, before now, had been foreign to him.

"You're right. I think if I was recognized last night and they may try to hit us this morning, before any meeting takes place. I'm sure Barajas has some idea that I was not what I represented when I disappeared several years ago. He wasn't happy then and is probably not happy now. If they're going to hit us, I would be more comfortable if it was at our choice of sites not theirs. They probably don't think I recognized the muscle and will feel safe hitting us here. We'll have the advantage because we know they may be coming. We can be, not only ready but, lying in wait."

"I understand. What do you want me to do?" Ronnie asked, her voice losing its edge.

"We don't know which of our rooms they'll hit, or whether they'll hit both. We also don't know how many of them there will be, although I think three, maybe four would be all they would have hired locally," John said, as he was thinking through the problem. "Did you bring a silencer for your weapon? I would hope the entire hotel wasn't alerted to our activities."

"Yes, I have the standard issue, but I'm not sure it's effective. The few times I've used it, it sounded really loud."

"Put it on and don't worry about the effectiveness. It'll be better than nothing." John hesitated as he was installing his own silencer. "Do you have a knife?"

A chill went up Ronnie's back. She always abhorred the thought of using a knife on another human being. "Yes, but do you think it's necessary when we have the element of surprise and the guns?"

"I don't know what we will need. I learned years ago that one doesn't eliminate a weapon because one thinks he may not need it. Get it out and have it available, where it can be used if necessary." John saw a look of fear cloud Ronnie's delicate features. He instantly had the desire to protect her from the events he was sure would be playing themselves out in the next few hours, if not minutes. John also realized that protecting her, no shielding her, was not possible in this circumstance. She was a trained operative. Although green, she was still a trained operative.

John had secured his stiletto, a longish blade sharpened on both sides, to his outer right leg and was stripping a thin wire from the seams of his luggage. He attached a somewhat flattened but roundish handle to each end and pulled the wire tight to insure all was ready and operative. Ronnie watched and copied his actions with her knife. She looked toward John as she was finishing.

"Am I supposed to have a wire also?"

"No, this is my addition to the standard package. You won't need one anyway." John arranged the wire around his neck with the handles hanging to the bottom of his breast pockets. "You are not to hesitate to use your weapon. They won't. We'll be outnumbered. All we have is the element of surprise. We'll deal with what the noise brings, if anything, afterwards. Can you handle that?"

"Yes, but what are we going to do when they show up? Where do you want me to be?" Ronnie asked, while she was adjusting her knife so it would be where she wanted it, yet partially hidden.

"Let's leave the door between our rooms open for now. They may attempt either door, or maybe both, but I think they will choose one attempting to gain entry through it. Whoever's door they choose, you will answer that door. I will be in the other room with the door closed but not latched. When they all have gained entry you say – 'What is it you want?' That will be my signal they are in. I will make an entry that will draw their attention to me. You take care of at least one hopefully two. By that time I will have eliminated at least one. If there are four of them, the fourth is either yours, if all has gone well for you, or mine if you can't get a clean shot off. Remember, these are hired killers. They won't hesitate killing you or me. If they hit both doors at once -- well, we'll each be on our own, but remember they won't be expecting us to be ready. If you don't hesitate this could be over in seconds."

Ronnie nodded her assent and understanding of her role in the events John was convinced would be playing out in the near future. She was unsure what she was going to do during the period of waiting or how long the period was going to be.

"Do you think they will be here shortly?" Ronnie asked, as she took a seat near the door separating the two sleeping rooms.

"They'll be here within the next hour if they're coming at all," John said, as he stretched out on the bed that remained unmade from the previous night. His weapon was resting on the bed beside him. Ronnie watched as he appeared to close his eyes with the casualness of one lying down for a simple nap. Instantly she was angry. They were about to kill three or four men, or be killed themselves, and he was napping.

"What the hell are you doing?" she said after she could not hold it in any longer.

John's eyes seemed to open a bit. "What do you mean,' What am I doing?' What does it look like I'm doing? I'm doing the same thing you are. Waiting for them to approach our rooms."

"It looks like you're taking a nap. Shouldn't we be doing something? I can't just sit here like it's some Pollyanna morning waiting for you to wake and make my day. Maybe you expect me to wait for them and wake you when they appear – John, would you please wake up. Our guests have arrived."

"What would you like me to do? Pace back and forth, join you and sit rigidly in one of the chairs, or possibly paste my ear against the door and listen for someone in the corridor. No, I don't think so. I've learned one should rest when one can because one never knows when the next opportunity will present itself. I suggest you find some way to relax and leave me to do the same." John adjusted his weapon to be at his fingertips as he tilted his head back and closed his eyes again.

Ronnie felt as though she the wind had been knocked from her. Her anger had been replaced with a feeling of inadequacy-- a feeling of fear. She just wasn't ready to accept the inevitable as cavalierly as John obviously could. She did admit to herself that it did no good to waste nervous energy and she should get comfortable and learn to wait. With her weapon in her lap she made a concerted attempt to use the time to rest while remaining alert.

As Barajas moved to the interior of his suite, he checked to make sure none of the maids or other hotel personnel were present in the area. He located his cell phone and dialed a number he had memorized more than a year before. The recipient phone must have rung several times before it was answered, because he began to scowl shortly before he spoke into the receiver.

"You didn't tell me others were going to be sent," he said without the customary greeting and then listened to the reply. "Yes, I know I'm taking a chance calling you like this but I have no choice. There's a man and a woman here in Rio that one of my most trusted men recognized. I think from what he said, it's a man I've dealt with before. I suspect he's one of your men."

Barajas hesitated as the person on the other end was saying something. "I intend to do just that, and I hope there will be no further surprises. I have committed far too many resources to this venture already for anything to go wrong now." Again the person on the other end was speaking.

"Yes, I will, and you can rest assured this whole matter will be brought to a conclusion within the next forty-eight hours." Barajas flipped the cell phone closed, terminating the conversation.

Barajas paced the spacious suite. It would have been clear, to even the most casual observer, that he was nervous or anxious about something. Within a few minutes Salvador was back with the two locals he had posted in the corridor along with the locals he had just retrieved from the lobby. Salvador directed the four to be seated. He motioned to Barajas that he needed to speak to him privately. Barajas stepped into a small hallway, which separated the main portion of the suite from the sleeping area. Both men positioned themselves so they could watch the men.

"I have spoken to them about eliminating two of the hotel's guests. Three of them were eager after I indicated they would each receive an additional thousand dollars if they were successful. The fourth was a little reluctant but agreed after some thought. He has some problem with eliminating a woman. I think we can trust them, at least for the time we will be in this city. I also told them if they were caught, we would have them eliminated in the jail. I told them our contacts went to high places, and their elimination would not be a problem. I can assure you, they believed me. What is your plan?"

"I'll leave that up to you but it must be done quickly. I don't know when Butler will arrive, but it must be done before he gets here. What will you do with the bodies?"

"I will have the men commandeer one of those laundry carts. There's an extra on this floor. I saw it as we came in. It's large enough to hold two bodies without showing. They will use the service elevator and dump the bodies in a trash bin outside the kitchen. It should be hours before they're found and at least an additional hour before they're identified," Salvador responded, still thinking the plan through.

"Good -- only one more thing. I don't want you involved," Barajas specified. "I need you here if things go wrong. I don't want us implicated in any way. Will they do it without your participation?"

"I hadn't considered that," Salvador said thinking. "I'll have to pay them after they prove it's done. An ear from each will do. I could meet them in the lobby or on the grounds in front. Let's see if they will agree to these terms." Salvador was still formulating his thoughts as he was speaking.

"Let's get it done. I'll arrange for more security. We won't want them around after it's over," Barajas said, as he reached out and squeezed Salvador's shoulder, indicating his approval of the way his new lieutenant was handling the assigned task.

Salvador turned and entered the main room of the suite, approaching the four men sitting in various chairs. The men were ill at ease in the suite, as it contained more opulence in one place than any of them had seen before. After explaining the plan and fielding questions from the men, he asked they show him their weapons. Each of the men had an old pistol varying from one thirty- eight caliber to a forty-four magnum. All were fully loaded. It was decided the smallest of the four would, using the service elevator, take the laundry cart to the twelfth floor. He would start before the other three went down. One was to take the stairwell while the other two would arrive last in separate main elevators. Salvador explained that the marks were in two rooms and entry should be as unobtrusive as possible but, in no event, were they to be refused entry to the rooms. Salvador suggested they try to determine which was the woman's room and hit it last, taking the man out first. All of the men nodded in agreement and holstered their weapons.

On the prompting of Salvador the smallest of the men entered the corridor, located the laundry cart, and disappeared into the service elevator. As the elevator door closed, the second and most athletic of the four left the suite and entered the staircase. Salvador gave the men two or three minutes before he dispatched the last two for the main elevator.

Ronnie was having trouble acting as though she was relaxed and resting in anticipation of an assault she wasn't sure was coming. She had started to wonder if John was being paranoid in his caution. As the minutes passed, she almost convinced herself John had not been recognized, and the anticipated attack was not going to materialize.

Then, as she was working herself up to confronting John with her thoughts, she heard a slight movement in the corridor outside her door. John must have heard it also because he was on his feet, his weapon in hand, and was heading for the door adjoining his room to hers. His reaction to the slight noise, really just a rustle, was noiseless and decisive. She vacated the chair and approached the door, placing her ear to its smooth interior veneer. She could detect the sound of hushed voices and whispers on the other side of the door. Ronnie turned slightly nodding to John, who was still in the interior doorway. He slowly and noiselessly closed the door, leaving it slightly ajar. It seemed like minutes, though it was only seconds, before there was a knock at the door. A man announced he was from room service and had a delivery for the lady.

"One moment please," Ronnie responded, attempting to make her voice sound natural. She had previously freed her weapon and was making sure it was hidden in the folds of her skirt. She quietly unlatched the door and stepped back. "Come in. The door is open."

As the door opened, she moved to the side where she would be shielded from the intruders by the door itself. Her silencer was securely attached to her weapon. Its extra length and weight made the gun feel awkward in her hand. Ronnie had a fleeting regret for the times she avoided the practice range where she could have gotten more comfortable using the silencer. As she held the weapon in the folds of her clothing, she saw a long barreled pistol appear, and immediately behind it appeared one of the men she had seen in the lobby. He was straining to see in the darkened room. She could hear others behind him. His actions suggested he was being prodded from behind.

He was looking straight ahead and had not detected her location in the room. As the second intruder became visible from her vantage point, she heard a muffled, almost guttural sound from the corridor. The first man started to turn and as he did, he saw her. His gun began to swing toward her. John's warnings and her instincts were governing her actions. She squeezed off the first round. The sound was not as she had remembered, but was more like a loud cough or sneeze. The man stopped and, with the weapon still swinging toward her, fell to the floor. The man following him was seemingly having trouble with something behind him because he stumbled forward, almost tripping over his dead confederate. Ronnie didn't allow him time to recover before her pistol coughed a second time. The man uttered a muted yelp while falling to the floor, partially falling over her first victim. He had a smallish hole in his forehead.

As Ronnie swung her pistol toward the door, anticipating a third assailant, she saw the reason for the awkward entry of her last victim. The third man entered with John's knife planted to the hilt in his upper back. He was dead and had been falling forward. As she continued to position her weapon in anticipation of others, she was not disappointed because a fourth man was being shoved inside his head was nearly severed from the rest of his body. John was behind him pulling the handles. He released the man and he collapsed on top of the other bodies.

Ronnie's hand and gun fell to her side. She felt revulsion for what had just been accomplished. She thought she was going to vomit. John was kicking at the dead men's legs, clearing them from the doorway, so the door could be shut. He looked at her, and could tell from the paleness of her face that she was not accepting the events of the last few seconds easily.

"You did well," he said. "Just remember, if you hadn't done your job it would be us here on the floor, not them. Now help me get this door shut."

Without thinking further, Ronnie holstered her weapon and assisted John in getting the bodies into the room.

"What in the hell are we going to do with these bodies?" she asked dropping the leg of the last victim as the door was shut.

"If things go the way I think they will, we probably won't have to do anything. We'll be out of here before the next maid service. To be safe though, I think we should dispose of them the same way they were going to dispose of us. They have a large laundry cart in the corridor. It almost got in my way, as I was slipping in behind them. We'll dump them in it and leave it on another floor, hopefully in a maintenance closet where they won't be discovered too soon. That will buy time for us. Even if they are found, there'll be no tie to our rooms or to us. John hesitated, noticing a pool of blood on the carpet. Not for a while at least." John stepped over the bodies and opened the adjoining door to his room. "I'll get the cart and bring it in through here. You get as many towels as we can spare."

Ronnie complied, acting more as a dutiful servant than a partner in the carnage before her. The laundry cart was quite large but getting four medium sized men in it was going to be difficult. John positioned it just inside Ronnie's room beside the bodies. Ronnie was sitting on the edge of the bed with four or five newly laundered towels in her lap. John looked at the four bodies and then at the cart.

"The biggest one first. I think he's the biggest," he said, pointing to the second man who had entered the room. John immediately started to move the corpses, getting to the largest of them. He was careful not to get any more blood on the carpet than was already there. As he freed the corpse he was going to load first, he looked up at Ronnie. "I could use some help here," he said, but without the venom his tone was so capable of exuding. "You get his feet, I'll get the top part. Let's make sure he fits fully in the bottom of the cart." Again, Ronnie complied, leaving the towels on the edge of the bed.

The man fit nicely in the cart occupying only the bottom section. The second man went in on top of him. John reached in, arranging the limbs so they took as little space as possible. The third man filled the cart almost to the top, and the smallest of the corpses folded around him, leaving ten to fifteen centimeters for a covering.

"Strip the bedding from your bed and bring it to me," John said, while still arranging body parts, insuring there were no extruding hands or legs. Ronnie complied and before long the cart appeared to be full of soiled linens. The only giveaway was the obvious weight. It could hardly be moved. "Go get the service elevator and signal me when you have it." Ronnie left the room and got to the service elevator. As she was about to call it, a couple got off the main elevators and turned toward where she was waiting. The woman, a middle aged lady who was obviously very friendly, smiled at her as they approached.

"You know you're using the service elevators don't you, Honey? You may have better luck down there, where we came out."

Ronnie smiled, thanked the lady, and started toward the main elevators but not before punching the call button. As she walked toward the main elevators, feigning just the right amount of indecisiveness, Ronnie glanced back over her shoulder to see where they were going. They were entering a room directly across from the service elevator. To use that elevator would be an enormous risk. As she passed the main elevator, she heard the service elevator's bell ring, signaling it had arrived. John must have heard the arrival bell also. He immediately pushed the loaded laundry cart into the corridor. Ronnie pushed the main elevator call button and the doors the couple had just occupied opened. She immediately entered the car and pushed the hold button. Thankfully, it locked in place and she was free to help John push the cart.

"Forget the service elevators. I met some people who have a room immediately across from it. We'll have to risk the main ones," Ronnie said in a hushed voice as she began pushing in an effort to help clear the floor quickly.

The cart pushed more easily than she had originally thought, especially after it was in motion. They reached the service elevator without incident and released the hold button. John pushed the button for the fourteenth floor and within seconds the car was slowing and the door opened. Ronnie stepped out, surveying the corridor. It was clear. She motioned John to roll the cart into the corridor and began to look for the maintenance closet. It was located by the service elevator on the twelfth floor and was probably in the same location on fourteen. Ronnie walked toward the service elevator trying to hurry, but not appear to be out of place if anyone came into the corridor. As expected, the service elevator and the maintenance closet were in the same location, but the door was locked.

Ronnie suddenly remembered that the stairwell, they had used late last night, had wide spacious landings. There was more than enough room for the laundry cart. Instinctively, she opened the stairwell door. The landing was just as she remembered. She motioned John into the stairwell. As the cart hit the concrete floor of the landing it moved much easier than it had in the carpeted corridor. John was slightly out of breath having pushed the cart, and all its extra weight, from the elevator to the end of the corridor without help.

"What was wrong with the maintenance closet?" he asked, as he made sure the door was closed behind him.

"It was locked. This may be a better place anyway. Look at the dust on the floor and in the corners. It's obvious they don't clean here on any regular schedule but they'll be in the closet daily. This could buy or a day or two, maybe longer."

John nodded and pushed the cart into the corner so if anyone were using the staircase, they would have plenty of room to get around without moving the cart. Both stepped back and surveyed the cart and the pile of would--be laundry covering the cart. The bed linens had been adequately arranged on the cart. Nothing betrayed its gruesome contents. Without saying anything both left the stairwell and proceeded back to their room on the twelfth floor. They entered John's, neither of them wanting to see the carnage that was in the adjoining room. John sat on the bed and Ronnie fell into a chair near the bath.

"We're still in danger," he said in a matter-of-fact tone. "The man that spotted me was not one of the four we just disposed of. He may have already been alerted to the failure of his henchman.

"I saw that also. What do we do now?" Ronnie responded, as she was thinking about the mess in the adjoining room.

"First, we need to clean up the room a bit, get a change of clothes, and pack our things so we won't have to come back here. We should also shower. I don't want any evidence of the last hour to remain on our bodies."

Ronnie nodded assent if not agreement. "I'll get my things and move in here. I'm not going to spend any more time in there than I have to, so you just acquired a roommate," she said as a declaration, which by her tone, John knew was not up for debate.

"Why don't you get started moving your things in here and take a good shower? I'll clean up what I can. My hope is there won't be much blood on the carpet. I think they bled more on each other than on the carpet.

Ronnie was relieved that John had volunteered to do the cleanup. She wasn't sure she had the stomach for it, literally. John got up and opened the adjoining door. The room was still as dark and gloomy as Ronnie had remembered leaving it. As he entered the room to survey the damage, he switched on the light. Other than the bed being stripped of all its sheets and blankets, the room didn't look much worse for the wear. The carpet was a medium to dark brown. What blood was on it had soaked in and blended with the natural tone in the carpet. Ronnie slid by John avoiding the area just inside the entrance where the bodies had piled up. John was right. They must have bled on each other, because not as much blood as might be expected reached the carpet.

Ronnie's travel bag was where she had placed it when she first entered the hotel room. The only items needing collection were a few toiletry items in the bathroom. She quickly gathered them and, together with her bag, escaped to John's room. As she passed John, he was cleaning up what evidence was visible with one of the only towels left in the room.

"Would you get the bedspread from my room and put in on the bed. If someone was to check on the room, I don't want the naked mattress to give us away."

Ronnie hated the idea of going back into her room – that room. She knew John was right, however, so she braced herself and stripped the bedspread from John's bed. She went back into her room, making a special effort not to go anywhere near the bloodied carpet. She made the bed. As she was finishing, she glanced at John. He was standing, evaluating the cleanup.

"Unless someone enters this room to clean, it would be hard to tell anything happened here," he said, with a certain amount of satisfaction in his voice. Ronnie agreed and they left her room through the adjoining door.

John brought the bloodied towel he'd used on the carpet. Using the knife he had taken from the back of the unfortunate he had impaled, he quickly cut it in strips and flushed the evidence down the toilet. As he returned to the main room, Ronnie was already stripped to the waist preparing for the shower. She dropped her skirt in the middle of the floor and headed for the bathroom, wearing only bikini panties. Even with the events of the morning still fresh in his mind, John could not help but notice the beauty of her naked body. She was breathtaking, at least in his opinion.

CHAPTER FIFTY-THREE

The morning dawned in the classic Caribbean style. There wasn't a cloud in the sky. The air had been softened by night sea breezes that never seem to fail to cool the island landscape. I checked my tickets to make sure of the departure time and confirmed that lift off was scheduled for seven-thirty a.m. All that was left was to get some breakfast and get to the landing strip the islanders referred to as an airport.

I had secreted the deposit and withdrawal numbers for my new account. I had also acquired a cell phone, which would keep me in touch with the rest of the world. The trip to the island had been a success and, better than a success, had not been stressful. I was rested and ready to complete, what might be, my last assignment. I packed my bag, making sure my weapon was secured in its special place, dressed, and went to the lobby to get a light breakfast. I found a small cafe in the corner of the lobby that catered to the early riser. There were about six tables, four of which were already occupied by tourists who were, obviously, excited about early excursions of one type or another.

A glance at my watch indicated, I had less than an hour to eat before the cab would be waiting for me. The proprietor was also the waiter. I assumed his wife was the cook. I ordered a bowl of local fruit, coffee, and a sweet-roll, which was displayed and certainly baked this morning. The coffee was thick and rich and the fruit was sweet. The roll was delicious. I paid the bill, tipping the owner generously. As I walked to the front entrance I stopped and paid the hotel tab which had been accumulating during my stay. As I exited the main entrance, the cab appeared. I was now ready to conclude my business.

The flight to Rio was as advertised. The plane was small, carrying about fifteen passengers when fully loaded. Today's flight was light with only seven people other than myself on the plane. Much of the flight was over water, but when we reached land the view from the plane's porthole window was spectacular. The rainforest seemed to grow right into the sea with sparkling white beaches around each bend in the shoreline. Approximately four hours into the flight, the pilot announced that we had encountered favorable winds. We'd be landing about fifteen minutes early. I finished my coffee and settled in for the conclusion of the flight.

As the pilot had announced, we landed in the Rio area ahead of schedule. The airport was a small airstrip with all the amenities of larger airports without the crowds and turmoil. My bag went through customs smoothly, and I was standing on the sidewalk outside the terminal fifteen minutes after I deplaned. Cab service was immediately available. I was on my way into Rio in short order. The cab driver was a local who spoke reasonably good English. I arranged to secure his services for the day and instructed him to take me to the city's banking district. He nodded suggesting that if I was looking for a good bank, the Rio de Janeiro Bank of International Commerce was the best. I needed to establish an account with a bank that would be able to give me access to my funds in a matter of hours. The recommended bank sounded like it would fit my needs, so I instructed him to take me there.

The bank was not all that different than others on the street where it was located with one exception. The building itself occupied two full blocks, and the main entrance seemed more appropriate for a four- star hotel than a bank. The cabby dropped me off at the entrance. He pointed out a lot a half block away where there were limos and cabs parked. He would wait for me there. I entered the bank and was immediately approached by an employee, inquiring as to the department I was seeking. I told him I was intending to open an account if the proper arrangements could be satisfied. The employee directed me to an elevator and instructed me to go to the third floor. A receptionist would help me there. I followed his instructions and as he had advised, upon exiting the elevator, a nicely dressed middle aged woman met me.

Evidently the employee had announced my arrival. She was expecting me. "What can the Bank of Commerce do for you, Mr. ---------?"

"Butler -- Butler is my name. I would like to arrange a transfer of money into your bank. It will be withdrawn within days so I will need credit which is verifiable within hours. Does your bank perform such services?" I asked, as I looked around the area. It was not unlike the Bank of Commerce in Aruba, just a bit on the flashy side.

"We can if all is in order, Mr. Butler. Would you follow me please?" The lady led me to a small office where she asked I wait, and a bank officer would be with me shortly. I complied with her request. In less than a minute a rather large man entered the room, introducing himself as Mr. Velasquez. He asked what the bank could do for me, and I responded with the same answer given the receptionist.

"What is the amount of money you will be transferring and where will it be coming from?" he asked, taking out a standard yellow pad such as one seen in offices all over the world.

"The sum will be ten million dollars American, and it will be transferred from the Bank of Commerce in Aruba, from a private numbered account," I responded, making every effort to speed the transaction along.

"We have a fine relationship with that bank, Mr. Butler. We can arrange the transfer when you are ready. Will it be to an account in your name, sir?"

"Part of it will, yes. I want six million to be placed in a separate account in joint names, which will be accessible by either one of two verified signatures, Salvador Barajas or mine. Four million will be in a separate account accessible only by myself. I also want the four million dollar account to be reachable by draft or check. I need the accounts to be established and verifiable by close of business today. Can that be arranged?"

"I see no problem, so long as the funds are verified and transfer made by your present bank. Will you be banking with us in the future, Mr. Butler, or is this an interim arrangement?" Velasquez asked.

"The six million dollar account will be of short duration, just a matter of days. I'm closing a business transaction with that account. The four million dollar account, my personal account, will be utilized over a longer period of time."

"Not a problem, Mr. Butler. We will need some basic information from you and then after the account is set up, the transfer can be made."

I gave him my information, where I thought it was any of his business. I used the bank address in Aruba as my personnel address, which he picked up on immediately. After some discussion, he gave up and didn't pursue a different address further. Utilizing the facilities supplied by the bank, I wired the Bank of Commerce in Aruba and, with the number code I had been supplied, arranged for the transfer. Velasquez also wired the bank verifying the Brazilian deposit accounts and codes. Before I left the bank he received confirmation the requested funds were being transferred. With the accounts set up and fifteen or twenty preprinted bank drafts for my personal account in my possession, I left the bank. It was getting into the late afternoon hours. I needed to contact Howard Baker as well as Barajas. As promised my personal cab driver was parked where he had indicated. I needed some privacy to make the calls.

As I approached the cab I noticed my driver was sprawled across the front seat of the cab. For a moment I thought he'd been killed. I tapped on the cab's roof and he jumped up, resuming his position behind the wheel.

"Thought for a moment you'd been robbed or something," I said, as I slid into the seat next to him.

"Oh, no I was just getting some rest. In this business you get rest when you can because one never knows when the next opportunity may present itself," he said in an obvious attempt to placate his fare. "Where to, boss?"

"I need to place some phone calls, but I'll need absolute privacy. I'll need no more than a half-hour but it must be uninterrupted. Can you find such a place quickly?"

"How private do you need? You could make them from here in the cab, if that's private enough," he responded.

"No, the calls are very sensitive and you don't need to be exposed to them. It's not that I don't trust you, but I don't want to cause you any trouble. Is there a cheap hotel around here where I can rent a room for the night? I won't be staying there but a room would be private enough."

"The Rio Arms is just a few blocks from here. It's not the best hotel but it isn't the worst either."

"That will work. Take me there. I'll need you back in forty-five minutes. Can you do that?

"You're the boss. I'll be in front forty–five minutes from when I drop you off," the cabby said, as he started the motor.

The Rio Arms was in the financial district. It was an older hotel which had at one time been very nice. It wasn't bad, as it was, but the owners hadn't kept it up as well as they might have and it showed. The desk clerk was ancient, but accommodating, and rented me a room on the top floor for fifty dollars, no questions asked. I got the feeling this hotel was utilized by the financial wizards to meet with their girlfriends for secret liaisons they didn't want their wives or bosses to know about.

The elevator to the top floor was an old- cage type with ornate iron slats that began at the floor level and ended about chest high. It had been renovated in recent years to operate automatically, but the mechanism for the elevator man to operate had been left intact, at least from outward appearances. I selected the fifth floor, which was the top, and pushed the button. Following a few small jerks and some distant groaning, the elevator car began to move upward.

The corridor on the fifth floor was what one might have expected of a hotel which had seen better days but it appeared clean and reasonably well kept. My room was the third from the elevator on the left side. I opened the door and entered. The room's contained a bed and a wash basin in the main room. A small water closet was attached. There was one chair, which had been very elegant, but was now threadbare, and there were visible repairs, which had been made to the chairs structural parts. The room was more than adequate for the need I had.

The small cell phone, I had purchased, indicated a strong signal but was getting a bit low on power. I hoped the power would be adequate for the two calls I needed to make. I made a mental note to find a place to plug it in for recharging at the first opportunity. I sat down in the chair and began to plan the calls. It seemed best to call Barajas before attempting to get Howard

Baker. The time was fast approaching for the takedown, and Howard would need any information I could give him on the operation. Barajas would be expecting my call and I should be able to arrange a meeting in short order.

I dialed the number I had memorized for Barajas's cell phone. It rang twice. On the third ring a voice came on simply saying - Hello. The voice was that of Barajas.

"Eric Butler here. Are you ready to complete our arrangements?"

"Yes, of course. Are you in Rio? I have arranged a room for you at my hotel."

"Yes, I'm here. I will be over within the hour. Is the product ready for shipping? I must notify my people to arrange for its delivery," I said, wondering when he was going to tell me the agreed amount for shipment would be light.

"We can discuss all these matters when you arrive. Should I send a car?"

"No, I will arrange my own transportation. Where are you staying?"

"I have made arrangements for us at the Brazilian Star. It's a nice hotel. We'll be able to complete our business here without interruption"

"I'll be there within the hour." As I disconnected the call I sensed a tone in Barajas's voice I had not heard before. It was almost imperceptible, but there was something that was different. I determined extra caution for the next four or five hours was in order.

My next call was to be to Howard Baker. I couldn't risk using the Company lines and would again use his private and, therefore, more public system. I hoped he would answer but knew in my heart that to have that happen on two consecutive occasions would be stretching the odds. I had to hope that if Mrs. Baker answered she wouldn't recognize my voice, as one of Howard's operatives and would simply connect me to Howard.

The phone in the Baker residence rang. Mildred was sitting in the kitchen doing what she often did in the midday and that was sorting through recipes, making plans for the evening meal. She went to the phone on the wall next to the coffee maker and lifted the receiver, announcing "The Baker residence." After listening for a moment she placed the receiver on the counter and went into the sitting room.

"Howard, the phone is for you."

Howard was in one of his favorite reclining chairs, studying the business section of the daily newspaper. There was an extension phone in virtually every room of the house, so he picked up a phone located on a table next to him.

"Howard Baker here," he blurted into the phone with some irritation in his voice.

"Howard, this is Eric. I'm in Rio and our deal is about to go down. Are you ready to get things rolling on your end?" There was an uncharacteristic hesitation on Howard's end of the connection.

"Eric, I wish to hell you wouldn't use this line. You know the risks and no I am not ready. The Company may not even authorize me to continue with you. You've been determined rogue. I don't know how far up the chain the decision was made, or even how far up the knowledge extends, but you have problems and I don't know if I can fix them."

"Have they inserted an extraction team?" I inquired knowing full well Company policy required it once an operative's loyalty or objectives were questioned.

"Yes, and my bet is they are in South America as we speak."

"Do you know who they are?"

"No, and you wouldn't recognize them anyway, you know that. Scott Steel ordered it. It seems he has an agenda of his own and eliminating you from the scene is part of it." There was further hesitation on the line. "I've no information on what's going to happen or where. I will do my best, but I can't guarantee anything."

"Assume for now the Company goons haven't located me and I have at minimum twenty- four hours before they do. I can arrange for the shipment to leave a small port in northern Colombia. It's located just north of a small town named Cartagena. The port isn't listed for deep-water vessels but Barajas has modified the facility so it can handle his shipments and the vessels he uses. He will have all the supply he could arrange on a vessel, leaving from there within the next twenty-four hours. The U.S. authorities should blockade the port in international waters, board the vessel, and seize the product. In making this shipment, Barajas has stretched his capability to the extent that when it's seized he'll have no product to sell for a long enough period to eliminate him from the market. That was our plan. If the Company wants him eliminated, they had better cooperate, whether I'm declared rogue or not!" Again, there was a long silence on the phone.

This will probably end my career, but I think I can get to the Assistant Director. He and I go a long way back. I think he will at least listen to me." Howard was making the statement, but it was couched in a tone that was more of a question than fact. "Is there a number where I can reach you in the next fifteen minutes, possibly half hour?"

"I have a cell number I can give you but don't attempt to trace it. I paid a premium to get one that will leave you at a dead end." I gave him the number, and told him he should try several times if he got a message I was out of the service area. I would be moving around a lot. Immediately, upon receiving the number, he disconnected the conversation.

With the calls made, the stage was being set to complete the mission. Howard was a question but one that was out of my control. I had no choice but to proceed forward and hope he could work his customary magic with the Company. I surveyed the room I had rented and found it was not as seedy as my first impressions had indicated. The furniture and fixtures were old, but not ragged and the room was clean. I went to the basin and began to draw it full of hot water. I wouldn't have time for a shower, but I could wash my face and feel a bit fresh. As the water was warming and it took a considerable time, thoughts of Sadie flashed across my mind. I really had not had any time to grasp the enormity of her loss. I knew how proud she would have been to take part in the demise of the Barajas Cartel. She deserved to be here and I missed her.

Insofar as I had paid for the night, it seemed to be better to keep the room, as opposed to turning it back to the management. I needed a place to hide the key where I would retrieve it later if a use were determined. I left the room and securely locked the door behind me. A quick viewing of the corridor established there wasn't a location where a key could be hidden. I certainly didn't want it on my person in the event I was to be searched by Barajas's men. A hiding place somewhere outside the hotel would have to be found.

The elevator cage was just as slow and squeaky going down as it had been going up. Upon finally reaching the lobby, I glanced at my watch. Only thirty minutes had passed. My driver wouldn't be here for another fifteen minutes. At first, I contemplated going back to the room so as not to be seen on the street. Howard had said there was an extraction team out and, while I didn't think that they would have found me yet, one could not be too careful. I needed to conceal the room key, however, and this would be a perfect time to do it. I exited the hotel and turned to the left. I could see a planter on the corner not fifty meters away. There wasn't much foot traffic so I should be able to secrete the key in the planter without being seen.

Walking as casually as I could, I approached the planter with the key in my closed hand. The small tree in the planter was obviously root bound, but the soil while, strewn with the expected small items of trash, appeared to be softer than the hard pan I was expecting. I stopped at the planter and lit a cigarette, while at the same time making sure no one was close or seemed to have an interest in me. Under the guise of making sure my match was completely out, I slipped the key into the dirt and covered it while arranging the trash so as to hide the recent disturbance. The key securely hidden, I relaxed and continued to enjoy my cigarette while strolling back toward the entrance to the hotel. I just about reached the entrance when a cab rounded the corner. Within seconds I recognized my friendly driver.

"I need to get to the Brazilian Star hotel, I have reservations there. I will want you to be accessible to me tonight. Is that a problem?" My driver looked thoughtful and after a short period turned in the seat to face me.

"The internal security at that hotel doesn't like cabbies hanging around, if you know what I mean. It's an expensive hotel and they have a few bungalows on the grounds that some of the guests rent for their staff. You might be able to arrange for one of those. I will be close and only a phone call away. I could use the rest anyway. What do you think boss?"

"I can do that. Let's see if they have the accommodations."

The trip to the hotel took about fifteen or twenty minutes. As we pulled into the covered entrance area, a bellhop signaled where we should park so the cab could drop me off. My driver signaled the bellhop to the cab.

"Hey, man, you got any of those shacks you keep for hired help? The boss wants me to be around."

"I think they're all occupied. Let me check," the bellman responded, while leaning through the cab's open window.

My driver inserted a twenty-dollar bill into the open fist of the bellman. He quickly closed the hand, straightened up, and indicated he was sure something could be worked out. He spoke on his hand held radio to someone, and after some conversation I couldn't hear, leaned back in and told us to park the cab in a space he was indicating. A room would be available following my registration. The cab driver was to remain with the cab.

I took that as my cue to exit the cab and go to the registration desk. The interior of the hotel was what one might expect from an establishment that catered to the world's rich and elite. The registration desk was at least thirty meters from the entrance with plush decor and eloquent furniture in between. Because of what Howard had told me my senses were on red alert. Instinctively I was searching for movement of any individual appearing out of the ordinary -- someone who didn't fit. I quickly scanned the faces of the patrons in the lobby area, noting their location. The training the Company had provided early in my career was helpful. The mental training and instincts acquired during years in the field was invaluable.

No one stood out but then I really didn't expect they would, at least not immediately. I approached the desk and announced I had a suite, which had been reserved by Mr. Barajas. The reservations clerk asked my name and I responded.

"Oh, yes, Mr. Butler, Mr. Barajas is waiting for you. May I ring his suite to announce your arrival?"

"No, I don't think that will be necessary. If you would just direct me to my suite, I will announce my own arrival. By the way, I have a man waiting outside. We were told we could arrange for his accommodations in one of your bungalows."

"Yes, of course, and will you be paying for that separately, or is that to be included on the Barajas account?"

"I'll pay separately. There's no need to bother Mr. Barajas with the details -- understood? The clerk nodded giving me a pass card to my suite and a brass key that was indented with the letters Unit D. "Give the key to the bellman. He will direct your man to his quarters." Having received the two keys, I turned to go to the cab and in passing I did I noticed there were two individuals sitting in the lounge area just inside the lighted entrance. I couldn't tell if they were watching the lobby or frankly, whether they were male or female. The one thing I noticed that seemed a bit out of the ordinary, given the style of the hotel, was one or both was drinking beer and not from a glass.

I needed to know whether they were my assigned extraction team. There was not a lot of time. I had to know if the enemy was in town or if I only had Barajas to worry about. In order to get an idea of their intentions I needed to have someone in the elevator with me. An elderly couple were unknowingly very accommodating, as they approached the elevators just ahead of me. I strolled into the car with them and they signaled for the sixth floor. That was good enough for me. I mentioned I too was going to six. As I was making small talk I leaned against the signal panel and pushed the button for the top floor. It must have appeared to be a mistake because the couple didn't mention anything and we went directly to the sixth floor. On arrival, I held the elevator doors for them to exit and then exited myself. As the doors closed, I feigned the loss of the newspaper I had just purchased and immediately called for an elevator car going down. One came within seconds. As the couple was heading to their room, having completely forgotten me, I boarded the car and pushed the button labeled lobby.

As the elevator dropped to the lobby level, I positioned myself in the car so that, upon reaching the bottom and the doors opening, I could see the entrance to the lounge area. If I were lucky there would still be two people sitting in the shadows enjoying themselves. The door opened. As my intuition had warned me, their table was empty. The bottles containing the partially consumed beer were still on the table. They had just left. I quickly stepped out of the elevator and looked at the dials above each of the cars. The elevator on my right was just leaving the fourteenth floor, en route to the lobby. If they were my extraction team, they would be in the staircase, climbing to the top floor. If Barajas had the security I expected, they would be walking into a trap.

A part of me was relieved Barajas was going to rid me of a problem I really didn't need. A bigger part of me realized that the two agents, if that's what they were, were innocent and just following orders. For them to be killed, when there was something I could do to prevent it, was something I didn't want to live with. I reentered the elevator I had just utilized and pushed the button for the top floor. My weapon was in its holster, which I brought a bit forward on my body unclipping the safety strap. As the elevator door slid open, I immediately exited with my hand inside my jacket resting on the butt of my pistol.

The corridor was empty. The feeling was anti-climactic. Had I made a mistake, and the two were not agents sent to extract me. Before I could fully comprehend the circumstance, the door to the suite across the corridor and on my immediate left swung open. In its place stood a man I'd never seen before. I'll admit I didn't study his face much, as I was focused on the weapon he held in his hand. It had the longest silencer I'd ever seen.

"I'm here to see Barajas. Who the hell are you?" I blurted out, relaxing my grip on the pistol and hoping he wasn't observant enough to notice the hand inside my jacket.

"Who are you, is a more appropriate question," he responded.

"My name is Eric Butler and Mr. Barajas and I have some business to transact. You have a problem with that?

"No, Mr. Butler, I don't and Mr. Barajas is expecting you. Please come in."

I approached the doorway as the man stepped forward, indicating I was to raise my arms so he could search me. I stepped back and showed him my weapon by simply opening my coat.

"Unless you intend to use that gun, step aside and let me through. As you can see, I'm armed, and I intend to stay that way. Now Mr. Barajas is waiting and, unless you need to check with him about the fact I'm armed, please do as I asked and step aside." The man acted confused but did as I requested and, without taking his gun off me, stepped inside the suite, allowing me to enter.

I hadn't gotten two steps inside when I saw that Barajas was not alone and my intuition had not misled me. Barajas was standing in the main room with a pistol trained on someone just out of sight. I could only see two legs of the person, the rest being obscured by the entrance hall. My first instinct was to drop to the floor, while taking my pistol out of its holster. I could feel the goon behind me, however, and knew that any suspicious move would cause him to react. I walked into the room.

"Mr. Butler, I was expecting you sooner. I hope nothing has gone wrong."

"Not from this end, but what the hell is all this, and who are these people?" I responded, making every attempt to appear startled.

"I was hoping you could tell me. Michael found them in the hall attempting to exit by the stairs. Both were armed and carrying considerable cash. They're not your men?   Excuse me lady. They are not in your employ?"

I looked at both of the individuals. They were sitting on a small loveseat just inside the entrance hall doorway. My interest was to see if they were familiar to me, even vaguely. The man was in his early forties. The woman was attractive and in her late twenties, possibly in her early thirties. Neither of them looked familiar to me, however, I wasn't going to admit it if they did.

"No, I've never seen these people."

"Michael, take these people to the back bedroom, tie them up, and make sure they can't make any noise. Mr. Butler and I have some business to attend." Barajas laid his pistol on the table in front of him and motioned me to join him for a drink.

CHAPTER FIFTY-FOUR

Howard Baker hung up the telephone and sat in the recliner for several minutes, deep in thought. He had been with the Company for longer than he cared to remember but never had he been so unsure of himself. The options were to go directly to the Director, a man named Nathaniel Adams. Howard knew him, but because he was more of a political appointment than a rank and file Company man, Howard didn't have the confidence in him he had in others. There was the Assistant Director Bill Morris, a man who had been through the ranks and had at one time worked with Howard in the field. In fact, Morris was present when Howard received the injuries ultimately placing him in the stagnant position he currently occupied.

Bill had always had good, if not exceptional, field instincts. He was more apt to understand what was going on and was in a position to act on what he perceived was the best course. Howard also had a personal relationship with the Assistant Director, and for that reason would be able to contact him outside the normal CIA channels. This was the man he would contact and, if Bill thought the director should be involved, then it would be his decision. A decision Howard knew he would have to abide by.

The telephone directory where Mildred kept the telephone numbers of family friends was in the kitchen. Howard dreaded going to the kitchen and retrieving the directory. It would prompt a series of questions from Mildred he didn't want to answer, at least not at this time. He had no choice, however, as personal telephone numbers were never kept in the office. Howard entered the kitchen, opened the refrigerator, and selected a root beer. The directory was kept on the counter under the kitchen phone. On the way out, he retrieved the metal index and began to make his way to the office.

"Who're you going to call?" Mildred asked, in the inquisitive tone unique only to Mildred.

"I need the home number for Bill Morris and it's business so don't ask any questions," Howard said knowing Mildred could not help herself.

"Well, they are personal friends. I have a right to know if you're calling them on a social matter which is something I should know. After all, I am your wife whether the Company likes it or not." Having said that, Mildred shut her recipe books and stormed into the sitting room, where she busied herself straightening the area and preparing to do her daily stint with the needlepoint projects.

As Howard reached the office, he did something he hadn't done often, possibly in years. He slid the soundproof door shut. Mildred didn't need a glimmer of the contents of the conversation he was about to have. Seating himself in the special chair designed for him, he contemplated whether to use the standard ordinary landline, or the special line with all of its security. He choose the secured line and dialed the number. After several rings, just before he was going to hang up, Beth Morris answered the phone.

"Beth, this is Howard Baker. Is Bill available?"

"Yes, Howard. Let me get him. You sound stressed. Is everything okay?"

"Yes, it is, Beth. Thanks for asking." I just need to speak to Bill. Business, you understand." Beth indicated that she would get Bill, and, like all well-trained Company wives with husbands in sensitive positions, she didn't ask any further questions. Within seconds Bill Morris was on the line.

"Howard, what's going on?"

"Sorry to bother you at home, but I have a situation needing your guidance, in fact, your help?" Howard said, waiting for permission to proceed. There was a noticeable pause on the line.

"Have you tried Scott Steel? Shouldn't he be in the loop?"

"Scott Steel may be part of the problem, in fact is part of the problem -- or I am," Howard responded. "Bill, you, better than anyone else, know I've had my problems with Scott. You also know me better than almost anyone in the agency. Regardless of my problems with Scott, you know I wouldn't come to you if I didn't feel it was absolutely necessary. Please hear me out. If you feel I'm out of line just tell me, and I'll back off."

"Go ahead, Howard, but this had better be something with substance."

"Firstly, let me tell you the sting on the Barajas Cartel is about ready to flourish. Our agent in the field is Eric Butler. As you probably know, he lost his partner in the undercover operation. Scott thinks he's gone south and has declared him rogue. I released operational funds to Eric several days ago, about the same time Scott released an extraction team to pick him up. I've known Eric since he first joined the Company, and I don't believe that he would do anything to jeopardize the operation. This is especially true since he lost his partner as a result of the undercover activities. She was more than just his partner," Howard hesitated.

"Assuming all you have said is true, what do you want from me?"

"It's simple, Bill. I need you to pull this operation from Scott and give the authorization to complete the takedown. Scott will never authorize it. Because it involves use of the Coast Guard, I can't do it on my own authority. Someone above my rate of pay must approve it before the boarding and confiscation can occur. I can direct the operation from here, but I must have your authorization." Howard's voice was assuming the quality of one not simply asking a superior for his blessing, but one of urgency, almost to the point of begging.

"What's the timetable?" Bill inquired after a considerable period of hesitation.

"Within the next twelve to twenty-four hours. It can't be delayed."

"Why is Scott being so – so hard to deal with on this? Do you have any explanation?"

"No, I don't, but I do know he has gone far outside Company policy parameters. It's like he has a personal vendetta regarding Eric Butler, or possibly me. I really don't know but, what I do know, is his actions will, if they haven't already, destroy the Company's objective in this operation, not to mention the loss of the investment. He has sent an extraction team to the field to bring back Eric Butler. Bill, you've known me for a long time, and you know I wouldn't go around my immediate supervisor if I didn't think it was the only way. I need your support on this, and I'm willing to face a review board after it's all over if necessary."

Bill Morris was silent for a long period of time. Howard was beginning to wonder if the telephone connection had been broken, when he began again. "The investment has been made and this is one of the priority projects. Scott should have come to me before he sent the extraction team into the field. There's no doubt he broke all the rules by making that decision without conferring with me. I will authorize the Coast Guard to complete the takedown, but I can assure you there will be a board of inquiry convened after this is all over. Are you sure you want to put yourself through that Howard? They're never fun."

"Just give me your authority to involve the Coast Guard and I will take my chances. Bill, I know I'm right about Scott. I think, for whatever reason, he's over the edge. I know also I'm not the person to make that decision, especially in view of my problems with Scott, but I'm willing to risk what's left of my career on this operation. Please now, give me the authorization code and make the necessary call. Time may be more of the essence than I anticipate."

"Use the code 'Omega.' I'll make the calls now. Give me an hour to get the pieces all in place and, Howard, good luck. Your career may well depend on the success of this operation." The phone went dead. Howard hung up the receiver and immediately dialed the number Eric had given him.

The cell phone in Eric's coat pocket rang as Eric and Barajas were approaching the bar in the suite's main room. Eric knew who was on the other end -- the timing could not have been worse. The choices were two, answer the call, or attempt to blow it off, and call Howard back at the next opportunity. Eric opted for the first choice. As he causally approached the bar he retrieved his cell phone, flipping the receiver open.

"Is there a problem?" Eric spoke in a tone that Howard would pick up and realize he was not where he could talk.

"I assume I've got you at a bad time so just listen. I will have the Coast Guard in the waters off the coast of northern Colombia. I need more information on timing, but you can get back to me on that. The Agency is behind you, but I've no idea where Scott is in all this. Get back as soon as you can."

"I'm making the final arrangements as we speak. Tell our buyer they will have their product within the next seven days at the delivery point." Eric closed the cell putting it back in his coat pocket. "Our buyers are getting impatient. I assume you can deliver today," Eric asked, looking Barajas directly in the eye.

"I can, but not the quantity we had originally discussed. I've had some problems with local factions which has reduced my available inventory. The quantity will be sufficient to satisfy them, with a second shipment to follow. A minor problem, but one which will be rectified." Barajas was obviously a bit nervous about the reaction to his admission. "But you realized this before you came to Rio," he emphasized.

"I knew you had some problems but not the extent of them. How short will you be? If you're too short this deal is over now," Eric replied.

"I am told by my people, we can deliver one half of the product now with the balance to follow within one month. We will solve our problems in Colombia. This will not occur again. I assume that will be satisfactory?"

"I might be able to make that work, but I was hoping the shipment would be larger. I had no idea your 'problems in Colombia' were as extensive as they obviously are. Can you ship tonight?"

"I can, but I need to know more information on the destination. We need to fit the vessel properly for the voyage, you understand."

"Your vessel need only be fitted to get one hundred fifty kilometers from the port. I will have it met and the product transferred in the open sea. We will transport from there. The money must also change because of your 'Colombian problem.' I am willing to give you five million American dollars with the balance to be paid when the transfer is made. We must see the product and assure its quality, especially, in view of your apparent delivery problems. I assume that will be satisfactory," I said, sipping the drink which had been handed to me moments before.

The blood in Barajas's face seemed to drain, leaving him with a pasty, almost waxy look. "That amount of money won't cover my expenses in this operation. I will need the full payment or there will be no delivery and you and your organization ...."

"Stop right there, Barajas. My organization will do just fine with or without you, so don't start threatening me about what you will or will not do. We also have expenses, and they have just escalated because of your internal problems. This is business not a charity. We will pay only for what we verify has been delivered. There's nothing you can do about that. The sooner you reconcile yourself to the fact that your organization is not the driver in this deal the better off you will be. I will deliver you a draft on a local bank for five million. Upon verification of the amount transferred to our vessel in the open sea, we'll pay you the balance. The extra expenses we are incurring will, of course, reduce your profits from the transaction. That's the deal. Take it or leave it."

Salvador Barajas had lost all the color in his face. His eyes were narrowed and piercing. It was obvious he was not accustomed to the tenor of the conversation that had just transpired. His bodyguard was standing slightly behind his boss with an expression which betrayed complete disbelief that anyone could speak to the head of the family in that tone. I finished my drink and approached the bar, keeping both Barajas and the goon in my field of vision. I retrieved the blank bank draft from my jacket, designated the amount of five million in the proper area of the document, and signed my name leaving the payee section blank.

"You may insert anyone you want as the payee," I said and slid the draft down the bar to Barajas. "Now, can you have your vessel in the open sea by dawn tomorrow loaded with what product you can arrange?"

"You may think you have all the cards, Butler, but you don't. You don't even control your own organization. Do you think I, my family, would enter into a business arrangement with you, especially one of this magnitude, not knowing anything more about you and your organization than you have told us? If you believe that, you and your people are more naive than we had suspected. I know who you are and I have been aware of your plan and activities from the beginning. This may surprise you, but we have a friend close to the Central Intelligence Agency. She has kept us informed on most, if not all, of your activities. My organization was never going to deliver the product to you or your organization. We simply wanted the money you were willing to give us, shall we say, donate to us. Even after the split with our Agency partner, the profits would have been considerable. The true benefit would have been the embarrassment to your country, resulting from your failed efforts to shut us down. This benefit isn't dependent on whether we get thirty million or five million." The color had gradually returned to the patriarch's face. The narrow slits that were his eyes had relaxed, evidencing the fact he was confident that he was having the last word -- his ultimate victory in this game we were playing.

Barajas' reference to the Company hit me like a sledgehammer between the eyes. Was I the pawn of some Agency trader? Had the last several years been a fraud designed to funnel money to some individual in the Agency? Was Sadie's death meaningless? I struggled to keep control of my emotions. My experience, gained from years in the field, had not prepared me for the situation I found myself in. My first instinct was to kill both of them and disappear. The anticipation and ultimate satisfaction of seeing Barajas lying in his own blood was almost overwhelming. I needed time to get control of myself.

"It appears we both have the same objective," I said as I moved down the bar toward the bottle of very expensive bourbon. "Mind if I have another drink?"

"Not at all, Mr. Butler. A drink may make the next few minutes less painful. You see, there's not a chance in hell I will allow you to live after what you know of our organization and, especially, after the way you spoke to me just minutes ago. I hope you understand. It's just business and business preservation."

"Then tell me, since it won't matter in a few minutes, did you order the death of my partner? She was killed a few months ago in Bogotá." I asked, realizing I had to get ready to act fast if I was going to live, but I had to know the answer to that question.

"My organization arranged for the death, but my U.S. partner actually requested it be accomplished. It seems she felt Sadie's banking knowledge and abilities in international finance would cause us some problems. I was requested to remove the problem. Our first attempt was botched and we lost an ally when your partner killed the policeman. We were fortunate, however, when the two of you returned and the job was easily completed. I understand the two of you were more than just partners. You were lovers also. I'm sure it was a regrettable loss for you, but it was a business necessity. Barajas was smiling as he sipped the drink he had refreshed while talking.

Somehow, I was gaining control of myself. The reference to the relationship Sadie and I had meant only one thing. It felt like I had just been stabbed in the stomach with a knife. The only person with any knowledge of our relationship was Howard Baker. Howard was abrupt, self-pitying, and somewhat bitter, but to believe he would orchestrate the death of an agent, one of his own agents, was not consistent with his character. Not the man I had known for many years, the man that had gone to bat for me as recently as an hour ago. I needed to buy some time, not much but a bit, so I engaged Barajas in further conversation.

"Why in the word would anyone think Sadie would be able to affect this operation with her banking knowledge? I was running the show, not her. Didn't you realize that?"

"I did, but my partner thought Sadie would be able to block the ultimate transfer of funds, evidently a skill you don't possess. I didn't question her judgment. I rarely question the judgments of an associate, especially one who stands to gain as much as I do given the success of the arrangement," Barajas said, in a tone evidencing he was feeling very secure, even a bit cocky about his position. His bodyguard was also enjoying the conversation and was leaning against the opposite end of the bar with his right elbow and forearm on the top of the bar.

"So based on advises of your 'U.S. partner' you had your men, or the police on your payroll, terminate my partner?" As I was speaking, I reached for my drink with my left hand. In doing so I leaned forward so the bar would mask my right hand, which I simultaneously slipped inside my coat securing my weapon. In one move, I drew the pistol and shot the guard in the neck. Blood went everywhere as he dropped to the floor. Barajas reached for his weapon. He suddenly realized he'd left it on the table across the room. He was unarmed and he knew it. Fear spread across his face as I swung the pistol to bear on him.

"Hold on, Butler. We can make some arrangement, after all we're businessmen aren't we. There's no need for us to act this way. What do you want? I am a powerful man and can get you whatever you would like." He was close to tears as he viewed his own mortality.

"I'm confidant Sadie faced her executioners with much more dignity than you demonstrate." I felt my finger tighten on the trigger. It was like I was outside my body, watching as the gun went off and the explosion filled the room. Barajas stood for a second or two before he slumped to the floor. The entire back of his head was gone. The Barajas cartel had just lost its patriarch.

After the smoke cleared and enough time had gone by to have some assurance the sound of two gunshots hadn't been detected, I went into the bedroom where the two individuals were being held. They were both gagged and securely bound by silver duct tape. I stripped the tape off the mouths of each of the individuals but left their hands and feet securely tied. The woman was scared but still had fire in her eyes which told me she was for real -- prepared for whatever was to come. The man, older than the woman, was not evidencing any fear at all and in fact was smiling at me. Not the defiant smile I somehow expected, but rather one that would come from a friend or good acquaintance.

"Who the hell are you?" I said, directing the question to the man.

"We were sent by the Company to extract you, but I'm sure you've probably figured that out. My name is John Sailor. This is Ronnie Matthews. We heard all the conversation. It confirmed a gut feeling I've had since we were assigned to this extraction."

"John Sailor – I've heard about you somewhere. You've done a lot of black ops in the last few years, haven't you?"

"That's all I do and I generally, I do it alone. Ms. Matthews was assigned to me for this mission but she's just a pawn. I would appreciate it if you'd release her. Do with me as you will, but it need not involve her. She has done nothing but follow my orders." John's demeanor indicated he was as close to begging as he would ever get.

"Hold on, I haven't decided to do anything to anyone. As far as I can tell, you both were just following orders. I'd love to cut the tape and release you. How do I know you won't continue to carry out your orders?"

"You don't, but I'm telling you I won't cause you any grief and neither will Ronnie. I heard what was said out there and, with the reservations I had coming in, I won't be attempting any extraction. That's my word and it's always been good but you don't know that. The choice is yours."

"How are you going to explain your actions to the Company? They don't like failures. I'm sure you know that."

"I don't plan on explaining anything to the Company or anyone else. It's time I retired from this game and this is a good opportunity. My hope is Ronnie will join me, but, in any event, I will get her back to the states in good health if that's what she wants. Now, as I said previously, the choice is yours. You can leave us here for the authorities to deal with, you can kill us and make it look like we did Barajas, or you can release us and between the three of us we should be able to get out of here and out of Brazil. It seems we can help each other but you first must believe me. By the way, you should know there are four more of Barajas' men dead in a stairwell. They will be discovered shortly. What are you going to do?"

For the first time in many years, I wasn't able to reach a decision with the quickness and mental agility I felt was one of my best assets. I knew if these agents were intent on extraction, they would, in all probability, either be successful or some of us would end up dead. I didn't want their deaths on my conscience and I certainly didn't want to die. By the same token, if I left them here they would spend the rest of their lives in a Brazilian prison or dead, again something which would be on my conscience. To release them would place me at risk, but I somehow believed John Sailor. He had a reputation for being ruthless and deadly, but he didn't seem to be a person who would be able to lie successfully. I cut the tape on John and gave him the knife to cut his partner loose. It was his test and I was ready. My hand was on my weapon. Any quick move and he would be dead. He cut the woman loose and handed the knife back to me, handle first. I suddenly felt more comfortable with the decision I had made.

"Barajas has some good whiskey. Let's get a drink and decide our next move, and whether it's joint, or whether we should go our separate ways," I said, keeping both of them in sight as they left the room.

One look around the main room and Sailor laughed. "You certainly know how to mess up a perfectly good suite." Ronnie was not so light hearted about it and had some obvious difficulty in viewing Barajas without the back of his skull.

I poured three drinks, using the same bottle on the bar, and we went into the sitting area. "What are your ideas and, more importantly, what're your plans from here. You know they will send more teams to extract each of us, especially if you decide to retire from here. Are you ready for that?" I said, wanting to see the reaction from each of them.

Sailor sat for a moment as though he was deep in thought. "I don't know much about you, Butler, but I am the best they ever had when it comes to black ops and extractions. They know anyone they send stands an extremely good chance of returning in a pine box. If Ronnie's with me, they will know the same odds apply to her. I don't think they'll want to embarrass themselves further by sacrificing perfectly good agents, especially since both Ronnie and I were not the type of agents that were, shall we say, advertised by the Company. What about you, Butler?"

"They may try to get me, but one thing you said, which is also true with me, is the embarrassment factor. I think the Company will want to bury this operation as quickly as they can. With Barajas dead they obtained their goal, although not in the way they planned. I don't see them as being anxious to spend any more money or agents for what would appear, at least on the surface, to be a successful operation. I might also be difficult to extract and they know that. It seems the only question is you, Ronnie. What is your desire?"

"I'm with John," Ronnie replied without hesitation. "I don't know what that entails or what is expected of me, but I do know if I was able to get back, and I'm sure John could arrange that, I would be released from the Company. I really don't have anything I can turn to which would make any sense."

"You realize if you go with John, it will mean you won't be able to return to the States without running the risk of imprisonment or worse. The Company may not hunt you but, if it learns where you are, they will arrest you," I said, attempting to gauge the commitment she was ready to take.

"Yes, I'm aware of all of that, but I need to get a new start, which I don't see happening in the States.

"How are the two of you fixed for money? John, have you been able to set up an account to handle this decision. You know what I mean. Consider that you may have the responsibility for two now."

"I've been around for a long time. I've been able to stash just under a million, which should go a long way toward making us safe and comfortable. We'll be fine."

I went to Barajas' body and reached into the front shirt pocket retrieving the draft I had just given him. Luckily, it was free of any evidence of the fate of its previous owner. "Here's a better start on your new career. I suggest that you arrange to get it deposited in an offshore account as soon as possible. If you have any questions regarding how to handle the funds, don't hesitate to ask. I've learned a lot in the last few weeks. By the way it would be good to put one of your names in the payee box so it won't be honored by just anyone presenting it."

John handed the draft to Ronnie, indicating she should put her name on the draft. When Ronnie saw the size to the draft she gasped, got control of herself, and wrote her name on the document, handing it back to John.

"Now, that we've all committed to where we are going and the finances have been arranged, how do you suggest we get out of here? It seems the three of us are responsible for, not less than, six dead bodies in various locations of the hotel. Barajas and his goon could go, at the least, twenty-four hours before discovery. I don't know about the others. What are your thoughts?" I asked, thinking out loud.

"If we're lucky they'll not be discovered before tomorrow, but they could be discovered at any time. The sooner we get out of here the better," John answered.

'Then let's get out of here. I have a cab driver on retainer so we won't have to make a big deal about leaving the hotel. I'll call him and have him meet us at a side door rather than the main entrance," I said, as I dialed his bungalow. He answered on the third ring and was clearly still partially asleep. He said he would meet us at the hotel side door in fifteen minutes. This was good timing for us, as we needed to work our way down the stairwell at least three or four floors before entering the elevator to avoid the elevator indicator on the ground floor showing where we came from. Prior to leaving the Barajas suite, I placed the "Do Not Disturb" sign on the door. Hopefully, this would buy us some additional time. Now my only remaining tie to the suite or Barajas was my suite, located on the same floor, but that couldn't be avoided now. We had to get out of Brazil.

The cab was waiting at the side door as he said it would be. I could tell from the look on the cabby's face, that he was somewhat surprised I had two friends with me. I slid into the seat next to him. John and Ronnie entered the rear seat. "Where to boss?" he said in the same way he always had.

I had to think for a moment. We needed to get someplace where we could plan our exit from the country. I also needed to contact Howard Baker. I estimated, notwithstanding the causalities John had indicated were in a stairwell, the suite would be left alone and the bodies undiscovered for several hours, if not until the morning.

"The hotel you showed me earlier and take your time. We don't want to draw attention to our leaving."

"Done," was his only comment. I could tell by his tone and body language that my cab driver wasn't sure what he'd gotten himself into. He was keeping a close eye on the passengers in the back seat, while at the same time keeping tabs on me.

The trip was uneventful, taking only fifteen minutes. As he pulled up to the front of the hotel, he partially turned in the seat and, as John and Ronnie exited the back, he indicated he needed to talk to me. I motioned them on and turned to the driver.

"What is it?" I asked

"Do you know the man is packing?" he said, wasting no time.

"Yes, and it's okay. He's a friend. You'll have to take my word for that. We may be as long as forty-five minutes. When we leave, we'll need to get to the airport where you and I first hooked up. Can you arrange that?"

"I'll be here in thirty minutes and, if you're not ready, I'll circle the block until you are. That work, boss?"

I nodded and exited the cab.

The key was in the pot just where I had left it. Following retrieval, the three of us entered the hotel lobby and went straight to the elevator. The desk clerk I dealt with earlier was still on duty. As we passed, he smirked in that knowing way only hotel clerks have mastered, signifying he thought we were nothing more or less than a kinky threesome in for the evening. Something in me made me put my hand on John's shoulder, confirming the clerks suspicions. John's reaction was that of surprise and, as we entered the elevator cage, bewilderment. "Relax, John. It's for the clerk's benefit," I said in a low voice only he could hear. The explanation seemed to be enough because John immediately relaxed, playing along with the charade.

The elevator, which had seemed so slow before now, seemed to barely move. Eventually, however, it did reach the top floor. I unlocked the room and we entered. As always, I had set an indicator to alert me if the room had been entered. It hadn't, so I decided we were safe there to conduct the business so necessary to our exit from Brazil.

Ronnie was the last one in, closing the door behind her. John did the things any experienced agent would do checking out the suite, while I used the sink to splash water on my face, attempting to bring some vitality back to my body. Ronnie had found the bed and was lying on her back with eyes closed. I couldn't help but notice that she had a wonderfully curvaceous body. John was a lucky man, and I hoped he was smart enough to keep her with him.

"I need to call my handler. The last two years of work have just come to a conclusion, and I don't want that to go to waste," I said as I retrieved my cell phone from the front pocket of my shirt. I considered which number I should call and decided, with the information I had learned, it didn't matter. I chose to call on the supposedly secure line. I dialed the number. The phone on the other end didn't ring more than twice.

"Baker here."

"Howard, this is Eric."

"About time. I thought I had lost you again. What's your status and what about the shipment? I pulled every string I could and got authority to use the Coast Guard. They're moving into position as we speak." Howard's voice was strained. I could tell he'd been under the gun since we last talked. "By the way I see you remembered the correct phone to use. Maybe you're not a complete loss after all.

"I'm a complete loss, Howard. Let me assure you of that. Are you alone?"

"What the hell are you talking about? Yes, I'm alone, no one is allowed in this room you know that."

"No, Howard, I didn't mean alone in your office. Are you alone in the house? It's important. Just answer yes or no."

"Well, no I'm not. Mildred is here but she always is. What's going on?"

"Never mind for now. Barajas is dead. It was either him or me and I chose to live. It's a long story but I also killed his only successor. You need to call off the Coast Guard because there won't be any shipment. His Cartel is out of business. What you need to do is contact the Colombian authorities we have been working with in this operation -- ones we can trust. Tell them the only remaining supply of Barajas product is located in a small resort north of Cartagena about sixty kilometers on the coast. If they can seize that product there will be no more from the Barajas organization."

"That's very good news. With this success, I'm sure when you get back we can arrange to have you cleared of any suspicions, which may have attached over the past weeks." Howard's tone indicated the sincere elation and relief he was feeling.

"Howard, you didn't hear what I said. I'm a complete loss and intend to stay that way."

"That's stupid. There's an extraction team out for you now. You'll be killed or bought back. However it happens, I won't be able to help and the success of your assignment will get lost in the shuffle. Use your head, Man!" For the second time in almost as many hours, Howard's voice was taking on a tone indicating ultimate frustration. He was virtually pleading.

"There are some other things you need to know, Howard. The extraction team is with me as we speak. They have no intention to proceed with their mission, nor do they intend on going back to the Agency. I don't believe the agency will want the embarrassment of sending extraction agents after them, especially when they know anyone they send will have inferior skills, and the chance of success will be nil to none. I think the agency will feel the same way about me, or I wouldn't have been here in the first place."

"What if you're wrong, and I'm not saying you are, are you willing to do what you may have to do to remain outside agency control? You know what I mean, Eric. Are you and your friends willing to eliminate anyone who comes after you?"

"We are willing to take our chances. In answer to your last question I'll … we'll face that if it happens, but I think the answer will be yes, and you should tell that to the director. It may have an effect on the decisions he makes." The phone was silent on the other end. I could tell Howard was trying to say something which would change my mind.

"There's one other thing I think you should know, Howard, and this is the hardest thing I've ever had to say. Barajas had a partner in the States. In fact, we were all being set up. He never intended to make the shipment. All the preparations he was making were a façade. Not that he wasn't accumulating product. He was. It just wasn't meant for us. He and his partner were intending to take our money and ship the product to the States. It was to be business as usual with the exception that he would be collecting twice for the same product. His partner was keeping him informed on the sting from the inside, well, almost on the inside. He and his partner arranged for Sadie's death and they would have eventually arranged for my death."

"Who do you think it was, Eric? These are serious accusations, which is another reason you should come back."

"Let me finish, Howard. This will be the last time I ever talk to you. At one point he referred to his U.S. partner as a "her." Mildred just lost a business partner. I think you can figure it out from there. What you do about it is all up to you, but I could not just disappear without telling you the truth."

I had an emptiness in my gut I hadn't felt since the loss of Sadie. I knew too well what Howard must have been feeling.

EPILOGUE

The exit from Brazil was uneventful. The three of us landed in Aruba with no questions asked. John Sailor and Ronnie both made the decision to leave the service, and disappear into the numerous resort areas of the world, where one's true identity was not as much of an issue as one's ability to pay the bills. There were plenty of those available. I helped them, although my help was not necessary, to get new passports and other identification. They chose to present themselves as man and wife which, after being with them for no more than two days, was no surprise. The identifications and passports were prepared accordingly. Numbered bank accounts were arranged to get the funds represented by the draft I had given them cleared. John was going to eventually consolidate the funds in an account he had previously established, one which would draw interest.

John secured a cell phone through the same little shop I utilized earlier. He arranged for security similar to that which I had acquired, although through a different country of origin. The three of us agreed to remain in contact with each other, if for no other reason than the ability to associate on any appropriate future job presenting itself. During our few days together on the island we had time to discuss the project which had just been completed, along with the details of how we both got to Brazil. John made a call to his friends in Colombia and arranged for the release of their abandoned partner. He was back in the States within hours, and the report he filed probably had no connection with the truth. I told them about the death of Sadie and how I was eventually going to complete my revenge.

Within a week of leaving Brazil, John and Ronnie were off to create a life for themselves -- somewhere where there was sun, beaches, and the accouterments necessary to lead the good life. I missed them. It was strange, but I felt an affinity with John which was uncommon in my experience. Maybe it was the shared identity created by the fact that our decisions relative to the Agency placed us in like circumstances. Maybe it was I realized that our philosophies of life and of the future were similar. For whatever the reason, a bond was formed and I felt a closeness and trust of John that was somehow comforting.

Almost a year has passed since John and Ronnie left the island. I think the time has come to let people, who might need the services of someone with my training and abilities, know of my availability -- people with the money to pay for those services. I have made a few calls to men I knew from my work with the Company. These men were generally good, well-intentioned men involved in trying to make positive changes in their countries -- men who have run into resistance from rebels, whose economic interests are served only by maintaining the status quo. In each case I have made it clear, they could contact me only through the Aruba Bank of Commerce where I continue to maintain a portion of my assets to insure I can use its facilities as an address.

I check with the bank several times a week to see if there have been any responses to my overtures. As in most businesses, the interest is more than what I anticipated, but the available cash was not sufficient. In each case I politely respond to their offers, telling them to accumulate the necessary cash and then contact me to work out the details of what they want done and how it is to be completed. If I hear back from one of the contacts, my efforts will be successful. In the meantime the fact I am in the open market is spreading. Eventually I will not have to make any overtures whatsoever, or at least that is the theory.

On one occasion, several months after the conclusion of the Barajas matter, I received an envelope that contained nothing but newspaper clippings, recounting the retirement of Howard Baker from the CIA. It contained a brief summary of Howard's career, at least as it could be printed in the mainstream press, and a notation that he had divorced his wife of many years just prior to retirement. A second article was a bit more guarded and dealt with a senior agent of the CIA who, after a spotless career, had been called before one of the Congressional oversight committees. It appeared, following the hearings, he had committed himself to a secluded sanitarium specializing in the rehabilitation of mental breakdowns. The agent was Scott Steel.

As I had suspected, the agency was covering its ass in an attempt to avoid an embarrassing situation regarding the expenditure of thirty million dollars which was non-recoverable.

Howard seemed to be the only individual affected who really didn't deserve what he got. I could make that right and did. Howard Baker became the beneficiary of a one million-dollar offshore account from an anonymous donor. I had the bank notify him through secure channels of its existence and access codes. Even if he lost his retirement, and I doubted he would, he'd be financially stable for the remainder of his life. Only he would know it was there, and he would know how to get to it in a way no one would ever find it.

Just recently I got an envelope, which from the outside, I knew was from Sailor or Matthews. Its postal markings indicated it originated in a resort on the western coast of Mexico, an area John had mentioned several times as being as close to heaven as he had ever gotten. The envelope contained a single article from a Washington DC newspaper recounting the "gangland slaying of Mildred Baker, the ex-wife of retired CIA agent Howard Baker." The article recounted that she had been shot multiple times while in her Washington apartment. There were no suspects or leads according to the article. At the bottom of the clipping someone had written, "Consider this my gift to you. I think the circumstances are sufficiently close to constitute revenge, don't you?" I reread the article several times before reducing it to ashes. I felt a combination of relief that she was dead and of resentment that I had not done it myself. John knew it would be extremely risky for me to re-enter the States and, while there was some risk to himself, with his experience it wasn't an unmanageable risk. After some thought and contemplation I was thankful it was over and I could get on with my life. Sadie's death had been avenged.

Today was to be a special day in my life. It's now slightly after six in the morning and at ten thirty a plane will land at the island's airport that will contain a very special woman, a woman from the hills of Colombia. Her name is Marie. I have certain reservations about bringing her into my world with all its uncertainties and complexities, but the alternative would have been to deny what has been on my mind for the many months since I boarded that pickup truck and left the solitude of a Colombian ranch. The adjustment to a life here and to a man like me may be difficult for Marie. Only time will tell.

CPSIA information can be obtained at www.ICGtesting.com
Printed in the USA
LVOW04s2244120415

434315LV00012B/168/P